The Danube Testament

THE
DANUBE
TESTAMENT

INGRID MANN

Elliott & Thompson
London

For R.

Prologue

Who, me, sir?
Yes, you, sir!
Not me, sir!
Then who, sir?

Children's game

A fatally marred infant was born prematurely to Hannah Fischer's daughter on the evening of Good Friday. Amy Fischer Hawkins, in the seventh month of an unacknowledged pregnancy, went into labour some hours before the aircraft carrying her and her aged grandmother landed in Vienna, where a waiting ambulance took them both to St Saviour's Hospital in the city's ninth district. There, shortly before midnight, she was finally delivered of a son.

It was a difficult and bloody birth. At first the doctors doubted that the blighted infant would survive at all. Somewhat to their surprise, it clung to life until six days later when, under circumstances still in dispute, its spirit found release.

Soon afterwards the police were in possession of a duly signed and dated confession in which a blood relative of the child on its mother's side, an individual who for the purposes of the present narrative will be referred to as 'S.', unequivocally claimed sole responsibility for the 'crime' of having restored the flawed creature to its maker before the stain of suffering could spread.

This confession was dismissed by the authorities as worthless, and the coroner's report gives the cause of death as, absurdly, 'misadventure'.

* * *

The precise circumstances of the child's demise have continued, however, to feed speculation – less so by now, to be sure, within S.'s immediate family than among friends formerly connected to the sanatorium at St Anselm which he has called home almost precisely since the twentieth century reached its mid-point. Many of these sceptics will be satisfied with nothing short of a comprehensive account of the entire 'baby affair', and it is chiefly for their sakes that S. has been persuaded to embark on the present memoir, thinly but deftly disguised as a work of fiction.

It is S.'s first ambitious work in English, a tongue he has studied and loved since boyhood and one which happily offers far greater marketing and distribution potential than the author's native German. It is his hope and desire that the fruit of his literary labours should reach as broad a readership as possible, reflecting everlasting credit on the institution that nurtured the talents of its maker. For it was here at St Anselm, soon after the cessation of the century's bloodiest war, that the Vienna-born Dr Helmut Rosen of Cambridge University pioneered his world-famous Creative Therapy for the mentally and emotionally disturbed. Without that vital impetus, the present work would never have come into being.

An unrepayable debt of gratitude is owed to the author's family, both here and abroad, and especially to his sister Frau Dr Eva Berger, for typing and proofing the manuscript, as well as for much earlier assistance in the preparation of a short fictional work published in *Die Presse* (Sunday supplement of 13 June 1982).

Finally, profound thanks are due to the author's friend and mentor Brother Sebastian (now, alas, stationed at an African mission so remote that he may never read these words) for decades of wise and patient tutelage in matters of English style, and for his untiring reiteration of the basic principles of good writing: (1) proposition, (2) development and (3) conclusion; remembering to lace all three with concrete facts, descriptive detail, plenty of action and *frequent use of direct speech*!

1

On a purely practical level the question that immediately springs to mind is why, six months into a pregnancy, Hannah's daughter or any other young lady in her condition should have set out on such a long, strenuous journey. An hour's drive from Maple Harbor to Bangor, Maine; a three-hour flight (with change of planes) from there to New York City; a forty-five-minute trip by taxi from the airport to her grandmother's flat; another, hour-long, taxi ride with the old lady (herself far from fully recovered from a second hip-replacement operation) to a different airport, followed by the exhausting eight-hour flight to Vienna. Not to mention checking-in of luggage, possible flight delays, likely loss or damage of luggage, time-consuming customs inspections, difficulties with taxis, etc. All this to be repeated in reverse order on the return journey. Such would have been the ordeal in prospect for poor Amy, had fate not prepared a terrible alternative.

What then could have been her motive?

The explanation, however unlikely it might sound at first hearing, seems to be that Amy may not only have concealed her pregnancy from others but actually refused to admit to herself that she was again with child.

'Oh, Amy absolutely adores Charles and the girls,' her sister Beatrice had told Eva and S. on her first visit. 'She's turned out to be a model wife and mother, to everyone's amazement. But no more kids for her, she says, two are enough. She's adamant on that point.'

Beatrice, who at the time was just finishing work on a photographic assignment in Venice, had stopped over in Vienna expressly to meet her mother's Austrian relatives. The 'stopover', however, stretched into a stay of fully eleven days as a result of Beatrice's professional zeal. Much to S.'s embarrassment, she had no sooner made the acquaintance of Brother Sebastian than she began coaxing him to arrange permission for her to do a so-called 'photo feature' on the sanatorium and its creative therapy wing, complete with pictures of 'inmates at work', for an American popular magazine.

* * *

'In fact, my little sister's something of a fanatic on the subject of family planning,' Beatrice had rattled on in her bland American English, unabashed by S.'s presence opposite her at the dining table, immersing himself as best he could in a *Kronenzeitung* editorial. (*Die Kronenzeitung*, Austria's oldest daily newspaper, is despised by many so-called intellectuals, but S. has never been unduly influenced by popular opinion.) 'She'll tell you it's nothing short of immoral in this day and age to bring more than two kids into the world. After Sally was born she went on the pill straight away. I suggested to her that for absolute safety she'd be better off to have her tubes tied, but she said Charles would never stand for it, he needs to feel fertile. I said it's your tubes I had in mind, not his, but she said, "Same difference." Well, what can you say to that? She was always a strange kid, our Amy.'

Eva muttered some reply, plainly as embarrassed as her brother that he should have to hear such talk, though as a creative writer he was naturally ever on the *qui vive*, eager to glimpse fresh facets of human experience.

'Oh, I'm on the pill myself,' Beatrice continued, apparently indifferent to the possible effect of these confidences on her audience. 'I do like being in control, and the pill's far less of a nuisance than a diaphragm. But I'll be honest with you, I'm not all that keen on messing up my body chemistry,' she added, making a rueful mouth. 'Last fall I missed two periods for no apparent reason. I didn't tell my boyfriend Brian, he'd have been over the moon thinking it meant wedding bells. Anyway it turned out to be a false alarm, very much to my relief. Not that I'd have married him if it hadn't. No, thank you very much!' A hard little laugh; then, suddenly winsome, 'I wonder if you'd reach me the sugar, S.? Oh, thanks!'

Complying, he was rewarded with a seductive smile.

* * *

Throughout that 'stopover', Beatrice had conducted herself towards S. (who as her mother's cousin was after all a sort of uncle to her) in a manner best described as provocative: her assumed boyishness of manner contrasting with her pronounced femininity of person in a way calculated to disturb him.

On another occasion, she and Eva were idly discussing the subject of family resemblances when Beatrice suddenly bounded up from the sofa and advanced on S., who had been standing by the window deep in thought, with a barrage of rhetorical questions.

'What do you say, S.? Do you set any store by Eva's notion of a Fischer face? Take me, do I really look that much like my mother? I've always thought I took after Daddy.' She stood so close he could feel her breath, their eyes almost on a level. As he had already noticed, hers were hazel like Hannah's, and they had the same slight upward tilt at the corners. Mouth and chin, though, lacked the sensitivity of the mother's, and the face as a whole was devoid of genuine charm.

S. prudently averted his eyes from her bold stare. 'My dear young lady, never having met your father I am hardly the best judge of that,' he answered dryly. (Though perfectly fluent, his spoken English is tinctured with the traces of a French-Canadian accent picked up willy-nilly from Brother Sebastian, who despite his advanced degree in English Literature from one of the greatest American universities, Villanova, has never lost his Quebecois twang.) 'My only memories of your mother date back to the days of childhood,' he went on in somewhat milder tones. 'I've not laid eyes on her since then, you see. We correspond but have never exchanged photographs.'

'How strange to think of you and Mama as children together!' Beatrice widened her eyes and tilted her chin roguishly. 'You look easily ten years younger. Easily. Both you and Auntie Eva,' she added tactfully. 'It must be some magic gene on your father's side.'

S. acknowledged the compliment with a small, ironic bow and glanced sidelong at his sister. Her relatively youthful appearance is in fact the hard-won reward of rigorous diet (even when taking S. to lunch, she shuns pastries), strenuous yoga exercises twice daily and an evening ritual of facial massage involving various expensive creams that has occasioned a certain amount of gentle teasing on her brother's part, since Eva considers herself to be opposed in principle to 'cosmetics'. She is a faithful reader of fashion magazines, however, and chooses her clothes with care despite a limited budget. With her immaculate coiffure and her aristocratic bearing, Eva would cut a fine figure in any company. More than once S. has heard strangers address her as 'Madame'. In all these respects she has probably become (so S. conjectures) very nearly the polar opposite of our famously untidy American cousin Hannah, who has reportedly aged rather a lot in recent years.

* * *

And Hannah too is not without her vanity. Evidence of that comes readily to hand in the form of an early letter to S. dated 16 April 1954, ten days after her twenty-eighth birthday, thanking him for his congratulatory note. At that time she was not yet a widow.

The previous autumn Hannah had opened a medical practice in a small town in Maine, the extreme northeastern corner of the United States of America. It was the third year of her marriage to one Jack La-Crosse, a young man of mixed American Indian and French Canadian ancestry who taught art at the local high school, painted at night and on weekends and believed himself and his work to be destined for greatness. At that time he was already planning (with the blessing of Hannah, who fervently believed in his talent) to 'follow his star' and give up everything, including wife and babies, for a life of reclusive creativity in Big Sur, California. Regrettably, before he could put his plan into action LaCrosse was killed, beheaded in fact, in a ghastly motorcycle accident that also ended the life of a young woman companion whose existence had been quite unknown to Hannah. Parenthetically, if Hannah's own daughters are to be believed, she didn't long lack consolation, intellectual or sexual, for the loss of LaCrosse.

To this day, however, the very mention of his name puts Aunt Mia into a rage at that pigheaded daughter of hers. Anyone with a grain of sense would have seen through that cheap trickster – him and his ugly daubs and his high artistic mission, pfui! But not Hannah, she wouldn't hear a word against him, she swallowed the whole thing hook, line and sinker and she'd have come back for more if Mr Michelangelo hadn't hit that oil slick at eighty miles an hour!

* * *

'Dear S.,' the youthful Hannah had written in English to her cousin, three weeks before that tragic event. (At his express wish, their correspondence has always been conducted in the language of Shakespeare, Conrad and Fenimore Cooper.) 'Dear S., many thanks for your birthday felicitations. Time, as they say, marches on, rather too briskly for me. Only fancy, this morning I pulled out three more white hairs! With two daughters still in diapers I find myself well on the way to becoming a snowy-headed crone. I know what you'll say: ageing is only another word for ripening, and ripeness is all. To which I say, with great respect, rubbish! I'm not ready for ripeness. For God's sake, I've only just got used to being an adult!' And more in the same vein.

S. found this tone unsettlingly out of character. Mostly, Hannah's letters were confined to family news, milestones in her professional life and comments on current events or books she had been reading. She was anxious to help fill the gaps the war had left in S.'s education, to keep him abreast of affairs in the great world and perhaps also to keep alive his awareness of the place each of them had had in the life of the other. But her letters were always so positive and self-assured in tone that this glimpse of personal vulnerability came as rather a shock.

* * *

Over the years of their separation Hannah had desired, it seemed, to gradually withdraw into the role of a kind of elder sister to S. Not for long had he been able to deceive himself with dreams of a distant soulmate, still less a sweetheart! Instead she had became a friendly counsellor who year after year tirelessly 'pelted' him with indiscriminate intellectual challenges and ideas. Apart from her regular personal letters, there was an unending succession of battered sea-mail envelopes and packets bringing books, magazines, clippings, theatre and concert programmes, even travel brochures (all in English, their principal redeeming feature!). They amounted to a sort of continuing documentary history of Hannah's interests and enthusiasms, all of which she wanted him to share. Often she had written to him about the events and experiences to which these items related, but since the packets reached their destination weeks later than the letters, S. had often forgotten the connection and might put the booklet or the programme aside unread.

What did kindle his interest, all the more so because Hannah rarely mentioned them in her letters, were the 'philosophical' and religious pamphlets that had increasingly begun to turn up in these shipments of assorted reading matter. For the most part they consisted of well-meaning mumbo-jumbo, which S. was nevertheless careful to keep away from Brother Sebastian's censorious Catholic eye. They had begun to appear in the packets about the time of Hannah's brief conversion to an eccentric form of Protestantism which apparently denies the existence of heaven and hell and enjoins its members to acknowledge the divinity of every creature, to instantly forgive any injury or offence and to extend this same forgiveness to the Almighty(!) with respect to wars, pestilences, natural disasters and no doubt smaller-scale atrocities as well, such as death by cancer or the birth of monsters!

Later on, Hannah's horizons expanded to include other, more dubious, doctrines. Anything 'alternative' or esoteric drew her like a magnet. Transcendental meditation, hypnosis, homoeopathy, scientology, Sufism, primal-scream therapy, ley lines, macrobiotic diets, anthroposophy – if normal people laughed at it, Hannah would want to look into it. After abandoning her flirtation with the 'Church of Mercy' movement she never became a proper convert to any of these doctrines, but she would always maintain that there was definitely 'something in it' that the sceptics were too perverse to acknowledge.

'I honestly don't understand how people can scoff at the idea of reincarnation,' she had written in one of the first letters addressed to S. at the sanatorium when he was already a patient of Dr Rosen. 'To me it seems highly implausible that this should be my first earthly existence, or my last for that matter. We've each made the rounds a number of times, and our paths will cross again. Wait and see!'

* * *

Professionally, too, Hannah was firmly committed to at least one unconventional school of thought, the so-called 'tender childbirth' movement, pioneered by her friend and colleague Dr Ilona Kovacs. She was an eager exponent of that distinguished physician's doctrines regarding the emotional and psychic (or spiritual) effects of the maternal environment on the fetus *in utero*.

In retrospect, one can only say: Poor Hannah! For how could her theories possibly have survived, at least without some very drastic changes, the horrifying outcome of her own daughter's third pregnancy?

* * *

'You distress yourself over nothing, my dear,' Eva would chide her brother when he gave voice to his annoyance at their American visitor's unmannerly talk. 'Times have changed, you ought to know that. Beatrice doesn't mean any harm. She's just very direct. She likes you and both of us are "family", that's all. You needn't stand on your dignity so much. Just take her at face value and forget all that nonsense about a "pass", it's pure imagination. I'm quite, quite sure such a thing would never enter her head.'

That was true to form. Eva had always gone to great lengths to soothe S.'s hurts and calm his worries.

'I still don't see why she persists in calling me by my first name,' S. had pointed out mildly. He had been prepared to make allowances for Beatrice's relative youth and her very different national and cultural background, but he failed to see why she for her part shouldn't be expected to make the modest effort required to address her mother's first cousin as 'Uncle'. Failing that, the young woman could easily have found some other courtesy title such as 'Brother', the form of address used by nearly every one of the younger staff persons here. To call by a mangled version of his Christian name a senior family member who was entitled to respect and had done nothing to invite familiarity seemed to S. indefensible.

But the point was lost on his sister.

* * *

Altogether, S. had noticed, Eva had a way of springing to the defence of anyone who became the target of his criticism. She had even tried to justify Hannah's refusal to teach her children the barest rudiments of their mother's native tongue. As if anyone had the right to deny children access to their linguistic heritage, leaving them unable even to pronounce the name of a blood relative whose love for her, despite age and diminished capacities, had survived decades of separation!

But, again, Eva had simply dismissed the indictment out of hand. No one, she had said, could blame Hannah for choosing to shut the door permanently on certain historical events, as any sensitive person would surely have to agree! And with that she had walked out of the room, leaving S. to meditate on the fragility of rational discussion.

◄ 2 ►

Whatever Amy's state of mind may have been when she agreed to accompany her grandmother to Vienna, whether or not she had actually succeeded in deluding herself about her own condition, there was no mystery about Aunt Mia's motive for the trip!

Much to her daughter Hannah's annoyance, the old lady had suddenly taken it into her head that, instead of sharing her husband's grave in Forest Hills, Long Island, she must and would, when her time came, be buried in Vienna. With Aunt Mia, decisions were swiftly followed by action, and this one was no exception. Nothing Hannah could say would alter her mother's determination to fly to Vienna within the week, hip or no hip, to make the necessary advance arrangements on the spot. 'While I've still got all my marbles, darling,' as she put it.

Most if not all of Aunt Mia's faculties were indeed in very good order. In her chic New York suit and high-heeled shoes, fully painted and powdered and with all her jewellery on, she looked much more like a distinguished old actress than like anyone's great-grandmother, at least until you saw her move. But she had always been impulsive, and old age had made her even less willing to listen to reason than she had been in her prime.

Perhaps her sudden decision had something to do, too, with a small fit of homesickness for Austria and the Austrian relatives, for card-playing and chatting with her nephew S., who for his part had always greatly welcomed the chance to practise his English on her!

In any case, she would not be put off, insisting that despite the hip she was quite able to travel alone. But here Hannah put her foot down. 'Alone? That's insane, Mother,' she must have told her (or words to that effect). 'What if complications set in with that hip and they have to hospitalise you over there? You've got no right to put me through that, Mother. No, you go with an escort or not at all. That's it, full stop.'

Aunt Mia grumbled, but she knew better than to argue the point. The problem was the escort. Hannah, she knew, couldn't afford to take a fortnight off from her job at Columbia Presbyterian Hospital. One granddaughter, Beatrice, was off somewhere in Wales on a professional assignment. The other, Amy, was at home in Bangor, Maine, and might be more available. Amy, however, had only just returned to the bosom of her family from her latest 'excursion' (this time to Acapulco), and Aunt Mia was more than a little reluctant to jeopardise her good relations with Charles Hawkins by dragging his wife off on another wild goose chase almost before she had unpacked from the last one!

* * *

Among her family Amy is famous for her predilection for sudden departures. On quite a few occasions in the past she has taken off alone, on the spur of the moment, with the first long-distance bus that happened along, and reappeared a week or two later with no explanation other than a fresh lot of her peculiar, sad, spidery drawings: a dead crow on a stubble heap, a derelict farmhouse, washing on a line behind a broken fence. The strain which these periodic absences had put upon Amy's marriage had appeared to ease over the years. Charles, evidently, had made up his mind to take the bitter with the sweet, but Aunt Mia knew that the resentment must still be simmering there under his surface good humour, and who could blame him if it was!

* * *

Having put the possibility of Amy out of her mind, Aunt Mia decided she would hire a nurse-companion for the trip, and began dialling agencies. A few calls convinced her, first, that it would be terrifyingly expensive, and, second, that the chances of finding a suitable person on such short notice were almost non-existent. So Amy was really her only hope. The likelihood of her saying no if asked, Aunt Mia reckoned, was slight; the important thing would be to square the whole thing with Charles in advance. Knowing that he usually went to work on Mondays, Aunt Mia took a deep breath and rang him at his office.

As usual, her son-in-law was immensely cordial; to her surprise, he not only made no fuss about the prospect of being deprived of Amy but actually seemed to welcome it, saying he had been thinking that 'the poor kid' needed another little break. 'Remember, Granny Mia,' he said, 'the girls and I have always got Bridie to look after us.'

(Bridie was the elderly Irish housekeeper whom Charles and Amy had, so to speak, inherited from old Mr Hawkins when he moved to Florida. There he would spend the final years of his lonely retirement playing golf and sitting on the patio of the expensive condominium he had bought in Del Ray Beach. The climate in Florida is subtropical and salubrious, with excellent beaches for swimming and not too much violent crime in elegant places such as Del Ray Beach.)

* * *

Amy, as expected, needed very little persuasion to come along. Like everyone else, she was fond of her grandmother Mia, she had never been to Austria, and she happened to be a great admirer of one of the most celebrated Austrian artists of the century, Egon Schiele, who painted some very nice landscapes among other things not so nice.

'And can we visit the catacombs?' Amy had asked. She meant the Kapuzinergruft under St Stephen's Cathedral, where the bones and inner organs of our country's famous rulers await the Last Day, standing like rocks in the river of tourists streaming through those solemn precincts. Amy must have read about the Kapuzinergruft in a book.

'Weird girl, that granddaughter of mine!' Aunt Mia had remarked some years ago to S. on one of their canasta afternoons. 'Such a sunny disposition, and such a morbid fascination with death and decay, brrr! When she was quite tiny there was this little dead mouse. I don't know where she found it but she hid it under her pillow for almost a week, until Beattie noticed a funny smell. Amy cried and cried when they took it away. Beattie said she'd told her she didn't mind the smell, she just loved petting it with her finger. Children, who can understand them?'

S., as it happened, had understood perfectly, but he merely smiled and shook his head in a baffled way.

'Anyway, now she's Charles's problem,' Aunt Mia said, laying down her cards with a flourish so that her bracelets jingled. 'No, I shouldn't have said that, I didn't mean it, Amy's a darling. And a good little artist too,' she added, tapping with one scarlet fingernail on the lid of the little ivory card-box. (This was a souvenir Eva had brought back years and years ago from India, where she had been invited by her former boss at the UN to attend the wedding of his niece and ward Lalitha.)

'When she was only ten our little Amy used to make us the prettiest little Christmas cards,' Aunt Mia went on. 'I remember one she did with a drawing of the Christ child in the cradle – exquisite. Your Uncle Ludwig was greatly impressed, he really was. Such talent, he said, such talent she can only have got from my side of the family. So I said, teasing him you know, how can you be so sure? I know I'm her grandmother but you're just guessing, aren't you? I said. And he said, Mia, are you telling me we've been living a lie? Joking too, you know. Oh, we used to have such fun together, your Fischer-Uncle and I.'

Aunt Mia sighed and began reshuffling the cards with her ring-encumbered fingers. 'You remember your Fischer-Uncle, don't you? Remember that Christmas when the three of us came to you, him and me and our Hannah, and how he sat down at the piano and sang the Ave Maria like an angel? Great-Aunt Mitzi always made him sing the Ave Maria, you know. I remember her saying one time, "That voice would melt a heart of stone." And it's true, he had us all in tears with it that Christmas day, even your own papa.'

Of course S. remembered Hannah's father: the satin waistcoat he always wore, the beautiful ties, his courtly manners and his rather melancholy blue eyes, the same colour as Hannah's. The Fischer-Uncle had told a lot of jokes on that Christmas visit, jokes S. didn't understand at the time though he can remember how hard they made his parents laugh. A nice man, the Fischer-Uncle, and a clever one. Even today you can sometimes hear one or another of his cabaret songs on the radio, in between the rocks. The Fischer-Uncle must, S. supposes, have been quite famous in Vienna in his day.

'He was a real trouper, your Fischer-Uncle,' Aunt Mia went on musingly. 'A man of the theatre through and through. Nothing ever broke his spirit, not even after that fiasco in New York.'

'Fiasco?' S. said enquiringly, although he knew the story.

'Well, I'd never have said it to his face,' Aunt Mia said, 'but fifty years later why not call a spade a spade? He spent six months writing and rewriting it, he put absolutely everything we had into it, he nearly killed himself putting it on, and what happened? A couple of good notices but they stayed away in droves, his beloved *émigré* public. They had other things to worry about, the nostalgia hadn't hit them yet … *Vienna*

Follies indeed! Fischer's Folly is what they should have called it. All your uncle salvaged from it was his illusions. I came across one of his old business cards just the other day. Ludwig Fischer, it said, international composer-producer. Gave me a little stab, it did. Because if brother Lionel hadn't come to the rescue we'd all have landed in the poorhouse within a year.'

'Your loyalty must have given him much comfort,' S. commented.

'My dear, what can you do with a man like that?' Mia asked rhetorically. 'My Ludwig had a heart of gold. Some people might have called him a womaniser but he was never anything but discreet and considerate and kind with me. A wonderful man he was. And in forty-nine years of marriage I don't think he ever said anything to deliberately hurt me. Never a mean word in forty-nine years, S.! Forty-nine years is a long time, my boy!'

Aunt Mia laid down her cards and dabbed delicately at her eyes, so careful not to smudge the mascara that a stranger might think grief had taken a back seat to vanity.

* * *

Actually, she and Ludwig Fischer had been a devoted couple. As Great-Aunt Mitzi always liked to say, theirs had been one of Vienna's great love stories in the years after the war. 'Why but for love should a rich Jewish playboy like him take it into his head to marry a poor Catholic girl like our Mia?' the matriarch Mitzi would demand of anyone within earshot. 'Tell me that! You can't tell me? Of course you can't, because love's the only answer. The two of them were simply besotted with each other, it's as simple as that.'

And Great-Aunt Mitzi herself had been a thoroughly sensible person and a real lady, even if she did, towards the end of her life, become shockingly crude in her speech and insensitive to other people's feelings. Thus when S., returning from the prisoner-of-war camp so thin that every thread of his old clothes would have to be altered, presented himself to Great-Aunt Mitzi, she at once told him that he looked like a scarecrow and warned Eva about his supposed mental instability. 'If the lad had a screw half loose in the beginning,' she told Eva in S.'s own presence, 'that damned Nazi war has certainly finished the job. Look at him! I'm telling you, the best thing you can do is simply to have him locked up before he harms himself or somebody else.'

(S., though shocked and hurt at this, recognised the signs of senility and took no lasting offence. He had been fond of the old lady and had often admired her keen observation and her readiness to share her vast store of knowledge about their side of the family. She died of pneumonia in the September immediately before S. was committed to the sanatorium.)

On past occasions, too, Great-Aunt Mitzi had been known to over-dramatise. For instance, it was quite true that both her nieces had been orphaned at an early age, but neither had ever really known poverty. The fact of the matter, as established by S. through careful sorting-out of family gossip and analysis of overheard conversations, is that his mother and Aunt Mia had been two of the most eligible young ladies in St Anselm, by virtue not only of their looks but of their prospects. Though admittedly without independent means, they were due to inherit Great-Aunt Mitzi's residence, an imposing two-storeyed building in Elisabethstrasse, just off the town's principal square. In days gone by, most of the ground floor had been occupied by the famous Café Allotria, of which Great-Aunt Mitzi had been manager and sole owner.

Up until the end of World War I, the Allotria's casino and billiard rooms had been much frequented by officers and the aristocracy. Afterwards it became a popular haunt of moneyed society people, until the Great Depression wrote finis to all such frivolity. Soon Great-Aunt Mitzi bowed to the inevitable and shut the Allotria's doors for good.

By then, though, both nieces were already suitably married. Barbara, the future mother of Eva and S., had caught the eye of an up-and-coming doctor of veterinary medicine, Hugo Zimmermann. After their marriage the couple moved into an apartment on the ground floor of the Elisabethstrasse house, behind the former Allotria premises. These soon became the Zimmermann Animal Clinic, a veritable gold-mine, according to Great-Aunt Mitzi, throughout the early nineteen-thirties.

But it was Mia, the younger sister, who 'struck in the black', as they say, when the dashing Ludwig Fischer dropped on one knee to ask her hand in marriage!

Great-Aunt Mitzi was delighted with the match, but it was far from popular with Ludwig's family, especially with Lionel Fischer, the bride-groom's elder brother, who at age twenty-eight was the head of the Fischer family. A keen businessman, Lionel was also a racehorse owner and an avid sportsman, with hunting lodges in Hungary and Slovenia. Opposed to the match at the beginning, he was only gradually won over by Mia's wit and charm. Gradually but thoroughly, for by 1938, when Vienna's Jewish population could no longer ignore the threat looming over them and the Fischers were already making plans to emigrate, Lionel had unexpectedly changed his will to make Mia instead of Ludwig his executor in case he should not reach America!

Yet fate had decreed that Lionel Fischer would not only survive but live to return to Vienna after the war and spend his last years secluded in a beautiful flat on the Rennweg, not far from the famous Belvedere Palace. There, some ten or twenty years ago, he died in his sleep. Never having married, Lionel left no children. His remains were laid to rest in the Fischer family mausoleum in the Zentralfriedhof (Central Cemetery).

* * *

Against this background the reader will understand why, a half-century later, Aunt Mia's nearest and dearest were startled by her sudden deter-mination to be laid to rest – when the time came – in Vienna. She had once planned to join her Ludwig in the expensive grave she had bought for them both at Forest Hills 'so that our Hannah won't have to travel so far to visit us', as she had said at the time to her Austrian nephew and niece. Now, it seemed, she had simply reversed herself. 'Nobody could be bothered to visit me way out there, even if they happened to remember All Souls' Day,' she had blandly explained to them on her previous visit. 'Over here a person can still count on somebody lighting a candle on their grave once a year, and maybe saying a little prayer.'

S. and his sister were touched by their dear aunt's confidence and determined to be worthy of it. If they survived her, her grave would not be neglected. Five times a year, so they had thought – on All Souls' Day, Christmas, Easter and the anniversaries of Mia's birth and death – the two of them would make the long journey to the Zentralfriedhof to lay flowers on her grave and light a candle for the repose of her soul. (Despite its name, the Zentralfriedhof is actually anything but central, being a good two kilometres from the Innere Stadt or Zentrum, as the heart of Vienna is now known to the world.)

* * *

Meanwhile, what had required Aunt Mia's personal presence in Vienna was a practical difficulty which she felt could be dealt with properly only by herself: the Fischer mausoleum had run out of space! To accommodate yet another coffin, the contents of two or more of the old ones would have to be consolidated; this would be a difficult business to arrange, with forms to be filled out, documents to be supplied, and appeals made to officials in various municipal offices before anything could be done. All this would be arduous enough to accomplish if you were on the spot; by mail it would be quite impossible, Aunt Mia was convinced.

'And let's face it, at my age there isn't that much time to waste,' she pointed out to S., having familiarised him with the situation. 'Somehow or other, my last hip replacement brought that home to me.'

S.'s worldly-wise sister had her own explanation of Aunt Mia's strange caprice. 'Right from the beginning it was Lionel she wanted, not Ludwig,' she will tell S. when in a gossiping mood. 'Lionel was the one who found her and hired her, and he can't have lost much time making her his mistress. But then Ludwig fell hard for her, and she settled for him because she knew Lionel would never make an honest woman of her. But Lionel was her first love, and he's the one she wants to lie with when her time comes.'

S. has heard this theory a number of times. Along with her occasional lapses from good taste, Eva has a most annoying tendency to repeat herself.

* * *

For all her preoccupation with funereal matters, Aunt Mia certainly neither looked nor acted the part of one nearing the end of her days. The morning after her traumatic arrival, she was already up at eight, bright-eyed, animated and in no way the worse for her ordeal. Perched opposite S. on the vast leather sofa, once Aunt Mitzi's, that had survived Eva's latest redecoration of the living-room, she won five games of canasta and was on the point of winning a sixth when Eva returned from her night's vigil at the hospital with the fearful news about Amy's newborn son.

◀ 3 ▶

The great mystery, of course, the dark question looming over all, is why any creature so sorely afflicted as Amy's baby should ever have been allowed to come into the world at all. Yet it is perhaps no less mysterious that the Danube should flow past Vienna and Budapest and not past Berlin or Bombay or – a third B! – Bangor, Maine, 'home town' of Charles Hawkins, the benighted infant's bodily father.

The name Hawkins was one of the oldest and most respected in that small American city on the banks of the mighty Penobscot River. Two centuries ago, two Hawkins brothers had amassed a fortune in the timber trade, floating the logs they cut from their northern timberlands down the Penobscot to the shipbuilders of Bath and Bedford, whose vessels would transport thousands of black captives from the west coast of Africa to the slave plantations of the American South.

* * *

Is it really so very unlikely, then, that the Hawkins family – respected business proprietors and bank trustees for five generations now – should still bear some taint of guilt for that great wickedness? May not some slender thread of responsibility still link the fresh-faced Charles to the horrors of the American Civil War, link him through his forebears to the slaughter of so many thousands of fine young men?

Or consider the ancestry on the maternal side, Hannah's side. There we find apostasy by a prince of the church, fornication, perversity, treachery, insanity, suicide: name the sin and you will find it flourishing at the roots of our Austrian family tree.

May not indeed the sins of one generation be passed on to the next, like silt carried seaward by the river?

Or, to express the thought in yet another metaphor: cannot the sea itself be held to account for the death of the fisherman swept overboard and drowned, in the act of hauling in his nets, by a single casual wave?

Yes, these are mysteries indeed; and mysteries they are, perhaps, fated to remain.

* * *

Very early in the investigation of the 'baby killing', one must surely ask
when it was that it first became apparent to the family that the birth of
Amy's son was in every sense, and for every person involved, a terrible
catastrophe.

Answer: On Day One.

Nearly everyone concerned will prefer, out of cowardice or mis-
placed compassion, to dismiss as the figment of a morbid imagination
any suggestion that any one of them might have acted on the logic of
that realisation.

Yet just as they had chosen to accept a purely material explanation
(hormonal imbalances!) for the child's atrocious handicap, so too,
ignoring conclusive first-hand evidence to the contrary, they cling to the
idea that its death must have been the 'tragic' result of some organic
failure.

Only Brother Sebastian sees it as the fruit of a plan designed by God
for man's salvation: but that is Brother Sebastian's interpretation of all
the dreadful things that happen in this world.

'Oh, what a fine God He must be, Brother!' S. had more than once
teased the good priest. 'What kind of God is it, Brother, that creates a
Devil to tempt man into sin and then punishes the sinners with hell-
fire? I maintain that God himself was the first sinner, and the greatest.
Can you prove He wasn't?'

Sadly, Brother Sebastian had never been one to sharpen his wits in
dialectics. Though still young enough in years to be possessed of a flex-
ible mind, whenever he felt intellectually challenged Brother Sebastian
would simply pull out his rosary and begin fingering it mindlessly.

* * *

Eva was first in the family to know the truth about the newest offshoot
of the ancestral tree.

She and S. had driven in her new Toyota car to Vienna International
Airport to welcome their Aunt Mia and their cousin Amy. To spare the
old lady needless walking, Eva had taken the Toyota right up to the kerb
by the arrivals hall, in a space reserved for the disabled. There she waited

in the car, alert and ready with her explanation for policemen and traffic wardens, while S. climbed out of the car to wait for the arriving pair to emerge from the customs hall. Some distance down the pavement an ambulance had drawn up, its red light flashing ominously.

The aircraft had landed only minutes before, and no passengers had yet emerged, when a side door suddenly swung open and S. spotted Aunt Mia being pushed rapidly in a wheelchair past the crowds waiting at the barrier and towards the exit outside of which the ambulance was waiting.

S., with his usual presence of mind, dashed after them and swiftly informed himself of the situation. To his huge relief the ambulance had not been called for Aunt Mia but for Amy.

Amy, it seemed, was already inside, and Mia was about to be taken aboard with her (the Escort Escorted, as S. wittily remarked to his sister some time later).

After some confusion Mia was rescued from the wheelchair, the baggage was located and loaded into Eva's little car, and the three of them drove off, following the ambulance to St Saviour's Hospital in Vienna's Ninth District.

Aunt Mia was naturally shaken by the circumstances of their arrival and worried about her granddaughter. She was convinced that Amy must have got food poisoning from the chicken chasseur, so called, which she had chosen for dinner on the plane against her grandmother's advice. 'For God's sake stick to the beef, I told her, with airline chicken you're taking your life in your hands. But no, she would have the chicken, and half an hour later the cramps started. We hadn't even had our coffee, the service was awful.'

S. started to explain that the ambulance men had said Amy was in labour, but Aunt Mia was paying no attention and an almost imperceptible shrug of Eva's shoulders seemed to tell S. that he was probably wasting his breath. Sitting alone in the rear, the old lady soon lapsed into silence. She was plainly exhausted.

Eva left her with S. in the downstairs lobby of the hospital while she went off looking for Casualty, where Amy would have been taken.

* * *

Twenty minutes later Eva reappeared with the news that Amy was all right; she was under sedation and quite comfortable, but it could be hours before anything happened and it was pointless for three people to hang about waiting for developments. Aunt Mia and S., she said, should go straight on to St Anselm in a taxi. Everything was in readiness at the house in Elisabethstrasse, and she could be sure S. would take good care of her.

As in fact he did. There was no difficulty about taxis; several were waiting at the nearby taxi stand and the driver scrupulously followed S.'s careful instructions. It did turn out that S. had inadvertently left his wallet at home: a potential calamity, but luckily Aunt Mia had brought along plenty of Austrian currency left over from her visit the previous year, so his anxieties proved groundless.

During the taxi ride it became evident that Aunt Mia had quietly dropped her food-poisoning theory. She fretted aloud about Amy's failure to take proper care of herself. She pondered Amy's possible reasons for keeping her pregnancy dark. She speculated about the sex of the coming child. 'I hope it's a boy this time, for Charles's sake. Men always want sons. Of course your Uncle Ludwig was an exception, he was absolutely jubilant about Hannah. We named her after his mother – you remember old Madame Fischer, don't you? But what am I saying? Of course you couldn't have known her! She died before you were so much as a gleam in your papa's eye.'

At home they had a sandwich lunch, then Mia took a nap. S. had been planning on an early dinner at the Wirtshaus down the street, but Mia said all she needed was sleep and more sleep. By nine o'clock they had both retired for the night, Mia in a nightgown borrowed from Eva's closet, since they had forgotten to transfer her overnight case from the Toyota to the taxi.

* * *

Eva herself did not return until nearly nine o'clock the next morning, when S. and Aunt Mia had long since put away the breakfast things and settled down to their long-awaited canasta session. She had spent the whole night at the hospital, with only two hours' sleep on a chair beside Amy's bed after they had brought her back from the recovery room.

A young doctor had given her the news soon after midnight. It was a boy. The mother was doing 'as well as could be expected'. The child – well, it was too soon to say. When a birth was three months early ... and this one had been earlier still. And there was the additional problem, the hydrocephalus, that further reduced its chances of survival.

In plain words: Amy had given birth to a monstrosity.

That was the 'bad news'. The 'good news' was that Amy was out of immediate danger, and the doctors regarded the prospects for an early recovery as excellent.

◄ 4 ►

Word of her sister's misfortune reached Beatrice a day later at the modest hostelry in mid-Wales where she was sharing a so-called working holiday with her English 'partner', a freelance travel writer who was working on an illustrated *Family Bargain Holiday Guide* to the British Isles for a small American publisher: text by Brian Whiting, photos by Beatrice LaCrosse.

Normally, second billing wouldn't have appealed to Beatrice, a successful independent journalist whose byline is often seen in American newspapers and popular magazines that are bought and probably read by numerous US citizens of every age, colour and creed. But the guidebook had been Brian's mind-child, and Beatrice was quite happy for once to concentrate on the pictures and leave the writing to someone else.

She was thirty-four years old and unmarried. Brian was thirty-eight, divorced and the father of two: Joel, a boy of fourteen, and a daughter Sherrill, a precociously mature fifteen-year-old of Mediterranean appearance who was already expert in the arts of self-adornment. 'Those crazy kids', as Brian called them, were expected to join him and Beatrice after Easter for a week's free pony trekking, arranged by courtesy of local tourism authorities who were well disposed towards Brian's project.

Beatrice couldn't have been greatly pleased at the prospect of his children's visit. She would probably have been glad to pay for the privacy of proper hotel rooms, for she could well afford small luxuries. But rather than offend Brian she held her peace. His stinginess, evidently born of childhood hardship, ran deep. Deeper still, it seemed, was a curious streak of prudery that she supposed must have something to do with his working-class origins and the mother he had once described to her as a deeply committed Christian. However that might be, the fact was that Brian had absolutely insisted on booking separate rooms (adjoining, to be sure) rather than registering as a Mr & Mrs, and though Beatrice scoffed at his concern for appearances, Brian made a point of rumpling his bed in the mornings for the benefit of the inn's sole chambermaid.

* * *

On the night of her nephew's birth, their last night alone before the 'crazy kids' were due to arrive, they had gone to her room right after dinner to watch an American-made comedy on the 'tele'. It had been running for nearly an hour when someone knocked.

Beatrice turned the set down. 'Yes?'

'Telephone call for you, Miss LaCrosse,' said the landlord on the other side of the door. 'From New York. It's a lady, a doctor I think she said. I didn't quite catch the name.'

'Thanks, I'll be right down – Damn, that'll be Mother for sure,' Beatrice said. 'Wiss her charming Cherman eksent. She makes no effort at all.' She swung her legs over the side of the bed, toes groping for her footgear. 'And so inconsiderate, calling me at this hour! As if she'd never learned that the world is divided into time zones.'

'Don't be too hard on your mum, love,' Brian said soothingly. 'You're lucky she cares enough to call.'

'I know,' Beatrice said wearily. 'It might not be a check-up call, either. Something could have happened to Granny.' She was tying her tennis shoes. 'Granny was warned about that hip, but what's the use, you can't tell her anything once she's made up her mind. I love her dearly, but sometimes I wonder if we aren't all mad in this family of ours.' (Gentle reader, take note!)

Brian grunted. 'Hurry up and get it over with. It's chilly in bed,' he added naughtily. Despite the early grey in his curly hair, the melancholy in his eyes and the beginnings of jowliness, Beatrice still found his mischievous smile rather appealing. It always reminded her of an innocent English school-lad of the sort one sometimes used to see in films.

'Best pop my jumper on first, though,' he added. 'It'll be perishing down there in the hall.'

'No thanks, I'll be fine as I am.'

Brian was sporting a bright red-and-black chequered nightshirt, really a hunting shirt such as North American foresters wear to avoid accidentally shooting each other instead of the animals. This shirt had caught Brian's fancy on his visit to Maine the previous summer, and he had bought it without trying it on. It turned out to be a tall man's model which fitted nicely around the chest but hung down nearly to Brian's knees. As a nightshirt Beatrice found it bizarre, but it amused her that he had bought such a flashy garment, by far the most flamboyant thing in an otherwise doggedly unimaginative wardrobe.

* * *

Although she was fond of him and he was plainly besotted with her, Beatrice had begun to feel faintly irritated by Brian's placid temper, his good sense and his sheer reliability. He had never hurt or insulted her, never even given her a really good reason to be angry. She wished in vain that she could detect some sort of wild streak in his nature, some element of unpredictability. They were too comfortable together, she told herself, and the thought made her despise both of them a little. But she knew that she could do worse than Brian; much, much worse.

Well into her thirties, with a trail of broken love affairs behind her, Beatrice had seen her choices narrowing. She had always imagined that after a few years of 'playing the field' she would settle down with an exceptionally desirable man and raise a brood of wonderful, gifted children. The possibility that she might never be a mother had not really occurred to her until a year or so earlier, and when it did it put her in a panic. A few months later she met Brian, recently divorced, lonely and susceptible. Early in their affair it became clear to Beatrice that he was hers to keep if she wanted him, and she let herself drift into a settled relationship.

Brian couldn't, at first, believe that he had really won the affections of such a brilliant and exciting woman. But he soon learned to accept it, then to preen himself on it and finally to take their future together for granted. Beatrice, he thought, would make an excellent new mother for his Joel and Sherrill.

Professionally, too, Beatrice and Brian made a first-class team. Brian had long cherished the dream of setting up a small news agency in America to serve British newspapers, and a skilled photographer such as Beatrice was precisely the partner he needed to make a success of it.

Despite herself, however, Beatrice was becoming increasingly bored with these prospects. Sometimes she found herself wondering whether she would be much upset if one day Brian just quietly evaporated, leaving her with a few agreeable memories. In fact the longer the two of them were together, the less keen on marriage she became, and the less inclined to listen to Amy's advocacy of Brian's cause. But her anxiety to have a child 'before the biological clock runs out' (a phrase familiar to contemporary audiences) was keener than ever.

* * *

'If you were me, do you think you'd go to bed with that little Englishman who's staying with the Shermanovskys?' Beatrice had asked her sister soon after having arrived for her annual summer vacation at Maple Harbor. She and Brian had been introduced the previous evening at the annual Yacht Club dinner-dance.

* * *

Maple Harbor, it should be said here, is a small Maine coastal community which is predominantly a summer resort for people who live elsewhere the rest of the year. Long before Amy and Beatrice were born, their maternal grandfather, the Fischer-Uncle, overriding Aunt Mia's objections, had bought a cottage there (long since sold) to enable her and Hannah to escape the heat of the New York summer. Maple Harbor was where Hannah had first met Jack LaCrosse, whom she was later to marry. Amy and Beatrice were born there; an old converted farmhouse at Maple Harbor had been their childhood home for several years, until their father absconded to California. At that point Hannah had moved to New York with her young daughters and set up a medical practice in Manhattan. Thenceforth she used the Maple Harbor property only for summer holidays.

The 'summering-at-Maple-Harbor' tradition had been kept up for some decades now: Amy, with husband Charles and daughters, in the Hawkins' stately old summer home on the far side of the harbour; Beatrice, with or without her mother, in the much humbler farmhouse that had been their home when she and Amy were little.

* * *

'Oh, Brian Whiting? He's Mama's discovery, not mine. Better ask her,'

Amy told her sister in the flippant, half-teasing tone they often adopted when the two of them were alone together. She was busy making up sandwiches for her two young daughters to take along on their sailing lesson. 'But he's quite a decent sort, actually. Did you notice how solicitous he was with Charles's poor old Aunt Clara? That made a great hit with Charles, of course. He adores her and I guess it's mutual, but she's made it quite clear to him that we're not in her will. Until and unless, that is … Not that we ever really counted on the money,' Amy added.

'Until and unless what?'

'Charles and I produce a son to carry on the Hawkins name. If you can believe it. The nerve of the woman!'

'Well, may success crown your efforts,' Beatrice said with a smirk.

'What bloody efforts?' Amy demanded, slapping down her spoon and giving Beatrice a furious look. 'Watch your language there, big sister. I've been on the pill ever since Juliet. Not that it's any of your business.'

'Only teasing, darling. The temptation was great,' said Beatrice sweetly. Then, after a moment, 'What do you suppose Mama sees in him?'

'Who, Brian? His tenacity for one thing, I suppose. The man would rather die of sunstroke than quit without a fish.'

Beatrice had heard the story. The second day after his arrival, Brian had been fishing off the public dock, hatless and shirtless, his shoulders scarlet with sunburn, when Hannah spotted him from the road. She had rushed down to the dock and dragged him home with her for a cool drink and a bit of medical attention.

'Well, there's something to be said for tenacity in certain situations,' Beatrice said. 'But you still haven't answered my question. If you were me, would you consider having an affair with our new little Englishman? Just say yes or no.'

'Yes or no.'

'Come on, Amy, be serious. Would you?'

'Yes. Or rather no, in retrospect.'

Beatrice's eyes widened. 'Don't tell me you've slept with him!'

'Cross my heart and hope to die.' (The sisters often reverted to childhood idioms when they believed themselves to be alone.)

'My God, Amy, you can't mean it!' Beatrice pretended to be horrified. 'How could you, with that funny little man!'

'Little? Not so little. Be fair, darling,' said Amy, mimicking their mother's accent. 'I would razzer describe him as short and compact. With razzer too muscular legs.'

'Too muscular for what?' said Beatrice, suddenly changing sides. 'I gather he was a keen footballer as a boy. It's the sport of the masses over there, you know. And he came of a poor family. You see he spilled all the beans about himself in the course of just ten minutes. Or would you call that another point against him?'

'Of course not, darling,' said Amy soothingly. 'And even if I did, people do change their style to suit their circumstances, as everyone knows.' She added a final sandwich to the stack. 'All Brian needs to do now is lose a little weight, tighten up his tummy, maybe – above all, though, no shorts, please, and no short nightshirts either – and voila, he'll be all set to please!'

They succumbed to a fit of giggling.

'But seriously, Beattie, let's not be too hard on Brian. He's a really sweet-natured person, I mean it,' Amy resumed as soon as she had recovered. 'You might not have noticed, but he's very attuned to children. Sally and Juliet think he's terrific. And you know, he's on the phone to his own kids nearly every day. Boy and girl. They're at boarding school in England somewhere, but he's got custody. He's planning to bring them here when he comes next year, it seems. Looks to me as if he might be one of the world's born fathers.' She turned on a torrent of hot water to rinse the mixing bowl and spatula.

Beatrice, standing by the window, stared at her. 'What are you trying to do, sell me a husband?'

'That's one way of putting it, I suppose,' said Amy, suddenly serious. 'Frankly, Beattie, I think it's time for you to settle down and think about starting a family. That is, if you want kids. You're not getting noticeably younger, you know.'

'So what?' Beatrice said sardonically, watching her sister wriggle out of the voluminous old-fashioned apron she favoured for kitchen work. Underneath she was wearing a yellow linen shift hand blocked in a pattern Beatrice recognised as Amy's own. Fabric design was now her only artistic outlet, apart from a few pen-and-ink drawings produced on the solitary bus journeys she still undertook from time to time 'to get back in touch with myself'.

* * *

Amy's artistic talent – inherited no doubt from her father, the ill-fated Jack LaCrosse – had been evident since childhood. While still in high school she had taken first prize in an important adult competition. Everyone expected her to go on to greater things, and she did in fact win a scholarship to the best art school in Boston, Mass. But she dropped out after two terms to marry Charles Hawkins of a well-known New England banking family. Six months after that, she gave birth to a daughter, Sally, and, barely a year after that, to a second daughter, Juliet. Both of them were now in early adolescence. Judging from one of the snapshots Aunt Mia had brought from America, they must be nearly as tall as their grandmother Hannah had been at that age.

* * *

'Drink?' Amy asked her sister.

'Yes please.'

Amy prepared the Martinis, as they are called (an entirely different drink from the bottled product sold here in Austria), handed one to Beatrice and perched with her own glass on the worktop beside the refrigerator. For a while both young women were silent, gazing out across the bay to the islands on the horizon line where the open ocean begins, the vast Atlantic that reaches five thousand kilometres from the American coast to the western shores of Europe.

(S. has in his possession an old photo, sent him many years ago by Hannah, of the 'summer place' at Maple Harbor, Maine, which her papa had bought for his family. That was many years ago, of course, but the view from the big shingled cottage overlooking the islands in the bay can hardly have changed with the passage of time.)

'Look, Beattie, don't think I don't know what you're thinking now,' Amy went on without looking at her sister. 'You must be thinking, it's easy for Amy to talk. She's had her way all along, she married this nice, rich, easy-going man, they've got a couple of lovely kids, a social position, lots of interesting friends, and the best of it is she's free to do as she pleases, travel whenever and wherever she likes, Charles wouldn't dream of objecting. She's even got that lovely chest of paints and brushes waiting up there in the attic – ' Her voice trailed off.

Beatrice gave her head a quick shake as if to clear it. 'Well, even if I was thinking something along those lines – isn't all that enough?' she asked after some moments, tracing the rim of her glass with a fingertip.

'No, Beattie, it isn't.'

'What rot,' Beatrice said under her breath.

'No, listen, Beattie. You don't understand, really you don't,' Amy said quickly. 'Because, please believe me, if I were offered the chance of living my life over again, but with lots more talent and energy and opportunities and plenty of exciting lovers and a brilliant husband, if I could have all that and more, I wouldn't take it. I'd still opt for exactly the life I've got now. Average husband, two kids to take care of, cocktail parties, PTA meetings, Planned Parenthood and charity work and all the other little busy-bee activities that occupy my days.'

She broke off to gulp the rest of her drink. 'Why, you ask. I'll tell you why, Beattie. Because they're the only things I can count on to fill the emptiness. If I didn't have them I honestly think I could crack up. You know: have a breakdown, go bananas. And that wouldn't be nice for anyone, would it? So that's why I say hurrah for the PTA. And a toast to the well-hung Master Brian, too. Long may his manhood wave!'

* * *

Gentle reader, if you count yourself among the elderly or the innocent at heart, do not at this point allow Amy's reckless language to shock you. Do not be tempted to draw hasty conclusions about her moral character. Regardless of what might come to pass after the death of her infant son, hers had until then been a happy and harmonious marriage.

But it was a modern marriage as well. The social and moral barriers of yesteryear were already crumbling when Amy and her Charles Hawkins exchanged their marriage vows. Thanks to modern medicine, venereal disease – once a mortal threat to life and sanity and a curse on future generations – had been reduced to a mere inconvenience. Contraceptive drugs had freed women to take their pleasure, like men, wherever and whenever they chose. The bonds of monogamy had been loosened if not cut, making it quite possible for a stable, superficially conventional marriage partnership to be spiced with the occasional erotic adventure.

Regrettably, this new morality denies modern man the thrill of transgression that was once inseparable from sex. Even the religious are free to indulge in the grosser fleshly pleasures without the need for elaborate precautions to guard their secret.

How about the Fear of Consequences, then, the reader may ask.

But that fear had never, of course, deterred our ancestors from sexual transgression, it had only made them skilled in the arts of concealment. Now all that is past. Yet all of us in the West still bear within us, well concealed from the outside world, the genes of our forebears. That being so, why should we not have inherited certain of their foibles, and perhaps the stain of their guilt as well?

(A peculiar expression, 'the West', especially when one considers that a traveller circling the globe westward from Vienna will eventually leave 'the West' behind him, passing through 'the Far East' and 'the Near East' before the finger of St Stephen's on the horizon tells him he is approaching, from the East, his original point of departure!)

Our liberal modern view of sex is, in fact, not so very modern after all. Even in our grandparents' day, the sternest piety and the grossest lechery seemed able to coexist in perfect comfort, especially in the provinces. Liaisons between priests and laiety were not uncommon in rural Austria, where illegitimate births were more the rule than the exception and even farm animals often became helpless victims of the vilest human lust. Or so we are free to learn, now that morality has been declared obsolete and censorship itself has become the only recognised obscenity.

* * *

Thus, midway in this fable, it will be well to pause to search out the roots of the evil that had befallen the family and reflect on the possible consequences had S. failed in his knightly errand to deliver the blighted neonate, after the briefest of sojourns here on earth, into the hands of its Maker.

Suppose the child had been fated to live on through the seven stages of man's life to its inevitable conclusion, suffering, and willy-nilly inflicting on others, worse tortures with every passing year. Would not that itself have intolerably increased the penance required of the family for its ancestral wrongdoing?

It goes without saying that 'intellectuals' like Professor Dr Rosen will try to convince you that all such speculations are purest fantasy; that all the guilt a man might feel himself called to atone for, from dim ancestral incest to dreams of infanticide, is a contrivance to escape the monotony of a featureless future: gobbets of flesh served up to nourish the void – or, in S.'s case, the writer's hungry imagination.

◄ 5 ►

On the paternal side, Mr Hawkins senior was the last person to learn of the new baby's birth. The chain of messages which had started in Vienna with a young doctor's brief announcement continued with Eva's telephone call to Hannah in New York, who in turn called Beatrice in Wales and Charles in Bangor, Maine, who then rang old Mr Hawkins in Del Ray Beach, Florida, his home since the death of his wife from cancer nearly a quarter-century before.

By the time the news reached Charles' father, all mention of handicap seems to have been filtered out – or, if not, it simply failed to register with the old gentleman, who had long nursed a hope that Charles and Amy would one day present him with a grandson. 'By God, boy, I was beginning to think you didn't have it in you!' he croaked jubilantly into the receiver, and having managed to secure the address of St Saviour's, immediately cabled three dozen red roses to his daughter-in-law, with love and hooray and congratulations on the new arrival from One Proud Grandpa.

'It was pure luck that I happened to be just walking out when they came with these,' Eva told S. when she entered his room with his evening medicine, holding the huge bouquet in front of her like a trophy. 'I simply gave the delivery man fifty schillings and brought them home with me. Just look at them, they're absolute beauties. We haven't a vase big enough to hold them, so you get them in a pitcher.'

She set it down carefully on the computer table between the bed and the window. 'Thank God I was there to intercept them. Look at this stupid card from the father-in-law. They can't have told him, can they? Poor old fellow! But the effect that card could have had on Amy doesn't bear thinking about. I haven't mentioned the roses to Aunt Mia, either, but I suppose she'd bound to notice them. Just don't call attention to them if you can help it, OK?'

'Why not?' S. asked drily. 'It's nothing to do with her, is it, if the baby isn't, well, quite what a new mother might want to take into her arms.' He swallowed his pill with a gulp of water. 'Anyway, isn't a fifty-schilling tip just a shade excessive?' And when Eva chose not to reply, 'But go ahead by all means if you've got that kind of cash to squander, it's entirely your affair. As for the roses, I don't really care for them. That's my work table, you know.' He emptied his glass and lay back, gazing at her from under half-closed lids.

'Wait, don't you want me to fluff it a bit first?' Eva said, but there was no need as she had given him an extra pillow. (When the head is well propped up, the circulation in the trunk and extremities is enhanced, conducing to healthy sleep.)

'Well, please yourself.' Eva turned to lower the venetian blind, taking extra care to get it, for once, precisely halfway down, the way S. likes it. 'Brother Sebastian can find a place for them in your chapel.'

S. propped himself on his elbows to look more closely at the drooping roses. Then he shook his head. 'Not for our chapel, I'm afraid. Day before yesterday they might still have been nice, but now about all they're good for is the compost heap. I'll be glad to perform that little office for you tomorrow morning.'

* * *

Though she might have been tempted to dispute S.'s judgement of the roses' condition, Eva accepted his offer without demur. As S. well knew, the compost heap was her bane. It had been started many years ago, in a back corner of the garden behind a laurel hedge, by her son Werner. She had disliked the thing from the beginning. It was smelly and untidy, and her prediction that Werner would lose interest and abandon it had soon come true.

Moreover, one evening in early summer when Eva, unable to fall asleep, had taken a stroll in the moonlit garden, a moan from the toolshed in the other corner of the garden had led to the discovery of Werner and two other youths sprawled in a stupor, possibly drug-induced, just inside. Someone had vomited copiously into a box of garden implements. It was a scene typical of the youth culture of that time.

'And who'll have to clean up your god-awful messes again? Me, of course!' she thundered at the boy periodically throughout the following day. 'You make me sick! You're a total egotist just like your father.

Neither one of you gives a toss for anybody else, you just go ahead and do whatever suits you and let other people clear up the wreckage. You think that's awfully clever, don't you, making somebody else pay the piper? Well, let me tell you, my lad, you might get away with it here at home, but out in the great world you're due for a rude awakening!'

Werner, as usual, didn't attempt to defend himself. He simply stood sullenly in the doorway until the storm was spent, then turned on his toe and disappeared up the stairs. A few days later, after another confrontation with Eva over the company he was keeping, the boy took his rucksack and guitar and left home for good. It was barely a month since he had turned eighteen.

* * *

All this, of course, took place long after the war, so there was no danger of Werner's disappearing without a trace as his father had done in the confused circumstances of 1945. Besides, Werner probably had no wish to distress his mother; he only wanted to escape into some sort of independent life, and having succeeded in that he did keep in touch after a fashion. From time to time the postman would bring a 'Liebe Mutti' picture postcard from yet another of Werner's ports of call, never with a return address but always, or almost always, with a postscript in English to please his uncle: 'Hallo, Uncle Stefan! Love from your travelling nephew Werner Berger', or words to that effect, a token that the boy had not forgotten his faraway uncle!

It was in Juares, Mexico, that Eva's son finally found whatever it was he had been looking for and wrote his first real letter home, this time with a return address. Eva at once cabled money. Werner's second letter asked her not to send any more; he had found work as a garage mechanic and things were going very well. A year later, he had mysteriously become the owner of a repair shop.

Soon thereafter a printed announcement arrived. S.'s Latin, though rusty, enabled him to work out the general drift of the Spanish text, which reported the betrothal of Sr Werner Berger to one Conchita Maria Supervia, daughter of Sr and Sra Antonio Supervia of Juares. This welcome news was followed a few (too few!) months later by tidings of the birth of a daughter, Petra Evita.

'Evita, that's the diminutive of Eva,' S. pointed out, thinking to please her. 'Eva, after you.'

His remark had quite the opposite effect. 'I find that extremely offensive,' his sister snapped. 'It's utterly unheard of, putting his mother's name in the middle, like an afterthought!' She rubbed the back of her hand fiercely across her forehead. 'It's like a curse, all my life having to take second place with everyone. Mama, Papa, Hannah, everyone. And with you too, S., and don't you dare deny it! A convenience to you, that's all I am, and it's high time I – ' Breaking off in mid-sentence, she flung herself face downward on Great-Aunt Mitzi's splendid leather divan, her body shaking with sobs.

Experience had taught S. that there was nothing useful he could say, but he sensed that his touch might comfort her. Kneeling beside the divan, he slipped off her shoes, took a foot in either hand and began gently massaging each toe in turn with a symmetrical rotary motion of his thumbs, working outward from the great toe to the small and concluding with a series of vigorous squeezes of the outer instep.

It was a ritual he had invented in their childhood to calm them both when they were cowering together in bed listening to their parents shout and scream at each other in the next room. Now, as then, it proved effective: Eva's awful sobs finally died away, and she put her head against his chest, as the welcome darkness slowly gathered in the room.

* * *

A similarly tumultuous scene, likewise reminiscent of early days, took place again a dozen years later, when Werner wrote to ask whether his daughter Petra might spend the summer with her grandmother in St Anselm, and learn a little German.

Eva, though not keen on the idea to begin with, had been finally persuaded to agree to it as a gesture of reconciliation, but she told S., 'You know, I hate to say it, but I just have an awful feeling that nothing good will come of all this. Somehow things have never turned out quite right for us in this family; it's as if there were some sort of jinx on us. Don't you think that's possible?'

'Nonsense. Don't talk of the devil!' S. had admonished her sharply.

* * *

Eva's premonition proved well founded.

In a small provincial town like St Anselm, strangers are noticed. With her dusky skin, her broad cheekbones, her almond-shaped eyes and heavy black braids, the twelve-year-old Petra drew stares wherever she went in her grandmother's company. And Eva, though she tried not to show it, was embarrassed to be seen with the child.

Petra for her part was lonely and bored; she needed playmates, and there were no children of her age in our neighbourhood. So she hung about the house most of the day, watching Eva as she went about her household tasks.

This was a source of great annoyance to Eva, who had expected help with the housework but discovered very early that beyond keeping her own room in order Petra was not prepared to provide it. Whatever her reasons, when asked to lend a hand the girl would shake her head firmly and waggle her hand in a gesture of negation, smiling apologetically as if she were being prevented by forces beyond her control. If the flood of Spanish which accompanied this behaviour contained a satisfactory explanation it was lost on Eva, who on these occasions would usually banish Petra to her room and repair to the kitchen to make herself a calming cup of tea.

Whenever S. came home for the day, as he tried to do as often as possible during the three weeks of Petra's stay, he would give her a German lesson. He had equipped himself with a German-Spanish dictionary and was intent on providing the child with at least the rudiments of a German vocabulary. She proved to be a willing but desperately slow pupil, and it was always a relief to both of them when the lesson was over and Petra could amuse herself helping S. soak off the latest batch of postage stamps or looking for the dozenth time through his and Eva's album of family pictures. Curiously, she showed hardly any interest in television!

And so the summer might have gone on if Eva had not made the mistake of taking the train alone to Vienna one afternoon to meet for tea with a Swedish lady with whom she had worked at the United Nations. Petra, who was afraid of being left in the empty house, begged and begged to be taken along, but Eva was adamant that she should stay at home. Unfortunately S., four kilometres away in his sanatorium room, knew nothing of all this, or the disaster might have been avoided. As it was, when Eva got home some three hours later, Petra was weeping in her room, and Eva's own room was in indescribable disorder: the bed pulled apart, drawers emptied, dresses from the closet strewn across the floor.

It was Petra's revenge. She had damaged nothing, but her act was beyond Eva's power to forgive. A cable went off to Werner next morning, and two days later Eva and S. were seeing the girl off on the long flight back to Mexico City.

They have not set eyes on her since and are unlikely ever to do so, though Petra, now married and the mother of two children (first boy then girl, in the so-called 'royal' order) has recently written S., in bad English, two letters of inconsequential family news. (Curiously, both were correctly addressed to S. at the sanatorium. One wonders who can have given her the address. Surely S.'s literary activities could not have been headline news in far-away Mexico City?)

Though he couldn't quarrel with his sister's decision, S. was sorry to see the girl go. The house in Elisabethstrasse seemed twice as big and twice as gloomy without her.

Eva, recovered from her shock, was now able to view the incident philosophically. She said, 'We might as well face it, young and old just don't mix. And when you throw in a language barrier and an alien, er, ancestral culture – well, I guess we were lucky nothing worse came of it. I should have known better than to give in to Werner. It was all his fault, really.'

'You're just as much to blame, in my opinion,' S. said severely. 'It takes two to tango, you know.' This saying, so apt that S. could not resist it at that moment, was a bit of ancient slang from the 1920s that had recently come back into vogue.

Far from appreciating it, however, Eva started to cry. S. instantly felt a pang of remorse. In his heart of hearts he was deeply sorry for his sister, for fate had indeed dealt out to her an undue portion of pain and sorrow as penalty for the ancestral fall from grace!

⚍ 6 ⚏

Eva Berger's misfortunes had begun in the closing months of the war when, aged eighteen and about to give birth to Werner, she was informed by the military authorities that the child's father had been killed in action on the North African front when his tank was destroyed by an American grenade. The report was false: in reality, Herbert Berger was 'alive and kicking' in a prisoner-of-war-camp in Georgia, USA. Eva, of course, had no way of learning this, and it suited Herbert to start a new life in America unencumbered by family obligations.

At the end of the war, Eva herself had no longer any family of her own to turn to. Herbert's parents had fled west long before the Red Army's advance on Vienna (they never returned to St Anselm), and Eva's own parents were dead. Believing that S., their only son, had died a hero's death in the fight for his 'homeland', they had done away with themselves only minutes before the first Red Army tank rolled into the main square of St Anselm.

So it should by rights have been a joyous day for Eva when her brother, miraculously alive as it seemed, returned from two months' American captivity in Salzburg to be her help and support in the difficult times ahead!

Instead, her brother's return had brought nothing but trouble, beginning with his revulsion from food and culminating, some three weeks later, in the shame of seeing him consigned to a madhouse as an alternative to going to prison for 'unacceptable behaviour' in public.

That was the way of the authorities in those dim days of yore, before the age of enlightenment was ushered in by great men like Prof. Dr Rosen. Nowadays, of course, the pendulum appears to have swung to the other extreme, as witness some male 'movie stars' and 'models' who are paid huge sums for fleetingly displaying their sex organs for the titillation of an imbecile public!

* * *

Aunt Mia did all she could to help her Austrian relatives after the war, sending money from America as soon as a reliable postal service was resumed. Since the death of her husband, she had journeyed to Vienna each year, around the time of All Souls' and All Saints' Days, to visit not only her two living blood relatives, but the family graves in Vienna and St Anselm. (The Fischer-Uncle had been laid to rest in Long Island, but Aunt Mia explained that she owed it to his memory to light a candle at the Fischer mausoleum in Vienna's Central Cemetery, where his brother Lionel was interred. 'They all need candles lit and prayers said for them. We're all sinners, nobody's exempt,' she told her favourite nephew.)

* * *

Eva's private life became a great deal more endurable for her (and thus for her brother!) after Brother Sebastian appeared on the scene in the mid-1960s. It improved even further a decade later, with the advent of Dr Hebbar at the Vienna United Nations.

'Brother Sebastian taught me the love of God and Dr Hebbar the love of the intellect,' she told S. on more than one occasion.

The nauseous complacency of that remark deserved to be punctured by a sharp retort. The words, 'Pity neither one is available for sex,' crossed S.'s mind but not his lips, for as a gentleman of the old school he would not dream of addressing a lady in such terms, even if she were his own sister! In the words of the famous philosopher Wittgenstein, 'Before the unspeakable one ought to be speechless.'

* * *

Much the same delicacy with regard to his sister made S. hesitate to bring up with her the subject of a certain member of staff at the sanatorium, a young Filipino woman who was entrusted with the duty of bringing round the patients' food-trolley at midday. Having learned that this young person, whose name was Teresa, had a brother in the refugee camp who happened to be a keen philatelist, S. occasionally gave Teresa a few of his own stamps that would otherwise have gone to Brother Sebastian. Her gratitude for these small gifts was touching. To say that a friendship had sprung up between Teresa and himself would, S. knew, be grossly overstating the case; but he had come to look forward to her daily smile and greeting, and he fancied that Teresa for her part looked up to him not only with respect but with some small measure of affection.

Now, some people here in Austria may have their reservations about becoming familiar with foreigners, but as for the Filipini, once one gets accustomed to their looks, they prove to be very nice, open-hearted people.

It would be useless to pretend that there are no important differences between them and ourselves. All the same, Oriental ladies are very often more understanding than our own. They never look down on you or expect you to behave with them in a particular way, nor do they ever make fun of you like certain ladies in certain houses on the Guertel which claim to cater for all sorts of special needs. (The Guertel, or 'girdle', is a ring road, enclosing the more central districts of Vienna, which is frequented by buyers and sellers of carnal pleasure.)

S. had more than once thought how pleasant it would be to offer Teresa and her brother, or perhaps Teresa alone, a taste of old-fashioned Austrian hospitality at the house on Elisabethstrasse. He was nervous about making any such proposal to Eva, fearing that she would be disposed to read unseemly motives into it. But when he finally did bring up the subject, the objection she actually raised was even more bizarre – the size of our house and its many empty rooms might, she thought, tempt Teresa and family to move in and stay with us for good!

Quite apart, though, from that imaginary danger, Eva is terrified of tropical germs. 'Remember the time I went to India,' she once said to her brother. 'I didn't tell you then because I didn't want to alarm you, but I was desperately ill in that hospital in Bangalore. I really thought my last hour had come. Poor Dr Hebbar was frantic. I'd sworn him to secrecy about my condition, you see.'

'All the same, he ought to have notified me,' S. replied sharply. 'As your brother I had a right to know. I must say I find it shockingly irresponsible of both of you.'

To this Eva offered no defence, although she must have been aware of the hurt behind his reproof.

* * *

Dr Srivatsa Hebbar, for many years Eva's deputy department head at the United Nations Atomic Energy Authority in Vienna, was a gentleman and a scholar as well as a distinguished bureaucrat. What drew him and Eva into an enduring intellectual friendship was a common interest in literature, and especially a shared enthusiasm for the English Lake Poets, going back, in Dr Hebbar's case, to his undergraduate days at Mysore University, where he had done his thesis on 'Wordsworth's Debt to Vedic Philosophy'.

From his first visit to the house in St Anselm, Dr Hebbar impressed S. with his intelligence, his social poise and his unfailingly correct and courtly manner towards Eva. To S. he was cordiality itself, bringing him Indian postage stamps on each visit to the house in Elisabethstrasse and several times taking the three of them to dinner at Lindmaier, a restaurant he had heard S. praise.

When Dr Hebbar was first posted to Vienna he was already a married man and the father of a teenage son, but he came alone. Having been told by a noted astrologer that disastrous consequences would ensue if she should set foot outside India, his wife, an orthodox Hindu lady, had flatly refused to accompany him. So it was that she and Eva had never met until the early autumn of 1975, that fateful year when Dr Hebbar went on extended 'home leave' to arrange for the wedding of his niece and ward Lalitha.

Eva eagerly accepted his invitation to the wedding. Despite her brother's reservations about the safety and propriety of a 'maiden' lady like herself travelling alone in such a distant tropical country, she was not to be deterred. Her intention was to combine her visit to the Hebbars with an all-India tour after the wedding in Bangalore, and she spent many hours at her desk poring over tourist brochures and plotting out possible itineraries.

But just three days after her arrival in India, on the day after the wedding in fact, Eva was stricken by a particularly virulent 'stomach bug' which actually put her in hospital for the better part of a week. She was thus effectively insulated from the distressing aftermath of poor Mrs Hebbar's tragic death.

* * *

Lalitha's wedding had taken place at the Jagan Mohan Hall, a local venue much in demand for important private 'functions'. It was a love match, Eva had learned from Dr Hebbar, a rare event among orthodox Hindu families and one frowned on by the Brahmins and other 'hidebound conservatives', as he described them.

'Even my wife, you know,' he had added, 'is not so very happy with the match. She likes the boy Chandra very much but her parents disapprove and she is worried about that. She is a very traditional minded lady, you see. Religion-wise, she feels she is married to a dangerous liberal. She even suspects me of eating meat when I am in Vienna! I am hoping you can set her straight about that, at least, while you are here.'

Eva said she would be happy to do so, but it occurred to her that testifying to the fidelity of Dr Hebbar's vegetarianism might not be the best way of ingratiating herself with his wife!

During the two evenings Eva passed with the family, Mrs Hebbar, a plump, rather pretty lady in her middle forties, had smiled a great deal, treated Eva with impeccable courtesy and an almost exaggerated concern for her comfort, but addressed hardly a word to her directly. Dr Hebbar had apologised for her, saying she was shy about her English but would soon 'come out of her shell'. Eva had her doubts of that!

All had gone well with the wedding arrangements, and the happy day itself dawned 'auspiciously', as the Indians would say. By midday all the seats in the Jagan Mohan Hall were occupied by guests (including, Eva was told, the Deputy Chief Minister of the state), and the barechested Brahmin priest with his two assistants were busying themselves on-stage with preparatory rituals in advance of the marriage ceremony proper. Mrs Hebbar seemed relaxed and in good humour, joking with her niece as she helped her with the final adjustment of wedding garments and make-up. She herself was attired in a splendid new red-and-black silk sari, heavily embroidered with gold.

The wedding ceremony lasted for several hours. Eva, fascinated at first by the colourful goings-on on stage, found her interest fading after the first hour. Of course she understood little or nothing of the ritual, and neither of the elderly ladies between whom she was seated – aunts of Mrs Hebbar, if she had understood correctly – was able to remedy her ignorance. The one on the right, it appeared, knew no English at all;

the one on the left was prodigiously fluent but spoke at breakneck speed in such a heavy accent that Eva could make nothing of it and resorted to a pretence of understanding, with nods and smiles and frequent exclamations of 'Really!' and 'How interesting!' as the lady rattled on.

Late in the afternoon the ceremony finally came to an end and the dining and entertainment began. The various dishes – totally different from any Indian food Eva had ever eaten in the West, she told her brother – was served on large green leaves set on long tables, and the guests really tucked into their meal as Mrs Hebbar bustled about, seeing to it that no one's leaf remained bare for more than a moment.

The main feature of the entertainment (arranged in defiance of custom and, it was understood, at the bride's particular request) was to be a rock group from Delhi, 'Kali's Kids'. The four wild-looking young men spent most of the mealtime setting up their amplification equipment in the front of the hall and were just testing their microphones as the guests wandered back to their seats.

No one, it seems, noticed Mrs Hebbar leaving the hall or remarked her absence for perhaps a quarter of an hour. 'Kali's Kids' had just finished their first set when shouts were heard outside and a young man burst in waving his arms and shouting something that electrified the hall. There were cries of consternation. Many guests leaped to their feet, others sat as if paralysed, a few burst into tears and a long wail went up from someone in the rear of the hall.

It was some minutes before Eva learned what had happened. Mrs Hebbar, having slipped away unobserved, had walked to a nearby railway crossing and flung herself under the wheels of the evening Madras express.

Her death was a shattering event for her husband and family, all the more devastating because the Hindus regard suicide as a sin equivalent to murder. In their eyes, the poor lady had probably assured herself of something close to our eternal damnation.

* * *

In the months and years that followed, much speculation as to motive and much philosophical discussion as to the meaning of the tragic event was to take place many thousands of miles away in St Anselm, accompanied at times by severe self-castigation on Eva's part. It was wrong of her to have taken the trip, she kept repeating; she should never have accepted the invitation. No Westerner had any business attending a Hindu wedding; the sight of a white face at what was to everyone else there a sacred and rather intimate occasion couldn't help giving offence.

Dr Hebbar had, of course, been aware of all this but must have decided to flout public opinion rather than allow it to dictate to whom he might extend his hospitality. 'You are my friend,' he had once told Eva, 'and I believe in sticking up for my friends whatever my enemies might say.' Certainly he had behaved towards her with conspicuous gallantry on the two evenings she had spent with the Hebbar family.

'I don't know why it never occurred to me that he could be hurting her,' Eva said to S. later. 'But it's so obvious, isn't it? She'd heard about me so much in his letters, and suddenly there I am sitting in his house – her house – letting him practically pay court to me. That's what must have driven her over the brink. What a fool I was, what a guilty fool!' *Et cetera*, on and on.

Fed up at last with his sister's palaver, S. finally set her straight in frank, not to say brutal, terms. 'What are you trying to prove?' he demanded. 'Listen, even if your charming presence was the very last straw for the poor lady, you didn't kill her. Her suicide was her choice, not yours. The Hindus believe in karma, you know, so she must have known that suicide was in the cards for her, no matter how she might try to escape it. So she chose to embrace it instead. And that's not your affair at all, as far as I can see.'

* * *

Three months after the death of his wife Dr Hebbar retired from his United Nations post and returned to Bangalore to take up a new job as general secretary of the state civil servants' association. He never revisited Vienna, probably because the cost of air travel was now beyond his means, but he kept up a lively correspondence with Eva, reflected in a steady influx of colourful Indian stamps for S.'s collection.

❧ 7 ❧

Dr Hebbar's departure was something of a blow to Eva on the professional as well as the personal level. She conceived a hearty dislike for his successor as department head, a chain-smoking Pakistani lady who ruled her little 'fiefdom' with an 'iron hand' and managed to impose a strict ban on social conversation during office hours. The following spring, when the department was reorganised and Eva's job became impossibly difficult, she decided to avail herself of the authority's generous early-retirement scheme and give up gainful employment for the life of a 'lady of leisure'.

Except in passing, Eva never spoke to S. of Dr Hebbar. Whatever news his letters might have brought she kept to herself, and out of delicacy S. never asked any questions. Aunt Mia, however, being of a worldly disposition, had no such inhibitions. Less than a year later, on her annual All Souls' Day visit to Vienna, when the three of them were seated together after dinner, she suddenly looked up from her Kronenzeitung to say, 'And that Indian doctor of yours, Dr Hobbit or whatever his name is: how is he doing?'

'He's all right from what I hear,' Eva replied brusquely, probably hoping that the old lady wouldn't pursue the topic.

'I expect he's none too happy, a man in the best years without a wife,' said Aunt Mia, undeterred. 'It doesn't seem right to me, not right at all. He really liked you, Eva, anyone could see that. Now if I were you I'd show a little more interest and concern, I'd take the lead a bit, if you understand me. What's the sense of two lives going to waste, I'd like to know?'

Eva cried, 'Dear Lord, Aunt Mia, what are you saying? What an idea! Hebbar and I are good friends, full stop. There wasn't and isn't anything more to it than that, I assure you. Why, I wouldn't dream of such a thing.' She spoke in a tone of light amusement, but a vivid flush had spread over her cheeks.

'Now don't you get yourself in a tizzy, darling,' Aunt Mia persisted. 'I'm only saying maybe you ought to dream about it, 'cause it's not such a crazy idea at all. You're well matched in age and interests, you seemed to enjoy each other's company, you're a normal woman and he's a normal man, you're both unattached – well, my goodness, what could be more natural? And Evalein,' she went on ignoring signs of increasing discomfort on her niece's part, 'I shouldn't have to remind you that you're not getting any younger. Getting a bit long in the tooth, as they say. Now here's an eligible man, ripe for the picking, so to speak, and you're seemingly too proud to make a move. Doesn't make much sense, does it, my girl?'

Eva, now very flushed, sat with compressed lips awaiting the end of her aunt's monologue, unconsciously twisting her clasped hands in her lap.

Aunt Mia drew breath and resumed, pressing her advantage. 'And if what's bothering you is that poor lady's misfortune or accident, whatever it was – well, I say forget it. It was nobody's fault but her own, poor creature, so you should just stop brooding about it and let her rest in peace. Let the dead bury their dead, that's what I always say.'

Here she gave Eva an appraising look. 'Now don't misunderstand me, I'm not saying there aren't any obstacles. You've got your culture and you've got your race and religion, and you would have to make allowances. As I know from experience. Your Uncle Ludwig had his own peculiar ways in some things as well. Granted he was European too, but he came from a different religion and that makes a difference, don't let anyone tell you it doesn't. But it really shouldn't keep you from marrying What's-his-name, not in this day and age it shouldn't, unless of course … ' (she put in a brief strategic pause, observing Eva over the tops of her rhinestone-encrusted spectacles) ' … unless of course his heart is already engaged elsewhere. Maybe he's already found himself a new wife in the meantime?'

It was then that Eva dropped her bombshell. 'Yes, luckily he has,' she said calmly. 'A nice primary-school teacher. Maybe a bit younger than him, it's hard to tell from the wedding picture he sent.'

S. was absolutely 'floored' by this revelation. He must have sat there staring at his sister open-mouthed like an idiot. Eva, who might have felt a twinge of shame for having withheld such vital information from a brother who had every right to know, avoided his eyes.

But his aunt, self-possessed as always, took Eva's revelation in her stride. 'Oh, indeed?' she said coolly. 'A love match, I take it?'

'Oh, I don't really think so,' Eva replied easily. 'You know in India it's very difficult for a man to live by himself. Widowers are practically obliged to marry again. Incidentally,' she added, 'I don't believe he has the least intention of starting a new family. Hebbar treasures his independence. As do I, by the way.'

Without giving the others time to collect themselves for a reply, she rose and made for the kitchen, saying over her shoulder, 'Don't forget Brother Sebastian will be here in an hour. I've got things to get ready.'

Presently, the rattle of an eggbeater gave notice that Eva was whipping the cream for Brother Sebastian's favourite apfelstrudel. It was their usual Sunday afternoon fare when the good Brother stopped by for tea before giving S. a 'lift' back to the sanatorium.

* * *

'It's a mystery to me why she took such a fancy to that little brown Dr Hobbit in the first place,' Aunt Mia remarked *sotto voce* to S. 'But she could certainly have had him. All she needed was to roll up her sleeves and go for it. And what stopped her? Pure pride and pig-headedness, that's all.'

'Could be,' S. said. He was tired and in no mood to argue. But the truth was that Eva would not have married Dr Hebbar in any case. What would have prevented her was not fear of the practical obstacles or the cultural and religious differences with which she would be faced. Rather, it was a positive reason: the heavy responsibility she bore in the person of her brother.

Had she been free of that burden, Eva might have packed her bags many years ago and said goodbye to a town where parents cautioned their sons not to get involved with Eva Berger. It wasn't so much that she would be bringing a baby into the marriage (though not everyone fancies playing father to another man's child!) as the common knowledge that her crazy parents had died in a suicide pact when the Russians came, and that she had a brother confined to the asylum just a few kilometres away.

* * *

* * *

But it's a well-known fact that people's attitudes change almost as freely as hairstyles or fashions in clothing. Nowadays very few are inclined to avert their eyes from unseemly sights like exposed genitalia, or object to others publicly engaging in activities that would have ranked in earlier decades as criminal misdemeanours. For this reason alone, life had become easier for Eva over the course of time, as people who had once shunned her on her brother's account gradually began to take a more tolerant view.

* * *

The great turning-point in the personal histories of both siblings, however, was to come years later, on 13 June 1982, when S.'s first story appeared in the Sunday supplement of *Die Presse*, Austria's most respected daily newspaper. Its publication had attracted much good publicity and drew felicitations from around the world for the author and the institution which, in a way, he represented.

Weeks later, people were still coming up to Eva in the street with such comments as 'Oh, I was so impressed by your brother's story in *Die Presse*, Frau Eva. Wonderful, really. Putting the sanatorium on the map like that, it's a boost for the town too. You must be so proud of him, Frau Eva!'

* * *

Individual successes aside, there can be no doubt that Mr & Mrs Average Citizen have become far more tolerant of deviations from the accepted norm. Today even Brothers dress like the laity when 'off duty', and the patients can dress more or less as they please, as long as their attire is clean and reasonably appropriate to the season.

Much the same holds for their behaviour. No one in authority appears to care in the least how unhappy the patients may be, or why they are making fools of themselves by singing some silly little song over and over again, or counting to a hundred and back again, or shouting nonsense or whimpering vain appeals such as 'Help me, oh, please, help me! Oh, please, please, somebody help me!' Not even the visitors care; they just avert their eyes and hurry off as fast as their dignity permits, as if to escape a contagious disease.

* * *

The picture changes drastically, of course, once you are enrolled in the Creative Therapy programme. From that moment, your mentor suddenly becomes a personal friend and spiritual guru. That gives him the right, even the duty, to spy on you, to explore you inside and out. 'Learn *from* your patient as well as *about* him,' Dr Rosen urges all his therapists. To him alone, to Dr Marvellous, will go all the credit for yet another miracle cure via the 'Healing through Creativity' method!

* * *

The deviousness of the good doctor may be illustrated by a scene from the life of S., dating from the late seventies when Dr Rosen came from Cambridge University, England, for a brief inspection tour of the institution he had co-founded the decade before.

Here we see him vigorously shaking S.'s hand. 'Hallo, old friend, what a pleasure to see you! But tell me, what are you still doing here? I had imagined you out there in the big world doing things, making a contribution, making a name for yourself, and instead I find you here just where I left you. All very nice and comfortable I'm sure, but don't you find it a bit limiting?'

Patient, screwing up his face in mock puzzlement: 'Limiting? But I see you yourself are here again, Dr Rosen, honouring us with a visit. Apparently you like it well enough.'

Dr Rosen's smile becomes a little less cordial, and his voice colder. 'Still a bit too contentious for your own good, I see. Look, S., don't waste your time trying to score points. Let me remind you who is the patient here and who is the doctor. You know quite well that I'm only here to help you.'

Patient, seemingly in increasing confusion: 'But if you've come here expressly for my sake, why should you want me to leave? Where would you be without me, doctor? Where would your wonderful institution be without a few star patients to be treated and exhibited and looked after?'

'Ah, very clever, my friend,' Prof. Dr Rosen replies with the ghost of a smile (the most such an important personage can permit himself). 'Though rather less clever than you imagine. Less clever than that entertaining story of yours, on which I must really congratulate you. But we will speak of that later, in my office.'

And with a benign pat on S.'s shoulder (some inches above his own), the great man moves on to the next patient.

Though praised in many other quarters, the story in question never received Brother Sebastian's wholehearted approval, since it stopped short of condemning an act which church dogma abhors as a mortal sin.

For the uninitiated reader of these pages, a brief résumé of the work may be of interest. It concerns a club, or society, whose members had committed themselves to ending their lives on their own terms when they no longer desired to live. It has a surprise ending suggested by Prof. Dr Rosen himself, who in fact had originally conceived the idea of the story and generously shared it with his prize patient S., the author-to-be. (For a translation of 'The Suicide Society' see the Appendix.)

* * *

Although he could not condone the story's content, Brother Sebastian had, as was his wont, unstintingly supported the author's arduous and ultimately successful efforts to complete it and bring it before the public.

(Alas that Brother is no longer here in bodily presence to perform the same services for the current work in progress!)

'You don't seem to understand, S.,' Eva remonstrated. 'You really cannot send Sebastian your manuscript and expect him to read it. God knows he's got enough else on his mind, with all those tribal killings and famines and sexual diseases out there! How could he afford to let himself be distracted?'

And she added, probably as much for her own consolation as to mollify S., 'The religious are supposed to dedicate themselves exclusively to God, and I'm sure Brother Sebastian has done exactly that. Their hearts are full of God, they've got no room there for selfish personal loves.'

* * *

Now, a truly wicked person might perhaps at this point suggest that Eva – with her history of repeated disappointments and rejections by her son, her lovers, etc. – could easily, in her heart of hearts, have felt a glow of malicious pleasure in ringing up cousin Hannah in New York shortly after midnight on that Good Friday to convey to her the terrible news of her daughter's blighted infant. For fate had, as it were, at last levelled the two of them out.

'Jealousy plain and simple,' such a person might say. 'After all these years Eva still resents Hannah. She can't forget that Herbert Berger had been making eyes at her beautiful cousin long before he took any notice of Eva's own existence. It's like a stone in her shoe.'

But such a person would be wrong on two counts.

First, Eva hadn't really been in love with Herbert Berger; in fact, for some time after he appeared on the scene, so to speak, she was seeing a boy called Werner Gerngross whom she had met at Ellmayer's dancing school. That came to an end when he became ill with cancer, dying that same winter at the age of seventeen. (His headstone in the lower city cemetery has since been removed, and last All Souls' Day, when Eva went there to light a candle for her old dancing-school partner, she was unable to find his grave.)

Second, Eva herself was far from plain; indeed, in her quieter way she was almost as pretty as Hannah and did not go unnoticed by boys, even boys in the lower grades. S. suspected that quite a few of his schoolfriends and comrades used to come to the house as much in hopes of catching glimpses of Eva as to be with S. himself.

Often Hannah was there as well, for Aunt Mia used to bring her along on her Saturday afternoon visits to Great-Aunt Mitzi, who was still living with us at that time. While the two ladies sat gossiping in the parlour, Eva and Hannah would shut themselves up in Eva's room to try their hair in different ways, experiment with lipstick and eye-shadow, and maybe engage in other experiments as well that made them giggle and squeal.

For a long time both girls were taller and looked more mature than S., who only caught up with them after the age of thirteen. By fifteen he had outgrown Hannah by nearly a head. But that was a long, long time ago, and they have not seen each other since to compare.

◄ 8 ►

Herbert Berger had not been among the boys who hung about their house for a glimpse of Eva.

All of them went to the same school, the Realgymnasium in Doebling, Hannah's home district, which was easily accessible from St Anselm by train. The boys' and girls' schools were in separate wings but shared the same schoolyard, so they all knew each other, at least by sight.

Herbert was three grades ahead of S. They first met in the junior section of the St Anselm rowing club, which Berger captained, but there had been little occasion for personal contact between them. Why, after all, should a star athlete like Herbert Berger interest himself in one of the weakest oarsmen in the club?

One day, however, Herbert unexpectedly strolled up to S. in the schoolyard during the ten o'clock recess and after a few moments of idle talk proposed a bicycle outing to Tulln for the following Wednesday, the first day of the Easter recess, 'if you can get your blonde cousin to come along'.

S., startled and flattered, readily agreed. He felt quite certain – rightly as it turned out – that Hannah would accept their invitation. She had recently been given a new cycle by her papa the Fischer-Uncle. It was the best ladies' touring bicycle that money could buy, with three speeds forward, multicoloured netting over the wheel guards and a real dynamo lamp that you tilted against the front wheel if darkness should overtake you on the road. S. had helped Hannah adjust the seat and handlebars to the correct height and made sure the tyres were properly pumped up.

Nothing was said by either boy about asking S.'s sister along. Eva couldn't have come in any case; she was due to leave on Monday with her classmates for a week's skiing course in Mariazell.

It was only early March, but the weather was already as capricious as in mid-April. Rain decreasing and a chance of some sunshine were predicted for the next forty-eight hours. S., checking the barometer on the outside gate of his father's veterinary practice, found that the mercury was indeed rising. He wished that taking Hannah for a bicycle ride had been his own idea; he certainly wouldn't have asked Herbert Berger along.

Then on the Tuesday, during the ten o'clock recess, Herbert had again come up to S. and said, 'Look here, Stefan, I've been thinking. Threesomes are stupid, don't you agree? No sense in both of us taking her – let's flip a coin.' S., feeling that this was a trick to get rid of him, said he thought they had better consult Hannah; but Herbert, ignoring his weak objections, spun the coin anyway.

Much to his surprise, and probably Herbert's as well, S. won the toss. He was fourteen at the time, and had never really been out alone with a girl before. But having got the idea from Herbert, he screwed up his courage to put the invitation to Hannah. To his delight and consternation, she agreed.

* * *

Wednesday was mild and sporadically sunny. Hannah and S. cycled some twenty kilometres upstream along the Danube past Krems, then scrambled down the embankment with their bikes to the river's edge, where they sat and ate the sandwiches and fruit each had brought from home. S. had a pear and Hannah a wedge of pineapple; she insisted they share. (Nowadays pineapple is nothing special, there is even such a thing as pineapple ice cream, but in those days only rich people even knew the name.)

After eating they lay back side by side on a sloping sandy patch and watched the river through half-closed eyes, a broad glistening sheet of grey-green slipping evenly from left to right, with frequent boats and barges passing in both directions, each flying the red-white-red of Austria at the bow and a foreign flag at the stern, each with a name painted on its side, often in Cyrillic characters which neither of them could read.

After a while his arm crept up to touch hers; then he took her hand and she let him keep it. So they lay there silent while a cold little breeze played above them and S. wondered whether she could hear the thumping of his heart against his ribs. He felt her hand stir in his and, afraid she was about to withdraw it, turned on his side towards her. The blood hammered in his ears. Hardly knowing what he was doing, he slipped one hand around Hannah's waist as if they were dancing, then slid the other slowly upward towards the mysterious shape of her breast. Her hand closed over his: to hinder or guide it? He never knew, for a moment later a burst of talk and laughter from people passing on the invisible towpath just above them put an end to this innocent beginning.

If anything of importance was said by either of them, before or after, it has left no trace in S.'s memory. He remember only how he explained to her about the Austrian national colours.

'Look, Hannah. The red stripes are supposed to represent the blood on a Crusader's garment – infidel blood, naturally – and the white part in between is where his shirt was protected by his big, broad battle-belt.'

'How ugly.' Hannah shivered. 'Why did you have to tell me? Blood really gives me the horrors.'

S. resisted the impulse to put his arm around her shoulders, sensing that it would displease her.

* * *

Curious that someone squeamish enough to shrink at the mere mention of blood should have chosen to become a doctor! According to the Eva of these latter days, however, the choice was not Hannah's: each person's fate is mapped out for them, long before birth, by good spirits, or at least with their help. Eva does not say whether these good spirits shape the destiny of monsters and murderers. Perhaps those are reserved for the bad spirits. Or do the good and bad spirits draw lots to decide which are to govern each soul's destiny?

* * *

There were two more bicycle rides, but no more picnics on the embankment. The weather had turned colder again and some strange constraint, almost a mutual embarrassment, kept them from any approach to intimacy; they were merely good comrades. S., in despair at his own stupid shyness, pinned his hopes on a fourth excursion they had planned, but it rained hard that day and the next.

And soon after that, Hannah had to leave with her parents for America. She kissed him goodbye on both cheeks, in plain sight of the family, and promised to write to him from America without fail. Then she turned hurriedly and dashed down the steps to the gate, as if she couldn't wait to be gone.

Two days later her first letter arrived, written that same evening and posted at the Westbahnhof before she boarded the train for Paris and Le Havre and the liner *Independence* that would take her to America. The letter wasn't as personal as S. had hoped; it was partly about a book she planned to finish on the train, although her mother thought it too old for her: *Victoria, the Story of a Love* by the Nordic writer Knut Hamsun. (Dr Rosen, as it turned out years later, knows this story too.)

'It's not very nice to say what I'm about to say, and I don't want to hurt your feelings,' she had written. 'Anyway, it's got nothing to do with you personally, or with the life I've lived in Vienna. Quite the contrary. I mean, I'd never, never have wanted to leave if it weren't for the Nazis and what they're doing to my father's people. But that has changed everything. Austria is my enemy now. I shall never forgive or forget, and [underlined] *I have sworn that I shall never go back*! So if you care to see me again you must come to America. Our home if we get there will be in New York. As you know my Uncle Lionel is already there and will help us get settled. Come and see me! *PS* From now on I shall be talking and writing *only English*, so you'd better work hard on your vocabulary!'

It need hardly be said that S. never breathed a word about having 'won' Hannah from Herbert Berger on the toss of a coin. Nor has he, throughout years of intimate correspondence with Hannah herself, ever so much as hinted at his knowledge of her post-war relationship with Herbert. The thought of his own duplicity in this regard is painful to him, and he wishes he could undo it, but that seems no longer possible.

Perhaps what made S. keep silent is the family pride that one sees in Aunt Mia, the kind of pride that won't acknowledge a fault in ourselves or in others, and neither asks nor offers forgiveness. He knew that Hannah's own 'infidelity', her clandestine relations with Herbert Berger, must have begun in St Anselm and been resumed in America. If Herbert was still alive, quite possibly the affair was still continuing.

In any case, Hannah must imagine that S. neither knew nor suspected anything. He had no wish to undeceive her, in fact the very thought of doing so was frightening to him. Whatever was between him and Hannah, he thought, might not survive the encounter with truth.

* * *

For accuracy's sake it must be recorded that there was yet another aspect of S.'s relationship with Hannah which had disquieted him from the very beginning. In those days, love between first cousins was frowned on as something not far enough removed from incest. Folk said that the offspring of such unions were often mentally retarded or, as they now say, 'disturbed'. Modern genetics has, of course, confirmed the wisdom of this supposed superstition.

Oddly, it seems not to have applied to Crowned Heads, since marriage between cousins (or, in ancient Egypt, even between siblings!) was almost the rule, and the fruit of such unions were regarded as embodying an especially noble and concentrated essence of kingship.

◀ 9 ▶

In this scene we are taken back to the 'guesthouse' or small hotel in Wales where Hannah's daughter Beatrice, lying in bed and watching her lover Brian prepare to join her, has just been summoned downstairs by the landlord to take a telephone call.

She already guesses that the caller is her mother in New York.

* * *

The guest telephone stands on a round table at the near end of the lounge. The receiver lies beside it, waiting, in the weak pool of light shed by a little brass lamp with a frilly shade. The landlord is nowhere in sight.

Beatrice lets some moments pass before picking up the handset.

* * *

Tensions between her mother and herself have increased in recent years. On the one hand, it is becoming ever clearer that Beatrice's work and her way of living would never measure up to Hannah's idiosyncratic ideals of personal and social integrity. On the other, Beatrice was becoming increasingly resentful of Hannah's aggressive eccentricities. She had often been hurt and humiliated by her mother's inconsiderate behaviour, she had confided to Eva on an earlier visit to Vienna.

Even in her dress, it seemed, Hannah had to flout convention. There were the shabby caftans, the tennis shorts revealing more than anyone wanted to see of bony elderly legs, the T-shirts spanning her generous bosom. And there was her deplorable readiness to hold forth to perfect strangers on the virtues of macrobiotic enemas, the occult significance of crop circles or the *vita sexualis* of the infant and young child.

Not to mention her penchant for picking up young men, which had led to Brian entering her daughter's life. Beatrice had more than once pondered how things might have turned out had Hannah decided to keep him for herself!

* * *

'Mama?'

'Beattie, darling, is that you?' Hannah always shouts on transatlantic phone calls, no matter how good the connection. 'Listen, darling, don't be alarmed, but your sister's just had a baby! Yes, in Vienna! Went into labour on the flight, it seems, and the pilot radioed ahead for an ambulance, so they got her to hospital in the nick of time. It's called *Zum göttlichen Heiland* – you know, Hospital of the Holy Saviour. In the Ninth District, if that means anything to you, darling. It's private, of course, with an excellent maternity wing as I recall. She couldn't be in better hands, I'm sure … ' Her voice trails off.

'Well, that's great news,' Beatrice says drily. 'Good for Charles, I say. Old Mr H. will be pleased as Punch. Boy or girl?'

'A little boy, darling. Quite premature, I gather – it was a Caesarean. But there's nothing to worry about!' Hannah trumpets out. 'Aunt Eva's been with her, in fact she rang me up from the hospital right after it happened. She sends you her love, darling.'

'I didn't even know Amy was pregnant again,' Beatrice says after some moments. 'My own sister.'

'Neither did I, Beatrice. The poor darling never has been awfully communicative, you know.'

'You can say that again,' says Beatrice sourly. 'But you've seen her, it must have been staring you in the face!'

'But darling, I didn't see her!' Hannah's voice rises. 'I didn't have a chance, she was only in town for a few hours and it was a Wednesday, so I was tied up at the clinic. Amy got in on the Wednesday morning plane from Bangor, and then she had to dash to Granny's and get her organised and get both of them into a taxi at four o'clock for the airport. She must have been terribly rushed, poor darling, she didn't even find a chance to ring me up at the hospital. I do so wish I could have been more helpful with Granny, but really and truly we had waiting lists a mile long. Those women come to us from far and wide, truly there was no way I could have called it off – '

'All right, Mother, calm down, nobody's accusing you!' Beatrice interrupts her. 'And do please turn down the volume a bit. We've got a wonderful connection, and it's really hard on the ears when you shout like that, I've got half a headache already.'

'I'm sorry, darling, there seem to be some interference on the line. Could you talk just a wee bit louder?'

'That's all right, let's just forget it, shall we?' Beatrice draws a deep breath as she reaches behind her for the chair and seats herself. 'But listen, Mama. Are you by any chance trying to lay some sort of guilt trip on me because you think I should have been the one to go with Granny? Because that's the impression I get. Don't think I don't know what you think of my work, you think it's all crap anyway.'

'Oh, Beatrice darling, how can you say that? Of course I don't, how can you think such a thing!'

'Come on, Mama, let's be honest with each other for once,' Beatrice says with a little laugh. 'Maybe the kid would have been born in its good time if Amy'd stayed home and either you or I had done the noble thing and volunteered as Granny's escort. Except of course that nobody could have expected you to do it, what with your clinic and your other work, and besides, we all appreciate how painful it would be for you with your Holocaust neurosis – ' she goes on rapidly, allowing her mother no time to object, ' – but what I'd like to know is why everyone just assumes that I should have been the one to call off everything and go off with Granny the moment it suited her whims! I've got deadlines in my life too, believe it or not, Mama, I'm under a lot of pressure. You've got no conception of how things stand with me.'

She breaks off, takes a deep breath and holds it for seven seconds (an Indian yogic technique for restoring one's inner calm). 'Sorry, Mama. Anyway, how is Amy doing?'

'Fine, darling,' Hannah says, and clears her throat violently. Though a fanatical nonsmoker, she is plagued much of the time by hoarseness and what sounds like a smoker's cough. 'Excuse me. No, Eva says Amy is fine. It seems she lost a good deal of blood, but that's only to be expected under the circumstances. Nothing to worry about.'

'How about the baby?'

Slight pause. 'I don't know, Beattie.' Another pause. 'I'm afraid he'll probably have to stay in an incubator for some time yet. Or so I gather from what Eva said.'

'Can't you call up the hospital? You haven't forgotten how to speak German, have you?' Beatrice demands sarcastically.

'Hospitals never give out information like that on the phone,' Hannah says equably, ignoring the provocation.

'Well, when do you plan to fly over there and see for yourself?'

'Oh, darling, I couldn't possibly. I'm on call at the clinic this coming weekend and all next week, remember it's Passover and then there's Easter upon us as well. I couldn't hope to find anyone to substitute for me over the holidays.'

'Really now, Mama! Don't tell me that anyone as inventive as you couldn't contrive to break loose for a week if she really wanted to! That clinic is a godsend, isn't it? The perfect excuse for leaving the responsibility for Granny to somebody else. Amy, or me. Daughters can be quite a help to their mothers, can't they?'

Hurt silence from Hannah. 'Beatrice, this isn't an emergency,' she says finally, clearing her throat again. 'Amy's in no danger.'

'I don't believe this!' Beatrice cries hotly, though it's precisely the reaction she might have expected. 'What kind of a mother are you? Here you've got a brand new grandson, your daughter is in hospital in a strange city, and you won't even make the effort to get over there! I bet if Charles or another of your favoured young men were in crisis you'd be on a plane tomorrow morning.'

Hannah clears her throat again. Another silence follows, one of such length that Beatrice begins to think she might really have wounded her mother, though Hannah – herself a passionate advocate of plain speaking – has always urged her daughters to be brutally frank with her.

'Beattie, you know better than that,' Hannah says at last, unexpectedly softly. 'You know that's not true.'

'Well, Mama, whether it's true or not I gather you're not coming,' Beatrice says, raising her voice slightly. There is now an intermittent crackle on the line, probably from the mainland part of the cable.

* * *

The transatlantic cables lie so deep on the ocean bed that even the severest storms cannot disturb them. The Austrian writer Stefan Zweig has written an interesting account of the laying of these cables in a collection of stories called *Sternstunden der Menschheit*, Star Hours of Mankind. Nowadays, however, cable transmission of transatlantic telephone conversations has been largely replaced by radio waves bouncing off satellites, an arrangement difficult for the layman to appreciate and one about which Stefan Zweig has nothing to say.

Perhaps we may one day learn how to communicate by mental telepathy. A very few genuine cases of that remarkable phenomenon have already been documented. Let us hope that scientists may yet discover how to control its strange power for the benefit of all mankind!

* * *

'Beatrice, I don't think I could be of any help to your sister,' Hannah finally says. 'I'm not even sure she wants me.'

'Don't be silly, Mama, of course she does,' Beatrice says quickly. 'She loves you, we both love you, you know that. I was just being horrid a minute ago, I didn't mean it.' She shifts the chair closer to the radiator to catch the last bit of fading warmth, wishing she hadn't been obstinate about Brian's jumper.

'I know, darling,' her mother says without conviction. 'Now how about you, are you all right?'

'Oh, I'm fine.' Beatrice has begun massaging her right shoulder with her left hand, in order to stimulate her circulation and thus raise the surface temperature of her body. (In the smaller English hostelries the heat is regularly switched off at nine. S.'s own sister caught the worst cold of her life at Stratford-upon-Avon, birthplace of the great William Shakespeare, as a result of this peculiar custom. Eva and three other ladies in her tour group had become so engrossed in a bridge game that they failed to notice how icy the room had become since dinner – or 'tea', as some of the old-fashioned English still refer to their evening meal.)

'Mama?' says Beatrice. 'There's something wrong with the baby, isn't there?' She feels that her teeth are actually on the point of chattering; the room is really frigid.

'I'm afraid there may be, darling,' Hannah says reluctantly. 'Eva said he might be handicapped. It doesn't sound very … hopeful.'

* * *

* * *

There are worse ways to be born, perhaps: limbless or spineless or as two heads sharing a single body. And worse horrors to witness or endure in hospital cancer wards, in the corridors of insane asylums, in secret-police interrogation chambers and punishment cells. Think of Auschwitz and Dresden and Hiroshima, the bloody wars of the ancient Greeks and Romans, the captives degraded and mutilated. Think of the killing fields of South-East Asia, think of the Aztec priests tearing out the hearts of living children to appease their cruel gods, think of the air-crash survivors feeding on the corpses of their companions.

Mercifully, few of the poor creatures who are born so severely maimed take very long to die. But some do linger on for years, and the saddest cases among them are those whose brains keep on functioning and whose senses have remained intact. For these the black abyss is always there yawning in the background, ready to swallow them up, no matter how nicely things may have been going for a stretch.

Yet it may have been only the tiniest hormonal imbalance that reduced his baby cries to an uncanny croaking and warped the tiny features under his bulging cranium. A single gene gone wild, a single bacterium, a virus so tiny that it escapes detection even under a powerful microscope!

* * *

In fact, it was just such a virus that had prevented Eva, on the afore-mentioned bus tour of Literary Britain, from visiting several important landmarks, such as the birthplaces of Charlotte Brontë (1818) and Thomas Hardy (1840), which she had once hoped to visit under different circumstances in the company of Dr Hebbar, a fellow devotee of the English Romantic poets as well as several others such as W.B. Yeats and T.S. Eliot, not to forget the great W. Shakespeare with his unusual Sonnets.

Their original plan to tour proud Albion together by hired car had come to nothing as a result of Mrs Hebbar's tragic death and her husband's consequent premature retirement from his UNO job. Thus deprived of her travelling companion, Eva had enterprisingly signed up with a tour sponsored by the University of Vienna which promised to include most of the historic sights on her list as well as several others she had never heard of. S. himself had very briefly considered joining her on the tour, for which his status as an adult student amply qualified him, but decided against it out of consideration for his sister. Other members of the tour party might, he thought, mistakenly take him for Eva's husband, and that would naturally deter any approaches by potentially interesting males.

Not that the possibility of attracting such males played any significant part in Eva's travel plans; but S. would have sincerely rejoiced to see such a thing come about, and the last thing he wanted was to hinder it. Unfortunately, as it happened the group consisted entirely of ladies. Even the bus driver was a woman.

◄ 10 ►

'Me stay on here while you're off to Vienna? Not a chance!' was Brian's reaction when Beatrice reported Hannah's news and announced her intention to take the next available flight to Vienna. 'I'm coming with you, full stop.'

'Well, if you put it like that,' Beatrice said wearily, feeling that she lacked the energy to oppose him. 'I don't suppose you'll mind being rather in the way.'

Brian didn't respond to that. 'Let's see now,' he said. 'We certainly ought to be able to catch an afternoon plane from Heathrow if we can make an early start.' He sat up in bed, swung his feet round to the floor and reached for his electronic personal organiser, painstakingly pro-grammed with airline and rail schedules, which he kept handy on his bedside table next to his water tumbler and his ulcer pills. He poked intently with one finger at the tiny keyboard.

Beatrice walked over to the dressing table and stooped to scrutinise herself in the small central mirror. 'I really ought to wash my hair, it looks a sight.'

Again Brian was too preoccupied to respond. 'There's a two-fifteen from Heathrow, but that means changing at Frankfurt. Or a Lauda from Gatwick at eight in the evening.'

'To tell the truth, I'm not all that keen on going there myself,' Beatrice said after a moment, running her fingers listlessly through her hair while keeping a watchful eye on her lover in the mirror.

Brian raised his sandy eyebrows. 'Oh, I wouldn't have thought you had a choice, love,' he said slowly, reverting to the Yorkshire accent that went with his Brian-knows-best manner. Even Eva, whose years of working with an Indian 'boss' in a UNO setting had accustomed her ear to exotic accents, was often baffled by Brian's dialect. 'Don't worry though, love, you'll have Brian there to look after you.'

'But what about the kids, Brian? You can't just get up and go like that,' Beatrice protested.

'Not to worry, love. I'll ring up at the farm first thing in the morning and arrange it. I'm certain Jilly and Albert won't mind keeping them. Or I could send them off to London to my mum's,' he added with less conviction.

'Oh Brian, come off it!' Beatrice cried in exasperation. 'You know very well she's hardly got room to swing a cat there, let alone two full-size teenagers, no matter how well they might behave. Why don't you just admit that they'll have to come along if you do? A nice little party we'll make, won't we?' she added bitterly as she disappeared into the bathroom (where, as in most English hostelries, the toilet was located – a sharp contrast to Austria, where until quite recently toilets and bathing facilities have been kept apart for sanitary and aesthetic reasons).

'Brian,' she called out some moments later. 'Remember last autumn when you were on that assignment with New England Tours Unlimited?' The toilet flushed, but Beatrice failed to emerge.

'Of course. What about it, love?' Brian replied in a low voice, as if the neighbours might hear. Actually they had no neighbours; on their left was Brian's own room, and the room on their right had been empty since yesterday.

'You stayed with Amy and Charles in Bangor, didn't you?' Beatrice persisted.

'For Thanksgiving dinner. Remember you were in Vienna at the time.' Brian said. (Thanksgiving is a holiday on which Americans overeat in honour of their pioneer ancestors.) 'Poor Charles, my heart goes out to him. Such a decent chap. A good sportsman, too,' he added. 'The sort of bloke who deserves to have a son.'

This display of male arrogance, innocent though it might have been, irritated Beatrice. 'Well, he seems to have got himself one now, doesn't he?' she retorted.

Briefly taken aback by the deliberate callousness of this remark, Brian didn't reply.

'Brian? Are you still there?'

'I think so.'

'There's something I need to know.'

'Try me.'

'It's just a factual point. Did you by any chance fuck my sister?'

Shocked silence.

'Well, did you? Did you sleep with Amy when you were staying with them over Thanksgiving? Surely it can't have slipped your mind. Because if you did, that could make you the proud papa. It just about figures. November to April, five months.'

Then, furiously, 'Oh, damn it, look at that, that's all I needed! I'm bleeding like a pig.'

'You all right in there, love?'

'No, I'm not all right in here,' she mimicked him. 'Damn you, Brian, fetch me a towel or something, this toilet paper's no good.'

As she stood up, feeling a warm clot sliding down her inner thigh, Beatrice suddenly remembered how she had once fainted at the sight of a mess of blood and feathers in the courtyard below her hotel window in Delhi. Then the white-tiled room tilted and went dark.

Brian's worried face, fringed with greying sandy curls, loomed ruddily over her. She was supine on the tile floor with a towel wadded between her legs and her head cradled in Brian's pudgy lap. He was stroking her hair and murmuring endearments, and his eyes were brimming with tears. Penitential tears, for it seemed she had guessed right.

* * *

'Charles and Amy had a lot of people over that evening,' he told her later. 'Five or six couples at least. Nice, respectable business and professional types, you know, but I had the impression that a few of the ladies had had more than a bit to drink already, and you know Charles, he kept everyone's glass filled. So it got a bit rowdy, and of course I was drinking too. And then someone suggested a game of forfeits, and then – well, it very quickly got rather sexual, if you know what I mean. And then it got very sexual, with couples going off in different directions. Charles disappeared with someone, and I found myself in the kitchen with Amy and someone else, and from that point on it's all sort of a blur. I can't honestly say whether I had it off with her or not, exactly, the whole thing was like a madhouse.' Brian clapped his hand to his temples in illustration. 'Mind you, I'm not suggesting Amy took the initiative. If anything did happen it was probably my fault. But the point is, love, the point is *it just doesn't matter*. Because I couldn't have made her pregnant, it's a physical impossibility. I've got no fish, full stop.'

* * *

Like it or not, Beatrice was obliged to listen then and there to her lover's maudlin confession. Eight years ago, it seemed, a severe case of mumps had 'gone to the testicles', leaving him permanently sterile. Fortunately it hadn't affected his …

'Performance?' Beatrice suggested bitterly. 'No, evidently not. But why in the name of God and all His angels didn't you tell me all this in the beginning, Mr No-Fish? Why did you let me go on taking the pill like a fool? Did you think I was playing around, or what?'

'I know it was rotten of me.' Brian stared at the floor. 'I guess I was just afraid it would turn you off. Unforgivable. Well, I suppose I should have known this was too wonderful to last. You and me, I mean.'

His weakness was Brian's most effective weapon. But for the pity she felt, Beatrice would have called it quits with him then and there. But with her courage sapped by two devastating pieces of news in quick succession, Beatrice forgave her lover and gave him that very night further 'proofs', as the saying is, of her continued affection – through it all, no doubt, praying that compassion might not bind her to a poor eunuch until her own time of fertility should run out.

❧ 11 ❧

On Saturday morning S. allowed himself an extra half-hour of sleep to recover from the upsetting events of the previous day. When he came downstairs for breakfast at seven-thirty Eva was nowhere to be seen, but her cream-coloured cashmere coat hanging in the hall showed that she had returned from her nightlong vigil at the maternity hospital.

Aunt Mia, like S. an inveterate early riser, greeted him from the drawing-room, where she had laid out a game of patience on Eva's writing table. She was apparently quite recovered from the traumatic flight from New York.

'Look, S.,' she said to him when they had exchanged good mornings, 'I don't see any sense in waiting breakfast for Eva, she'll be down when she's ready. So why don't I go ahead and fix us a nice pot of coffee while you skip down to the bakery for a bag of those lovely pastries? And after breakfast we'll have our game of canasta, what do you say, lovey?'

Tactfully, S. refrained from reminding the old lady that sweet things didn't agree with her. He also decided to save for the breakfast table the news that Eva's father-in-law, the master-baker Karl Berger, had died eight months ago and that the bakery, though retaining the prestigious Berger name, no longer baked its own pastries and wouldn't be open before ten o'clock anyway. Fortunately there was a little supermarket two blocks away, on the way to the post office, that had quite a nice baked-goods counter. It was the only shop in their neighbourhood now that opened before eight.

'So the old master-baker is no more, fancy that,' was Aunt Mia's reaction to the news, when he finally did tell her over their second cup of coffee. 'I'll tell you something funny now, S. You may not believe it, but your mother and I both had big crushes on Karli Berger when we were girls. Imagine that!'

She smiled to herself and shook her head. 'My goodness, that was such a long time ago it seems like a fairy tale. Karli was just a young lad then himself, you know. He was apprenticed to Great Aunt Mitzi's pastry-cook. You know that back room beyond the kitchen, the one your Dad used as a consulting-room? The one that stank so of cat and dog pee before Eva went to work on it last year?' She shook her head and blew out her cheeks to remind them both how bad the smell had been. 'Well, that's where all the baking was done. In the summer they always had the door open because of the heat, so your Mama and I spent an awful lot of time sunning ourselves on deckchairs in the back courtyard, just to catch a glimpse of Karli Berger.'

Aunt Mia had picked up a spoon and was now idly stirring her coffee as if to dissolve a sugar lump, though in fact she takes neither sugar nor cream. Eva puts their auntie's preference for black coffee down to vanity; she thinks that Aunt Mia, well into her ninth decade, is afraid of spoiling her figure! But this theory seems at odds with the old lady's stubborn fondness for pastries. Or perhaps she only indulges in them on visits to Vienna.

* * *

It must be said in any case that nobody would guess Mia's age from her looks. Although a little shrunken (she had been taller than most in her youth), she is hardly bent at all. Her hair (all her own, though not her own colour) is carefully arranged, her make-up and perfume aren't put on with too heavy a hand, and with her glittering jewellery – the splendid engagement diamond that the Fischer-Uncle had given her, her big golden hoop earrings, her garnet-and-gold bracelets and two heavy gold necklaces, one set with emeralds – she really cuts quite an impressive figure.

Most important of all, though, Aunt Mia has remained amazingly youthful in her outlook: alert, vital and interested in everything. You can talk to her as if she were your best friend instead of an elderly relative.

It might as well be admitted at once that S. is really rather proud of his American auntie, even if she does sometimes try to cheat at canasta!

* * *

'Not that Karli Berger was the only young lad we girls had a crush on,' Aunt Mia went on, daintily dividing a pastry into bite-sized bits with her fork. 'We were young girls – fourteen and fifteen. The world was our oyster! Anyway, at the end of that summer your mama went off to secretarial school – she was the brains of the family, God rest her – and I'd got myself a job with the Fischers, so our lives really ran on different tracks after that. But believe it or not, my boy, after all these many years your old auntie still has a soft spot for that Karli Berger. Probably it's sinful to feel that way after being given such a husband, a man with a heart of gold. But there you are, that's what I feel.'

She finally put a forkful of pastry into her mouth, followed by a too-hasty gulp of the coffee (lukewarm by now), which went down the wrong way, causing an alarming fit of coughing and choking.

S. hurriedly thrust at her the glass of water he keeps beside him at breakfast to wash his medication down. Thanks to this quick intervention, she soon recovered enough to continue, although in retrospect S. has wondered how differently things might have turned out had not his lightning response enabled Aunt Mia to continue her reminiscences with hardly a break. What if the coughing fit had been allowed to distract her from the theme of 'Karli Berger' and its unsavoury sequel, until then unknown to S. himself?

'So imagine my shock when young Herbert Berger turns up on my doorstep in New York fifty years later,' Aunt Mia went on with relish, fairly licking her lips. 'I could hardly believe my eyes. Spitting image of his dad, he was, even after all he'd been through. Same tall, sturdy build, same clumsy manners, same deepset eyes, with long lashes like a girl's. I'd have known him by those eyes alone.' A nostalgic sigh. 'But what a sight the lad was otherwise! Dirty hair down to his shoulders, smelly clothes, no socks – I'm telling you, S., if you've ever seen a real hippy, you've seen Berger Junior. Shocking! I'm telling you, I nearly shut the door on him and rang downstairs to the doorman to see him out, and that's the truth!'

She nodded, to underline the truth of it. 'But I remembered him so well as a boy, the image of his father at that age he was, standing with a bunch of roses on the platform at the Westbahnhof, all trim and tidy in a fresh white shirt and clean *Lederhosen*, hair short and neat, waving goodbye to Hannah and me as our train got under way – .' And so on, and so forth.

* * *

Of course the old lady could have had no idea what forces her reminiscences had summoned up, like the horrid winged things released from Pandora's box. (For that matter, with only eight years of schooling she probably had never heard the story of Pandora and why the half-goddess had to carry a box like that; though in fairness it must be said that even a person with an advanced academic degree might be unsure of these matters and be obliged in the end to consult a reference work for detailed information.)

Thus, despite years of formal higher education and an unusually high intelligence (defined, ironically enough, as 'ability to perceive and imagine relationships'!), S. did not immediately grasp the full enormity of what had been revealed in Mia's last words: the long-ago liaison between Herbert and Hannah, and the depth of treachery it implied!

* * *

'But in the end of course I offered the poor lad a bed and a bath,' the merciless monologue went on. 'In fact, I told him he could stay on with me at the apartment as long as he liked. There was only me rattling about there at the time. Your poor Fischer-Uncle had been called to his reward in the prime of his manhood, and Hannah was already in Chicago at medical school, so to be honest I'd have been glad of the company. But you know something? It wasn't little old me that he'd come to see, it was Hannah. He made no bones about it either, that boy. He thought she'd be living with me, and he could just pick up again with her where he'd left off, you see. You should have seen his face fall when I told him she was in Chicago and I couldn't guarantee she'd be alone. I told him about that Jack LaCrosse and how disturbed I was about the whole situation, I mean Jack coming down all the way from Maple Harbor, Maine to spend Memorial Day weekend with her in that stuffy little room. Say what you like about changing times, I still can't come to terms with this new generation and their make-love-not-war. It'll all come to no good, S., you wait and see.'

S.'s nod of mute assent did not betray the tumult in his poor heart.

Aunt Mia heaved a deep sigh. 'Well, I was beginning to feel sorry for Karli's boy. I might as well admit it to you, S., my lad. And that boy just sat there listening to me without a word, but his face was getting longer and longer. And then he looked at his watch and said, "Dear Lord, I must be going, I've got a bus to catch for Boston tonight." And then he suddenly spilled the beans. He'd got this girl waiting for him in Boston, he called her his fiancée, an American girl he'd met in his prisoner-of-war camp in Georgia. She'd worked in the camp infirmary, he said. And as soon as the war was over she'd arranged for him to get a temporary permit to stay until they could marry and he could apply for permanent residence. So I said to him, "That's all fine and dandy, Herbert, congratulations and I mean it, but you've got no business to come knocking at Hannah's door when you have a bride waiting for you in Boston!" In the end, though, I relented and told him that he could come by any time, and if he brought that fiancée of his along I'd treat them to a real Viennese *Jause*. Needless to say, I never heard another peep out of him.'

* * *

The flow of Aunt Mia's words, seemingly directed at an unseen audience as much to her silent nephew, suddenly died away as something in his demeanour caught her attention. 'But what's the matter, my boy? You look awful all of a sudden. Have you got a tummy-ache or something?'

S., realising that he had been biting his inner cheeks during her monologue, recovered himself with dignity.

'No, certainly not, why should I?' he said evenly. 'I'm just a trifle perplexed, because I don't really see how you could have let Berger talk in terms of a fiancée when you knew perfectly well that he was still married to Eva. You knew she would have been eligible for a war-widow's pension unless there had been a divorce, and you knew that she would never cheat on things like that. Of course the pension was just a pittance, but at least she and the baby wouldn't have starved to death. Even if you hadn't helped them out,' he couldn't resist adding.

His voice betrayed no trace of his inner turmoil.

The only effect of this calm and rational objection, however, was to provoke a tirade from Mia. 'Don't you start sounding off about matters you haven't a clue about, my boy!' she cried, glaring at him so fiercely that it was easy to imagine what a shrew she must have been in her younger days. S. remembers Great-Aunt Mitzi remarking to his mother that Ludwig Fischer must be a saint to put up with that demon sister of hers!

'Let me tell you here and now, S., our dear Eva knew perfectly well that her precious husband was alive and kicking in America! Only she never had the courage to tell you that,' she went on more and more heatedly. 'considering the state you yourself were in at that time. But you can believe me, your sister never gave a damn about Herbert nor he about her, and don't you let her tell you otherwise! It was just a mail-order marriage between a front-line soldier and a girl he happened to get pregnant in a one-night stand on his last leave … Sorry, lovey, I don't mean to shout at you like that. You're just a poor loony yourself, you can't help it either, can you?'

In the silence that followed this outburst, the last crumbs of Mia's pastry were herded by a withered forefinger into a tidy little heap.

'Well, for all we know he might indeed be dead by now. What difference does it make? Anyway, may God rest him if he is.' She pursed her lips briefly. 'But if you want my honest opinion it's this. Good looking though young Berger might have been, and I don't deny he had a way with him, either, I personally never had any use for him,' she went on, warming to the subject. 'He had no education, no manners and no sensitivity. Or sense, come to that. And to think that he actually imagined that our Hannah would still be carrying a torch for him! To tell you the truth, S., I can't see any self-respecting girl going for an oaf like that. Pitying him, maybe, but falling for him? Never!'

'Don't expect me to swallow all that,' S. said at last more calmly than he felt, for there was literally a painful lump in his throat. 'Do you think I don't know you're lying to me? You, too?'

'But my dearest boy, you are so terribly wrong!' Aunt Mia was suddenly all tender concern.

'What baffles me is why you always took Herbert's side,' S. continued, not to be put off. 'Just as Hannah did.'

He shook his head several times, then clasped it with both hands as he went on, with ever-increasing fervour, 'My God, why couldn't you people see what a devious, deceitful creature you were dealing with? Only a fool would ever trust Herbert Berger! Dear Lord, Aunt Mia, how could you let yourselves be duped like that? But you did, you did! And don't try to convince me that Hannah had no way of knowing what was going on! Of course she did, in fact she deliberately set out to use me as a pawn in her little game with Herbert. She thought she'd be more desirable in his eyes if he saw me hankering after her. Betrayed! And all the time I thought ... '

Here emotion got the better of S. Hearing his own voice climb to a childish high pitch, he broke off on the verge of a sob.

* * *

It might be in order to mention here that S. had been cruelly mocked in the American POW camp on account of his emotional volatility and his highly strung nerves. Twice he had been unfairly disciplined for the involuntary scream that escaped him when, with the platoon standing at attention, he had been surreptitiously prodded in the backside by a bully in the file just behind.

Some modern schools of psychiatry, including some with whom Hannah has maintained close professional contact, employ screaming as a valuable therapeutic device for the relief of internal stress, but only under proper professional supervision.

* * *

Thanks to modern medication, poor old Aunt Mia had never before witnessed one of S.'s 'spells'. With no idea what she should say or do to calm him, she could only lean across the table and pat his shoulder very, very gingerly, as if it were made of some exceptionally fragile material.

'Of course I won't try to tell you that you're utterly mistaken, my darling,' she tried to soothe him. 'And I won't deny that there could be something in what you say. But don't blame your old auntie too much, darling,' she went on. 'Look, what could I have done? It's a thankless business, intervening like that in a daughter's life, my boy. She wouldn't even have listened to me. Besides, I had enough troubles of my own at the time, didn't I?'

At last she lifted her hand from S.'s shoulder and leaned back in her chair. 'Your Fischer-Uncle wasn't the easiest of men to live with,' she resumed in her familiar, expansive storytelling mode. 'And our Hannah in her teens – now there was a handful! She was all right until we were properly settled in America, then the fun started. Running around with the wrong crowd, you know? She'd bring these awful boyfriends home with her – druggies, dropouts, blacks, you name it. Awful. And then the grand climax, actually marrying that greasy-haired nogoodnik Jack LaCrosse. Good riddance, I said to myself when he left her. She may have had one kid on her hands and another on the way, but I can tell you, I was glad to see the back of him. And two years later he was dead. Good riddance, I said again.'

She leaned forward. 'Believe you me, S. darling, Herbert Berger wasn't the worst of the lot, far from it. All he and Hannah ever did was exchange letters, nothing ever came of it really, but can you blame me for wishing it had? Instead of marrying that wretched LaCrosse,' she added, evidently oblivious to S.'s growing agitation. 'First turning her head completely with his artful ways and then cheating on her right and left the minute her back was turned. Hannah's so stubborn in her feelings, you can't budge her. I'm sure she'll cherish that man's memory until the day she dies. That's the way women are – But what is it now, my boy?' she interrupted herself, noticing his signs of renewed distress. 'Have you got a pain? Don't you try to fool Aunt Mia any more, I can see something's wrong.'

S. raised his head from between his hands. 'It's all right, I've just got a bad headache.'

Aunt Mia, saying, 'Oh, poor lamb,' got to her feet stiffly and painfully and moved behind S.'s chair, where she began massaging the back of his skull with a feather-light touch, her fingers moving in tiny circles. Soon he felt calm enough to grope in his jacket pocket for the unopened packet of cigarettes he habitually carries there.

(Smoking is an indulgence S. has very rarely permitted himself since his days in the American POW camp. Cigarettes don't mix well with his medication, in fact they make him feel nauseous, but the knowledge that they are there in his pocket, awaiting his pleasure, gives him a peculiar sense of confident well-being.)

'There now, my boy, that feels good, doesn't it? Your Fischer-Uncle used to massage my scalp like that when I felt one of my headaches coming on. He had good fingers, your Fischer-Uncle,' Aunt Mia murmured, slowing the rhythm ever so slightly. 'Oh yes, your Auntie Mia knows where it feels good. And you needn't think I didn't know that something was going on between you and my Hannah that spring before we left! But remember, darling, you two were first cousins as well. It would have been a sin for you to marry, and goodness knows there was enough of that in our family without you adding to it. Am I right or not, darling? So you see, you've got no reason to upset yourself over anything. What's past is past and there's no way to call it back. So we might just as well take what's handed out to us, and accept it all with good grace.'

She gave his neck a last little pat and withdrew her hands. 'There now. Feeling better? That's good, I thought so.' She hobbled back to her chair and lowered herself into it with sigh that was almost a groan. 'Ah, that feels good too, I can tell you – So since we can't change the past, darling,' she said cheerily, 'how about another cup of coffee, then, if there's any left?'

Since Eva's four-cup electric coffeepot was already empty, S. suggested using freeze-dried coffee. It tastes almost as good as real coffee, in fact some people cannot tell the difference. And it contains as much caffeine as regular coffee but is easier to make: no need to empty the coffee pot, get rid of the old coffee grounds or clean the kettle afterwards to get rid of that stale coffee smell.

◦ 12 ◦

Nephew and aunt, having finished their breakfast, were about to settle down in the living-room for a game of canasta (their first of the season, so to speak) when Eva, looking weary and drained, appeared in the doorway.

'It's a little boy, four months premature,' she said, even-voiced, and dropped down heavily on the ancient but lovingly cared-for leather sofa. 'They had to give Amy quite a lot of blood, but she'll be all right.'

Aunt Mia stared at her. 'Well, did you ever! I ought to have guessed.' She clasped her poor old ring-encumbered hands in evident agitation.

'I telephoned Hannah,' Eva went on. 'She'll notify the others. So I expect we'll have quite a crowd descending on us.'

'Some coffee?' S. asked her.

'No thanks, I had more than my share in the small hours. Just a glass of juice.' (S. quickly poured one and handed it to her.) 'So the first thing for us to do is to get ourselves organised here,' she resumed. Eva's amazing self-possession must largely account for her professional success as assistant deputy administrator at the UNO. 'There'll be at least three, maybe more.' She counted them off. 'The father, maybe – what's his name? Charles. Hannah. Beatrice; that makes three. There could be others too, I don't know. They'd have to stay at a hotel though, I can't put up more than three here.'

She sat up, straightening her back, and briefly ran her hand through her blonde-streaked hair, staring into space for a moment before she dropped the 'bombshell'. 'Chances are that the poor little thing won't survive for long, though,' she said, in the same calm voice. 'It seems there's something badly wrong. I'm not sure exactly what, but it sounds like brain damage. They've got him in a special care unit.'

Silence, during which Aunt Mia bowed her head and crossed herself quickly, while S. stood motionless, merely clenching and unclenching his fists in his trouser pockets. Neither asked any questions at the time, and Eva did not elaborate further.

She rose from the divan, suppressing a yawn, and hugged her arms as if for warmth. 'But right now I'm going to go back upstairs and lie down again for a bit. I've only had a couple of hours sleep and I'm really dead on my feet.'

She disappeared in the direction of the stairs, followed a short time later by Aunt Mia, who had decided she'd better have a little extra lie-in too, as her hip was acting up a bit.

So their canasta was put off until, tentatively, that same afternoon.

Anyway, there was no hurry about it: this year, because of Mia's visit, S.'s Easter weekend at home had been extended to a week. Dramatic advances in pharmaceutical science now make it possible for certain patients to enjoy prolonged absences from the sanatorium, provided the prescribed schedules and dosages of their medication are rigorously observed and they are closely monitored for signs of adverse reaction.

* * *

As it turned out, however, that Saturday afternoon before Easter saw yet another postponement of S.'s canasta game with his Aunt Mia! Because, on learning that Eva planned to drive into Vienna to visit the patient at St Saviour's, Aunt Mia decided that she too must come along and bestow 'a big hug' on her poor granddaughter. S., given the choice of joining the ladies or amusing himself 'at home', decided to make it a threesome.

No one had any reason then to guess that this 'family' trip to St Saviour's was destined to lay the groundwork of S.'s strategy for liberating the tiny sufferer, some five days later, from the shackles of earthly existence.

* * *

All three of them were nicely dressed for the visit: S. in suit and necktie, Eva, teetering on her favourite high-heeled shoes, in a wine-coloured woollen dress, and Aunt Mia in a striped suit with a short, narrow skirt in the Parisian fashion – unsuitably short for so old a woman, some might think. Her face, made up with as much care as if she were going to the opera, could have been that of a far younger woman. But her hands shook as she fingered the rosary she had fished from the depths of her expensive new American crocodile bag.

Having left St Anselm at two-thirty, they parked in a underground public garage, diagonally across the street from the maternity wing, at just seven minutes after three; very good time, as Eva is an expert driver who knows all the Vienna highways and byways and short-cuts better than most of the so-called 'professionals' who drive the sanatorium's VW minibus.

S. frequently avails himself of the minibus service for transport to and from Vienna. As well as to staff members, it is available to selected patients from the creative wing wishing to visit museums and galleries, hear lectures at the university and other educational institutions, and occasionally attend special evening performances by world-famous artistes such as the International Ice Revue or the Chinese National Circus.

* * *

Special-category patients like S. are free to use public transport – bus, tram, train or underground – for daytime travel to and from the city. S., however, has avoided all forms of public rail transport since suffering a panic attack in the underground a few years ago.

His irrational fear of trains goes back to the spring of 1945, when the remains of his infantry regiment were captured by the Russians in the small Saxon village where they had made their last stand. Together with most of the able-bodied villagers – adults and children – they were herded into a barbed-wire enclosure where they spent eight days under unspeakable conditions, told only that they would be soon be taken by train to the east 'with many others' to work 'for the reconstruction of the Motherland'. Had the muddy field in which they were penned been at the other end of the village, that would have meant, for most of them, a lifetime of slave labour. What saved them was the hastily agreed demarcation line between the American and Soviet military zones, which happened to pass some thirty metres to the east of their enclosure. That meant that the villagers had to be released, and the military prisoners handed over to American custody.

So S. came to no harm. But for months after that experience images of the train he had never seen, the terrible cattle train to the East, had haunted his dreams.

* * *

At the hospital the visitors from St Anselm were directed to take a lift to the sixth floor. S., for obvious reasons, would have preferred the stairs, but there were none in sight and he was determined to betray no weakness before the two women.

They found the new mother in a private room at the end of a long sunny corridor. S., seeing this daughter of Hannah for the first time, studied her with keen interest. The vivid pink of a blanket drawn up under Amy's chin contrasted cruelly with the drained lips and papery pallor of her sleeping face. He could detect little resemblance to Hannah in the facial structure, though the angle of the closed eyes might have held a faint reminder. The damp hair was fair like Hannah's, likewise the eyebrows (reliable evidence, according to Eva, that a woman's hair colour is her own).

Altogether, his inspection showed a woman plain of face, worn of body and virtually devoid of the female magnetism with which her sister Beatrice was so freely endowed. Of course, it had to be borne in mind that hospital patients are rarely at their physical best, and Amy had had less than a day to recover from a severe physical and emotional ordeal, culminating perhaps in the bleak awareness that her suffering had only brought more suffering into the world.

The infant, of course, was elsewhere, a circumstance no one questioned or referred to in the course of the visit.

* * *

Amy's eyelids presently fluttered open, and as she became fully aware of the presence of her visitors she stretched up her arms (pale-skinned, with a faint golden down) to hug her grandmother and her Aunt Eva in turn. And S., even before being introduced, got a nice smile from the patient.

It was all very strange, this encounter between a child of Hannah's, lying in a hospital bed thousands of miles from home, and the tall, awkward stranger looming at her bedside, no doubt with necktie askew and hair in disarray, despite repeated careful grooming during the car journey. Stranger still, everyone behaved as if nothing in the least unusual were taking place!

'And this is Uncle S., darling, that you've heard so much about,' Aunt Mia was saying. 'A very, very special person, and my favourite ever since he was so big,' and stooping slightly she demonstrated, with her crimson-nailed, bejewelled hand held at knee-level (well out of the invalid's range of vision), the height of the infant S.

Now, hearing these sentiments expressed by his dear Aunt Mia, S.'s heart swelled with pride. At such moments he felt capable of any feat of courage, any sacrifice, to shield her from harm!

The women's small talk, however, didn't greatly interest him. Were Amy's nurses nice? Very nice indeed. Only one of them could really speak English, but Amy hadn't had any problem making her wants known. How about the food? Was there anything she would like Eva to bring along tomorrow? A book? Some nice grapes and bananas? Time magazine?

At last, having heard as much of this as he cared to 'stomach', S. whispered in his sister's ear that he must briefly excuse himself – inferentially, to respond to a 'call of nature'.

He strolled down the corridor. The matron's station, three doors down on the left, was manned by a youngish, pleasant-looking sister of Filipino or perhaps Vietnamese origin. There are plenty of such ladies working at the sanatorium, and S. has always found them genuinely friendly, obliging and agreeable, despite his sister's dark suspicion of the motives and intentions behind their niceness.

This one, in any case, was a nun. Introducing himself as 'Brother S.', he said that he desired to have a brief look at his newborn nephew. The nun nodded her assent and beckoned him to follow her back down the corridor, then down another on the right that led to the special care unit. In the vestibule he was handed a white cotton cap, such as a baker or a surgeon might wear, with a white gown and a mask to cover his nose and mouth, and directed to remove his shoes and don special footgear, which turned out to be nothing but thick-soled white cotton socks.

It should probably be mentioned, entirely without vanity, at this point of the story that on quite a number of occasions S. has been mistaken by patients from other wings for Brother Sebastian himself – understandably, in view of their remarkably similar height, weight and colouring. Since the dress code has been relaxed to allow the religious to wear ordinary civilian clothes when bound for activities outside the sanatorium, he has even been occasionally addressed as 'Brother' by sanatorium staff (kitchen helpers and the like).

S.'s physical appearance, it should be said, belies the severe blows that life has dealt him, such as being obliged to supervise the rounding-up of several score of would-be deserters for summary execution, and being captured and sexually misused by enemy troops, an experience which had certainly contributed to the condition for which he was, in effect, condemned to serve a life sentence at the sanatorium.

Through it all his eyes had remained a clear and piercing blue, his cheeks unlined and his chestnut hair full and abundant, with hardly a streak of grey.

* * *

The baby was in a tiny chamber all by itself, imprisoned in a box of clear plastic resembling (but for the tubes sprouting from one end) the glass coffin in which the Seven Dwarfs had laid the supposedly dead Snow White, so that they might gaze on her beauty forever. The difference was that the baby's 'coffin' was only a fraction of the size of Snow White's, and the tiny occupant was so encumbered by life-support devices that S. couldn't even make out its face. Except for the bulging cranium, the poor little worm could as easily have been the infant of some other mammalian species.

What most saddened S., however, was the reflection that the creature in the plastic box couldn't forever stay there, immobile and secure as it now was. It – he – would have to grow up and take its place (if it could be said to have a place!) among its fellow human creatures, adding their suffering to its own.

Having himself been 'on' a respirator in the wake of his first amateurish suicide (in the days before the advent of Dr Rosen), S. was fully familiar with the workings of these devices. The awareness that he would know exactly what to do when the time came was immensely reassuring; between then and now, he had only to wait. From the moment of Hannah's arrival in Vienna, all things would take their pre-destined course.

⊰ 13 ⊱

Midway in this narrative the reader is asked to pause and reflect, under the author's guidance, on the reason why the authorities, armed with all the tricks of their respective trades, should perversely have invested so much of their time in efforts to discredit S.'s confession. With the *corpus delicti* there, so to speak, for all to see, these officials occupied themselves with efforts to pick holes in the logic of his presentation, examining every aspect of the confession for technical flaws or potential inconsistencies that could be exploited to eliminate S. as a 'self-declared' prime suspect; or, if the case should come to trial, to ensure his full and unqualified acquittal on all counts.

* * *

The St Anselm police, notified by S. himself of the 'crime' once he had recovered from the emotional strain of a week of painful partings, were obviously prejudiced against him from the start.

His main interrogator, Inspector Novak, was a potbellied detective in civilian dress (blue jeans!), sitting behind a bare table in a very small office. He acknowledged S.'s entrance with a curt nod, motioned him to a seat and reached for a paper in his 'In'-basket which S. recognised as the form filled in by the long-haired uniformed youth at the reception counter. There he had been obliged to declare his name, address, occupation, marital status, citizenship and 'purpose of visit' before being admitted to the so-called waiting-room, a short ill-lit corridor with benches on either side crowded with humanity of all shapes, colours and sizes.

Most of them, S. supposed, would be traffic offenders, people with petty complaints or foreigners wishing to have their work permits renewed; no one else, certainly, with a purpose as momentous as his! Here they all sat, patiently waiting, while nameless officials in secret chambers checked and crosschecked their data on computer screens before each in turn was called into this bleak little *sanctum sanctorum*, or another like it.

It had not always been so. Once upon a time everything had been simpler and more human. People had known and respected each other; everyone had his place and had been treated accordingly.

But that was before humanity had multiplied beyond control.

* * *

At last Inspector Novak looked up from his papers and leaned back in his chair, fingers interlaced at the nape of his neck. 'Well, now, Herr Zimmermann,' he said jovially, in the dialect-inflected speech which has lately become fashionable among the upper echelons of official-dom. 'So you are here to tell us that you caused the death of a five-day-old male infant in – ' he consulted the paper again – 'the maternity ward of St Saviour's hospital.'

S. assumed a military posture. 'Yes, sir, that's correct,' he confirmed in his best educated High German, out of respect for the authority embodied in the unprepossessing person of his *vis-à-vis*. 'Three weeks ago, on the Friday after Easter to be exact, at approximately sixteen-thirty hours. Illness and recent upheavals within my immediate family have prevented me from reporting to you earlier. I do apologise for any resulting delay in the judicial process, but I trust my coming forward voluntarily will be taken into consideration as a mitigating circumstance when I am charged.'

The inspector consulted his papers again, a slight frown creasing his fleshy brow, before raising his eyes to S.'s.

'My dear man, you're wasting your time. There's nothing we can do for you here,' he said finally. 'The police weren't born yesterday, you know. My colleague has already checked your story against the central police computer in Vienna. Pure routine. Doesn't take ten minutes, and more than once it's saved us from wasting our time checking out hoaxes. Take this case, now. Any death that takes place in a Vienna hospital, whatever the cause, that death's got to be reported to the police within six hours. That's the law as it stands now, see? And it goes straight on to the central computer.'

Leaning back in his chair and half-closing his eyes, the inspector permitted himself a strategically timed pause.

'Now then, Herr Zimmermann,' he continued, 'I'll have you know that no deaths whatever occurred in St Saviour's Hospital after midday on that particular Friday, April the fourteenth. So why don't you just calm yourself, Herr Zimmermann, go back home to your sanatorium and forget the whole thing? You don't want us to charge you with wasting police time, that's a bookable offence, you know. You look to me like a nice intelligent chap, Herr Zimmermann. Believe me, I'd hate to see you get into trouble like that.'

No deaths, indeed! Preposterous as the assertion was, S. sensed that to the mind of this petty functionary, the central police computer was infallible; merely to challenge it would be to sacrifice his remaining credibility. Was there any other possible explanation that wouldn't be instantly rejected?

The idea that then suddenly leaped to his mind might, S. realised as he considered it, be more than a clever tactical argument; it could be the true explanation. He had been sitting for the past few moments in silence, head bowed as if in acquiescence; now he raised his eyes to the inspector's and straightened in his seat. 'But there's one thing that may not have occurred to you, Herr Inspector. You say no death occurred. But allow me to point out, with all due respect, that all you can really say is that no death was reported.'

'Same thing,' the detective said impatiently. 'Let's not be splitting hairs.'

'Ah, but wait,' S. pressed on. 'Just suppose a child does die at the hands of an intruder one afternoon because the hospital got careless with security and there was nobody about. Maybe a nun who was supposed to be watching was praying instead, who knows? Well, think of the scandal if such a thing got out! A real feast for the press, wouldn't it be? And an awful blow to the hospital. To say nothing of the political repercussions. Now, I'd suggest that it must have occurred to somebody that they could avoid a lot of awkward questions simply by changing the reported time of death to morning instead of afternoon. Because in the morning the place is so busy, you see? Plenty of medical staff about, no question of anyone slipping in and out unobserved.'

In all modesty it must be said that this analysis was a genuine spur-of-the-moment inspiration, though it owed something to the memory of an incident in the past. Some years ago a fellow patient at the sanatorium had committed suicide by hanging himself from a window bar in a locked toilet. His family had successfully sued the sanatorium for a large sum of money, and its reputation and income had suffered.

Whatever its sources, S.'s argument appeared to have had an effect. The impatient drumming of the inspector's fingers on the table-top slowed to a gentle patter, then stopped, and silence reigned in the little room. S. began counting mentally up from one, substituting the syllable 'Bim' for seven or any of its multiples. (Indulgence in intellectual exercises of this sort is said to be a manifestation of exceptional intelligence.)

Finally the inspector raised his chin and gave S. a penetrating look. 'Now let's just suppose, Herr Zimmermann, that you're telling us the truth here,' he said with the air of someone offering an absurd concession to an unreasonable interlocutor. 'You must surely understand, Herr Zimmermann, that if you'd really brought about the child's death and you'd done it deliberately, that would make you a common murderer in the eyes of the law. You understand that, don't you, sir? A common murderer. Think it over, sir. Don't tell me you want to do that to your family! You don't want that, surely? Of course you don't. Look, sir, your last bus leaves from the station here at four-twenty. Why don't you just run along like a good chap and have another think about this whole business, and then when you've come to your senses we can have another little chat. If you're so inclined, that is. And now good day to you.'

He rose and held out his hand. For a moment S. kept his seat. He was frustrated by this perfunctory dismissal, chagrined at having overestimated his opponent's intelligence, and deeply reluctant to give up. But at the same time he sensed that the other man, having made up his mind that he was dealing with a lunatic, was now impervious to both facts and reason. So he rose, smiled, grasped the extended hand, and took his leave. You could say that they parted on the best of terms.

* * *

Another staunch linesman for the defence (i.e. another supposed ally intent on denying S. the responsibility for his act) is Brother Sebastian, spokesman for the Religious.

His tactics are, of course, entirely different. 'My dear S., whether the child died of natural courses or because you actually interfered with its oxygen supply really doesn't matter so much. But it's absolutely beyond me how an intelligent, sensitive person like yourself could ever have harboured such a terrible intention,' he says, distress furrowing his lofty brow. 'In God's name, S., how could you persuade yourself that putting an end to any human life, whatever its quality, would benefit anyone – the poor little fellow himself, his family, humanity at large? You know that deliberate killing is a mortal sin, whatever the circumstances. For the love of Christ, man, how could you set yourself up against Our Blessed Lord and court your own damnation?'

His deepset blue eyes gaze questioningly at S., who sits stony-faced. 'Trust in the goodness of Our Lord, S. Trust Him as a child trusts its father, for He is all-loving and all-knowing and everything He does is for the best. How can you doubt that, how could you presume to set yourself against His plan? Humble yourself as God humbled Himself when He was man. Pray to Him for forgiveness, my friend. You will not be refused. Come, S., let us pray to Our Lady to help us resist the evil in our own hearts. She has never yet failed a sinner who sincerely sought her help!'

Et cetera, followed by a series of fervent 'Hail Marys', for which Brother Sebastian extracts a black-beaded rosary from a trouser pocket beneath his immaculate white habit.

Brother is a demon for cleanliness, washing his hands perhaps a dozen times a day, as if a smudge without were as grave a threat to his immortal soul as a stain within. How, S., has often wondered, will he ever manage to cope with conditions in his African mission, where there may be little enough water to drink, let alone maintain a lofty standard of personal hygiene?

But dear Brother Sebastian has always meant well, and in this instance there can be no doubt that he thought he had S.'s best interests at heart. His mistake was only to underestimate his adversary. As the Book of Job teaches us, he who would oppose insanity is battling in a lost cause. God is too great to be challenged by human logic. He will not stand for it!

* * *

Last but by no means least in this impressive array of unwelcome witnesses for the 'defence' comes the medical profession, represented by no less an expert than Professor Dr Helmut Rosen himself. Dr Rosen had hurriedly set out from his residence in Cambridge, England, on a mission of mercy to extricate an old friend and ex-star patient from grave, if self-imposed, difficulties.

Of all the authorities involved in S.'s case, Dr Rosen was probably the most perceptive and certainly the most akin to S. in background, age and temperament, although their paths had diverged so sharply many years ago.

Being of Jewish blood, Helmut Rosen had left Austria soon after it became a part of Greater Germany under the Führer (Adolf Hitler). It turned out to be an unexpectedly fortunate move, enabling him to spend the war years in pursuit of learning and professional qualification in England, whilst his erstwhile schoolmates in Austria were being conscripted straight from the classroom at seventeen or even sixteen to serve their country in its hour of need. Where battle lines were crumbling, even younger lads were often thrown in as reserves.

Surely, then, it must be obvious that quite apart from the formidable barrier of the doctor-patient relationship, the gulf that now yawned between the two men, otherwise so much alike, could never really be bridged, no matter how much goodwill might be invested in the attempt.

Never himself having worn a uniform or smelled the smoke of battle, how could the good Dr Rosen guess at the demons in S.'s brain? How could he imagine what it might mean to be commanded to shoot dead a fellow soldier from the same regiment, company, a miserable creature in mud-caked fatigues who had been caught sneaking off to join the enemy and was now staring at his appointed executioner with the eyes of a cornered animal?

Your bowels turn to liquid when you hear the order. You have never killed anyone and you have convinced yourself that somehow, even though you carry a rifle and have been trained to use it, you will never be faced with the obligation to take a human life. Yet suddenly the unthinkable crouches there before you in the form of a straw-haired Swabian farm-boy, drooling with terror. Surely you must hold true to the oath you gave and faithfully carry out the captain's order. Surely deserters must be shot, lest they betray to the enemy the secrets of our front-line defences. If you let them escape, you not only risk the firing squad yourself for refusing an order but you endanger the lives of your brave and honest comrades – who, true unto death, continue to defy the vicious assault of barbarian forces which know no mercy and take no prisoners from regiments such as yours.

Have you ever seen a soldier's body despoiled by a brutal enemy?

So if you shot the deserter, your conscience ought to be clear. And if your mental discipline should have faltered, that was no reason for others to look askance at you. We are, even the best of us, only fallible human creatures.

Author's note: All men of good will are asked to reread the foregoing paragraphs and ponder their implications.

* * *

Professor Dr Rosen's therapy sessions followed a well-defined pattern. Having listened with keen professional attention for forty-five minutes or more to his patient's personal reminiscences and/or philosophical speculations, having offered a few trenchant comments at appropriate points and dropped in the odd leading question to guide the subject's outpourings, Dr Rosen would utilise the next pause to lean forward on his desk and gently shut the lid of his old-fashioned wind-up gold pocket watch (an absurd affectation in an age of quartz movements) to signify as discreetly as possible that the allotted hour was over.

It is worthy of note that their sessions were nearly always conducted in English at the express desire of S. He was eager to improve his knowledge of the Anglo-Saxon tongue, which within his own lifetime had become the principal vehicle of communication between nations, even continents. By unspoken mutual consent, intimate autobiographical vignettes of a sexual nature had rarely been on the bill of fare at these sporadic therapy sessions in Dr Rosen's office – which, having begun with a failed suicide attempt, were fated to end in a death nearly a half-century later.

* * *

Paradoxically, perhaps, but not unnaturally, a friendship of a sort developed between patient and therapist in the course of this long if much interrupted history. They soon found that they never lacked matter for lively intellectual exchanges. Love, lust, justice, duty, renunciation, the right to die – over the years these and many other great questions had furnished inexhaustible food for discussion between doctor and patient.

One topic they had pondered deeply was the interdependency of the human and the divine, as seen in Homer's *Iliad* and again in Dante's *Divine Comedy*, which is not a comedy at all but a deeply serious account of the author Dante's imaginary journey through the after-world, guided by the spirit of his great Roman predecessor Virgil, one of a number of great souls (Socrates being another) condemned to Limbo because they had had the bad luck to be born before the Christian era. Yet another fine example of divine justice!

Author's note: Readers impatient for swift plot development are advised to skip the following paragraph.

Dante's vision of the afterlife comes about through the spirit of an utterly sinless young lady of heavenly beauty whom the poet had ide-alised from childhood on, though for reasons well understood by S., at least, the poet had never ventured to approach her. The point being that this young lady's spirit was so pure and perfect that her place was right up there with the angels, and she was able to offer Dante a glimpse of the ultimate Divinity. Further evidence, if evidence were needed, that the worlds of the flesh and the spirit are profoundly, one might say hopelessly, entangled!

* * *

Even more poignant and significant, perhaps, than their analyses of Dante's love for Beatrice were the many pleasant hours that Dr Rosen and his patient had spent together reflecting on the great suicides of antiquity and their relevance through the ages. They considered Socrates and Cleopatra, Zeno the Epicurean and Seneca the famous Stoic, who had set an example to all Rome by the dignity of his end.

This had naturally led to a briefing by Dr Rosen on how the classical ideal of a dignified exit had influenced the thinking of successive enlightened Humanists, such as the open-minded city fathers of the ancient city of Marseilles, France, where cups of poison for an honourable exit were offered to those who could offer a plausible reason for wishing to end their lives.

'Sanity might be well served in our own time if only our legislators were to follow that example,' he remarked in the exaggeratedly theatrical tones he chose to affect lest S. think he was being talked down to. 'But alas for us, our modern civilisation has steadily regressed in this as in other moral issues. Did you know that in England, during the so-called Age of Enlightenment, deliberate failure to prevent a suicide was treated as a crime comparable to murder?'

* * *

These discussions between therapist and patient remained in the realm of theory for a year or two, until at last the day came when S. made his second attempt to 'take arms against a sea of troubles' by consuming a whole bottle of Perdormal tablets. He had managed to steal them from the pharmacy a week before, when old Brother Oswald – now long since retired to his 'mother house' in Upper Austria – briefly left it unattended. This episode further enhanced S.'s familiarity with respirators and also provided Dr Rosen with an excellent opportunity to put his therapeutic theories to the test.

In the present situation he dispensed with preliminary pleasantries and began as soon as the patient was seated. 'You know, my friend, reflecting on your case it has occurred to me that you may very well be one of those individuals who have completed their allotted share of life's experiences long before their physiological and biological clock-work has run down.'

The narrow blue eyes glinted sharply over the tops of his gold-rimmed half-spectacles. 'So let me assure you first of all that in principle I'm entirely in sympathy with your desire to destroy yourself.'

A thin-lipped smile.

'But in principle only, mind you! The way you chose to go about it was deplorably ineffective,' the professor went on, adopting an increasingly severe, almost scolding tone for better effect on the patient. 'It was a practical certainty that you would be found before the barbiturates could finish you off. And you must have known that from the outset. All of which means that you are far from ready to take your leave of life.'

End of lecture? Not at all; another of Dr Rosen's melancholy smiles signalled yet another change of tactics. His eyes above the gold-rimmed half-spectacles took on a watchful look as he went on briskly, 'In the meantime, though, may I suggest that for a start you apply your considerable talents in a more creative way and methodically put down on paper your troubled thoughts on the subject? Writing is a better way than most of thwarting those little demons that torture us, you know,' he explained, as if he were presenting S. with a novel and rather abstruse set of ideas. Whereas in reality every idiot knows that creativity therapy for the insane was Rosen's own idea. That was precisely what had made him such a famous man!

* * *

At the time, however, even Dr Rosen could hardly have divined that this offhand suggestion would secure him a small share of literary immortality as a leading character in a short story, *Die Sozietät der Selbstmörder* ('The Suicide Society'), published in the 'Feuilleton' section of *Die Presse* (see Appendix).

* * *

From the very beginning S. had acknowledged freely and without reservation that Dr Rosen's familiarity with the great thinkers, writers and philosophers of antiquity was incomparably greater than his own. At the outset, many of the names the professor mentioned in the course of their discussions were virtually unknown to S., a consequence of the premature termination of his schooling. Yet it would be undue modesty to deny that once he put his mind to it, S. was soon in a position to challenge his mentor in the field of classical learning!

Constantly urged onwards and upwards by his sister, his cousin and other well-wishers at home and abroad, he advanced rapidly in his extramural university-level studies. A decade and a half after first enrolling he had earned a 'magister' degree – a recognised academic title in Austria, second only to a doctorate.

Needless, perhaps, to add that however lofty his intelligence, S. could never have aspired to catch up academically with his mentor, who had not one but two doctorates (in Philosophy and in Medicine) under his belt, not to mention a full professorship at Cambridge University. He had also been a co-founder of the Austrian branch of WORLD ALERT!, a director of the Carl Jung Foundation and, briefly, president of the Stoic Society.

* * *

These distinctions as well as a number of other, minor, accomplishments were listed in Dr Rosen's death notice in *Die Presse*, Vienna's oldest liberal newspaper, which has always been supportive of abortion as well as of euthanasia and assisted suicide. The obituary noted that Professor Rosen had recently been presented with the keys to the city of Vienna. The deceased left a wife and a daughter in England, where he had 'made his home' for the past fifty or so years. The obituary concluded, 'Future generations will see in the creative programme at the sanatorium at St Anselm, of which Prof. Dr Rosen was co-founder, a lasting memorial to this great healer.' Equally generous memorial tributes appeared in leading German and English journals.

* * *

Mankind being what it is, there were a few so consumed with envy of Dr Rosen's exalted status that they did not hesitate to call him publicly a fool, a dangerous dreamer, an opportunist or a charlatan. Even today, shame has not yet entirely silenced their slanderous tongues.

◁ 14 ▷

In the tradition of painfully scrupulous honesty set by the great Professor Rosen himself, it merits mention that S.'s interlocutors were all, by and large, well-meaning people, very much on his side, as they mistakenly thought.

Paradoxically, it was for just this reason that many of those wielders of authority were so anxious to frustrate S.'s efforts to testify against himself. Such testimony, so their argument ran, might well cause him, in the end, to be transferred at this late stage of his life from the 'creative' wing to the west wing of the sanatorium, with the consequent loss of all the special privileges accorded a creative-wing patient (visits to museums, PEN Club meetings, trips to the Schönbrunn Zoo, etc.), no human contact but the company of the mad and no 'challenge' but the contemplation of four bare walls.

As if such solitude could ever constitute a threat!

Had the authorities shown better sense – as they did in the end, to the immense relief of everyone concerned with the case – S.'s insanity could once again be officially confirmed and certified, enabling him, after decades of senseless ambition and futile struggles against mind and heart, to attain his ultimate earthly goal: perpetual immurement in the heavenly quiet of the west wing, that Nirvana where nothing is demanded, nothing expected, nothing offered or laid before one except the saffron-yellow tablets that automatically avert the least tremor in the perfect stillness inside one's head.

Perfect except for visits from one's sister, and the need to keep up with far-flung correspondents in the USA, Africa, Australia and the Philippines!

* * *

S.'s replies to his questioners had been brief and concrete, but in the trial scenes that are still played and replayed in his head during wakeful early morning hours, he has been able to make the philosophical basis of his act more palatable to uninitiates.

'Ladies and gentlemen, you are far off the track, I fear,' he would address the judges. 'May I be permitted to set the record straight? Let me first categorically assure you that I was not, and never have been prompted, as you seem to imagine, by any humanitarian impulse, still less by anything describable as love for the "victim" of my act.

'Let me assure you as well that in my endeavour to deliver the Hawkins infant from future misery I had given no thought to sparing his family any inconveniences such as those my own existence has brought upon my loved ones!' he would flatly assert. 'No, ladies and gentlemen of the jury, common sense will tell you that the driving force behind all my actions is insanity. The same insanity that has been medically attested to and certified since the Year One; an insanity that was and still remains sadly impervious to reason, love or any other therapeutic measure.

'For this reason, as far as I am concerned the whole of humanity can go to the dogs. Let volcanoes erupt – bravo! Let war and pestilence stalk the land – encore, encore! Let the very ocean rise from its bed and drown the seven continents – hallelujah! I couldn't care less. In fact, the worse the catastrophe the more I shall enjoy it … '

And so on and so forth, ranting on to his captivated audience until the bells of the abbey ring in the midday hour.

Soon lunch will be brought to the rooms and all other activity will stop.

* * *

'S., you know quite well you had nothing to do with that infant's death,' Dr Rosen would say to him when at last, later in the day, they found themselves *tête-à-tête* in the professor's office. (His former office, now normally used for staff meetings, is still 'his' for consulting purposes whenever he visits St Anselm.) 'You are neither a killer nor a lunatic, my friend, so do me a favour and stop this nonsense. You are far too intelligent to imagine that I can't see through you.'

Predictably, Dr R. reached into his waistcoat packet for the gold cig-arette case before imparting further morsels of wisdom to his patient. No personal weakness or defect of character could stop him from playing his favoured role of the blunt, all-seeing, all-understanding Great Man whose own wounds have been long ago replaced by healthy scar tissue!

'And as for that new notion about your family bearing some ancestral taint,' he went on, pronouncing the last word in a voice dripping with scorn, 'it's pure, unadulterated, obscurantist poppycock. Forget it, my friend, don't demean yourself by uttering such rubbish.'

The cigarette he had extracted was still unlit between his fingers.

'Let me repeat, there is no clinical insanity in your medical history. Nor, according to all the records we could discover, are there any attested instances of madness in your family. Neurosis, undoubtedly; psychosis, no. As for your parents' violent death, theirs was a rational, well-thought-through plan. Credit where credit is due! Their only mistake was believing the report of your death. But maybe it was just as well for them that they did; if they had know the truth it would have given them reason to cling to life … In any case please don't try to justify your bizarre behaviour by pleading insanity. It cuts absolutely no ice with me.'

He leaned back in his chair, lit the cigarette, inhaled and blew out a long plume of smoke towards S., who remained immobile, hands on his knees.

'The harsh reality, my friend,' Dr Rosen went on in somewhat milder tones, 'is that spending the rest of your life in an isolation ward for the sake of those little fantasies you choose to indulge in isn't exactly the sort of happy ending you envision for yourself. All you can achieve by your stubbornness is absolute loss of your personal freedom. Worse still' — holding up a hand to forestall comment — 'worse still, you will eventually become so dulled and desensitised that you will be unable to experience such a vegetative existence as the fruit of your own free choice.'

The good man paused to tap his cigarette against the ashtray. 'If your pride prompts you to insist on destroying yourself despite everything, you are perfectly free to do so.' The unstained teeth revealed by his sudden smile bore witness to the excellence of English dentistry. 'But do try to bear in mind, my friend, that you have at your disposal more elegant means of self-destruction than those you've experimented with so far.'

'Ah, Herr Professor, if it were only that simple: vegetative existence I want, vegetative existence I get!' S. retorted wittily, relishing the English vernacular construction. But this spurt of humour yielded almost at once to the usual feelings of boredom and fatigue.

'I'm tired, Rosen, do you understand? I no longer care what happened to me, or how. Or why it all keeps on happening. Or why I was ever born! Believe me, I'm tired of everything and everyone, past and present. I'm sick of vanity and deception, sick of my family and their craziness' – pressing his knuckles into his eye-sockets to check the tears – 'sick and tired to death of my whole life … '

'Rot,' Dr Rosen broke in brutally. 'You're not insane, and you don't in the least want to die. So kindly get a grip on yourself and don't dare to come to me again whimpering like a beaten dog. Stop blubbering, straighten up, tuck in your shirt and wipe your face. You're not a little boy, you know.'

S. managed to remain outwardly calm during this outburst, and it may be surmised that his composure had a chastening effect on the other man. Dr Rosen's voice trailed off on the last words. Presently he again took out, but did not immediately open, the gold cigarette case which he had described as an inheritance from his grandfather – a suspect claim, in S.'s view, since the grandfather in question had been only a poor Galicean tailor.

The professor now stubbed out his half-smoked Gauloise in the ashtray and leaned back in his chair, thumbs hooked in the armholes of his waistcoat, ready to resume his harassment.

His next question was preceded by the ghost of a smile, at once conspiratorial and benign. 'Don't you agree that it's high time for you to take on the responsibility for your own life, for what you are and what you will be? And to forget all this nonsense about insanity and ancestral sin? Alternatively, if you really want to end your life, end it with my blessing. But end it in a way that does credit to us both. A gentlemanly way.'

* * *

The attentive reader will by now have discerned that it is not in S.'s nature to concede defeat. In the face of such an unjust suggestion, it was impossible for him not to challenge Dr Rosen, to save his own honour if not his therapist's.

'And how, pray, Herr Professor, can you ever be entirely sure whether I'm telling you the truth?' he asked, gently and diplomatically. 'How, for that matter, if I have been lying to you now, can you have confidence that I've ever told you the truth about anything?'

Still calm and in total control, S. permitted himself a well-timed little smile before continuing relentlessly, 'You are a monster of arrogance, Dr Rosen. You think you can lord it over me, you think you've got life all wrapped up. Sitting up there on your throne, you see it all, know it all, nothing can touch you. Even when your favourite patient, your model patient in fact, has managed to turn himself into a killer without your help or your knowledge, all you have to offer him is platitudes! Meanwhile another part of your mind is busily sifting the "material" for yet another scientific paper to add to your academic laurels. Your heart is cold as stone. If human beings perish before your eyes, that matters not a whit to you, because you're above all that, you're invulnerable.'

Here S. choked with the force of his emotion and broke off, bowing over his knees so that his face was no longer exposed to his inquisitor.

* * *

Gazing thus motionless at the floor between his feet, S. saw with a shock that his shoes were badly in need of cleaning. He had always been very particular about their appearance, a trait he must have learned or inherited from his father. Throughout his childhood, S.'s father had never left the house without having his shoes freshly polished by his wife. She would fetch the metal shoeshine box from a shelf in the WC and kneel down before him, like a devotee before her deity, to buff his shoe-tops to a high gloss with a ball made of old stockings and socks. Yet the night before they might have been at each other's throats.

S. and Eva's bedroom adjoined the living-room where their parents' terrible quarrels most often took place. Their mother would begin with a series of loud, bitter reproaches about Papa's late hours, punctuated by his increasingly angry retorts. This would build rapidly to a furious shouting-match, she accusing him of consorting with bad women and exposing his family to nameless shameful diseases. The curses would follow, rising to a scream: Let the Devil come and fetch them all and put an end to their misery! Then his half-strangled shout, the thud of a blow, a muffled cry.

Unable to bear it, S. would pull the pillow over his head. Then he might feel a hand on his neck and look up to find Eva standing beside his bed in her long white nightgown, trembling as if with cold. Then he would move over and she would slip in beside him and they would hold each other for comfort, as they used to do when they were both tiny and frightened of ghosts, and their parents' awful quarrelling had not yet begun.

(In those days all the girls had worn cotton stockings from October until May. When after many mendings they were hopelessly worn out, these stockings would find a use as shoeshine cloths or polishing cloths for brass door handles and window-locks. Nowadays, of course, all this has changed: you simply go out and buy a special cloth for cleaning. And when any object has served its purpose it is discarded 'like an old shoe'!)

* * *

Over the years Dr Rosen had succeeded with his dubious methods in 'worming out' some of the more intimate details of S.'s life, thereby no doubt providing his own academic circle with a certain amount of vicarious titillation and, perhaps, satisfaction at some of the shabbier details revealed by his star patient in the course of this extended debriefing.

Let us not begrudge him these pleasures.

Rosen himself, needless to say, had freed himself decades ago from the stubborn ignorance and narrow-mindedness of his parents, Galician immigrants apropos of whom Dr Rosen himself, in a rare jocular mood, had once observed to S. that you can take a Jew out of the *shtetl* but you can't take the *shtetl* out of the Jew.

One of the shabby details referred to above concerned S.'s own mother. Barbara Zimmermann had been a plain woman very unlike her sister Mia: tall and rather bony, with large hands and feet and masses of rebellious dark hair that S. remembered as perpetually untidy despite her putting it up every night in leather curlers. In S.'s memory she is not distinguished by any special charm of speech or manner. Yet she had at least one secret admirer.

* * *

Herr Alberich was a little balding man, a widower, who owned a solid-fuel business and probably for that reason had a noticeably grimy complexion. He had been our coal supplier for a long time and always made his deliveries in person. On these occasions S.'s mother would invite him in afterwards for coffee and cake and a bit of neighbourhood gossip. She did so, she said, 'out of human feeling', for the poor man had neither kin nor kith. It was obvious that Herr Alberich valued these invitations, because he frequently stayed for quite a long time.

'What a nuisance Herr Alberich is getting to be,' Mama might complain. 'Thick-skinned as well, you wouldn't believe. I told him today was my laundry day and I had a whole basket of washing to hang out to dry, but do you think he'd take the hint? Not Herr Alberich! And of course he tracks all that fine coal-dust into the kitchen. I always feel I have to give the linoleum a good scrubbing afterwards.'

But the following month the visit would be repeated. This had been going on, S. now reckons, for at least two years.

Until one summer morning S.'s father, who always scanned the *Kronenzeitung* over breakfast, said, 'Barbara, listen to this. "The body of the well-known fuel merchant Anton Alberich was discovered yesterday afternoon by police in a bathtub at his home, Koppstrasse 44, where they had gone to investigate a neighbour's complaint. Pending an autopsy, the cause of death is thought to have been a heart attack. There were no indications of foul play." A decent chap, Anton Alberich, even if he couldn't take a hint,' Papa said with a penetrating look at S.'s mother.

He handed her the paper, but she laid it down without so much a glance at the story, rose from the table, leaving her breakfast unfinished, and fled to her bedroom, where she spent the rest of the morning incommunicado, not even emerging to braid Eva's hair for school. Great-Aunt Mitzi had to do the best she could with her arthritic fingers, and Eva went off to school looking like a 'scarecrow'. S. was sent to the apothecary's to fetch some extra-strong camomile drops, Great-Aunt Mitzi's favourite remedy in times of stress. Eventually Mama emerged from seclusion with swollen eyes, and things gradually got back to normal. As far as S. can remember, Herr Alberich's name was never mentioned again.

❧ 15 ☙

For anyone so keen to excavate a patient's past in search of discreditable morsels, Dr Rosen played his own cards notably close to his chest.

In fact, only once in all their years of intimacy, and that towards the end, did he feel secure enough to speak at all openly to S. about his own life and family. Perhaps internal pressures had been building up until they had to find an outlet, or perhaps it was a last desperate effort to find a way of helping his friend. Be that as it may, his confession touched S. deeply.

The good professor had been trying to persuade S. that his insistence on confessing to infanticide would inevitably have unhappy consequences for his family. 'You love your sister, do you not? Have you considered how she will have to suffer from this pig-headedness of yours?'

S. was girding his loins to ward off this 'sneak attack' from a fresh quarter when Dr Rosen suddenly leaned across the desk and attempted (unsuccessfully, since S. was slightly out of reach) to lay a hand on his patient's shoulder.

'You may wonder why I should be concerned about your sister in particular,' he said in a much softer tone. 'You might suspect a personal feeling, and you would be right. I too had a sister, S. Her name was Mathilda, we called her Tillie. She was twelve years old when she died, I was thirteen.' He paused and gave S. a challenging look.

'How did it happen?' S. asked, as he was evidently expected to do.

'An accident, you might say. She jumped out of a window.' Dr Rosen had, surprisingly, lapsed into a German tinged with demotic Viennese. 'We had a third-floor flat in Fasangasse. It was in 1938, just after the Nazis had come to power in Austria and were beginning to round up Jews for deportation.'

He settled back in his chair and began drumming the desktop with his fingers, perhaps in lieu of lighting another cigarette.

'I know Fasangasse. Third District, near the Belvedere,' S. said, to break the silence.

Dr Rosen nodded absently. 'She was younger by more than a year, but people used to take her for my big sister. Tillie was tall for her age. A redhead. We used to play music together. She was studying the cello and I played the piano after a fashion, but I was far below her standard. Actually we had been playing together the previous afternoon, preparing a piece to surprise our parents, a thing by Bruch, I don't expect you'd know it.' His voice trailed off again.

'They say redheads have a passionate temper,' S. remarked, tactfully suppressing the other observation that occurred to him, namely that some people still tend to avoid them.

His own sister, for example, has confessed to S. that she will choose to stand in a crowded carriage rather than squeeze into a seat beside a redhead. S. recalls Eva's horror when her Mexican granddaughter, on her one and only visit to Austria, decided to dye her hair red, 'like Fergie' (a favourite 'pop star' of the day). The transformation had been achieved in two stages: black to blonde, then blonde to scarlet. In combination with her heavy eye make-up it made the girl look, so said Eva, like an underage streetwalker. That was not quite fair, in S.'s opinion. Red hair was very much in fashion that year, so much so that even many of the Asian and Central European nursing staff at the sanatorium had briefly a similar transformation.

Dr Rosen made no response to S.'s remark about redheads. It was impossible to tell what he was thinking, especially since the light was behind him and his face in shadow, the classic setting for a Grand Inquisitor.

'On the 3rd of May, at a quarter to eight in the morning, someone rang our doorbell,' he resumed. 'It was a Tuesday, an ordinary school day for us, though Tillie was to have had her weekly dancing lesson at Ellmayer's after school. Life went as usual, you see, despite all the ominous signs around us in the wake of the Nazi takeover. But we had all heard a lot of stories. Tillie was scared; she thought it was crazy to stay on and hope for the best. But Father refused to acknowledge the danger. He wouldn't even discuss it, other than tell her not to worry her head about it. That put her in a real panic.'

He cleared his throat. 'Well, we had about finished eating our breakfast that Tuesday when the doorbell rang. Tillie knew that early morning callers didn't bode well for Jews in those days. She whispered, "Oh, my God!" and started to her feet. Father told her quietly, "Sit down, my child," but she didn't, she just stood there trembling. I reached out and took her hand, I was frightened too. So Father got to his feet and walked down the hallway to answer the door himself. We no longer had a maid, you see. I noticed that Father walked slowly and somehow uncertainly, like a much older man, and when he got to the door he didn't open it, he just said with his usual politeness, raising his voice only a little, "Yes, please? What is it?" '

(Here Dr Rosen broke off briefly to grope in various pockets of his tweed jacket, presumably for his cigarette case.)

'And someone on the other side answered, "Rosen? Gerhard Rosen? Open up at once!" Well, our visitor turned out to be a partner in Father's law firm, come a day early with passports and exit visas for all of us, but first he had to have his little joke. But Tillie didn't wait to find out, she tore her hand free and dashed to the window. I was right behind her but I didn't catch her. She was too quick for me, too determined. She practically vaulted the sill. It was all over in an instant. People were shouting and crying down below. I wasn't allowed to go down.'

Dr Rosen rose from his chair and faced the window, hands clasped behind his back. It was the longest speech S. had ever heard from him.

'How awful,' S. said finally. 'I'm sorrier than I can say.'

Dr Rosen bowed his head in acknowledgment. Seen from the rear he presented a much less formidable figure.

'She must have thought about what she would do in an extremity, mustn't she?' S. suggested gently. 'In a sense she must have planned to take her own life. And she must have decided not to put that burden on you. I'm quite sure she wouldn't want you to torment yourself over it now, either. If I were you … '

Absurd as it may seem, for a moment or two S. felt an impulse to go to the other man and put a consoling arm around his shoulders. What restrained him was a sudden suspicion that the therapist's story had been merely an attempt to manipulate his patient's feelings. Besides, Dr Rosen was already resuming the Grand Inquisitor's seat behind his desk, where he presently lit up a Gauloise and drew in a double lungful of the poisonous smoke with obvious relish, apparently unashamed of

the repeated glimpses of sick self-hatred in a supposedly sound personality which this little pantomime kept affording. S. had a momentary
vision of a mange-ridden dog, obsessively licking its sores, unable to let
any lesion scab over and heal.

* * *

'I can't deny that I am deeply moved by your story,' S. said at length.
'And in a way I feel honoured by the confidence. But why, I wonder, do
you feel driven to reveal such things to a patient? It seems very unpro-
fessional. What could be your motive? Obviously you can't expect me to
grant you absolution. Being omniscient you must see that. Or has it
escaped you?'

At this Dr Rosen, who as usual had been leaning far back in his
chair as S. spoke, started to his feet as if about to leap over his desk and
physically attack his patient. S. involuntarily raised a defensive arm in
anticipation. But the good doctor merely leaned forward, his hands on
the edge of his desk, and fixed S. with a steely look.

'I am your therapist,' he said harshly. 'Therapists like patients are
human and capable of error. I addressed you, briefly, as a friend. Your
reply shows that to have been a mistake. It will not be repeated. So let
me remind you again of why I am here. It is because of your disturbed
state. I am endeavouring to help you, but I need your co-operation. I
cannot tolerate frivolity. If you are wise you will remember that I have to
safeguard my reputation, and that imposes certain constraints on your
own behaviour.'

He produced his heavy, old-fashioned gold pocket watch. 'Ah, we
have overrun our time.'

There was nothing for S. to do but get up and take his leave, with
thanks and a rather perfunctory handshake.

* * *

But for his premature demise, Professor Dr Helmut Rosen's faith in his
therapeutic methods might well have been at least partly borne out by
his patient's literary output.

Despite the inevitable clash of personalities, S. felt deep gratitude
for all the professor's efforts to help him therapeutically, efforts which

had in important respects been crowned with success. It must have been difficult and painful, for example, to speak so openly of his personal tragedy and the heart-rending death of his beloved sister. Such unflinching exposure of a vulnerable heart, solely to advance a troubled patient's chances of recovery!

Considerations such as these lie behind the author's decision to dedicate this book to the memory of his mentor and friend, Professor Dr Helmut J. Rosen MA (Oxon), MD, FRCP.

◦ 16 ◦

That Easter week following the birth of Hannah's doomed grandson turned out to be an exceptionally happy time for S., possibly the best few days of his life, preoccupied though he was with the problem of how, for its own good and that of the family, the poor little mite could best be returned to its Maker. The very best and most tranquil hours of that week – far more tranquil, certainly, than those spent in anticipation of a meeting with Hannah – fell between the arrival of Aunt Mia and the influx of house guests later in the week.

Because Eva spent most of those two and a half days at the hospital with Amy, S. had his Aunt Mia all to himself. That meant not only his fill of canasta, but – even more apropos under the present circumstances! – ample time for drawing a wealth of details about the family's past out of his dear auntie, a panorama of persons and events all faithfully recorded in her marvellous memory.

'Tell me again how it used to be when you and Mama were young girls,' he cleverly suggested to her, hoping to divert them both from thoughts of poor Amy and the fresh blight that through her had fallen on the family.

As he had foreseen, Aunt Mia's face immediately brightened as she set off once again down Memory Lane.

'Oh, we had such fun together when we were girls, your Mama and I. We even slept together in the same old bed until the day I was married, did you know that? Imagine what the psychiatrists would say to that nowadays, two growing girls sleeping under a single coverlet!' She chuckled briefly. 'We couldn't have been closer if we'd been twins. Oh, the deviltry we used to get up to together, teasing your Great-Aunt Mitzi, playing tricks on shopkeepers and neighbours. Nothing mean, you understand. People liked us. They used to say that Mia was the smart one but Barbara was the sweet one. And she was. Sweet, with a touch of psychic mixed in.'

'How do you mean? My mother was psychic?' S. asked, not having heard this before.

'Oh, she used to guess my thoughts all the time. She'd say, "Oh, Mia, stop worrying about that exam," or, "Mia, I know you like that Komar boy, but I hear he's already spoken for," and I wouldn't have said a word. It was weird. She could read my mind from my face or something. And once or twice she foretold something that actually happened afterwards, like your Great-Aunt Mitzi getting hit on the head by a soccer ball one Sunday when we were walking past a football ground. I mean, she didn't foresee it in detail, she just said, "I wish Auntie would stay at home this afternoon, I have this feeling she might get hurt if she comes along with us." And she did. Not badly, she was just stunned for a minute, but you see it had come true.'

S. said, 'It could have been coincidence. Anyway, if my mother ever had psychic powers she must have lost them after she married Papa. She was always being overtaken by disasters, as I remember it. Not disasters exactly, crises. They were mostly money problems or health problems or problems with the housekeeping. The thing about them was that she was never prepared to meet them, they always put her in a panic. It used to drive Papa wild. They fought like cat and dog a lot of the time, you know. Eva and I hated it.' He stopped and cleared his throat.

'Of course you did, lovey,' Aunt Mia said, 'But it was in the cards, wasn't it, with your poor mama's jealous nature. He was a good looker, your papa. He couldn't help it if women threw themselves at him. I don't mind telling you I could have made a play for a man like that myself, if your Fischer-Uncle hadn't appeared on the scene.' A dreamy look came into her eyes. 'Anyway, your papa couldn't say no to a pretty face, and he made a lot of ladies happy. Your mama was a saint to put up with it as she did, but she wasn't one to suffer in silence, no indeed … Anyway, the important thing was that they were good parents to you both. Always there for the two of you, weren't they, whenever they were needed? With a guiding hand and a loving heart.'

'Only up to a point,' S. said bitterly. 'In the end they abandoned us both, didn't they? They put themselves first.'

She said, 'Darling S., we've been through all this before. Nobody abandoned you. They'd never have done it if they'd even suspected that you could still be alive. And Eva didn't need them any more. You must see that.'

'And they were afraid,' S. said. 'It was pure cowardice.'

'Easy for you to talk, my lad. But just try to put yourself in their shoes, with you supposedly killed in action and the Red Army at the gates, ready to hang every Nazi they could find from the nearest lamp-post, and plenty of people just waiting to denounce their neighbours and save their own skin. Sin or no sin, I can't blame him for it. And as for your mama – well, he couldn't leave her to the mercy of the Russians, now could he?'

'No, she had to go too,' S. said with bitter irony. 'He didn't even bother to ask her.'

'Now that's something nobody knows at all, nor ever will. But it's my belief they had a pact, the two of them. And even if they didn't, it was what she'd have chosen,' his aunt said. 'Have a heart, my lad.'

'I try, believe me,' S. said quietly. He cleared his throat again.

'Of course you do, darling,' Aunt Mia said heartily. 'And I'm a selfish old thing to be arguing with you about your own papa. But one thing I must say: politics or not, your father was a good man at heart. Many's the calf he delivered for poor farmers that couldn't afford to pay. But people can be so vicious. I know what I'm talking about, I speak from experience. When I remember how people treated us after the Anschluss, just because your poor Fischer-Uncle was a Jew! And there were quite a few of his friends and relatives driven to suicide by the neighbours, and that's the truth.'

'That doesn't excuse Papa,' S. said. 'If he wasn't wicked he was mad. And according to you he wasn't wicked. Ergo … '

Aunt Mia waggled her finger. 'Ergo, yourself! Excuse me, my lad, but I just don't want to listen to it again, this madness-in-the-family theory of yours. It's the craziest thing I've ever heard of. Just don't let your psychiatrist get wind of it, that's my advice.'

'If I value my liberty, you mean,' S. said sardonically. 'You're not exactly subtle, are you, dear Auntie? But the evidence for my theory, as you call it, is clear enough, isn't it? His act, her complicity. I inherited it from both sides. The cards were stacked against me before I was ever born.'

'Oh, get along with you! Now you're being naughty, and you know it,' Aunt Mia said airily, giving him a playful little kick on the ankle with the toe of her shoe. 'Your nerves are kaput from that damned war, that's all, and sometimes you get funny ideas. Who wouldn't, if they'd been through what you've been through? But crazy? Don't make me laugh! And your mama, with all her little quirks, she had her feet on the ground, I can tell you. And she did love your papa, I know that for a fact. Never mind his philandering, there was never anyone else for her. Take it from me, she went out the way she wanted to.' She took a sip of her now cold coffee.

'All right, enough, I give up!' S. made a humorous pretence of surrendering to superior force. It had in fact comforted him to hear Aunt Mia categorically insist that there had indeed been traces of love and sweetness underneath the lies and treachery that formed the background of his childhood. Perhaps, he thought, Aunt Mia was right to focus on the surface of things and avoid the challenge of opening up the hidden depths and attempting to divine the deeper nature and significance of everything one might find buried there. Perhaps all that should be left to people with stronger stomachs: people like Dr Rosen. Or the Pope.

* * *

But once a writer, always a writer! Rebel as he might against his own nature, S. was fated to continue exploring the depths while others basked on the sunny surface of things. The course of his destiny was as fixed as that of a holy martyr, a great psychiatrist or a moribund infant.

* * *

If, for S., Aunt Mia stood guard over the portals of the past, he liked to imagine that she also held certain keys to the future. Although he disapproved of palm-reading and fortune-telling in principle, he was never able to refuse an offer from Aunt Mia to consult the cards for a glimpse into his own personal fortunes.

'Mark my words, my boy, one of these days you'll strike it rich as a writer,' she might say, looking up from the table where she has just laid out a dozen or so cards from the canasta pack. 'No two ways about it, you're going to be famous and people are going to believe your crazy yarns,' she added, with a fond smile. 'Just you wait and see.'

'And how is that supposed to come about, exactly?' S. demanded good-naturedly. 'I'm well past sixty, and all I've got to show for the work I've done is one lightweight story in a Sunday supplement. Who's going to discover me, do you suppose?'

'I don't know anything about that,' Mia said crisply. 'All I know is, the cards never lie.' Her eyes glowed with confidence. Mia was extremely proud of the talents of her beloved nephew, there could be no doubt of that.

* * *

S. had, as in former years, been granted home leave for the Easter weekend. Normally he would have returned to the sanatorium on the Tuesday. But unexpected complications – first the arrival of house guests from abroad, then Eva's accident – were to keep him in Elisabethstrasse for the entire week. Far from being a burden on his family, he was now actually needed at home! And there was no real risk to his well-being. Eva kept unerring track of his complicated medication schedule, and Brother Sebastian, always helpful and obliging beyond the call of duty, even for a religious, could always be relied on to come by and lend a helping hand.

* * *

Naturally, S.'s *tête-à-têtes* with Aunt Mia as described on earlier pages were not always pure sweetness and light. How could either of them fail to be preoccupied, if only at the very back of their minds, with the fact of the malformed infant, the manifold ins and outs of the affair and its possible consequences for others in the years to come?

'Poor Amy, such a good little mummy she's always been to her girls, and now that it's a boy this has to happen,' Aunt Mia would suddenly remark, apropos of nothing, midway through a game of canasta. Then she'd sigh and shake her head. ' A blessing that the poor little chappie's in a Catholic hospital where there's a priest around to baptise him! Nowadays you hardly ever find a hospital that's got a priest on duty around the clock. Although, I must say, in my time they wouldn't make such a fuss about a five-month foetus,' she added mercilessly, probably to cover up her own distress over the ill-starred birth. 'Flushed him down the drain, that's what they'd have done! But now, with all the progress they've made, I guess maybe they'll pull him through. God help him, the poor little tyke!'

S. fanned his cards. 'Don't pray too hard for him,' he said without looking up. 'It's not just that he's premature. There's something terribly wrong with that baby. It's got a cranium almost as big as an adult's. I saw it with my own eyes.'

'Well, I don't think your opinion is worth a hill of beans where my great-grandson is concerned,' Aunt Mia retorted with unaccustomed sharpness. 'And what's more, you should never have gone and sneaked in there by yourself, pretending to be a priest. Shame on you! As if there weren't damage enough already done to the family name … ' She checked herself before her garrulity could get her into deeper water. 'Whose turn is it, anyway? Mine, I believe, so here's an eight of spades for you. See what you can do with it, it's certainly no good to me.'

* * *

Of course his dear old auntie hadn't meant to wound him with her sharp tongue, but there was no mistaking the suggestion that S., through his long residence in the local loony-bin, had already brought enough shame on his family to delight its worst enemies.

She herself evidently became aware of this inference as soon as the words had escaped her lips, for she hastened to add, 'Mark my words, though, darling, whatever might be wrong with the poor little kid, it doesn't come from your side of the family – our side, I mean. There might have been a few of them too highly strung for their own good, but nobody crippled or really mental.'

She leaned back in her chair. 'But on the other hand I wouldn't be a bit surprised if there had been a bad gene or two on Amy's papa's side,' she went on, pursing her lips. 'That no-good French Canadian person from Maine, you know. Jack LaCrosse the self-styled artist, pfui! He certainly had a screw loose, a screw and a half, I'd say. You should see his so-called paintings: worse than Picasso, I'm telling you! I've told Hannah a hundred times, she must have been off her rocker to let herself be taken in like that. But love is blind, and that's the truth!'

S., feeling he was expected to nod confirmation, did so.

'But apart from that person, you couldn't say there was anything amiss on Amy's side,' Aunt Mia went on. 'The Fischers are all good stock.' She shook her head vigorously, as though to fend off any possible objection. 'Lawyers, bankers, doctors, businessmen wherever you look in the Fischer family tree. Even your poor Fischer-Uncle wasn't as daft as some people made him out to be. What if he did live with his head in the clouds most of the time, obsessed with his operettas? He saw to it that his family didn't starve, and when it came to the pinch there was a shrewd businessman inside your Fischer-Uncle. He left me well enough provided for, as anyone can see. I don't think that bespeaks a crazy person, do you? Of course it doesn't.'

She leaned forward and laid her right hand on the table, being careful not to show her cards.

'And as far as our side of the family goes – well, lovey, you know as well as I that there's been a good deal of misfortune and, yes, some peculiarities here and there, maybe a bit of immorality and plenty of unhappiness and pain too, but what of it? Let me tell you, my boy, there are all kinds of wickedness going on all over the world every minute of the day, and I guess there always will be, so why should we be any different? I'm sure our dear Lord must turn a blind eye, otherwise there'd be no end to the punishment He'd have to deal out … All right, S., enough idle talk, back to business!' she ended resolutely, fanning her cards again and fixing her eyes on them as if she had really put everything else behind her.

≈ 17 ≈

Say what she might to her favourite nephew, Aunt Mia's mind (like everyone else's, no doubt!) was evidently churning away in an effort to find some half-plausible reason for the tragedy of Amy's baby. And so she was soon off and away on the theme of sin and retribution, apropos of the infant's parental line.

* * *

The baby's father, Charles Hawkins of the timberland Hawkinses of Bangor, Maine, was his parents' only issue, the fruit of a course of intensive treatment at a famous fertility clinic in Switzerland, where they had spent three months in mid-1945, soon after the end of the war in Europe.

Here is Aunt Mia's account of the circumstances.

'Ted Hawkins was getting on for sixty when little Charles came along,' she told S., 'and Winnie was no spring chicken either. Goodness only knows what they did to which of them at that clinic! They were silent as the grave on that particular subject, believe me. All I know is what I heard from little Bridie Kelly. She worked at the Hawkinses; Winnie always referred to her as the parlour-maid, very grand, you see. Bridie was just a young girl then, straight off the boat from Ireland, and the Hawkinses didn't pay her much, so she used to work odd hours for me, cleaning. And she let it drop one day that Winnie and Ted weren't living together any more as husband and wife, if you know what I mean. And they had this friend, or she did, from Chicago or somewhere, who used to come and visit them for weeks at a time. Livingstone, Homer Livingstone his name was. A dapper little man with a big booming voice, and a little moustache like Hitler. You'd see the two of them out horse-riding in all kinds of weather. Ted didn't ride, you see. All quite innocent, possibly, but people used to wonder. After she passed away, the Livingstone fellow never showed his face again at Maple Harbor. They said it was lung cancer that killed her, but I have my doubts. Charles was only three at the time, poor little soul.' A sad shake of the head.

'You think she didn't have cancer?' asked S. 'I've heard of people keeping it a secret, but never of anyone saying they had cancer when they didn't.'

'Oh, it was cancer all right, and maybe it spread to the lungs. But I have a hunch it started with something that happened in that clinic, with those doctors playing God.'

'It's a role they enjoy, some of them,' S. remarked. 'But I take it the father never remarried?'

'No, Bridie was offered the nanny's job when Winnie first got ill, and she stayed on and brought Charles up almost single-handed. She's been the mainstay of the family, really. Looks after Charles and Amy's girls now. She must be over seventy. And they say she's never had a day's illness since she's been with them. Nor never seen the doctor.'

'Lucky woman,' S. said with feeling.

'You call it luck, I'd call it good sense,' Aunt Mia said. 'You know, my Hannah's got plenty of harebrained ideas. I don't hold with vegetarianism as you know, and all that stuff about migrating souls is just rubbish. Once you're dead you're dead and that's that, you stay dead till Judgement Day. But I have to give Hannah credit for a bit of good sense now and then. She's one hundred per cent right when she says watch your step with these modern medicines, they can do more harm than good in the long run. Sometimes it even skips a generation or two, the damage I mean, but there comes a day of reckoning. Believe me, my boy, I know! Your Aunt Mia has seen a lot in her long life … That's why I didn't want another child after Hannah,' she added after a brief pause, 'though goodness knows your Fischer-Uncle would have loved to have a son. Most men do, you know: it's their vanity, I say. No good trying to force God's hand, though. He sends children when the time comes for them to be born, takes them back as and when it pleases Him. Mark my words, it never comes to good when man tries to interfere with nature's law.'

S. nodded his 'Yea and Amen' to all this at appropriate intervals but refrained from any comment of his own, sensing that the old lady wasn't prepared to listen to a dissenting opinion. The last thing in the world he wanted was to hurt or offend Aunt Mia, whom he loved dearly – better, almost, than any other person in the world, not excepting parents, sister, and true friends like Brother Sebastian.

And yet, he somehow found it in his heart to remind his dear auntie of the heavy burden of mortal sin accumulated by our ancestors ever since man's first disobedience in the Garden.

* * *

In Room 315 of the Rathaus, where all Vienna's birth records since the middle of the last century are kept, a researcher will find on page 1238 of Volume 255 (Shelf 18, Aisle B) the following entry among the 29 births recorded for 20 April, 1874 (a set of numbers which once won S. 500 schillings in the Austrian State Lottery):

> Weber, Maria Anna, female. 3 p.m., Vienna General Hospital.
> Mother: Johanna Franziska Weber, 34, widowed.
> Abbey Yard, St Anselm, N.O. Parish cook. Father: Unknown.

That entry contains the cue for the pregnant question: *Unknown to whom?* – in S.'s childhood a perennial topic of speculation among S.'s mother, Aunt Mia and Great-Aunt Mitzi, their voices dropping as usual when a delicate theme was broached, though rarely so low as to be inaudible to a listening child.

And to think that at that very time – was it the mid-1930s? – their sinful forebear was still living, though probably long since withdrawn from the world! The records show that Pater Aegidus Demel, *Chorherr* of the Abbey – which made him, if not a prince of the church, at least a princeling! – had died in 1937 and been laid to rest in the catacombs beneath the cathedral.

Later research into church archives and correspondence has turned up earlier references to one Aegidus Demel, Latin scholar, scion of an obscure aristocratic family, who after his ordination becomes parish priest of the village of Stoizendorf. It is then that the childless widow Johanna Weber enters his employ as cook and housekeeper.

Nothing sinful there, or even unusual.

Nothing unusual, either, about the widowed Johanna having borne a child. That sort of thing happened too often in those days (as in our own) to be considered scandalous. Johanna Weber carried on cooking for his reverence while bringing up her child as a member of the household; and when Aegidus Demel was appointed to the post of Chorherr, she and her little Maria naturally came with him to take up residence in the cloistered precincts of the Abbey.

* * *

Pater Aegidus never acknowledged the paternity of his housekeeper's child, but it is reasonable to suppose that the fact was strongly suspected in the community, and known to the pater's church superiors. According to Brother Sebastian this would not necessarily have jeopardised his continued pursuit of his religious calling, nor even have damaged his prospects of advancement, provided there had been due repentance and no repetition of the offence, which is not counted among the seven deadly sins.

In any case, Pater Aegidus had been a steadfast benefactor to Johanna Weber and her offspring for the rest of his whole long life. He stood godfather to the infant Maria Anna (S.'s maternal great-grandmother!) and later officiated at her wedding to a respectable widower, the vintner Lothar Wollzeiler, and was also instrumental in the purchase of a large house with an across-the-counter wine-bar, later to be converted by our Great-Aunt Mitzi, Maria Anna's older daughter (again with the pater's blessings and support) into the Café Allotria.

This went on for many years. Aunt Mia herself still remembers from her childhood days the spare, black-clad figure of the old eminence from the abbey coming to pay a call on Great-Aunt Mitzi and her orphaned nieces Barbara and Mia, and the two of them being summoned to the parlour to kneel before the old priest, kiss his hand and receive his blessing.

'Your mama and I hadn't a clue that he was our own great-grandpapa,' Aunt Mia told S. 'It would have been an awful shock to us in those days. Believe it or not, we only found out when I broke the news to Aunt Mitzi that I was engaged to your Fischer-Uncle. What a fit she had about that! "A Jew in the family!" she said. "First an anointed priest, then a Jew! Good will never come of it," she said, and then, after all those years, she let the cat out of the bag about those two old sinners. You know, I've often thought that was why our own poor mother had to die so young. God's punishment on a sinful brood!'

Several vigorous nods affirmed the truth of these words.

'I was only two, you know,' she went on, 'and your mama was three when our mother died and Great-Aunt Mitzi took us in. She was such a good Catholic, you know, mass five times a week and lengthy confessions. No wonder, with a priest for a grandfather, blood will tell, they say – ' (here Aunt Mia gave S. a quick wink, to show she wasn't entirely serious about this) ' – and there was this story she used to tell about a serious suitor of hers, a Guards officer, who refused to come with her to Sunday mass. Well, guess what happened! A week after he'd proposed marriage to her he was struck by lightning on Leopoldsberg and that was the end of him.'

'Had she accepted the proposal?' S. asked.

'No, that was the strange part,' Aunt Mia said. 'She'd told him he could have her answer in a week's time. He was going to see her the evening of the very day he was killed. "It was God's answer," she'd say. "I never got a chance to give him mine, but it was going to be yes. And I believe to this day," she'd tell your mama and me, though of course not in front of you children, "that divine providence saved me from a marriage that wouldn't have been pleasing to God." So you can see how someone like that would carry on about me marrying a Jew. Let me tell you, it took me forever to persuade her that the Fischers had really converted and your Fischer-Uncle was as good a Christian as anyone.'

* * *

At last Aunt Mia came to the point. 'But to tell you the truth, S.,' she said, 'and just between you and me, I'm not a bit superstitious myself, but I just wonder what your Great-Aunt Mitzi would say if she could see the two of us here and that poor little mite in the hospital, born to my own granddaughter! And your poor mother – her heart would have broken if she'd known what fate had in store for you, poor old lovey, and what a heavy price you'd be asked to pay for the follies of others.'

She broke off, groped in her sleeve for the tiny embroidered handkerchief she keeps there against emergencies, and dabbed at her eyes. 'It's a fact, the mills of God grind slow but fine. And it all could have come out far worse in the end. God never sends a heavier burden than we can bear, and He certainly gave you a good broad pair of shoulders, lovey!'

* * *

Dear old Aunt Mia! Never before had she had the courage to acknowledge openly S.'s manifest disabilities, much less connect them with divine punishment for mortal sin. Yet, as the Bible tells us, 'The Lord shall chastise them unto the seventh generation.' And does it really matter, in the end, for whose sins their children's children were meant to atone?

The more S. pondered on this, the clearer became the task at hand: here and now, for its own sake as well as that of the others, to strike the newborn from the rolls of the living.

* * *

Needless to say, no word of his intention passed S.'s lips in the course of his conversations with Aunt Mia about divine retribution for human sin. He would never have shared such a burden with anyone, not even her. He knew that he could trust her to protect his secret, but she could have opposed his plan or even tried to frustrate it, even though in her heart of hearts she would probably have rejoiced had she been able to foresee the poor little creature's early exit from this vale of tears.

But other events and concerns, not directly related to the impending act of liberation, were crowding in upon S., interposing themselves between the intention and the deed. He found himself obliged to wait until the time was ripe and circumstances favourable. And this, miraculously, came about without much planning on his part – almost, a pious soul might say, by Divine Intervention – on the Friday afternoon seven days after the birth of Amy's ill-omened son.

S. had set out early that afternoon by train for Vienna (having, for Aunt Mia's benefit, invented a session with Dr Rosen), with the intention of meeting his cousin Hannah Fischer at the Café Landsmann in the Inner City, as suggested by Hannah herself in a written communication which had reached him earlier that week. But he was not destined to reach the meeting place at the appointed time. Arriving fully a quarter-hour late to find no trace of a waiting Hannah, he saw the hand of providence at work and decided on the spot to seize the opportunity it offered. Catching a northbound D train, he was carried clockwise on the Ringstrasse for seven stops, then changed to the J line, which brought him, three stops later, almost to the threshold of St Saviour's Hospital.

As they say, the rest is history.

The other events of that week can be fitted only loosely into the week encompassed by the two Fridays which framed the brief earthly sojourn of Amy's baby.

How futile, in the face of such prodigious events, to quibble over the minutiae of precisely when and how the deed was done, or split hairs over such questions as whether Beatrice had handed Hannah's letter to S. on Tuesday evening or Wednesday morning, or, for that matter, ten years earlier or later! Why should S. struggle so hard to recall for them the precise timing of the infant's transition? Why must they persist in torturing him with their ridiculous questions?

* * *

'Look here, Herr Zimmermann, let's be logical about this,' his old friend Inspector Novak urged S. on his second visit to the St Anselm police. 'You've got to concede that there's no way you could have done the little chap in late Friday afternoon if he died on Friday morning. Well, just to satisfy myself I had somebody check the actual hospital records the other day. They put the time of death at nine-forty a.m. Signed by two doctors. So that's that. So just shut up about it and let's have no more nonsense out of you.'

And S., in conciliatory tones, 'Of course, inspector, I see that perfectly. I suppose I could be mistaken about the time. We all know that to err is human, and besides everything was at sixes and sevens that week, I was in a complete muddle and I still can't sort it all out in my own mind. It's possible Miss Beatrice had already given me Dr Fischer's note on Tuesday. In any case,' he added, 'I'm absolutely certain that it was towards the end of the week that Dr Fischer rang from Dr Kovacs's flat to notify us that they would all be leaving for America in a day or two. Ask my sister, she's the one who took the call. I'm not a liar, you know! Put any label on me – schizophrenic, fool, killer if you please, but don't call me a liar!'

'Come now, dear sir, let's not be talking a load of rubbish,' the inspector broke in coarsely. 'What's the sense of you trying to mislead the police? Nobody believes a word of it, you know. Look, if you were a normal person we'd have arrested you a long time ago for making a nuisance of yourself and wasting police time. Take care, you're trying my patience!'

'So I'm misrepresenting myself, am I? So you doubt my word? You forget that I have proofs, proofs in black and white!' Inwardly calm and self-possessed, S. here chose to feign heated indignation. 'Proofs,' he repeated, patting the wallet in his inner jacket pocket. 'In here. But that's my private business, inspector! Private, do you understand? There are such things as private matters, areas where the state has no right to meddle!'

'There, there, no need to get excited,' the inspector said soothingly. He stretched out his legs, undid the last two buttons of his uniform jacket and hooked his thumbs easily under his belt. Notwithstanding his potbelly, he was in fairly trim condition like most of the present-day Austrian police, though his longish hair gave him a faintly dissolute look. 'Look, I've got nothing against you, Herr Zimmermann. But if you're determined to get yourself locked up, you'd better go at it some other way. Listen, old chap. If you're so set on cooking up crime stories, you'd best just toddle back to your sanatorium. That's the place to do it, understand what I'm saying? Maybe you can even sell 'em to *Crimewave* or *Scary Tales*.' A quizzical grin. 'That's the best way for both of us, you see? … Well, I knew you would. So you go on home now and forget the whole business. All the best, then.'

Another benign smile, then the commissar leaned forward to press a button. 'Next, please.'

As etiquette dictated, S. rose promptly to go and touched his finger to his brow in the ghost of a military salute. 'So long then, Herr Inspector. Until we meet again.'

S. spoke briskly, but his heart was no longer in the affair. He was, in fact, rapidly losing not only heart but interest; the whole baby-killing affair, strenuous and heart-rending as it was, now seemed more and more like a farce!

* * *

For the truth is that S., now far beyond the midpoint of his allotted biblical span, had begun to feel his age.

His urge to strive against fate was on the wane, as were his sexual needs and his capacity for ardent emotion, positive or negative. The leisure-time pursuits that, until lately, had so absorbed him – correspondence courses, serious reading, television drama – held less and less attraction for him now. Even his beloved stamp collection was beginning to lose its charm. In the company of others who had shared his enthusiasms, he was more and more often assailed by lethargy and a deadening sense of futility. Only Brother Sebastian might have been able to rekindle his spirits, but Brother always seemed preoccupied now with other things, probably (S. now sees in retrospect) with arrangements for his impending transfer to the jungles of darkest Africa.

* * *

In a way, the last straw for S. was the loss of his good friend Sister Kim at the sanatorium. She had got married just before Easter to a gentleman from China and thereafter vanished from the scene. (The couple have since opened a restaurant called China Gardens in Margareten, one of Vienna's grimier quarters. They sent S. a card announcing the opening and promising the bearer a Special Peking Feast at half-price, but he has not yet taken advantage of the invitation.)

* * *

More than once, in the days that lay between the baby's death and his confession to the police, S. had seriously considered ending his life.

Perhaps it is true, as some studies seem to confirm, that most men in their middle years experience a change of life similar to the female loss of fertility, a change that seems to drain away the meaning of life and robs one of the taste for going on.

Even such an intelligent and enlightened personality as Helmut Rosen, S.'s precise contemporary and psychic or spiritual counterpart, had been sorely tried by the effects of this 'male menopause' for some months before his untimely demise, which came as such a devastating shock for all who knew him. It was that event, the death of his mentor, which had given renewed urgency to what S. now recognised as his own mission: to distil the helter-skelter clutter of raw, often brutal and incomprehensible experience that constitutes the daily life of the sufferer (life is suffering, said the Buddha) into the classic, ordered purity of all-seeing, all-forgiving Art.

But enough of philosophising. Back to the plot of our story, to events presented in orderly sequence! Back, above all, to action, the very stuff of the storyteller's craft!

⊰ 18 ⊱

Beatrice, with Mr Brian Whiting and his fifteen-year-old daughter Sherrill in tow, reached the house in Elisabethstrasse late Saturday afternoon.

They had come by taxi all the way from the airport, stopping en route at St Saviour's, where Beatrice, locating Amy's room with some difficulty, found her sister under heavy sedation and decided not to stay. The taxi driver had charged them two hundred schillings extra for the fifteen-minute wait! Brian had wanted to protest, but he had no German and the driver pretended not to understand English. That, Brian said, was certainly a lie, since the man's beard and turban marked him as a Sikh, and any Sikh must have at least a smattering of English after having lived for years under the British Raj.

'I'm really sorry about all the nuisance we're causing you, Aunt Eva, but I saw absolutely no way out of it,' a considerably chastened Beatrice told Eva after supper, over the washing-up. 'I couldn't just run off to Vienna and leave Brian to cope by himself, and he was really keen to come. He needs to play the protective male, you know. And besides, he cares a lot about Amy and Charles. He got to know them quite well last summer in Maine.'

She and Eva were alone in the kitchen. Brian and Sherrill, tired out from the long day, had retired right after dinner, and Mia had gone up soon afterwards to watch television. S. himself, having finished his allotted task of clearing away the dishes, had resumed his place at the dining table and immersed himself in the English newspaper Brian had thoughtfully saved from the plane.

(The *Mirror*, as it is called, seems to be quite a serious paper, though written in a racy popular style like Aunt Mia's favourite Vienna daily, *Die Kronenzeitung* ('Crown Paper'), to which she is an airmail subscriber. This particular issue offered several thought-provoking articles on political and cultural matters. Regrettably there was also a rather large photo, unconnected with any item of news, of a partially unclothed young lady smiling provocatively at the camera while mounted on a carousel pony. Such pictures often appear in the *Kronenzeitung* as well, giving offence to some people – Aunt Mia, for example – but probably not to others. S. himself finds amusement in the laboured captions which accompany them, invariably containing some sly and silly innuendo.)

'I ought to explain about Sherrill,' Beatrice was saying to Eva. 'I know it's an imposition but there was really no alternative. Her mother flatly refused to have her for the rest of the Easter recess, you see. She didn't mind taking the boy, but she was adamant about no Sherrill. Not that Sherrill was keen to go there. It seems she doesn't get on at all with her stepfather. Brian says she's frightened of him; I gather he's a bit of a brute. To tell you the honest truth, it wouldn't greatly surprise me if … ' Here the tap was briefly turned on full force, drowning the rest of the sentence.

'But really and truly, Aunt Eva,' she went on, becoming audible again, 'you must tell me whether this invasion might not be too much for Uncle Stefan. We're not hardship cases, you know. Of course it's lovely being under your roof, but it wouldn't kill us by any means to put ourselves up somewhere in town. I'm sure there must be decent places. So if it gets to be too much, please don't suffer in silence.'

This new sensitivity to the feelings of others raised Beatrice several degrees in S.'s estimation. She seemed a changed young woman, a far cry from the hoyden of less than a year earlier, who had respected neither the taboos of blood nor the vows of a celibate priesthood.

Predictably, Eva lost no time rejecting Beatrice's offer. 'A hotel, dear? Never! That's completely out of the question. We've got rooms to spare and beds enough for everyone. And it's a real treat for us, having you here, you must know that. So put the idea right out of your head.'

At no point, the reader will have noted, did Eva make any motion to consult her brother and joint owner of the house, who was seated hardly a dozen steps away. Without so much as a glance at him to ascertain his feelings, she had taken it up on herself to extend to Beatrice an invitation that implicitly included two total strangers, at least one of whom had made a distinctly negative impression on her prospective host.

* * *

This young person, Sherrill, was a saucy little minx with a shock of wild, curly black hair like a gypsy and what seemed to be a permanent scowl, dressed in a too-large jumper and a too-small 'miniskirt'. Her manners matched her appearance: she had barely addressed a civil word to anyone since her arrival and seemed totally absorbed in listening, via a headset, to her Walkman, an escape mechanism to which she, like so many of her contemporaries, appeared to be addicted. Only once since she walked in the door had Sherrill addressed herself to S., and that was to ask him (in English) whether he could provide an extension lead for her room.

This little chamber at the head of the stairs had been the 'maid's room' in Great-Aunt Mitzi's time and now normally served as Eva's study. It was just big enough to accommodate a single bed, two chairs and Eva's writing desk. At her brother's urging Eva had recently replaced her old electric typewriter with a modern computer and printer. At the outset she despaired of ever learning how to operate either machine, but she soon mastered them and now finds them indispensable for household accounts, correspondence and, of course, manuscript preparation.

Not one word of thanks to her host fell from Miss Sherrill's pouting lips when he brought her the extension lead from his own room, thereby depriving himself of the possibility of background music for his reading. No, she simply took it from his hand, ducked her head, muttered something incomprehensible and bang, shut the door firmly in his face! The girl's evident aversion to adult company remained on display in the following hours and days.

'Sherrill seems to be afraid of me,' S. complained to Eva on that first evening when she brought his medicine to his room. 'It's understandable, I suppose. Most people are afraid of loonies, aren't they? Probably I would be too, if ever I came across one!' he added jokingly.

But his sister came at once to the girl's defence. 'Fifteen is a difficult age, you know,' she said, fluffing S.'s pillow. 'Think how you and I must have seemed to others at that age. And the poor child's a total stranger here. She's got no one here but her father, and he doesn't seem to bother himself about her. She must feel terribly out of place.'

'Well, as I recall it, Petra wasn't much older when she was with us,'

S. had to remind her. 'Think how she must have suffered, with her dark skin and her struggles with the language.' He raised himself on his elbows. 'Half the time she hadn't a clue what was being said to her, for God's sake! Some nights she cried herself to sleep, poor child. But I didn't notice you showing much affection or sympathy for your own flesh and blood. In fact, as I recall it, you gave a big sigh of relief when the door closed behind little Petra for the last time.'

He hadn't really intended to hurt his dear sister in any way, but the presence of all those house-guests had put him in a bad temper. He had even lost patience with his beloved Aunt Mia that morning, for cheating at canasta. Twice he had caught her slipping him a good card, as if he weren't capable of winning on his own. Yet now it seemed that his bluntness had genuinely wounded Eva. Without a word in her own defence, she busied herself counting out his pills, compressing her lips to control their trembling as she bent to wish him a shaky 'Good-night.' Some people find the truth about themselves extremely painful to hear!

* * *

On the next afternoon, Easter Sunday, S. and Aunt Mia were 'at it' (canasta!) again when Eva strolled in and sat down beside S., idly observing the progress of the game (and probably wishing that there were a three-handed version). In the ensuing chitchat, neither she nor S. made any direct reference to their conversation of the previous evening, but it soon became evident, albeit in a roundabout way, that at least some of S.'s points had made their impression on his sister.

It seemed that after having chauffeured Beatrice to visit her sister at St Saviour's, Eva had chosen to pass the time in the Visitors' Gallery just outside the glass-walled children's ward rather than intrude on the sisters' reunion.

'Really and truly, Aunt Mia, it's such a happy place, with all those new babies in their baskets; there must have been twenty at least,' she exclaimed, her eyes shining as if Amy's tragedy, the sole reason for her presence, had completely slipped her mind. 'For me there's nothing nicer in the whole world than a newborn baby. Oh, I remember it so clearly, how wonderful it was having Werner,' she rushed on, oblivious to any disinclination her brother might feel to share with her the intimate details of her birth experience. 'As a child I used to think that there couldn't be anything nicer in the world than having babies. Lots and lots of them: four, five, a dozen! Of course, right after the war people thought nothing of having big families. It was more or less the thing to do in those days.

'But do you know, Aunt Mia,' she went on after a swift sidelong glance at S., who was absorbed in sorting out his hand, 'I really don't understand it myself, but the fact is I miss Werner less and less as time goes on. My only child, and yet for weeks at a time it slips my mind, in a manner of speaking, that I was ever a mother at all. Let alone a grand-parent. S. will tell you what a disaster I am in that role – a regular mon-ster of unfeeling!'

Her joking tone deceived neither of them. 'Oh, come, Eva, don't be so hard on yourself,' Aunt Mia said briskly. 'Who said you have to waste your time worrying about your children, once they've left the nest? Listen, that boy of yours couldn't wait to shake the dust of Austria from his feet. See the great world, that was his idea since he was a little lad. It's in his blood, he's a born adventurer like his father. So don't worry about Werner, he'll do fine wherever he goes and I'll bet you wild horses couldn't drag him back from Mexico just now.'

'I know, Aunt Mia, but that's not what I'm saying,' Eva tried to protest.

But the old lady was not to be deflected. 'And as for that grand-daughter of yours,' she continued in the tone of someone delivering a clinching argument, 'she's got her own roots over there in Mexico, so that's nothing to do with you at all. Nobody in his right mind could blame you for sending her home. I could have told you in the beginning that it was never going to work, not in this part of the world. They say Vienna's such a cosmopolitan place, but when you get right down to it what do you find? Provincialism and stupidity, that's what.'

Eva nodded vigorously and would have added a comment, but Aunt Mia hadn't finished.

'Now, take this cemetery business of mine, just for an example,' she went on. 'You wouldn't believe the red tape and the regulations. It's not as if I was out to buy the whole blasted place – all I want is a little spot for my ashes. Doesn't seem too much to ask, does it, seeing I've paid the bills for all the upkeep over the years? But just try to get anything done here by mail. It's hopeless, I tell you. You've got to be right here on the spot, so they can send you from office to office on a devilish paper chase! I tell you, I've had it up to here with Austrian bureaucracy.'

She paused and examined her cards before adding roughly, 'Well, no use getting worked up about things you can't change. Whose turn is it, anyway?'

'Mine,' S. said, 'but maybe Eva would like to take my hand. I don't mind sitting on the sidelines for a while.'

Almost impatiently, Eva waved the offer away. 'Well,' she said in an oddly tense little voice, almost under her breath, 'I expect you're right as usual, Aunt Mia, but I still feel it can't be normal. Perhaps I didn't make myself clear. What I'm saying is, Werner means absolutely nothing to me any more. I don't think about him, I don't miss him, I wouldn't particularly care to see him. Actually I wouldn't mind if he never set foot in Austria again. It's not as if we'd quarrelled, or he'd hurt me in some way. It's as if he'd never had anything to do with me. I can't feel anything for him. That's abnormal and you know it.'

Aunt Mia shrugged her shoulders. 'You're talking nonsense now, my dear. Evalein, Evalein, who in the world would want to break their heart over a grown child? That wouldn't be normal either, would it now?' she demanded. 'Never mind the past; what's done is done and there's no sense crying over spilt milk – I'll tell you what we'll do,' she added with sudden animation. 'We'll see what the future holds for you two darlings!' And with that she gathered up all the cards, shuffled them rapidly and began laying them out to read their fortunes.

* * *

Now, as it happens, Aunt Mia really can foretell the future from the cards. As a rule the news she has for them is good: fame and fortune for S., perhaps, and for Eva 'a dark handsome stranger in the offing, but watch out for the seven of spades!' Even after she and Dr Hebbar parted, the dark handsome stranger and the seven of spades still figured in Aunt Mia's predictions for Eva, who finally plucked up courage to ask whether there were anything else bad in store for her.

No one guessed at the time that Eva was deeply troubled, even then, by the thought that Brother Sebastian might some day be recalled by his order to California, or perhaps to its Mother House in his native Canada. Neither she nor anyone else outside the order was aware that nearly four years earlier he had applied to his superiors for a transfer to the mission in the Central African Republic, where filth, brutality and rampant disease are said to eclipse the worst horrors of medieval Europe.

Could Aunt Mia have had an inkling of all this from the cards? She studied them for several minutes in evident puzzlement before confessing, 'It's no good, Evalein, I can't seem to make out what they're trying to tell me.'

'I don't believe you,' Eva said. 'You must have seen something in those cards, I know you did. What was it?' It's always like this with Eva; she likes to think that she despises everything occult, but she can't help taking Aunt Mia's fortune-telling half seriously.

Aunt Mia shook her head. 'As God is my witness, nothing but a jumble. Sometimes a lot of what the cards tell you is rubbish anyway, you know, like static on the radio. All that's coming through to me is that you need to keep a cool head at all times and above all look after your health.'

'They always say that, don't they? What makes them think I need to be reminded, I wonder?' Eva said half teasingly. 'Look at me, I'm a living testimonial to the virtues of diet and exercise. Why, I've got to keep in shape, haven't I, to keep up with S. here! What would he do without Big Sister to cosset him and keep an eye on his literary outpourings and see that he takes his pills? He'd get himself into all sorts of pickles. Wouldn't you, brother dear!'

Her obvious attempt to raise his drooping spirits may have won a faint smile from S., but he was inwardly in anguish at the mere thought of ever having to cope without her! Needless perhaps to say, her callousness in even implicitly suggesting such a thing added to his distress.

* * *

It was on another occasion like this, when the terrible thought of life without his sister had presented itself vividly to S., that he had first really and truly considered in practical terms the mechanics of doing away with himself.

What were the alternatives?

One was self-starvation: lengthy, painful and uncertain, since others could easily prevent it.

Another possibility was death by drowning (preferably in the Danube, on a sunny day); but that too could be frustrated by a well-meaning passer-by.

A third would be to jump from a high window, as Dr Rosen's sister had done. But the sanatorium had only two storeys and the house in Elisabethstrasse only three. It could best be done from a place like the restaurant at the top of the new Danube Tower, a hundred meters above ground level. But they were probably on the lookout for would-be suicides and would pounce on him before he even got a leg over the parapet.

Was there a parapet? S. thought so but could not be sure. Dr Hebbar had once taken him and Eva there for dinner. For all the fine linen and candlelight and flowers, it was not a comfortable place to be. At times the whining of the wind outside had threatened to put an end to conversation, and S. had fancied he could feel the tower swaying beneath his feet.

⊰ 19 ⊱

Hannah Fischer arrived from New York City, USA, in the early hours of Easter Monday, three days after her younger daughter Amy had given birth to a severely handicapped infant.

Her presence in Vienna augured no material change in the lives of her cousins in St Anselm, since she had chosen to stay with her friend Frau Dr Kovacs, whose flat happened to be within reasonable walking distance of St Saviour's. She had no time to inform other relatives of her arrival, let alone make a personal appearance at the house on Elisabethstrasse. Because Amy was now suffering badly from depression as well as from postnatal complications of a physical nature, her mother felt duty-bound to spend most of her waking hours at the bedside, taking turns with Charles and Beatrice so that the patient would never be left alone.

* * *

S., though confident that he would hear from Hannah in due course, was nevertheless filled with anxiety in anticipation of the actual event. He successfully concealed his state from Eva, Beatrice, Brian and the reclusive little Sherrill – from everyone, that is, except Aunt Mia – but he was twice obliged to deny to his perceptive old auntie that he was suffering from a 'tummy-ache'.

His intuitive belief in Hannah's fidelity did not deceive him. On Tuesday afternoon Beatrice, returning from St Saviour's, handed him an envelope addressed to him in Hannah's familiar hand. 'For you, from my mother,' she said, with a meaningful smile which in another context might once have been perceived as seductive, but which the present circumstances exonerated of any such intent.

Mastering a nervous tremor of the hand, S. took the cheap blue envelope and, with a gracious inclination of his head in lieu of verbal thanks, turned on his heel and departed with measured steps for his bedroom. Once there he locked the door, switched on the bedside light, drew the curtains, slipped off his shoes and settled down on the bed with two pillows under his head for support before proceeding, with due deliberation, to peel back the flap and extract the contents for perusal at his leisure.

They consisted of three small pages torn from an address book or engagement calendar, covered on both sides in Hannah's neat, rounded script.

My dear [she had written], 'I'm all tied up here at the hospital with Amy but hopefully could arrange to meet you Friday at the Café Landsmann on the Ring, just across from the university. According to my city map there's a direct train from St. Anselm to the Franz-Josef-Bahnhof, and from there you can take the D tram to the university. The Landsmann is right there next door to the Burgtheater, you can't miss it. One o'clock would suit me nicely, as Charles will be relieving me here at St Saviour's just after midday. Give me a ring here at 94 65 515 to confirm. I'm staying with Ilona Kovacs, my friend from medical school. She's got an answering machine, so you can leave a message. Sorry about all these complications. Everything seems a mess – wrong place, wrong timing. Too late? Too early? We shouldn't let that bother us, though. [The last sentence was in German: *Doch das soll uns wohl nichts bekümmern.*] – Ever your H.

Having read and reread this letter until he had thoroughly digested every nuance of its contents, S. consulted the Vienna telephone directory to confirm Dr I. Kovacs's street address. Not that he felt the slightest stirring of a desire to call there, or to linger in the neighbourhood in hopes of catching sight of Hannah, as he would certainly have done in the days of his youth. What he did want was to imagine her daily surroundings and mentally to trace her journeys, by tram or by foot, between her friend's flat and the hospital.

Frustratingly, he found only one listing for an I. Kovacs, without the Dr or other academic credentials, as is common practice in Austria. The address was not Werdetorgasse in the Inner City as Aunt Mia had mentioned, but Saikogasse somewhere in the 22nd District, and of course the telephone numbers didn't correspond. At first S. was puzzled. The thought fleetingly occurred to him that this lady friend of Hannah's might be a medical imposter or a practitioner whose licence had been nullified for some medical misdeed.

But Aunt Mia, to whom he confided his problem, pointed out a likelier explanation. 'She's ex-directory, that's what it is. She probably just doesn't fancy being constantly rung up in the middle of the night, I know I wouldn't. But she's a doctor all right, she graduated with Hannah at the Pennsylvania Medical School. They even shared a flat there in their final year. Well do I remember some of those weirdos that used to hang about them. There was one young fellow with his hair tied back in a greasy ponytail who didn't even have the manners to get up from his chair when I walked in, and another one as black as coal. I swear, it gave me a real fright to see this huge black man looming there by the window. He was Ilona's friend, thank God. Not that what Hannah ended up with was much of an improvement over those two. No way could she have shown her face in polite society with that LaCrosse specimen!'

After qualifying, Aunt Mia related, both young women had gone on to specialise in paediatrics. That was a fine thing for a woman to do, Aunt Mia thought; she had no quarrel with it. The trouble was that they both had their heads full of this so-called 'gentle childbirth' nonsense, which was basically just a lot of hocus-pocus tacked on to the idea of home birth without anaesthetics, supposedly a deeply fulfilling experience. When it didn't go wrong, that is. And some years ago, as a sort of sideline, Ilona had opened a women's clinic where she practised some kind of therapy based on 'healing the forgotten child' that was supposedly trapped inside the patient. Articles on her work had already appeared in American scientific journals such as *Omni* and *Psychology Today*, Mia added.

S. was not overly impressed. Two or three articles about Dr Kovacs and her theories, though not the ones Aunt Mia mentioned, had been among the hundreds of clippings and tearsheets that Hannah had sent him over the course of the years, touching on nearly every topic that interested her and she thought likely to strike a responsive chord in him. It did not escape him that Aunt Mia had given a rather biased account of Dr Kovacs, but that was understandable. It must be painful indeed, he reflected, to see one's only child fall under the influence of someone whose ideas and values one deeply mistrusts, and who threatens to draw away that child to a foreign environment where, with the passage of time, she may well become increasingly a stranger not only to her mother but to her own children and grandchildren as well.

* * *

All things considered, S. was relieved that his dear cousin was evidently not intending to introduce him, in the course of her brief visit, to her exotic colleague. It was, in fact, largely to avoid any possibility of an encounter with this person that he chose not to avail himself of the telephone to confirm the rendezvous at the Café Landsmann; what he had heard of her from Aunt Mia filled him with distaste. He was also, if the truth be told, more than a little apprehensive of a meeting because he sensed that the contact, if it occurred, would not be purely social. He could imagine nothing more disagreeable than to have to fend off any attempt by Hannah's friend to heal the forgotten child within him. Doubtless Dr Kovacs herself was no model of emotional health. Damaged personalities, S. had observed, were more the rule than the exception among those in her profession.

Accordingly, instead of telephoning, S. wrote Hannah a brief note of acceptance on a postcard of 'Old Houses in Krumau', a painting by the controversial Austrian artist Egon Schiele. (There are several places in Austria called Krumau; the one in Schiele's painting is a little town rather like St Anselm but situated on a much smaller river, the Kamp. It would probably take twenty Kamps to make a single Danube.) He then placed the card in an envelope, sealed it carefully, and handed it to Beatrice that same evening, asking her to convey it to her mother personally at the hospital the following day.

Is it possible that Beatrice, in all the turmoil surrounding her, might have forgotten to carry out these instructions? That is a tempting hypothesis. It would explain why S. had not found Hannah waiting at the Landsmann when he arrived, perspiring and out of breath, a quarter of an hour late for their meeting. Her letter had asked him to confirm; if his confirmation had gone astray, she would naturally think that he would not or could not be there.

If, on the other hand, his note had indeed reached her, then there were two possible alternative explanations for her absence: one, that some unforeseen circumstance had prevented her from coming; two, that she had in fact been there at the appointed time but had not cared to wait for as much as fifteen minutes to see and talk with him face to face. The second of these possibilities was too hurtful and humiliating to be borne; S. quite simply did not believe it.

Whatever the cause, it was the fact of her absence that sealed the hour of the infant's death.

◀ 20 ▶

In the early evening hours of Easter Monday Amy's husband Charles made his first and only appearance before his wife's Austrian relatives in St Anselm.

He had arrived on a flight from Boston at Vienna airport in the late afternoon, checked into the Intercontinental, a large and expensive businessmen's hotel in downtown Vienna, and after an unsuccessful attempt to see his wife at the hospital, had rung the house in Elisabethstrasse to let them know he had finally made it to Vienna.

Eva, who had reached the phone a split second before her brother, told Charles to take a taxi out to St Anselm and join them for a bit of supper. He accepted but entreated her not to delay the meal on his account.

The trip from Vienna normally takes less than half an hour by taxi, but it was nearly an hour later when Charles rang the doorbell. The taxi driver, a young Turk who had never before had a fare to St Anselm, had taken Charles by a roundabout way over the Kahlenberg; consequently, by the time Charles turned up the rest of them had nearly finished their supper.

S., who had expected a beefy American type, was agreeably surprised by the actual Charles, a tall, thin, wiry man with a bald spot, whose nervous smile reminded S. of a figure from the distant past: the American corporal Chuck who had befriended him in the prisoner-of-war camp and had then been disciplined for fraternisation with the enemy and transferred to another unit, causing S. much distress.

The newcomer's arrival was followed by a lengthy round of greetings, with hugs for Aunt Mia ('Granny' to Charles, it seemed) and his sister-in-law Beatrice, followed by a warm handshake and a slap on the shoulder for Brian Whiting, whom he had met the previous summer at Maple Harbor but whose presence here as companion to Beatrice evidently came as a bit of a surprise to her brother-in-law.

At last, spotting his host, who had chosen to melt into the background during these preliminaries, Charles introduced himself, vigorously pumping S.'s hand. 'Hi, I'm Charles. You must be Hannah's cousin that I've heard so much about. Hannah thinks the world of you, you know.' (Note the familiar 'Hannah' when speaking of his mother-in-law!)

Strangely, during these first few minutes no one so much as mentioned Amy and the baby. Instead, there were rearrangements of chairs, S. and Aunt Mia moving theirs so as to squeeze in Charles between them, and hospitable gestures by Eva, whose attempts to press a slice of home-smoked Easter ham on the newcomer were tactfully warded off, though Charles did accept a quarter-litre of wine, *Grüener Veltliner* from a local vineyard.

'You should've seen the gourmet meal they fed us in first class,' Charles remarked to the company in general. 'Four courses, plus seconds if you don't stop them, and I didn't. That's what it's all about in the airline business these days: fancy food, caviare and champagne. Personally I'd rather they put the money into maintenance.'

He looked as if for confirmation at his wife's much-travelled grandmother, but Aunt Mia only compressed her lips. She always travelled economy class on principle, S. remembered, wondering briefly whether it could have been the cramped seating in economy class that had caused Amy to go into labour months before her proper time.

Charles would have arrived earlier, he told the party, if it hadn't been for difficulties in organising a baby-sitter(!) for his two daughters, aged twelve and thirteen. Gerti, their new au pair fresh from Switzerland, had flatly refused to take the responsibility, and Bridie, the mainstay of the family, had already left to spend the Easter weekend with her brother and his family in Connecticut when the news from Vienna had reached Charles in Bangor. So he had been obliged to spend the best part of Saturday organising Bridie's emergency return to duty and making travel arrangements for himself: first, finding a travel agency that stayed open at weekends, then booking a seat from Boston, always a problem at short notice on a holiday weekend. In the event all economy and business seats were already booked, so he had been obliged to fly first class.

'At double the price, no doubt,' S. remarked in his elegant English – a signal, as it were, for Brian to chime in with an account of his own difficulties in securing three seats on a London-to-Vienna Saturday-morning flight for Beatrice and himself and Sherrill. 'Not one tourist-class seat left on the entire plane, no last-minute cancellations either,' he said, 'but luckily I thought of an old classmate of mine from boarding school who works for British Air, so we ended up with Beatrice taking Sherrill with her on Royal Class and just me tourist, on one of those fold-down bulkhead seats the cabin staff use at take-off and landing. Very comfortable it was, too.'

'Actually it was more like three times the going rate for economy,' Charles said, addressing S. 'You know, I don't think I'm what you'd call a stingy person, but it really hurts me to pay that kind of money for a bigger seat and a so-called gourmet meal. I don't know about anybody else, but I've got better ways to spend the stuff, personally.'

'So have I,' S. said automatically, an absurd remark prompted by the wish to make himself agreeable to this new American friend.

No doubt more of the same pleasant, diverting chatter among the three men would have followed had not Beatrice turned the talk back to the stroke of fate that had brought them all together here.

'So what time was it when you tried to get through to Amy?' she asked Charles.

'Just before I phoned here,' Charles said. He took some time looking at his watch. 'Maybe two hours ago. It feels like more when you're jet-lagged. First thing after I'd checked in I tried to get through to Amy at the – God, I can't pronounce it – the hospital she's in – '

'St Saviour's,' S. offered at once. '*Zum göttlichen Heiland*, in German. Which means the same thing,' he added unnecessarily.

Charles nodded. 'Right, Gottlicken Highland, that's it. Anyway, I had a hard time making myself understood, and I couldn't make out much of what the charge nurse was trying to tell me. My two years of high-school German really let me down,' he added with a rueful little chuckle. 'But then the reception girl came on and I was saved. She told me she was Russian, and boy, does she have an accent, but she was completely fluent in English, a terrific interpreter. Seems she'd spent a couple of years modelling or something in New York.'

Here Eva and Aunt Mia exchanged glances.

'Excuse me,' S. said, taking a deep breath to calm himself. 'But you might have been connected to the wrong nursing station. You see, the hospital consists of two main units, the general building and the maternity wing. Their regulations differ.' He fixed his eyes on a point infinitely distant behind Charles's head. 'Your wife and son are in the maternity wing. You can visit them there at any hour of the day or night. Nobody will stop you. That is a fact. Believe me, I am absolutely certain on this point.'

'Gee,' Charles said in evident puzzlement, 'maybe I didn't get it right – '

'No, no, you made no mistake,' Eva said quickly. 'I hadn't mentioned it at home for fear of upsetting Aunt Mia and S. here, but Amy was moved a couple of days ago to the general wing. She's quite all right, it's just that she needed some special care that they're not set up to provide in the maternity wing.'

'And the baby?' asked Aunt Mia anxiously.

'Oh, he's still on life support.'

* * *

This was, of course, terrible news for S. If Amy was now in a different wing and they hadn't moved her baby, who knows what obstacles he might encounter on his next visit to St Saviour's? What if he were challenged in a corridor of the maternity pavilion, asked what patient he wanted to see? He would have to give a name; not Amy's, of course, since he'd then be sent to the other pavilion. It would have to be an unusual name; anything as common as 'Frau Schmidt' would risk the danger of being conducted to a real patient's bedside and instantly exposed as an imposter. 'Frau Yamaguchi' would avert that danger but arouse suspicion on other grounds. Something like 'Frau Ziska', unusual but not impossible, might enable him to escape without being suspected of anything worse than an honest mistake.

But that would mean the collapse of his mission!

And what if there were, by ill fortune, a real Frau Ziska in the pavilion?

Even if sheer luck enabled him to avoid these hazards, there remained the worst of all dangers, that of being caught too early in the act of disconnecting the infant's life-support devices. As a faithful follower of an American TV series where such procedures are shown in graphic detail, S. was confident that he would be able to manage this swiftly and efficiently. It should take, he reckoned, no more than twenty seconds. If he were caught after that it would not really matter, though he would prefer to acknowledge the act at a time and place of his own choice. But to accomplish his purpose without violence, twenty undisturbed seconds would be essential.

* * *

'What about his condition? And where have they got him?' S. managed to ask.

'They say he's stable, whatever that means,' Eva said. 'But do calm yourself, S. He's getting the best of care and there's really nothing we can do.'

'Except pray,' Aunt Mia put in.

'That's absolutely right. You know the saying, S.: Man proposes, God disposes,' Eva said sententiously.

S. took a deep breath, yoga-fashion, a highly effective means of restabilising the nervous system. 'I asked you what they've done with him,' he said quietly, 'but you haven't told me. I want to know, Eva. Please don't play games with me!'

'What makes you think I'm playing games?' Eva demanded in evident irritation.

'The fact that I merely asked a simple question which you have not yet answered,' S. persisted, as calmly as he could. 'Questions are still allowed, I hope?'

'Don't be ridiculous,' Eva said sharply. 'I didn't understand what you were asking. No, they haven't moved the baby. Apparently there's no question of that while he's still on life support.'

'It's not that big a deal, I think,' Beatrice put in quickly, in her quaint American way. 'Amy's the number-one concern for all of us, I think, but she's going to be OK. They weren't a hundred per cent happy with her progress a day after the birth, so they've moved her to where she'll be getting more nursing care, that's all. She's not in intensive care or anything.'

S. shook his head, as if unable to quite take in this information. 'So you too knew about the transfer,' he muttered at last, without looking up from his plate. 'It seems that everyone else in the family has been kept informed except me.' He couldn't repress another head-shake. 'It's really beyond me. I know I'm a mental case, but people like myself have feelings … ' Here he broke off in distress.

Charles, no doubt sensing the charged atmosphere and seeing Beatrice at a loss to reply, resumed his account of his problems at the hospital. 'Anyhow, the message finally got through that there was no way for me to see Amy today, she'd be tucked in for the night by the time I could get there and I'd better come by in the morning. Fair enough, I suppose. Poor kid,' he added, 'she's really been through a lot this last couple of days. But I guess that goes for the rest of us too. Doesn't it, Granny?'

Aunt Mia's first response was a faint smile and a slight raising of the eyebrows in token of her displeasure at his chosen mode of address – which was understandable, even though she was in point of fact not only a grandmother but a great-grandmother, and that three times over, counting the unfortunate newborn! But in the end she decided to take it lightly. 'Don't you Granny me, darling,' she said, wagging a finger at him. 'I'm a tough old bird, and you should thank God your wife seems to have inherited my gumption and my strong constitution as well as my good looks.' Perhaps her perky response could be considered inappropriate or even callous under the circumstances, but it made people smile and restored peace around the table.

Charles nodded. 'It was touch and go there for a few hours, wasn't it? But Amy's a fighter, bless her heart!'

'Listen,' Beatrice called to him across the table. 'What about a toast to my darling sister?'

Charles got to his feet and raised his half-empty glass. 'Now that's what I call a sensible idea. Ladies and gentlemen, I give you … Amy, my beloved wife!' he ended with a flourish.

'To Amy,' Eva echoed, and they drained their remaining wine or mineral water – all but S., whose habit it is to minimise his intake of liquids in the two hours before bedtime, for reasons the reader will readily surmise.

* * *

Soon, however, the merrymaking was cut short when Aunt Mia began complaining about a ringing in her ears which, she only now confessed, had plagued her during the flight and had steadily got worse ever since. 'It's loud as anything,' she said. 'Loud enough to drown out the conversation. Like a buzz saw. I'm amazed you can't hear it, because it's driving me around the bend. I'm going straight up to bed.'

So the party broke up then and there. Aunt Mia retired to her room upstairs, while Eva and Beatrice cleared the table and busied themselves in the kitchen, rinsing and stacking the plates in the dishwasher and putting away the perishable leftovers, such as the remaining potato salad and half a Malakoff-torte, an extremely rich dessert which Eva had mentally earmarked for Brian's daughter Sherrill – who, however, hadn't shown her face downstairs since her arrival, although the thump of rock 'music' had issued intermittently from her room since late morning. ('Don't let it upset you,' Eva had responded to S.'s complaints about the noise. 'Of course, it's thoughtless of her, but she's only a teenager after all. And the music won't kill you; it's what they all listen to nowadays.' Clearly Eva was prejudiced from the start in favour of Brian's unruly adolescent offspring.)

* * *

Left by the ladies alone with Brian and Charles, S., despite grave initial apprehensions, assumed the role of host with ease and grace. He invited the other two men to bring their wine glasses to the adjoining sitting-room and help themselves freely from a newly opened bottle of so-called 'Prelate's Wine' from the Abbey's own vineyards – which he had uncorked easily with the aid of a so-called 'Never Fail' American corkscrew, a hostess present to Eva from her friend Dr Hebbar.

Seated again, sipping his own glass gingerly for fear of discomfort in the night, but freely enough to loosen his tongue, S. proceeded to entertained his two guests with interesting bits of historical information about the locality. On impulse he launched into a story about how he and Eva and Hannah had gone sledding on the forbidden meadows of Abbey Hill adjoining the vineyards, the only young people ever to have defied the ban.

'The first time we went there with our sleds we were challenged by a black-robed young guardian monk,' S. related. 'Hannah might have been twelve or thirteen at the time. She went straight up to him, looked him boldly in the eye and told him he was making a big mistake: we had come there at the invitation of our grandfather Monsignor Demel, who wouldn't be a bit pleased to hear about our unfriendly reception. She actually used those words: "*unfreundlicher Empfang*". Well, it worked like magic. The poor young man was so rattled by the mention of his grace's name, or by Hannah's pretty face, that he just stammered some kind of apology and took to his heels. I guess he returned to his austere monastic cell, to lick his wounds in solitude! We never saw him again.'

Amusement registered on the faces of his audience.

'It wasn't strictly true, of course,' the narrator conceded with a wry smile. 'Monsignor Demel wasn't our grandfather but our great-grand-father, and at the time he was already very ancient and too ill to set foot outside his quarters in the abbey. He had at some point asked that we should be brought to him to receive his blessing, but he was certainly beyond caring where we went with our sleds.'

This elicited chuckles from both gentlemen.

S.'s lively presentation of the above anecdote had made for a con-genial atmosphere in which conversation could flourish. The principal topic was wine, Brian enthusiastically championing the merits of New York State wines against the 'run-of-the-mill local stuff you get every-where in Europe' while Charles evinced some scepticism but showed himself more interested in the soil conditions and climate most favourable to growing the *Grüner Veltliner* grape.

After a quarter of an hour or so Brian excused himself briefly, prob-ably to ease his bladder. His absence gave S. the opportunity to ask Charles the question uppermost in his mind: 'And how long are you thinking of extending your sojourn in our charming capital, if one may ask?' It was vital for him to gain a comprehensive knowledge of every-one's movements over the next few days.

Charles's answer was vague if not actually evasive: 'I guess I'll just stay around until Amy's well enough to come home with me.' After a brief pause Charles went on, as if he could thought-read S.'s next ques-tion, 'I was talking with Hannah on the phone last night, and that's what she advised. She may be here tomorrow or the next day herself, she said, if she can get a colleague to stand in for her at the hospital.'

Nothing more than that was forthcoming from Charles on the subject of Hannah, but S. sensed in his use of her Christian name, and in particular the curious little lilt with which he spoke it, a degree of intimacy that went beyond the usual bounds of a son-in-law–mother-in-law relationship.

Apart from 'the girls', who would be well looked after by Bridie in their mother's absence, there was nothing of importance awaiting his attention at home, Charles explained.

'At forty-four I'm a free man, you see,' he said. 'Hawkins & Hawkins virtually runs itself these days. I'm keeping my seat on the board, but basically I'm no longer involved in day-to-day management, so my time is my own. I'm a lucky fella, no doubt about that. Being born on April Fool's Day must have something to do with it.'

Charles had also been a keen birdwatcher as a boy, 'until peer pressure forced me out of it in high school,' he admitted with an embarrassed smile. Recently, though, he had been doing quite a bit of fund-raising for wildlife conservation work, and he was thinking of going into it on a semi-professional basis. 'I used to think I'd kind of enjoy being an odd-ball, but what do you know, ecology is "in" right now. One of life's little ironies, I guess,' he added, with a self-deprecatory smile.

* * *

It is a strange fact, incomprehensible perhaps to the literal-minded, that from the moment S. first set eyes on Charles, he had experienced a strong sense of kinship and sympathy with the man, an attraction devoid of any sexual dimension and without any obvious basis in common experience or interests. Hannah would diagnose it, no doubt, as instant recognition of a kindred soul. S. wasn't satisfied with that, but he had no better explanation.

Having learned Charles's age from his own lips, S. did some mental arithmetic in bed that night which yielded an amazing result: Charles must have been conceived in mid-1945, in the wake of six years of horrific bloodshed and suffering, after a spring which marked the end of World War II with the surrender of the Wehrmacht, S.'s imprisonment by the Americans, the commencement of his life sentence at the sanatorium and therewith the end of his Third Age of Man: youth.

He had read somewhere of a statistical study which provided scientific support for the common observation that wars or great natural catastrophes are followed by a great upsurge in births. There is an ancient belief that the souls of these children are those of the dead who perished before their time and have sought out new bodies in which to live out their allotted season on earth.

Now if this is viewed in conjunction with the spontaneous mutual attraction and affection that arose between Charles and S. practically from the moment they met, and – perhaps most tellingly – their respective feelings for Hannah Fischer, then one begins to gain an inkling of the strength of the predestined bond between them, a bond which will endure even if their paths never cross again in this life.

* * *

The doctrine of the transmigration of souls was first explained to S. by his sister's boss at the UN Atomic Energy Commission, Dr S. (for Srivatsa) Hebbar, who as a good Hindu believed implicitly in rebirth. 'The soul, anybody's soul – yours, mine – goes through many lives bound to the wheel of existence,' he declared, as usual speaking so rapidly that S. had trouble following the oddly accented English. 'Eventually, through successive reincarnations, it can purge itself of earthly ties and accumulate enough merit to win release and union with Brahman. Brahman is the Absolute, the ground of all being, God if you prefer. Now then, what is the catch? The catch, my dear fellow, is that this process is not automatic. Oh no, very far from it. What kind of body you will get the next time depends exactly on how you have behaved in your present existence. If you have been good and noble and served others to the best of your ability, you may be reborn in a very high state, with very nice body. But if you have behaved like a dirty fellow you may come back as the lowest of the low, even as a dog or pig. Brrr!'

Dr Hebbar liked to spice his talk with humour, but there can be no doubt that he took his religion very seriously. He neither smoked nor drank, and would not knowingly eat flesh, fish or even egg. When S. and Eva dined with him at a fish restaurant in the Prater which affords a glorious view of the Danube, their host scrupulously avoided everything except the vegetables and filled up instead on dessert.

Doubtless it was his devout Hinduism that kept Dr Hebbar, after the suicide of his first wife, from proposing marriage to Eva, despite all they had in common.

In any event, when it comes to the crunch no amount of philosophical speculation can explain why, to this day, S. should bear feelings of such warmth and depth for Charles Hawkins, a man he has met only once, a man devoid of any evident intellectual distinction and unconnected to him by any circumstance less tenuous than the life-breath of a newborn infant bearing the genes of both.

And yet, truly, given the choice, S. would never have changed places with Charles, even for the sake of physical propinquity to Hannah. How much better to nurture a mutual love, ever growing, developing and deepening through decades of faithful, truthful correspondence, than to be forced to witness the fleshly decay of the loved one: her honey-coloured hair turning grey, her slender waist thickening, all her beauties yielding to the grim advance of age!

Above all, S. counted himself fortunate that his relationship with Hannah had progressed no further. How dreadful if he had been fated to share in the creation of another being, an offspring doubly blighted, born of two rotting branches from a ruinous tree! Then how exuberantly the evil would have bred and multiplied down the years, from generation to generation, world without end!

Unless it should be cut short by a single loving act, like a thunderbolt from Heaven: not, indeed, an act of the Almighty in whose hands the whole world rests, but of another poor, blighted creature, 'despised and rejected of men': a stone spurned by the builders, a miserable loony with no hopes, no expectations or claims to love or honour or responsibility – a person, in short, with nothing to lose.

'There you go again, getting carried away with yourself,' Eva would tell her brother. But deep down she envied him his rich inner life and his ability to capture in 'winged words' the very essence of the human condition.

◀ 21 ▶

The evening of Charles's first and last visit to Elisabethstrasse ended with a near disaster. This is how it came about.

Charles had dismissed his taxi on arriving at the house. Soon after his *tête-à-tête* with S. following dinner, he confessed to being 'dead on his feet', and Eva telephoned for a radio taxi to take him back to his hotel in Vienna, but learned that there would be at least a half-hour wait. At that, overriding their guest's objections, she insisted on driving him back to the city in her car – welcoming, perhaps, the opportunity to have a quiet word with him about his newborn son.

She delivered Charles safely to the Intercontinental and drove back to St Anselm without incident, only to meet calamity within a few metres of her own doorway.

S. had switched on the outside porch light as usual for their departure, then switched it off again, awaiting the three short hornblasts that would signal his sister's return.

That evening, however, when Eva got back to Elisabethstrasse she decided not to disturb anyone by sounding the horn. That meant reversing into the garage beside the house in darkness, or near-darkness. Unfortunately Eva's reversing is rather erratic, and on this particular evening she was too tired to be careful. The result was a violent collision between the rear of the vehicle and an antique fire-hydrant that had stood at the corner of the drive since the days of Great-Aunt Mitzi and should have been removed by the authorities decades ago, when new hydrants were installed at either end of the block.

The impact of the collision, which had been audible from inside the house, brought both S. and Brian dashing to the door. The hydrant had been demolished and the rear of the Toyota severely damaged. Eva, though shocked, seemed to be unhurt. But a few minutes later, entering the house, she felt a sharp pain in her back, and over the next hours it got steadily worse. Since Eva flatly refused to see a doctor, S. was obliged in the end to walk downtown to the only chemist on duty over the Easter weekend, twenty minutes by foot from Elisabethstrasse, for a strong over-the-counter painkiller. It was not until the late afternoon of the next day, Easter Monday, that Eva could walk comfortably enough, with the temporary help of a cane, to resume most of her household functions.

The new Toyota was, surprisingly, a total write-off. The insurance company even paid for a week's rental of another vehicle while the purchase of a new car – this time a French Renault – was arranged.

* * *

Ten minutes after the accident Aunt Mia was urging legal action on Eva. 'Look, child, we can't let the town fathers get away with this. I'll get us a good lawyer and we'll sue for negligence. There's at least a hundred thousand schillings in it, mark my words.'

Overnight, however, she had quite changed her mind. 'Look, S.,' she said to him over the cards soon after breakfast, while they were playing canasta in her room, 'I've been thinking. Why waste money and energy on a lawsuit, just to prove a point? Quite honestly, darling, that accident was your sister's fault from beginning to end. She knew the hydrant was there, it's been there for ages. How could she have forgotten? No, darling, I have a hunch it could be a kind of sign to her to be a bit easier on herself, not to take on too much ... I worry about you both, you know, and now I've got something new to worry about. How on earth is she going to go on coping with this big house? And the garden!' She shook her head sadly. 'Not with a bad back, it's out of the question.'

'Bad back?' S. said dubiously. 'Aren't you being a trifle pessimistic? People do recover from injuries, you know. And Eva doesn't seem to have been badly hurt. She said it was a lot better when I looked in on her this morning.'

'Well, pray God you're right,' Mia said, rapping the edge of the table with her knuckle so that the bracelets jingled. 'But back or no back, none of us are getting any younger, you know. Believe me, Eva'd be doing herself a favour to find a smaller place with no stairs to climb, like one of those new two-bedroom Residency Bungalows they're putting up at the foot of the Kreuzberg. Didn't you see that story in the paper? They've got central heating and a full-time warden. I thought they looked very attractive, just right for Eva and pleasant for you too. And later on, if her back's all right and she feels like a bit of travelling, why, all she needs to do is lock the place up, and off she goes without a care in the world.'

'Very nice for Eva, but aren't you forgetting something? How about me?' S. demanded bluntly. Sometimes one owes it to oneself and others to let people know exactly how one feels! 'I may be a mental case, but I am also a sentient being. Not a doormat or a piece of furniture that you can move about as it pleases you!'

'Oh, you'll be all right, lovey,' Aunt Mia said brusquely. 'Don't you worry, now, she won't run away for good!' She picked up the cards and shuffled them with a flourish. (She was scrupulous about shuffling for canasta, though when it came to fortune-telling she barely went through the motions. She cut the pack only once!)

'I'm going to tell you something else now, sweetheart,' she went on, as if the last exchange hadn't taken place at all. 'I've put my apartment on the market. I want to leave New York for good and move to Florida. It's only a couple of hours further from Vienna,' she added, as if to fend off a predictable objection.

'Wonderful,' S. said drily. 'Twelve hours instead of ten.'

'I've told you about my flat in Fort Lauderdale, haven't I?' his aunt went on, ignoring this negative response. 'Two bedrooms right on the ocean, in a lovely co-op complex with absolutely all the trimmings. Olympic pool – that's an extra-large swimming pool – and doctors and hairdressers and shopping right on the premises, you name it. Plus round-the-clock security to keep the riff-raff out. Your Fischer-Uncle bought it ages ago. For the winters, you know. But the first winter we spent there was the last. He couldn't stand the climate, you see. So after that first winter we let it out, and it's been a nice little income earner ever since, I must say. No, Florida didn't suit your Fischer-Uncle at all. "Give me a real Austrian winter any day," he'd say. "Remember our honeymoon, remember how hard it snowed on the Semmering, how cosy we were in our little room?" Ah, I guess he must have still been in love with me, the dear man, mustn't he?'

She sighed and closed her eyes for a moment or two while S., wincing inwardly with embarrassment, prayed to be spared whatever intimate revelations his elderly relative might be tempted to impart.

A brief silence followed, Aunt Mia doubtless calling up tender scenes from memory's book before resuming her brisk, practical manner. 'Anyway, personally I've got nothing against plenty of sunshine. In fact the more of it the better I like it. So why shouldn't I give myself a break and retire to Florida like everybody else instead of staying on in Forest Hills until I get mugged and raped and murdered? What's to stop me from saying "so long" to the Big Apple forever, I'd like to know?'

'Big Apple? What's that, a restaurant?' S. interrupted.

'No, it's just an expression people use for New York City. Someone probably invented it to attract the tourists, and it caught on.'

'But why "Apple"? "Big" makes sense, but "Apple"?'

'Listen, darling, I don't know why "Apple" and I don't care. Why should it make sense? If you bother your head about everything in this world that doesn't make sense you might as well forget about living. So don't worry about it. Let's just see what Lady Luck will hand out to us this time.'

Aunt Mia started dealing out the cards, chattering a blue stream the while. 'OK, in Forest Hills I've got Hannah half an hour away, and a fat lot of good it does me. All that daughter of mine can think of is work, work, work. She'll go on until she drops. D'you know the latest? Listen to this. When her contract runs out at Beth Israel next summer, she wants to quit hospital work and go into a practice partnership with that Hungarian friend of hers from medical school, that Ilona Kovacs. Now there's a strange bird for you. Who ever heard of a doctor growing herbs according to the phases of the moon, and making her patients wear amulets to rebalance their auras, I'd like to know? But she's built up quite a following in eastern Europe, it seems. She's got a big flat in Budapest and a pied-à-terre in Vienna, in the Werdetorgasse. As a matter of fact, I've got a standing invitation to stay there whenever she's in town. Of course she knows she's safe, I'd never take her up on it.'

'So what is this partnership with Hannah?' S. tried to sound casual.

'A lot of nonsense, if you ask me. That "gentle birth therapy" they're both so wrapped up in. Meditation and massage and prenatal this and that,' Aunt Mia said with evident distaste. 'The idea is to open a big clinic in Budapest and let the world come to their door and learn how to have babies. But you know if Hannah goes through with that, I might as well be living in Timbuktu for all I'll see or hear of her.'

'Why couldn't you come here and move in with us?' S. felt his face tingling with a sudden wild hope. 'Then you and Hannah could meet here. There's a daily boat service now to Budapest. Only three hours from Vienna. The return trip takes longer, because it's upstream, against the current. Or there's the train.'

Aunt Mia nodded absently, evidently so preoccupied with her own thoughts that S.'s suggestion had failed to register. 'Well, no matter how you look at it Budapest is a long way from home, my boy. And it's not as if she'd be there when I wanted her. Half the time she'd be on the go like that Kovacs woman, heading off to conferences in Brazil, Mexico, Australia, you name it. It's a big thing with the wealthy these days, this natural childbirth racket. In my day respectable people had their babies in hospital. Home delivery was for the hoi polloi.'

'Not *the* hoi polloi,' S. corrected her gently. 'Hoi *means* "the". You should say, "Home delivery was for hoi polloi." '

Aunt Mia gave him a look. 'Myself, I had Hannah in St Saviour's,' she went on. 'Your Fischer-Uncle insisted on it. The most exclusive hospital in Vienna it was in those days, maybe still is for all I know. It cost him a pretty penny, but the money didn't matter. "Nothing's too good for my Mia," he used to say. Worshipped the ground I walked on, your Fischer-Uncle did. He had foolish ideas like his daughter, yes, but a heart of gold. He'd never have dreamed of deserting his old mother that way … But wake up, my sweetheart, it's your play.'

'I know, I know,' S. replied a little sharply, for it could hardly have escaped her that he was still arranging his hand. 'D'you think I've lost my wits?' He was trying to take it all in good humour. His voice was shaky and he was not far from angry tears, but he managed a humorous smile.

And Aunt Mia smiled as well. 'Oh, S., you're a real clown, you know,' she said with a shake of her head, as if he had intended a witticism all along. 'But look at me, I must be getting senile, here I am discarding the king of hearts when I've got the king of clubs right here in my hand! Lord, if I'm that bad now I hate to think how I'll be three years hence. If I'm not dead by then. Well, what can you do?'

She sighed, laid down her cards and extracted from her alligator handbag a roll of her favourite American wintergreen mints. 'Here, have a life-saver,' she said cheerfully. 'And let's just forget about the Grim Reaper. There's life in the old girl yet, as they say. Who knows, down in Florida I might find myself a nice partner for my old age. Actually – ' (she laid a finger on her cheek) ' – actually, there is one person I know in Fort Lauderdale. An older man, but still lively: Ferdinand Chasins. We were practically neighbours on 41st Avenue in Queens; I was a member of their bridge group, that's how I got to know them. His wife Juanita was a lovely person. She got cancer three years ago, and when she died he sold the house and moved to Florida. Ferdy and I have kept in touch. We're very compatible. So maybe we'll get together, who knows? Actually he's already sort of invited me to go on a cruise with him next Christmastime. So we could get to know each other better, you know. I've got more than half a mind to accept.'

S. felt stricken. He said hesitantly, 'I hadn't realised that you might be thinking of marrying again. I know I should want you to be happy and I do, but somehow the idea of you married to a total stranger makes me feel sad.'

'Don't be a ninny, he's not a total stranger. I've known Ferdy for going on six years, as I told you. And besides, who said anything about marriage? Getting together was the expression I used. We might move in together, but marry? Not on your life. He's got his money and his heirs, and I've got mine, and that's the way it's going to stay. So don't you worry for a minute about your inheritance, my darling, it's sacred. Nobody's going to lay a finger on it.'

'Sometimes I wonder what you think of me,' S. said bitterly. 'To imagine that I'd waste a single thought on that. You ought to know that I never want to inherit a penny from you. I just want you to live forever!'

Aunt Mia's face softened, and she patted his hand tenderly. 'You're a silly old darling, that's what you are. Listen, did I ever tell you what a gypsy woman in the Prater said to me once when I was sixteen? A fortune-teller, you know. She foresaw everything that's happened to me since. She told me I'd marry money, and have a child before I was twenty, and that I'd live to be a hundred. Well, the first and the second came true all right, so why not the third?'

She held out the mints once more. 'Go ahead, have another. But don't chew them, it's bad for your teeth. Anyhow, as you can see, your old Auntie isn't quite ready to start pushing up the daisies yet!' She fanned out her cards swiftly, surveying them with falcon eyes, and presently rearranged them with a satisfied little smile.

S. again noticed the liver-spotted hands and the time-worn face, puckered and riddled with little furrows and worry wrinkles which her make-up and her fancy spectacle-frames could not hide. He felt a sudden stab of sorrow at the thought of how very ancient she was, his dear auntie, the only person in the world who really loved him. Old and infirm, with two artificial hip joints that wouldn't last forever and a mind that might already be starting the long slide into senility, leaving her pitifully muddled like the patients in the Pavilion for the Aged by the south gate of the sanatorium, just across from the Arts Pavilion. There would be no more Vienna trips for her then, no more canasta, no more chatting or reminiscing with her near and dear ones.

* * *

Why not admit that for an instant or two S. toyed with the thought of how much better it would be for Aunt Mia to die, as her great-grandson was to die, quickly – yes, here and now, while she was still ahead of the game, with her dear nephew standing behind her chair, murmuring fond words and embracing her with all the power of his boundless love, delivering her from all the pains and ills of living – yes, literally loving her to death, as he loved that innocent little creature branded with the mark of Cain!

Such was indeed S.'s state of mind at the time.

Yet it would be a tragic error to imagine that even in the remotest recesses of his brain he could have caught a glimpse of himself as the possible agent of anyone's involuntary departure from this vale of tears whilst said person was in control of his or her faculties. Only in the case of malformed infants and others powerless to escape their suffering could such an act be warranted.

⊰ 22 ⊱

It was not surprising that Dr Rosen, in his professional arrogance, should have refused even to consider the possibility that S. had ever seriously planned the death of Hannah's infant grandchild, much less actually carried out the deed. Day after day, session after session, the good professor kept harking back to the same theme, ever on the alert for the tiniest technical flaw in his patient's story, the smallest inconsistency that he could exploit to penetrate what he regarded as S.'s armour of delusion.

'Very well then, on Tuesday Beatrice gave you Hannah's invitation to meet her on Friday at the Café Landsmann,' he would begin. 'You sent back a note through Beatrice, promising to meet her at one. Knowing your compulsiveness Hannah expects you to arrive at least ten minutes early for this so important meeting. She waits and waits. Half an hour later you are still not there. She concludes you are not coming, pays and goes. What could be simpler? Yet typically you make a great mystery out of it rather than admit to any fault.'

'With respect, I find that rather a shallow analysis,' S. said, 'and plausible only to someone without any insight into the long relationship between the persons involved. Hannah and me.' On the last three words, uttered without forethought, his voice unexpectedly cracked.

Dr Rosen said softly, 'Long, but is it so very deep? Are you yourself so sure about her motives and intentions? For example, her returning to Vienna: that surprised you, did it not? Breaking, for her daughter's sake, that famous vow never to return to the country that persecuted her people and expelled her family?'

S. shrugged his shoulders. 'My dear Herr Professor,' he replied coolly, 'I have learned long ago to expect these twists and turns, they are in Hannah's nature. And believe me, she would have changed her mind about returning to her old homeland long ago if, for instance, someone more attractive than myself had been waiting for her here!'

There was a brief silence while Dr Rosen drew heavily on his cigarette.

'All right,' he retorted at last. 'Go ahead, start picking at your scabs again. Lick your sores like an mangy dog.' (This in the brutal manner the good professor deems necessary from time to time in the course of therapy. To the discerning ear, his Cambridge-accented English was again tinged by the faintest possible hint of a vulgar Viennese inflection.)

'I agree it would hardly be surprising if she had found your footloose friend Herbert Berger more interesting than yourself,' he went on heartlessly. 'By your own account he was a better cyclist and a better all-round sportsman than you: handsome, self-confident, quite a lad, in short. Who could blame her?' He laid his cigarette down in the ashtray and settled back in his chair to await S.'s rebuttal, eyes shining expectantly behind his gold-rimmed half-glasses.

'On the other hand, if I mean so little to Hannah, why should she have kept up an intimate correspondence with me all these years?' S. retorted sarcastically. 'Why the urgent invitation to a rendezvous in the Café Landsmann as soon as she set foot on Austrian soil?'

'Except that it never came to a meeting, if I understood you correctly,' Dr Rosen remarked drily.

'Because I lost my way,' S. returned swiftly. 'I was feeling rather nervous, as perhaps you can imagine. And I have a great aversion to public transport. You could refresh your memory on that point by consulting some of your early notes regarding certain things I experienced as a prisoner of the Americans just after the war.'

He drew a deep breath to steady himself. 'Let me assure you that I would have been at the Landsmann on the dot of one if I'd stayed on the tram for one more stop, but you see I got out by mistake at Waehringerstrasse. I had to wait through two full cycles of traffic lights before I could even cross the Ring. I don't know if you have been there in recent years,' he added, allowing himself a veiled allusion to Dr Rosen's preference for permanent residence outside his fatherland! 'But the Ring is now extremely busy and extremely dangerous to cross!' he continued. 'And then I walked on very quickly, but when I finally reached the Landsmann it was full of strangers, and I suddenly realised how stupid it was that we had no agreed way of recognising each other. It simply hadn't occurred to me, you see, and possibly not to her either, that we would have to pick each other out of a crowd. So all I could do was ask the headwaiter if he had seen a single lady. He was very helpful, he led me past the tables so I could see for myself, but none of the single ladies I saw, and there must have been a dozen, looked as if they were expecting anyone. They were all absorbed in their various newspapers and magazines, and none of them looked young enough to be my cousin. So I left.'

Here S. put in a strategic pause. 'On my other errand. At the hospital, you know. The time was opportune, and it was only a few streetcar stops away. No problem, as they say.'

Dr Rosen, cigarette in hand, had listened without comment and now remained obdurately silent.

After some minutes of this passive provocation, S.'s patience snapped. 'Has it ever crossed your mind, Herr Doktor,' he demanded bluntly, 'that you could be disastrously wrong about all of this? Oh, I know well enough what you're thinking now. Poor, helpless fool, you're telling yourself, he likes to feel important. He has these delusions of grandeur, he sees himself as master over life and death. Poor deluded fool, he gets his ideas from storybooks! Now then,' S. continued in a voice that seemed to have lost its normal resonance, 'here we have a text-book story of two lovers who fix a rendezvous after many years of separation. Each catches sight of the other from afar, and the upshot is that the meeting never takes place. Because neither of them has the strength to accept what the other has become.'

Hitherto a stony-faced listener, Dr Rosen allowed himself at this point an ambiguous little smile.

'Or again,' S. went on harshly, 'you might have come to the learned conclusion that any feelings Hannah herself may have harboured for me must have been some mixture of compassion and sentimental nostalgia for the never-never land of youth. Or maybe you've decided that they were nothing but guilt feelings.' (Another strategic pause.) 'Because even at the tender age of fourteen she was already deceiving her poor clod of a cousin with his best friend.'

At this point S. paused for three deep breaths, which as usual proved a reliable means of stabilising the breathing, calming the nerves and refreshing the spirit in times of stress.

'But for all your theories and learning I pity you, Herr Professor,' he went on with renewed vigour, enunciating each word clearly and firmly, as if he were training for the lay readership for Sunday mass (though the conversation was conducted in English; owing to the recent influx of native English-speaking house guests, his own English had gained greatly in fluency and expressiveness.) 'Yes, I really pity you for the ignorance you have displayed on both the personal and professional level! You seem to have no clear conception of who I really am or what I think, or how things stand between Hannah and myself.'

He held up a hand to forestall any interruption. 'Oh, I know, now you'll be telling me that Hannah might have had reasons of her own for keeping the relationship alive over the years. And why not? All that diligent letter-writing must have been rewarding for her too. Therapeutic, you might say. But a personal confrontation must never be allowed to cast the shadow of a doubt on the memory of that first love, forever unmarred by space and time! Even though there may be no such thing as true love. I sometimes think that everything we call love is nothing but a form of camouflaged self-gratification!'

Again S. paused strategically before continuing with a vigour and fluency reminiscent of the late great Austrian actor Albin Skoda in Shakespeare's *Hamlet*, which S. had studied in depth in an extramural course at the University of Vienna. 'Yet on the other hand it is entirely possible, too, that my true love Hannah and I should have missed each other because of a subconscious wish on both sides to confine our relations to correspondence. For our reciprocal feelings should remain unsullied by half-truths and troublesome intimacies.'

Professor Rosen smiled.

'Or maybe you have something else on your mind, as well, Herr Professor,' S. said coldly. 'Maybe the thought has crossed your mind that all my actions, including the elimination of Child X, were prompted by a subconscious wish that Hannah might leave – yes, leave Vienna, go back to America for good. With the baby dead, what reason could she have to stay on? Oh, of course it isn't the bodily presence that matters to me and her! But how could she have borne the sight of me now in the flesh? Or what's left of me. A caricature of the image she has held in memory – '

A dull ache behind his forehead was becoming more insistent, but S. pressed home his attack with undiminished vigour, in a voice unhampered by the righteous emotion that filled his breast! 'You are a vain man, Rosen, too vain to admit it, but you know in your heart that you were wrong in your diagnosis, Dr Rosen, utterly and disastrously wrong! I have no vanity left, no desires of a personal nature. I am acquainted with grief, at home with pain and humiliation. My cup of gall runneth over. Have you heard of "blissful unhappiness", Dr Rosen? Perhaps not. But you see before you a rare example of that.' The self-mocking smile that followed this assertion acknowledged his debt to another living Austrian artist, a writer whose works would hardly be known to the other man. 'Which means that your theories and your therapy have come a cropper. Oh yes, Professor Rosen, your theories have made you famous. Scholars confer honours on you everywhere, they invite you to their congresses and hang on every word you utter. And here am I – your guinea-pig, your pride, your star patient – and I'm the walking proof of your failure, your intellectual bankruptcy!'

Dr Rosen, who had been listening with mild interest, elbows resting on the desktop and fingertips joined under his chin, suddenly leaned forward. 'Bravo! But let's not forget the real issue at stake here. Your writing – that's where the battle is joined. Let us keep this in mind for our next session.' He settled back in his chair, arching his chest as his hand sought the watch nestling in his waistcoat pocket.

The stage was set, the lion back on the prowl, eager for the kill.

◈ 23 ◈

On the Tuesday morning after Easter, S. and Brian breakfasted together in the kitchen. Beatrice, breakfastless, had taken the nine fifty-eight train for Vienna to visit Amy in St Saviour's; Eva and Aunt Mia were still in bed, putting in a well-deserved day of rest after all the excitement of the past seventy-two hours. S. had brought each of them breakfast on a tray: coffee and fresh buns from the Berger bakery. Both had declined the offer of butter and strawberry jam.

There was still no evidence of the youngest house-guest. Apart from occupying the bathroom continuously for almost three-quarters of an hour in the morning and again in the late afternoon, the only sign of life from Sherrill over the past twenty-four hours had been occasional blasts of extra-loud rock 'music' from her room. 'Leave her alone,' was Brian's advice to S. 'No point in taking her anything, she won't touch it.'

'I don't understand,' S. said. 'She must be hungry. It seems heartless not to offer her something.'

'I'm afraid it's quite useless,' Brian said wearily. 'When Sherrill gets into one of her moods she shuts herself up in her room all day long to listen to her tapes. And when I say shuts herself up, I mean she literally won't open the door. As for food, she's probably got enough chocolate bars in her suitcase to keep body and soul together for a couple of days. I've never seen her eat breakfast anyway, not since she was about ten.'

'A rebellious teenager,' S. observed sagely. 'It must be very difficult for you.'

'For about a year after the divorce I tried to keep house and be mother and father to her and Joel,' Brian said, 'but I couldn't just drop my work, and the two things were always getting in each other's way. My mother helped out as best as she could, but the situation went from bad to worse and in the end boarding school looked like the only feasible solution.'

'How sad,' S. said. 'That must have been painful for you.'

'Oh, it's all worked out well enough,' Brian said. 'It's a very liberal boarding school, a lot different from my own old one. It was Joel I worried about, much more than Sherrill. Joel was only thirteen when his mother left, and he'd always been a bit of a loner, so I wasn't sure how it was going to affect him. But he seems to be all right now. His big thing is computers. Like most young people nowadays he knows more about those damned things than you or I ever will. I say,' Brian paused, looking around the kitchen, 'is there another place to plug in the teakettle?'

'At the other end of the shelf, right over the sink,' S. told him. Apart from the coffee (which he had already made in advance in the twelve-cup percolator), and fresh rolls from the bakery, each man was on his own regarding the rest of the breakfast menu: for Brian, eggs and fried bacon and two buns; for S., muesli with skimmed milk and extra raisins (a tried and true recipe for regularity).

Altogether it was a very nice, relaxed breakfast at the kitchen table, with the Vienna Boys' Choir singing over the radio from the Stefansdom, though at that hour of the morning it was probably a recording.

Brian told S. that he too had been a boy treble at 'prep school' (so called because it is designed to prepare pupils for university). 'It was a boarding school near Sheffield, in the north, but they had a few day students too,' he recounted in his nice English accent as he broke a second egg into the frying pan and put the lid on. 'Normally my mother could never have afforded to send me there, not even as a day student, but I had quite a good voice and could kick a ball as well, so I got in on a bursary. Sports play an important part in a English schoolboy's life, as you probably know.'

'I was good at football too when I was a boy,' S. could not refrain from boasting. 'And rowing and skiing as well. Rowing on the Danube in summer, skiing in the Wienerwald in winter. The Vienna woods, you know. And a bit of ice-skating too, but the girls were better at that. Meaning Eva and my cousin Hannah. Dr Fischer, that is,' he added, though the clarification was probably unnecessary, Christian names being the fashion nowadays.

Brian nodded. 'That skiing sounds great to me,' he said, characteristically using an Americanism. 'I once went on a school skiing holiday in the Tyrol. Great fun.' He turned off the gas under the frying pan and leaned against the windowsill, waiting for the kettle to boil. With the light coming from behind, it was hard to make out his face. 'Actually school wasn't so bad,' he went on. 'I got along all right, really.' He turned and gazed out at the garden, which didn't look very pretty at this time of year, before the bushes had come out enough to hide the dustbins in the left rear corner. 'But I can't say that I ever felt completely accepted. Somehow I just didn't cut the right figure, and my accent wasn't right. Not that I got bullied a lot. On the contrary, they tended to ignore me. I'd have welcomed a bit of bullying, even if I'd had to fight. Not that I'm such a brave fellow, you understand,' he added with the shadow of a grin.

At that moment a high whine from the teakettle gave notice that the water was boiling. 'Care to share my teabag?' Brian enquired a moment later, lifting it steaming in his spoon. 'I want only the one cup.' When his offer was refused with thanks, he laid the envelope carefully in a clean saucer, presumably for future use. This seems to be a typically English trait: S. remembered Eva reporting on her return from England that even in a three-star hotel like the one where she had stayed in Stratford-upon-Avon, only one teabag was provided for a two-cup quantity of boiling water.

'Cheers,' Brian said, raising his teacup like a wineglass. 'Good talking with you, old chap.'

'Thank you.' Better to accept a compliment, even an unwarranted compliment, with simple grace than to squirm and protest.

'You may very well have been wondering what a brilliant girl like Beatrice could see in a character like me,' Brian resumed, having emptied his steaming cup in a single draught. 'I marvel at it too, believe me. But somehow we "clicked" from the first moment we met. Mind you, it was her mother who introduced us, Dr Fischer. She rescued me from death by sunburn, or so she thought. Total stranger that I was. Quite a lady, isn't she?'

He did not wait for S.'s assent to what was possibly a rhetorical question. 'Even on a professional level Beatrice and I are amazingly well-matched. The two of us pulling together in harness would make a terrific team. You know, I've given some thought to the idea of setting ourselves up like that in America. New York or possibly Los Angeles. As a photo-journalism team, you see. Stringers for overseas dailies, for instance. I've already got quite a few good contacts, and I see no reason why it shouldn't work out.'

He proceeded to describe, with boyish enthusiasm, Beatrice's New York flat. It was on the sixth floor of a very well-maintained apartment building on West 84th Street, five minutes' walk from the subway station, with shops of every description practically around the corner. The flat was centrally heated and consisted of two rooms, one bedroom plus a very large 'lounge', i.e. sitting-room, that could easily do duty as an office *cum* study, with a convertible divan for the kids to sleep on when they came to visit.

'Or how about you, S., why don't you come over for a couple of weeks?' he added enthusiastically, sounding more American than ever. 'You know we'd love to have you. Beatrice is a great fan of yours. And to think you've never been to the Big Apple,' he babbled on, choosing to ignore S.'s head-shake of refusal rather than give him a chance to explain. 'It's an incredible city, really, quite an experience just to be there. It could be quite conducive to your story-writing as well, you know, it's quite true what they say about travel broadening the mind. But, to be honest, I'm looking forward to the day when I'll be rich enough to forget all this reporting rubbish and do some serious writing of my own. I have some ideas. I'll tell you some day.'

'Sounds great,' S. said, choosing the fatuous Americanism for its sheer meaninglessness. Brian's raptures over Beatrice had made him uncomfortable. Whilst building his castles in the air, Brian had all too clearly failed to take into account the possibility that Beatrice might not be as besotted with him as he was with her, or worse, might already be in the process of writing him off!

As the reader will doubtless recall, S. had found himself in the role of captive audience for the confessions of Beatrice, who, with the easy candour so typical of her generation of young American womanhood, had freely described to Eva various private idiosyncrasies and personal weaknesses of her partner, including matters normally regarded as bedroom secrets, in a manner which made it quite clear that any romantic feelings she might once have harboured for him were dead. Amusement had become contempt; indifference had shaded into distaste; and the poor fellow had no inkling that his happiness hung on a fraying fabric of illusion!

* * *

Having conceived a sincere liking for Beatrice's lover, S. was profoundly distressed to see him standing unawares in the path of impending catastrophe. Would it not be better, he wondered, for Brian to depart this life with his illusions intact than to awaken to reality some fine day and be confronted by the devastating truth?

* * *

'What do you have in mind, then, for your friend Brian?' had been Dr Rosen's only response when his patient gave vent to his concerns on that point. 'Anticipatory euthanasia at the hands of your good self, to spare the poor fellow future suffering? Is that your idea of friendship?' he challenged S. point blank.

'I ask myself that,' S. said earnestly. 'Mightn't it be a friend's service? You see I'm fond of Brian, he's a true friend. My only true friend, I think sometimes. So it would be painful to me for him to be deceived and injured by someone he trusted, even in fiction! The mere thought of it appals me,' he added, for good measure.

Merely giving S. a quizzical look, Professor Rosen took some time to settle back in his chair, extract his cigarette case from an inside jacket pocket and a Gauloise from the case, tap it on the desk, light it, inhale deeply, and pronounce on the second exhalation, each syllable accompanied by a tiny puff of smoke, his professional analysis of the situation before him.

'Perhaps, then, you'd better make it quite clear at the outset, this sympathy of yours for Brian,' he said finally. 'Establish the fact that you identified with him. Projected your own death-wish on to him, *et cetera*. That's not so very unusual, as you know.' He briefly smiled at his well-manicured fingertips, evidently amused by this insight.

'Ah, but is it likely that a sexual innocent like myself would really identify himself with an accomplished, ah, ladies' man?' S. objected, having in the twinkling of an eye mentally weighed and rejected the term 'stud'. 'Doesn't that rather stretch the imagination? Even if I must as a writer be able to identify in a certain sense not only with any of my own characters but with virtually anyone, friend or foe or mere stranger, who's ever crossed my path. Ironically enough, even with an eminence such as yourself, Herr Professor!'

The alienist nodded, lacing his fingers together gently, and let another little smile flicker across his otherwise impassive countenance.

'Ironically, I say,' S. went on with unerring intent, 'because you are the one person in my life to whom I owe nearly everything: what I think, what I write, even who I am – in short, I'm painfully aware of my vast indebtedness to you. But here, you see, is the heart of the contradiction, Dr Rosen. For no matter what you have been to me – indeed still are, my mentor and my best friend, surely I can call you that without embarrassment or apology – despite all that, Dr Rosen, I utterly reject you. I reject everything you are and everything you stand for, in its totality. You are abhorrent to me. But I'm still able to identify with you. That is not so difficult for a writer.'

Here S. placed his hands on his knees and leaned forward in his chair to narrow the distance between them (a deliberate invasion of the good doctor's 'personal space'). 'Yes, I can empathise with you, Dr Rosen. I sense your concern and your sorrow for me. Yes, and your love for me. But underneath it all I can also sense the disgust and disdain that I've inspired in you from our first meeting. We are enemies, Dr Rosen. That has been ordained from the beginning.'

'Yes. Go on, please,' Dr Rosen urged him on, stony-faced. The tiger was on the prowl again!

S. shook his head wearily. He had, he felt, already said all that he had wished to say. Said it well, too, his delivery easy and relaxed – perhaps, he reflected, because he had temporarily gained the upper hand over the Great Man by having (as he remembered later) made his little speech not in English, their invariable protocol in these sessions, but in their native tongue, using the German second-person singular form *du*, with its alternative connotations of intimacy or blatant disrespect.

* * *

For the edification of future readers of these pages it should be explained here that many years ago, in the first months of their friendship, Helmut Rosen (as the senior of the two, if only by a few months) had proposed that the two of them address each other with the comradely *du*. In those days Rosen was a young doctor afire with radical new ideas about the treatment of the mentally disturbed. Obsessive in his pursuit of opportunities to test his revolutionary theories, he had little patience with conventions and formalities. Hence, perhaps, their mutual attraction.

But the intervening years had worked a transformation in Helmut Rosen. Along with professional recognition and an honorary degree or two, he had acquired a portentous bearing and an absurdly inflated notion of his own genius and of the deference due him from all and sundry. It was this swelling bubble of personal vanity that S.'s revival of the intimate *du* had been intended to prick.

* * *

Characteristically, the good doctor chose not to respond in any depth to his patient's analysis of their relationship, lest S. guess how deep the barb had gone. He merely nodded slowly, as if observing the confirmation of a long-held theory, and murmured (also in German, also with their old *du*): 'Hm, yes. You identify with me, and you feel that I despise you. I don't suppose the significance of that escapes either of us.'

To which S. returned only a subtle smile.

The rest of the session proceeded along familiar lines: S. relating some trivial incident of life at the sanatorium, Dr Rosen nodding his head at appropriate intervals and at a certain point fishing in his waistcoat pocket for his big gold watch, the signal that S.'s hour was drawing to a close. As he did so, S. was struck by the look of weariness in his eyes and felt a throb of pity. It was, he thought, the look of a man who was beginning to lose his faith in himself and in the value of his whole life's work.

Sadly, it was not given to Helmut Rosen to take his leave of life in the manner of the ancient Stoics: rationally, calmly and with the dignity of one in full possession of his (or her) faculties. That ideal manner of death had fired the young S.'s imagination, and his enthusiasm had, he has always believed, infected the young Dr Rosen as well.

However that might be, the doctor's professional vanity, his personal arrogance and his very autonomy as a human being were fated to be swept away in the twinkling of an eye.

⊲ 24 ⊳

There is something uncanny in the suddenness with which circumstances can reverse themselves. You find yourself at the mercy of events that you have never reckoned with or dreamed of. One thing leads to the next until suddenly all hell breaks loose and the whole structure of what you think of as your life begins to shiver and lurch like a sailboat on stormy waves.

As usual, Brother Sebastian had looked in on S., his patient-on-leave, late that Tuesday afternoon. His duty at the sanatorium being over for the day, he had let himself be persuaded by Eva to stay on for a bite of supper with the siblings and three of their house guests: Aunt Mia, Beatrice and Brian. Sherrill had still not condescended to show herself below stairs, but she hadn't been missed, since everyone was busy with other matters: Brian closeted in his room sorting out some work on his and Beatrice's British Isles travel guide, Beatrice at Amy's bedside at St Saviour's, Eva nursing her injured back, dear Aunt Mia in her darkened bedroom with a migraine, and S. himself fully occupied with food shopping and other household chores.

Small wonder, then, that Sherrill's absence elicited no comment from the others until shortly before dinner. S., who was in charge of setting the dinner table, interrupted Eva's chat with Brother Sebastian to ask whether he should lay a place for the young English lady as well.

'Sherrill?' Eva said. 'Yes, of course – at least I think so. Now that you mention it, I haven't seen her all day.'

Nobody else had, either, it seemed.

Brian calmed their fears. 'Oh, Sherrill's probably just dozed off with her headphones on,' he said lightly. 'Best let her be.'

His smile of reassurance couldn't have been entirely genuine in view of some of the things that came to light later that evening. Even at that point, when her mother's grounds for refusing to take her for the rest of the Easter holiday had not yet emerged, it was already apparent to everyone that Sherrill was a problem to herself and others.

Sherrill's downfall was, in a word, drugs: the curse and damnation of children of her generation worldwide. That part of her history, as recounted by her father that evening, would have distressed anyone of normal sensibilities.

Her stepfather Albert, it seemed, had banned her from the farm on Good Friday, ruling out any future visits, after what Brian described as 'a nasty argument about religion'. He, Albert, was a member of a small millennialist Christian sect that attributes the world's present ills to the Father of Lies, lately escaped from Hell and now wandering the earth sowing the seeds of man's damnation: socialism, fornication, rock music and drugs. Albert made no secret of his concern for Sherrill's immortal soul and had unwisely confiscated her tapes on this last visit to the farm. In attempting to take them back by force, she had scratched Albert's hand, provoking him to a towering fury in which he called her an accursed Jezebel and swore she should never darken his door again.

'And of course I'd never let her go there again,' Brian concluded his tale. 'And it's Joel's last time there as well. The farm is fini. If their mother wants to see them, fine, it's in the divorce settlement. But not at the farm!'

With the exception of Aunt Mia, who was seated next to S., the others appeared to take this account at face value. She murmured in S.'s ear, too softly to be accidentally overheard, 'Believe me, my boy, where there's smoke there's fire.'

Under cover of a lively conversation between Brian and Brother Sebastian, S. replied softly, 'But perhaps it's not the fire you think it is. All sorts of nasty things happen in this world of ours, dear Aunt. It's nothing so remarkable when a sinful father, a stepfather in this case, lusts after his daughter, or a brother after a sister, or a doctor after a patient. It's the way of the world, you see.'

'Oh, get along with you, that's naughty!' the old lady admonished him, but you could see that she was struggling to keep a straight face at his witticism.

At that point no one had an inkling of the dreadful bind young Sherrill had got herself into. Except for Brian, who took a long time eating because he deliberately chewed every mouthful twenty times to aid digestion, everyone had finished dinner, but no one made a move to quit the table until Eva asked her brother to 'be a dear' and run upstairs to fetch her handbag. She wanted to repay Brother Sebastian, she said, for the sixty-hour candle he had lit at her request in the Brothers' chapel for poor Amy's recovery and that of her baby.

Although he was eager to be of service to his sister, S. never got as far as her room. As soon as he reached the head of the staircase a peculiar rasping noise from Sherrill's room stopped him in his tracks. It was a human, not a mechanical sound, a kind of rasping snore that S. had never heard from a normal sleeper, even in his Wehrmacht days. He went straight to her door and knocked, at first softly, then a little louder, but there was no answer. He knew it was most unlikely that Sherrill had locked herself in. The bolt that had once secured the door from the inside could now no longer be worked without tools, so the door was never bolted; S. could have opened it without difficulty and walked straight in. But a certain delicacy of feeling, or perhaps it was a premonition, prevented him from entering alone and without authorisation. Instead, he sprinted back down the stairs to seek assistance.

His intuition had not misled him. When, in Brian and Brother Sebastian's wake, he finally did enter Sherrill's room, a shocking sight presented itself: the child on the bed, pale and dishevelled, eyes closed, mouth dribbling saliva on the pillow, breathing in stertorous snores, covers thrown off and the flimsy nightgown in disarray, exposing a little pale-nippled breast, a far cry from the ample beauties one sees from time to time on late-night television! And on the bedside table, the damning evidence: an opened twist of thin brown cigarette paper, a razor blade, a tiny spill of whitish powder.

* * *

As a youth in California, long before training for the priesthood, Brother Sebastian must have learned a lot about drugs. Now his knowledge and sophistication instantly came into play.

Confronted by the daunting sight of an unconscious, perhaps fatally drugged Sherrill, he 'swung into action', with Eva and Beatrice and the girl's father at his heels.

'Frau Eva,' he ordered crisply, 'give Dr Müller a ring. Tell him he's needed here as quickly as possible. Tell him I said it was urgent.'

(In retrospect, this must have been the moment S. first became aware that Brother was in the habit of addressing Eva by her Christian name.)

But hardly had Eva completed the call when the girl Sherrill groaned and opened her eyes. Seeing S. standing by the door on guard, she let out a shriek, snatched up the bedclothes around her neck and started screaming obscenities at S., or possibly at the world at large, in a startlingly powerful voice, drumming on the mattress with heels and fists like a madwoman meanwhile.

Brother Sebastian, returning quickly from the hallway, fearlessly bent over the thrashing girl, laid his hand on her shoulder and murmured some words to her. The screaming died to a faint whimper, then silence, and a moment later she lay back and closed her eyes, all signs of distress gone from her features. Brother Sebastian seated himself on the side of the bed and remained there for a few minutes in silence (praying, probably, as his eyes were closed). Then he gave the others a sign, and everyone tiptoed out. Twenty minutes later when Dr Müller arrived, a brief consultation with Brother Sebastian convinced him that his services were no longer required.

* * *

A sceptic might easily suggest that Brother's success in healing the hysterical girl could have been due to the trust and respect inspired in many persons by the sight of a priest in clerical garb. There is, on the part of many older Brothers, a regrettable tendency to wear civilian clothes off duty. Without their habits, they tend to behave like ordinary people when assailed by mundane temptations (boarding a train without a ticket, for example, and quickly getting off when a conductor comes in sight). But no one, not even the shrewdest of sceptics, can claim exclusive possession of the truth!

* * *

Early the following morning, Sherrill was still sleeping the 'sleep of the unjust' when S., returning to his room after having responded to a 'call of nature' at the other end of the corridor, softly opened the door of the girl's room and approached the bed, wishing to reassure himself as to her continued welfare.

Sherrill lay very still, her eyes closed as if in peaceful sleep, breathing gently through parted lips, her dark hair in disarray on the pillow. But suddenly, as S. bent a little closer to listen to her breathing – always a good index to a person's state of health – she sat up, flung both arms about his neck and pressed her face hard against his chest. It was only for a moment; then she let him go, fell back against her pillow and resumed her 'sleeping beauty' posture as if nothing had happened.

No word was spoken by either during this brief episode, but her unprovoked and utterly unexpected act had so shaken S.'s composure that he had to fumble with the latch for several seconds before he succeeded in escaping to the safety of his own room, there to ponder on the girl's disturbingly provocative behaviour towards someone who could easily have been her uncle, even her grand-uncle (though in the child's defence the reader is asked to recall that S., even at this late stage, looks a great deal younger than his chronological age).

Could she have been hallucinating? Could she have mistaken him for her father? Though unlikely, that seemed well within the limits of possibility, and if so they had all been mistaken in thinking her safely on the way to recovery from the drug. It was equally possible, though again unlikely, that she had taken another dose of whatever it was; no one, he realised, had searched the room for further supplies. It seemed to S. that, as the only adult now awake, he could not entirely shrug off responsibility for this situation, much as he might wish to do so. After perhaps half an hour of tossing and turning, he flung off the bedclothes, rose, pulled on his dressing-gown once more and again made his way quietly down the hallway to the girl's room.

* * *

Sherrill was awake, lying supine with one knee drawn up and eyes half open. 'Hallo,' she said in a small voice, obviously quite sober, as he approached the bed. 'Paying me a little visit?'

Nonplussed by this greeting, S. stood stock-still beside the bed, literally bereft of speech. Sherrill looked questioningly at him for a moment or two, obviously expecting a reply. When none was forthcoming she gave an almost imperceptible shrug and rolled over on her side, away from him, in what is known to medical science as the embryo posture.

Now, S. can testify with absolute certainty that at no point during this encounter (if that is the correct word) did he approach within arm's reach of the bed, let alone its occupant. Only in the act of leaving was he moved by the sight of the child's exposed shoulder to reach down and gently draw up the duvet to cover her. But in that instant she twisted violently away, crying, 'Get away from me! Don't you touch me!' and, 'Get your filthy hands away!'

Stunned speechless, S. swiftly withdrew to the doorway and called down the stairs, in as loud a voice as his shock-constricted voice would allow, for Brian to come to his daughter's aid.

But a few moments later when he appeared, bounding up the stairs like an athlete, Sherrill had already fallen silent. 'I'm sorry, I must have had a bad dream,' she told him meekly, but her eyes, fixed on S.'s, held a curious expression of complicity, as if, absurdly, she were lying to protect him.

* * *

Whilst remaining outwardly calm, S. himself could not help being severely upset by this incident. No one in the house remained unaware of the disturbance, but of course they all took at face value Sherrill's 'bad dream' explanation, from which S.'s blamelessness logically followed as the night the day. But now, against all reason, he found himself tormented by strange and troublesome thoughts; in particular, the fear that Sherrill's display of terror and revulsion might have been deliberately staged in order to entangle him in some obscure game of sexual blackmail.

Yet, he told himself over and over again, Sherrill was after all still only a schoolgirl, only a child. A child would hardly be capable of such wickedness. Even if she were, what conceivable motive could she have in seeking to destroy the character of a mature male whom she hardly knew, and whose goodwill and spotless morality were beyond reasonable question?

No, he decided each time these thoughts ran through his head, Sherrill's fright must have been genuine. She might well have had a frightening dream, and waking in a half-stupor to the sight of a man's face bending over her (even a kindly and far from ugly face), have been thrown into a sudden blind panic. That was surely the truth of the matter, whatever different message S. might have thought he had read in her eyes.

At all events, S.'s attention was soon diverted from the trivial episode of a young girl's hysteria to the ever-growing pressure of his felt responsibility to take early and decisive action.

◃ 25 ▹

With all the confusion in Elisabethstrasse, Beatrice remembered only on Wednesday morning to give S. the letter from her mother. Once he had sufficiently acquainted himself with its contents, most of S.'s succeeding thoughts and energies went into detailed route planning in preparation for his Friday-afternoon rendezvous with Hannah at the Café Landsmann.

Needless, perhaps, to remind the attentive reader of the tribulations this journey would involve, first and foremost among them, travel by public transport, necessitating changes of train and streetcar and presenting the problem of getting out at the correct stop on the Ringstrasse, which meant pressing the hard-to-find button that operates the now automatic doors of the carriage. All this, however, was simple compared with the planning and timing and careful thinking that were required for the success of his subsequent trip to St Saviour's maternity ward, there to quench a feeble flame that a benign celestial power would never have lit.

Small wonder, then, that on that Wednesday evening S. was too exhausted from these intellectual labours to play the role of genial host convincingly when dinner-time came!

* * *

They were a small and rather dispirited company at table that evening. Neither Sherrill nor Aunt Mia had come down for supper, the girl for obvious reasons, the old lady because of a migraine that she said had robbed her of all appetite, though she did consent to tea and Melba toast, personally prepared and brought to her room by her loving nephew. Eva was quiet, almost morose; S. guessed because of continuing back pain. Beatrice had returned from St Saviour's 'all washed out', as she put it, from her long vigil at Amy's bedside. And Brian, who had spent most of the day in his room redrafting parts of the manuscript he and Beatrice had promised to deliver to their publisher in less than a fortnight, also seemed somewhat drained by his labours.

A supper of cold cuts and left-over potato salad was eaten in near silence. Everyone but Brian, who favoured tea, took a second cup of coffee.

Even over coffee the talk was desultory.

It looked like a long, dull evening, and S. would have been quite happy to take his leave of the company and retire to his room, there to read or listen to the BBC World Service, perhaps with a ear cocked for inauspicious sounds from Sherrill's quarters.

But just as he was about to make a move Beatrice turned to him and said brightly, 'You know, Uncle Stefan, I'm awfully impressed with that Brother Sebastian of yours. I thought he was really wonderful with Sherrill yesterday. We chatted for just a few minutes after that, and I was struck all over again by his intelligence and the range of his interests. I can't help thinking that his cloistered life must feel a bit stifling at times.'

'Oh, I hardly think Brother feels frustrated or confined,'

Eva put in from her side of the table. 'He has a very fulfilling life, right where he is.'

'Oh, I'm sure you're right, Auntie Eva. You and Uncle Stefan have known him for ages, after all. Anyway, I didn't mean to suggest that he was frustrated, exactly. Just that maybe he doesn't have quite the scope that his talents deserve.'

She paused for a large sip of coffee. 'No, strike that. All I really wanted to say was that I'm a big fan of Sebastian's. I guess I have been ever since last spring, but seeing Sherrill respond to him like that put him in a new light.' S. nodded. 'There's more to him than meets the eye.'

'Exactly, that's what I feel.' There was an assertiveness in Beatrice's tone, as if she were defying anyone to challenge Brother's merits. (No one, of course, had the slightest impulse to do so, least of all Eva, at whom Beatrice was now directing her words.)

'Well do I remember the struggle I had last spring getting permission to take pictures inside the sanatorium for my *Times Magazine* story! But once Sebastian stepped in my troubles were over. He sorted everything out for me just like that, and he was really knowledgeable about the technical side of things too. Of course you know that he's a bit of a photographer himself, or was when he was living in San Francisco.'

'Los Angeles,' Eva corrected her, stony-faced. 'That was before he entered his order.'

'Yes, of course, Los Angeles,' Beatrice said. 'I gather he was in advertising for a while.'

'Public relations, actually,' Eva said. 'For one of the movie studios. He hated it.'

'Oh, public relations, was it? Yes, that certainly fits. He must have charmed the pants off the ladies and gentlemen of the media. Especially the ladies.'

Her words were followed by a brief silence.

Was it possible that Beatrice hadn't set out to torment Eva, that she had drawn blood by accident, as it were? Perhaps. But now she was deliberately twisting the knife.

Sometimes the left hand may not know what the right hand is doing. Now, in retrospect, Eva says she forgives Beatrice, if indeed there is anything to forgive. S. accepts that these are now her feelings. What they may have been on that Wednesday evening is quite another matter. But even the artist in S. shrinks from probing too deeply into the innermost heart of another human being!

'Gosh, Beattie,' Brian finally said. 'You'll make me jealous, there, if you don't watch out!'

'Don't be silly, Brian, the man's a priest after all,' she retorted. 'I just happen to think he's terrific. And I owe him a lot for opening doors for me at the sanatorium last year. Without him there'd have been no pictures, and without the pictures they would never have taken that piece. And you might not be sitting here today either.'

' "And all for the want of a horseshoe nail," ' S. quoted, thinking that a note of light humour might ease the tension.

'Listen, he might have got you in there, but they were your pictures and bloody good ones too, excuse the language,' Brian said loudly. 'She's a brilliant little photographer, you know,' he added in an aside to Eva. 'She really is, I'm proud of her.'

'And so you should be. I'm sure that Beatrice can accomplish anything she sets her mind to,' Eva said, but not with her usual kindness. It sounded more like a criticism than a compliment!

Whichever it was, Beatrice was not to be diverted from the subject of Brother Sebastian.

She turned to S. 'Remember the day I finished up there and

Sebastian took us to the abbey's garden restaurant? A really, really lovely lunch. There was a wedding reception or something going on in the room next door,' she told the others, 'with a gypsy fiddler playing. All very jolly, people sang along. Of course, I didn't understand a word, but Sebastian translated it all for me, and I do mean all of it. Imagine him knowing all those not-so-holy songs! And in German, as well!' she added roguishly.

S. nodded, unsmiling. He wished he could forget that lunch! It had pained him to witness Beatrice practising her crass coquetry on Brother Sebastian, a man of the cloth who was also S.'s own best friend, and it hurt still worse to see the Brother's innocent, enthusiastic response to what he imagined was merely a display of friendliness and high spirits.

Poor Eva, too! Seeing from her pale face and compressed lips that the anecdote had stung her to the quick, he felt he must set about presenting the company with plausible explanations for Brother Sebastian's rather free behaviour on that unfortunate occasion.

'Brother loves to show off his German,' he observed casually. 'As well he might. His command of the language is really superior to mine of English.' (A slight exaggeration which, however, drew no protest from Eva.)

'In fact,' S. went on with deliberate pomposity, 'Brother is indeed a man of many talents. I believe he could have succeeded in any career of his choosing. But in fact he chose to become a religious, and he has repeatedly said that he has never looked back and never will. He has embraced his calling heart and soul, and I believe he will never falter in it – no matter how great the magnetic power of worldly things!' he ended, with a solemnity proper to the occasion.

This little speech, intended as the last word (for that evening) on the theme of Brother Sebastian, had the desired effect of diverting the conversation into other, less controversial channels. Presently Eva rose from the table and enquired whether anyone would care for a *Bailoni* (an apricot liqueur from the so-called wine quarter, not too many miles upstream from St Anselm). When no one responded to the offer, she looked up at the old-fashioned pendulum clock on the mantel and exclaimed over the lateness of the hour. Suddenly, it seemed, everyone was very tired, and the party soon broke up, much to S.'s relief and perhaps to that of all three of the others.

* * *

Once in bed, S. found to his great annoyance that he was unable to fall asleep. He rehearsed Hannah's letter over and over in his head; he ruminated on the evening's conversation; he remembered the stricken look on his sister's face as Beatrice recalled her shameless familiarities with Brother Sebastian.

And that triggered a chain of reminiscences about the Brother. How youthful he had looked on his arrival at the sanatorium twenty-five, no, thirty years ago: gaunt and faintly forbidding, but still, at twenty-eight, little more than a boy. How very approachable he had turned out to be, how he had not hesitated to say yes that very first Sunday when, after the usual twelve o'clock mass at the sanatorium, Eva had asked him to join them for a nice home-cooked lunch and a pleasant chat in his native English! He had opened up so easily, it was as if he had known the two of them for years. Eva, S. remembered, had even had some difficulty dissuading Brother from lending a hand at the washing-up!

That had been the start of a long and rewarding friendship.

They had been a congenial threesome on Brother Sebastian's off-duty days, a threesome that was to become a foursome when Eva went to work at the United Nations Atomic Energy Authority, and her boss Dr Hebbar became an occasional visitor to Elisabethstrasse.

Oddly enough, the middle-aged Hindu and the young Catholic priest had hit it off from the beginning. Being a man of real cultural and spiritual refinement, Dr Hebbar had found the company at Elisabethstrasse much to his taste, and in his day had contributed his full share to their conversational pleasures.

Much later, after Dr Hebbar had departed and Eva's hopes had been blighted by the news of his impending marriage, Brother Sebastian had been there to bring her strength and comfort, driving the order's little car over to St Anselm whenever he sensed that he was needed there for an hour of prayer and meditation. As indeed he had done at other times of crisis, such as the painful fiasco of the visit from Eva's Mexican granddaughter Petra!

Eva had done her best to repay his support with warm hospitality and motherly concern on those increasingly frequent occasions when Brother Sebastian himself showed signs of low spirits. Eva might have her reasons for denying it to Beatrice, but the truth was that Brother was quite often 'down in the dumps'. Sometimes he even lacked appetite to enjoy his favourite dish, the apricot dumplings which Eva made a point of preparing for him nearly every Sunday in season.

More than once, on such occasions, Brother had confessed to his two friends that much as he loved Austria and rewarding as he found his chaplain's role, he felt too comfortable and too cosseted at the sanatorium for his own spiritual good.

'I need austerity,' he told them once. 'I need discipline. Silence, prayer, hard physical labour, that would challenge me. So I may be applying for a transfer back to my mother house in Quebec. It's almost like the Trappists there.'

The strange thing was that when Brother did apply for a transfer to new duties, it was not to a house of prayer but to a mission in central Africa where disease was rife and five monks of his order had recently lost their lives in an attack by marauding tribesmen. The story had been in all the papers.

Could it be, the modern reader might ask, that the young monk's decision to embrace hardship, disease and danger was a gesture of expiation for something he had done that he knew would be displeasing to God? Could he conceivably, after two decades of chaste friendship with a woman twelve years his senior, have allowed a carnal element to creep into that relationship? Or could he be tormented by guilt because once, in a setting of wine, gypsy music and nuptial celebration, he had permitted himself to experience a few fleeting moments of illicit excitement?

* * *

How strange it all is, S. marvels, as he tosses and turns in his bed, trying to sort out all the material at hand so as to make some sense of it all and work out a credible structure. So that, God willing, this manuscript might grow into a book which would, at least, not shame him.

❦ 26 ❦

Future readers of these pages are asked at this point to permit the author a little self-congratulation on the extraordinary skill and instinct for timing (not to mention the phenomenal good luck) that had enabled him so successfully to administer the *coup de grâce* to the poor blighted infant.

Gaining access to the infants' incubation ward had been child's play for S., thanks to the knowledge of the terrain gained on his initial visit. No one questioned him. Impeccably attired for the (aborted) rendezvous in dark-grey flannel trousers, fresh white shirt, dark blue four-in-hand bearing the crest of a distinguished American university (Harvard!), and the fine, rarely worn Scotch plaid jacket Eva had bought him two years earlier at the annual post-Christmas sale at Loden Plankl, an exclusive establishment in the Inner City, S. must have looked quite the university-trained professional – as indeed he was!

At the hospital entrance, he strode past the porter's glass cubicle with a brief nod at its occupant. Rather than risk waiting for the elevator, he took the stairs, briskly mounted the two flights to the maternity floor, and turned left down the corridor towards the incubation ward.

At the nursing station he greeted the elderly Asian nun with a cheerful, '*Grüss Gott, Schwester*,' and was rewarded with the same pious greeting. The good sister raised her eyes to him for only the briefest of moments before returning her attention to whatever she had been reading, probably her vesper prayers.

No problem there, in the current lingo. No problem, either, with the execution of his mission, complex though it might be. And it was clearly no easy task for a layman – even a layman of measured high general intelligence and thus the capacity to relate cause to effect – to locate the control panel governing the various life-support lines on the right-hand wall just within the door of a darkened room, to confirm with a swift glance the unchanged position of the cot, to calmly and methodically turn off all the appropriate controls and switches, and to make good his escape from the floor and the building, all without raising the alarm.

Common sense alone tells you there could be no confusion about any of this.

Ask the porter. Enquire of the nursing sister. (Granted, to Asian eyes all Austrian faces may well look 'alike as two peas'; but distinctive clothing such as the elegant and unusual Harvard University necktie would surely be noticed and remembered.)

It must have been about two-thirty in the afternoon when S. left the hospital, or so he concludes from having encountered, on the way out, another Asian lady pushing a tea-trolley – or rather, a watery-coffee trolley, coffee being much preferred to tea here in Austria. (Well aware that the good writer shuns generalities, S. nevertheless feels it part of his responsibility to the reader to supply certain bits of significant background information.)

Leaving the hospital by the door at which he had come in, S. felt a rush of intense exhilaration which lasted for only a few moments before fading to a dullness and then to a sense of emptiness and loss such as he had once or twice experienced in the wake of certain episodes of what the immortal Shakespeare has described as 'the expense of spirit in a waste of shame'. It was the sense of a purpose brought to fruition, of vital energy expended, of tension discharged, direction lost, meaning extinguished.

* * *

Of the journey home S. has no recollection. He must have wandered about aimlessly for a little while, or perhaps taken the wrong streetcar and got to the train station by a roundabout route; at all events he reached Elisabethstrasse, in a state of near-exhaustion, only at dusk, and retreated at once to his room for a nap, awaking much refreshed when summoned to dinner by Eva half an hour later.

* * *

At six-thirty the next morning, when all but S. and his sister were still abed, the telephone rang in Elisabethstrasse. To pin down these events for the benefit of the reader and of any well-meaning but misguided persons (like Dr Rosen) who might insist on precision of detail in their enquiries into the baby's death, let it be clearly stated that the ensuing conversation took place on Saturday after Easter, i.e. the day following the failed rendezvous at the Café Landsmann.

To ease her still painful back, Eva had been reclining on the leather-covered horsehair divan that had once graced the foyer of Great-Aunt Mitzi's Café Allotria. Although it sagged a little at one end, this divan was still one of the most comfortable pieces of furniture in the house, and one of the handsomest; common cooking lard, sparingly but faithfully rubbed in over the years, had kept its leather looking almost like new.

When the telephone rang, Eva struggled to her feet and made her way across the room to the spindly-legged rococo table (another Café Allotria heirloom) on which the extension telephone stood. S. himself, seated at a card table in the corner, could admittedly have reached the phone more easily than Eva, but when it rang he happened to be absorbed in the wearisome but necessary task of reordering his collection of Mexican stamps and could not afford the interruption. Besides, he had guessed the caller's identity. It could only be their cousin from America; a native Austrian would never dream of disturbing family or friends so early on a weekend!

His guess was soon confirmed by Eva's excited interjections. 'Hannah? My goodness, what a lovely surprise! You sound just the same as ever … I've been meaning to … ' she positively babbled with excitement. 'Oh, please don't … I know, Hannah … Yes of course I do … My God, what d'you need to explain, she's your daughter, isn't she? … Up and about so soon? Wonderful. The marvels of modern medicine! Coupled of course with your own methods … So lucky you could be there to care for her … No, of course you can't, I wouldn't dream of asking you. What? … No, out of the question, I'm afraid. This damned back of mine … I suppose you heard about my accident. So stupid of me, wasn't it? … No, it's getting better now, I ought to be getting around again after a fashion by next week. But how are you, my dear Hanny? Ah, wonderful! … What?'

Hannah's next words wiped out the eager smile. Eva's forehead wrinkled in distress as she sank on to a nearby chair (a fake Louis-Quinze, courtesy once again of Great-Aunt Mitzi) as if physically stricken by the news. She listened intently to the insect-like voice from the receiver, repeating fragmentary phrases in a quavering old woman's voice. 'No chance really, of course not … Poor, poor thing … For the best really, do you think so? … But poor Amy … So early? Is that wise? … Oh. Oh, if she says so … But what about the – the poor little body?'

Pause as the insect-voice at the other end prattled on.

Then Eva again, 'Oh. Oh, I think that's very appropriate … She is? … Afford it, yes, but still … Up to Charles I should think … What a tower of strength you've been!' Pause and sniffle. 'Oh, Hanny, when shall we ever see each other again? … Yes, of course I'll try. I'd love to see New York again. Next spring perhaps? Or the spring after that?'

And more of the same. But at last: 'S.? Oh yes, he's very well. Would you like to – '

A swift glance at her brother, who emphatically shook his head and crossed his forearms on his chest, signifying that he didn't want to be disturbed.

'Or better, write to him, you know how he is about the telephone … yes of course I'll tell him, you know how much your letters mean to him. They're his lifeline, really … Oh yes, Hanny, me too, me too … I'm so sorry about everything that's happened, darling … Do give Amy my best love … I wish so much I could see you all before you go, but I'm really a cripple at the moment … Yes, darling. God bless!'

With a heavy sigh Eva replaced the receiver in its cradle and pulled herself upright on her seat, knees and feet pressed primly together and back as erect as her injury permitted. She looked as if she were literally holding herself together, a dummy-like posture that reminded S. of the way schoolchildren were made to sit at their desks in his day: a far cry from what goes on in schools nowadays, especially schools with a high concentration of foreign children with alien cultural backgrounds – Turkish, Pakistani, Gypsy, Vietnamese – many of whom are unable even to speak our language. No wonder teachers can no longer maintain classroom discipline! Almost daily Die Kronenzeitung carries one or more alarming stories about these problems.

'So what was all that about, calling at such an hour?' he asked non-chalantly.

She turned and looked at him as if she had seen a ghost.

'Poor little Stephen died,' she said with a quaver.

'I know,' S. said without raising his eyes from the stamp album.

CHAPTER TWENTY-SIX

'And I say good riddance! One freak in the family's more than enough.'

'Why must you be so hateful?' Eva burst out. 'That kind of talk really disgusts me!'

S. ignored the rebuke. 'Any other news?' he enquired. 'You seemed to be all excited about something.'

'As a matter of fact, yes,' Eva said. 'It seems that Hannah and Amy and Charles are all flying back tomorrow afternoon.' She sighed. 'Amy's been pronounced fit to travel, which sounds crazy to me, but they must know what they're doing. Hannah's bosom friend Dr What's-her-name is involved in it somehow, I gather.'

'What about Aunt Mia?' he asked in sudden apprehension. 'She can't possibly fly back alone!'

'No, of course not. Hannah said Beatrice has agreed to take her this coming week, as soon as she's ready to go,' Eva said.

'And what about the, uh, "remains"?' S. enquired sardonically. 'Will they be going as cabin luggage, or disposed of with the hospital waste?'

'Funnily enough it doesn't bother me when I know you're being deliberately vile,' Eva retorted. 'Since you ask, the casket will be flown over early next week. That Hungarian doctor woman is taking care of the formalities. Anything else you'd like to know?'

'I'd love to know why you can't be bothered to remember people's names,' S. snapped. ' "That Hungarian doctor woman" is Dr Kovacs, Ilona Kovacs. It's an early sign of senility, you know, not remembering names. Not to mention a really effective way of giving offence.'

As usual, irritation made his hands tremble. He buried them in the pockets of his blue denim jeans and stared out of the window to calm himself. The sky was overcast, and Eva's shrubs in the strip of garden between house and street looked dank and dispirited. Beyond this border, the cobblestones had a greasy shine. To the left, through the branches of the still leafless trees, you could make out part of a side arm of the Danube, and beyond a further bar of wooded land a tiny glimpse of the river itself, nothing to compare with the sweeping view of grounds and river from the sanatorium on the hill six kilometres to the north.

'Well, go on. What else did our dear cousin have to say?' he finally demanded, his back still turned to her. 'Any other fascinating details?' And then, when no immediate answer was forthcoming, more sharply: 'Don't tease me, Eva, I'm warning you!'

'Oh, S., don't be an idiot!' Eva retorted 'As if I'd keep anything from you! She said Charles and Amy are planning a regular funeral service next Sunday in Bangor. The poor little thing will be buried there beside his paternal grandparents. It seems quite appropriate, really.'

'What else?'

'Nothing. Only how sorry she was to have missed seeing us.' Suddenly tearful, Eva mourned, 'Oh, S., who'd ever have thought that life could separate us so! And yet she sounded just like the old Hannah, so warm and caring – '

'Well, her caringness never got her as far as St Anselm, did it?' S. remarked drily. 'With all her globe-trotting she's had opportunities enough for a little side trip to Austria to visit her so-called beloved cousins. Somehow that never seems to happen, does it?'

'Don't be stupid S.!' Eva retorted. 'You can't be so dense you don't understand it. How Hannah feels about the place and the people, I mean. When you consider her background. I'll tell you one thing: if I'd had her chance to get away, I'd have taken it like a shot. And wild horses couldn't have dragged me back to this wretched place with its sickening hypocrisy and its idiotic customs and conventions.'

'Utter rubbish!' S. struck back. 'You know perfectly well, sweetheart, that it wasn't Austria that sentenced you to life as a spinster. Name me one country where a respectable family would want their boy to marry a girl who's got a brother in the loony-bin! You can't, there isn't one.'

'There you go being stupid,' said Eva wearily. 'Feeling ever so sorry for yourself, aren't you? When you know quite, quite well that I love you far too much to ever leave you. Such silliness! You really make me sick!'

'So it's finally registered, has it?' S. returned, deadpan. 'That's exactly what I've been trying to make you realise all these years, sweetheart. You can't stand me. I make you sick. All right, what do you expect me to do about it?'

That silenced her, but not for long.

'Dear Lord, S.!' she finally burst out. 'Talk about bearing grudges! As if you were the only one that had to suffer! There are plenty with more to complain of than you, and not by their own doing either. Try for once in your life to think about others! Try to imagine how Hannah must have felt, seeing her own father humiliated in the street. Imagine how all of them felt, having to steal out of the country like criminals, leaving their home and almost everything else behind. Just for the crime of being Jews.'

'What about yourself, then? Our papa – '

'Never mind Papa, we're talking about Hannah!' Eva cried. 'You really can't imagine, can you, what it would mean for a fourteen-year old to have to pack up her life in three suitcases and leave behind the only home she ever knew, and all her friends and schoolmates? And say goodbye to her own native language? Can you possibly imagine that?'

'Well, she consoled herself soon enough, I gather,' S. put in drily.

'Oh, you're so stupid, S.!' Eva launched into him like some mythological fury. 'Don't you dare malign Hannah! You know she loved us, she was practically a sister to us. How dare you talk about her like that – Oh, don't just sit there!' (She was nearly shouting now.) 'I'm talking to you! At least turn around and look at me! Please, S., darling brother! Look at me, don't turn away!'

Eva's theatricals, however, availed her nothing, since by this point in her tirade it had become clear to S. that his best course would be to get up and leave the room before her sentimental distortions about their dear American cousin could provoke him to remind her of some home truths she would no doubt have preferred to forget!

* * *

S. could, for instance, have said to his sister bluntly, 'Have you really forgotten, then, that this same dear loving Hannah was in effect writing us both off for good when she vowed she would never again set foot on Austrian soil? And that she held to that perverse intention for five decades, never setting eyes on yours truly here, whose freedom of movement has been curtailed not by choice, frivolous or otherwise, but by fate itself!'

'Ah, don't be a pompous ass, S., for pity's sake!' Eva would probably have snapped. 'If you knew what a pathetic figure you cut with those rhetorical flourishes of yours!'

And not content with that, she would, at this point in the debate, doubtless have trotted out another ludicrous assertion about their supposedly idyllic youth in some Cloud-cuckoo-land of her imagination – some fantastic nonsense that would, to everyone's detriment, shatter the steely self-control that had so far enabled S. to suppress certain revelations about their beloved cousin that would have made the floor fairly rock under his sister's feet!

* * *

What, for instance, if S. had had the heart to reveal to her at last how their dear cousin, perhaps even before she entered her teens, had been systematically deceiving them both, keeping secret rendezvous with their mutual 'friend' Herbert (Eva's own future betrothed!), cycling with him along the Danube, 'resting' in God knows how many deserted, shrub-screened spots!

And how Hannah had compounded that early treachery by resuming her affair with Herbert in America after the war, as soon as he was discharged from the prisoner-of-war camp in Minnesota, USA.

And, moreover, that the present-day Hannah – a mother of two grown daughters and a grandmother twice over – had not scrupled to trifle with her own daughters' respective sexual partners! One only had to consider the way in which Hannah had caught Brian in her net: catching sight of a sturdy, half-naked young stranger fishing off the dock at Maple Harbor, Hannah picks him up and takes him home with her on the pretext of treating his 'sunburn'. (That she later introduces him to her family, and that he becomes the lover of both daughters is merely a peripheral detail.)

* * *

Might there have been mitigating circumstances? Might Brian indeed have been at risk, and Hannah's action have been motivated at least in part by a genuine medical concern? Possible, but unlikely.

Even more unlikely, though not quite inconceivable, was the possibility that Herbert Berger had never admitted to Hannah that he had got Eva with child and married her in a proxy ceremony in the last year of the war, when he was serving on the North African front. Given

Hannah's temperament, that little revelation would only have added spice to their affair!

And even if Herbert had preserved silence on the subject, Hannah could never have remained ignorant of the facts. Even in the war's darkest days, Aunt Mia had never wholly written off her Austrian ties, and as soon as possible after it was over she had resumed contact with her dearly beloved niece and nephew in St Anselm. Self-evidently, whatever she heard from Eva (which would have been everything), Aunt Mia would have shared at once with her daughter. So Hannah must surely have known.

Her very first letter to S. after the war had been addressed to him at the sanatorium's creative wing, proof that in mid-1946 she must already have been *au courant* with every detail of his post-war circumstances.

◃ 27 ▹

The original of Hannah's letter was 'accidentally' discarded several years ago in the course of a too-zealous clean-up of S.'s overflowing desk drawers. (The author encloses the modifier in inverted commas in tacit tribute to his immortal mentor and guide, the late Professor Dr Helmut Rosen, whose doctrine of 'radical scepticism' holds that where human behaviour is involved, the reasons given almost invariably conceal, consciously or not, a very different pattern of cause and effect.)

But its physical loss is a matter of no moment, since many readings and rereadings had, as it were, imprinted its words indelibly on S.'s mind. Here, then, is the text, transcribed from memory:

New York, 17 August, 1946

Dear S. –

I know now what has happened to you, and you might as well know that I find it shameful and disgusting. Mama says there are mitigating circumstances, and I am sure it must be so. But there are many others who never lost their dignity, even in the face of death! The war was over, you were no longer in danger, you were quite safe.

I know you must have had some reason, or at least some need. I suppose it may have been a bit like being drunk. But I can't believe that you were really unable to stop yourself. Could you not have spared a thought for the shame you would be bringing on your sister? And the hurt you would be doing to me?

My poor dear S., forgive me. I know you must be suffering, asking yourself why? why? and finding no answer. But I'm going to help you. I'm determined to find the answer, for us both. I want you to find it with me, through me.

Then comes a part where she says that in seven years' time she'll be a doctor: four years of university, then three years of medical school.

* * *

That letter was the first of nearly a thousand she had written him over the next forty-five years. It had been an almost wholly one-sided correspondence, Hannah having made it clear that she did not write in any expectation of regular replies. ('Think of my letters as pages of a diary,' she had written. 'You owe me no answers. Write only when you wish.') Taking her at her word, S. had hardly written a dozen times in all those years, apart from an annual Christmas letter, Easter greetings, formal felicitations on her university matriculation, her graduation from medical school, her marriage and the births of Amy and Beatrice, and condolences on the death of her father. (The Fischer-Uncle had died quite unexpectedly of a massive heart attack in a New York taxi on his way to lunch with a prospective backer.)

Perhaps because she had taken S.'s failure to reply to her first letter as a rejection of the help she had offered, Hannah never pursued the matter further, so that early promise remained unkept.

Quite in keeping with the extraordinary one-sidedness of this correspondence was an almost total absence from Hannah's letters of any questions or comments on affairs in St Anselm. Virtually their sole substance was Hannah herself and Hannah's world: her failures and successes, her fears and hopes, her ideas and opinions, and (with the notable exception of any *vita sexualis*!) her interests and pleasures.

In fact, these letters were indeed very like pages from a diary, or issues of a newspaper to which S. happened to be the sole subscriber! And so, like a newspaper, they did not reach out to him, and he felt he was guilty of no discourtesy if, because of fatigue or preoccupation, he sometimes failed to read or (rarely) even to open them. He saw that they had served their purpose, in a sense, before they were even posted.

* * *

Be that as it may, one can safely assume that Hannah had had at all times, through her mother, at least a general knowledge of events and circumstances in St Anselm. It was, for example, hard to imagine that Aunt Mia, who is not known to be reticent about her good deeds, could have failed to brag a little to her daughter about her role in securing S.'s present status as a private patient. Or that Hannah had been left in ignorance of Eva's plight just after the war. Orphaned, penniless and with a small child to support, she might well have gone under if Aunt Mia hadn't come to the rescue. For Werner's father, of course, never sent a penny. He was too busy roaming the length and breadth of America, casually bedding any complaisant young woman who might cross his path – including, of course, Hannah herself, Eva's own beloved cousin.

In short, it was the continuing monthly allowance wired to her bank account by Aunt Mia that enabled Eva to keep the family home in Elisabethstrasse, bring up Werner properly, and eventually prepare herself for a career as an executive secretary by taking evening classes at college level. And that was not the limit of Aunt Mia's generosity. The year Werner was six, she had also paid Eva's fare and expenses for a three-week visit to America, including the wages of a child-sitter, a big-bosomed Polish refugee woman from across the street who moved in to take care of little Werner while his mother was kicking up her heels in America!

All of which, self-evidently, would have been known to Hannah.

* * *

Yet in the end S. said nothing of this to his sister. Poor Eva! he thought. Assailed by troubles from every quarter – her back injury, the shock of Dr Hebbar's remarriage, the ever-deepening gulf between her and the Mexican family – she had more than enough on her plate to be getting on with. The last thing she needed was to hear her brother dredging up ancient hurts from his own stock of petty grievances – hurts that cannot be healed, memories that will burn in his brain until the day they are erased by death!

* * *

Better not to think back. Forget about the past! As an old but still popular Viennese song advises us,

> *Glücklich ist*
> *wer vergisst*
> *was nicht mehr zu ändern ist –*

Chapter Twenty-Seven

Happy he
who forgets
what can no longer be changed.

Not so, said Dr Rosen. Your past is what you have to work with, what you have to deal with. Call it up again. Confront it. Suffer them again, all those pains and hurts and humiliations. You have survived them once, you'll survive them again, and this time you will have the means to control them, to gain the mastery. Language and imagination. They are what you must rely on. Your pen moves on the paper, and the miracle begins to happen. Pain is refined into beauty. Life is transmuted into Art!

Good advice!

In the following two separate, but equally disturbing, vignettes, Life and Art are perhaps inextricably intertwined.

Caveat lector!

Vignette number one: Eva and S., with their cousin Hannah, were still young children. Eva, the eldest by almost a year, would be eight on her next birthday. Aunt Mia, paying her usual Sunday visit to the house in Elisabethstrasse, had brought Hannah along, and Hannah had brought a plaything, a baby doll that closed its eyes when you laid it down and said 'MAMA' when you pressed a certain spot on its belly.

On previous visits Eva and Hannah had usually played house with their dolls in the rear garden while S. (who, being a boy, had to despise dolls) sat watching on a swing suspended from the larger of their apple trees. When the girls wearied of their dolls, all three children would amuse themselves with a ball or play hide-and-seek until Aunt Mia called to Hannah that it was time to go home.

But on this visit the girls were in a different mood, whispering and giggling between themselves and turning their backs to S., so that from his vantage point on the swing he could see very little of what they were doing. When he jumped down from the swing and approached them, they dashed straight into the house and up the stairs to Eva's room, with S. in hot pursuit.

They had slammed the door and shot the bolt behind them, squealing with excitement, before he had cleared the landing, and no amount of knocking, banging or begging would induce them to let him in. Shouts of 'NO!' from Hannah and storms of excited giggles from Eva met his pleas for admission and his tearful threats to tell Mama.

Until S. had an inspiration: If the girls wouldn't let him in, he could get even by spying on them. Shouting, 'Oh, all right, see if I care!' he tramped loudly down the stairs to the landing, then crept back up and put his eye to the crack under the door. The girls had stopped giggling, in fact there was complete silence in the room and all S. could see was a stretch of floor, an empty white sock and a caster of Eva's bed, on which the two girls must be lying. This was presently confirmed by a stifled giggle and a muffled, 'Don't!', followed by more giggles and sounds of feigned protest which soon lapsed into silence.

All at once a pair of feet, Hannah's, hit the floor just in front of him. S. scrambled to his feet in a panic, missed his footing on the stairs and fell, banging his head against a railing as he ended in a heap on the landing. He heard the door open above him and saw both girls standing there, Hannah looking scared and penitent, Eva wearing her older-sister's spiteful smile. He picked himself up and rushed into the garden bawling with pain and humiliation.

* * *

He had cried, yes, wept girlish tears, as if in rehearsal for the tears of shame he had wept a decade later, in a different country, for a different reason: bitter, stinging tears. Tears of a nightmare that now (as Dr Rosen would be pleased to hear) can be conjured up, confronted, analysed and dismissed again at will.

* * *

Vignette number two: Eleven years later, S. found himself on a two-man detail to execute the deserter Alois Heigl. He had actually volunteered for the detail, mainly to impress the platoon commander with his courage, soldierly spirit and resolve. Or something of the kind.

Alas, he had failed to reckon with the miserable Heigl's tears and howls for mercy as they tied him against the stable wall, or with the way he had tried to embrace S. as if to use him as a human shield. That must have been why, when the moment came for him and Corporal

Schiedmayer to take aim and fire, S. had actually soiled himself and dropped his rifle and wept, leaning against the corner of a shed with his face in his hands while Schiedmayer finished the ugly business alone. He escaped being court-martialled for cowardice only because Schiedmayer disdained to report the incident to the platoon commander.

* * *

In the evening of that same Saturday which had begun so discordantly following their cousin's early morning phonecall, Eva had lingered at the foot of S.'s bed after bringing him his medicine for the night.

'Look, S., I'm sorry about this morning,' she said rather hesitantly. 'I mean, we don't really want to quarrel and hurt each other like that, do we? So let's please just forget and forgive. After all – I mean, all we've got is each other, isn't it?'

'There'll be no making up if you keep on abusing me as you did this morning,' was S.'s stern reply. 'You called me an idiot, you called me dense, you said I disgust you. Also that I make you ill. So I suggest that you spare yourself an attack of nausea and leave me in peace. Good night!' he added in a tone calculated to put a stop to conversation. Pulling the eiderdown over his shoulders, he turned pointedly to the wall.

He was conscious that his show of anger was grossly disproportionate to the provocation, and that nothing could really mar their mutual love and devotion. But to have confessed frankly to the hurt would have risked a loss of emotional control that he could ill afford. Far better to show no weakness and Keep a Stiff Upper Lip, as Englishmen are supposed to do.

Upper-class Englishmen, that is. Brian, Englishman though he may be, is of an overtly emotional cut. According to Eva, who had it from Beatrice, Brian shed tears when told that Amy's baby was no more.

◀ 28 ▶

When Aunt Mia learned of the tragic death of the newborn and of the parents' funeral plans, the urgency of arranging for her own obsequies – the business that brought her to Vienna at the outset – seemed to evaporate into thin air. She and Beatrice must, she insisted, fly together back to Maine at once, to be there in good time to attend the last rites. Their presence would be such a comfort to Amy and Charles!

Aunt Mia's sudden *volte face* came as a great relief to Beatrice, who had resigned herself to staying on in Vienna until 'Granny'(!) had finished her business with the central cemetery authorities. That would have meant flying with the old lady straight back to New York, where Brian would be sure to follow her by the first available flight after delivering his daughter back to her Hertfordshire boarding school. The next day the doorbell would ring in Beatrice's flat, and there Brian would stand with his boyish grin, his indestructible plastic suitcase-on-wheels and his leather-look attaché case containing the latest final revision of *Touring Britain with Your Teens*.

A few days in Maine would provide at least a brief postponement of that reunion.

'Frankly, the whole project is beginning to bore me to tears,' Beatrice had confided to Eva early in the week, before Eva had been put off by her too-enthusiastic account of Brother Sebastian's role in her article project the previous spring. And it seemed that Beatrice was beginning to tire in earnest of her present partner.

* * *

Having pressed one granddaughter into service for the outward flight from America, Aunt Mia had successfully co-opted the other as nurse-companion for her return. S., a silent witness of these developments, found it difficult to refrain from challenging the old lady on this latest of her numerous whims, telling her outright that he regarded it as a betrayal of duty if she didn't stay to finish the cemetery business that had brought her to Vienna in begin with. But he prudently postponed his rebuke until Sunday morning, when he had her all to himself.

'My own personal feelings don't matter in the least, and why should they?' he said. 'But for heaven's sake, Aunt Mia, why not finish what you began? What's the sense in dropping the whole thing, when you went to so much trouble and expense to get here?'

Was she reversing her plans to oblige another person, he wanted to know, or was she really so fickle in her purposes as it seemed?

'Look, my boy, the situation has changed,' Aunt Mia replied soothingly, as if he were the unreasonable one. 'I've lost a great-grandchild and nearly lost a granddaughter, and I want to be there for her if she needs me. And what about the little angel's funeral in Bangor next week? I wouldn't miss that for the world. Plus, what use am I here? None. A burden, if the truth were told. No, you keep quiet, dear, I know what I know,' she raised her hand. 'Eva's not feeling all that great just now with that back of hers, you know. The last thing she needs is house guests to cook and carry for! And as for that cemetery business, now that I've had a word with the deputy director and got the ball rolling I don't really need to hang about here, it can all be done by post. Herr Romulka and I understand each other. He'll take his time about it, but I'll get exactly what I want in the end, you'll see. Of course it'll cost me a pretty penny, but you know what they say, the end justifies the means,' she concluded with a little smirk, as if she had just uttered a particularly telling *bon mot*.

'I didn't know you were so eager to get away,' S. said, unable to keep a trace of bitterness out of his voice.

'Don't talk nonsense, child!' she retorted crisply. 'I was counting on a long stay here, a month at least, but you can see for yourself, it wasn't in the cards. I couldn't desert my own flesh and blood at a time like this, now could I, darling? But listen, we're going to make up for it, aren't we? Because one of these days you're going to get on a great big jumbo jet and fly straight to Miami for a good long visit with your old Auntie Mia. Aren't you now?'

She spoke as if to a small child in need of consolation, and S. could only nod dumbly in reply.

'Of course you are, sweetheart.' His dear auntie laid her diamondberinged old hand on his sleeve. 'So there's no need for tears, it's not goodbye forever or anything like that.' Her own voice shook a bit as she said it.

She too must have known how slender the chances were, even assuming that S. could secure permission to travel from the sanatorium authorities, that she and her nephew would ever see each other in the flesh again, let alone sit together cosily, as now, over a game of cards! S. could have persisted in forcing her to confront painful realities, but he didn't want to hurt her. So he chose, instead, to scrutinise his cards and complain about the terrible hand she had dealt him. Which, of course, successfully diverted the old lady's attention.

⋍ 29 ⋍

When Brian, with Sherrill in tow, had accompanied Beatrice to Vienna, he had assumed (naïvely, as it turned out!) that the three of them would be returning to Britain together once the emergency was past.

'So it was quite a shock when Beatrice told me she'd be flying to America with the others,' he confided to S. that Friday afternoon as he took time out from his manuscript for a cup of tea with his host. 'But under the circumstances of course I wouldn't dream of disputing her decision. She says she'll meet me in Cardiff or London when Amy no longer needs her. Of course she can't commit herself to a date.'

Brian managed to sound confident and relaxed about it all, though he might already have been visited by a premonition that Beatrice could be cooling towards the prospect of a return to the *status quo ante*. S. and his sister shared a suspicion that the revelation of Brian's sterility, coupled with the thought of stepmothering Joel and his appalling sister, might already have determined Beatrice to make a clean break!

(References to Brian's sterility and other aspects of his sexuality that might occur in this manuscript should on no account be taken to suggest that the man himself ever overstepped the bounds of propriety and decency in any of his conversations with S. or in S.'s presence. Such was never the case. These reflections are based purely on authorial inference, well documented though it might be! It should also be made quite clear that none of the principal characters involved have ever, in real life, used dirty language in the author's hearing, or spoken openly of intimate matters. His knowledge in these areas has been derived almost exclusively from reading, TV-watching and general observation. Much can be learned these days by the simple habit of keeping one's eyes and ears attuned to what is going on around one, and relying on creative imagination to fill in the gaps!)

* * *

'The best laid schemes o' mice an' men gang aft a-gley.' (Robert Burns.) The truth of the poet's insight was demonstrated once again the next day in Elisabethstrasse. The planners (in this instance Beatrice & company), had made the mistake of reckoning without the temperamental Miss Sherrill, who was soon to claim centre stage once again. For no sooner was the drug crisis over and done with than a fresh storm blew in from the same quarter!

It all began just after breakfast (boycotted as usual by Sherrill), when Brian went up to her room to acquaint her with his plans. He had already booked two seats on a Sunday morning flight to London, where he intended to collect Sherrill's things from her grandmother's place, hire a car and drive her back to Carrollton Hall in time for the start of classes after the Easter recess.

Brian had not been long gone when shouts from Sherrill's room signalled that something had gone amiss. A short while later Brian, looking shaken and embarrassed, came slowly down the stairs. 'Well, I expect you all heard most of that,' he said hesitantly, looking round at the others. 'My daughter just won't listen to reason. Eva, I can't tell you how mortified I am to be the cause of all this upset.'

'It's hardly your fault,' Eva told him gently. 'Anyway, nobody's really upset except you. And of course the poor child herself, she's obviously under a lot of strain.'

Brian nodded gratefully. 'You're very understanding. I only wish I knew how to handle her when she gets into a temper like this.'

'Forgive me for asking, but what exactly is the trouble?' S. enquired boldly of his new friend.

'Oh, I thought you'd heard,' Brian said. 'She's suddenly decided she won't go back to school. I've no idea what's come over her, she simply won't listen to reason.'

'Was she having trouble at school, then?' Eva asked, probably sensing his need to talk.

'No, not really – Oh, well, her marks haven't been wonderful, and there was a bit of a fuss last year as well. Some girls had smuggled a bottle into the dormitory and Sherrill was thought to be one of them. Her mother was called for an interview with the head. But it eventually blew over. I don't know the details, I was in the States on business at the time.' He paused briefly. 'But no, she's got along fine. I really thought she was happy there. And now this.' Brian shook his head heavily.

CHAPTER TWENTY-NINE

'Doesn't she give any reason at all?'

'She refuses to discuss it. All I can get out of her is that she's totally fed up, she's through with being a puppet on a string, whatever that might mean, and wild horses won't drag her back to that concentration camp, as she calls it. She swears that if I try to force her, she'll run away for good this time.'

She was a pretty stubborn young lady, that Miss Sherrill!

It seemed that all her father could do for the present was to abandon attempts to persuade her and hope that as she cooled off she'd become more amenable to rational discussion.

That hope, however, was not to be fulfilled. Sherrill never stirred from her room for the rest of the morning, even to visit the toilet. Each bedroom in the house is equipped with an old-fashioned chamberpot, along with soap, a hand towel and a stoneware basin and pitcher which Eva fills daily with fresh water for the convenience of any guests who might prefer to wash in the privacy of their own room.

* * *

In the end it was Eva who sorted things out. Towards noon she hobbled over to Sherrill's room with a clean towel, a fresh cake of English lavender soap, from the hoard she'd brought back from her literary trip to England, and an innocent request: Would Sherrill be good enough to help her raise a stubborn window in her, Eva's, bedroom?

'I should have had a carpenter in to put it right ages ago,' she must have said (or words to that effect). 'But I've always managed to raise it myself. Now with this stupid back of mine I don't dare risk it. Would you be an angel?'

Somewhat surlily, Sherrill acquiesced, and from then on it was plain sailing. Eva's window duly yielded to Sherrill's superior strength; Eva insisted that the girl sit down for a small glass of her own home-made egg cognac – which, being a lot more potent than the commercial product, must have suggested to Sherrill that she was being treated as an adult at last!

Having tried with little success to get a conversation going, Eva had burst out with her usual impulsiveness, 'Your dad tells us you're balking at going back to school in England. Listen, I just want you to know that

I've got a lot of sympathy for you. I know a thing or two about those English girls' boarding schools, you see.'

This caught the girl's attention.

'And I've had an idea,' Eva rushed on heedlessly, too carried away by her own enthusiasm to wait for a response or to see the folly of what she was proposing. 'How would you like to stay on in St Anselm for the school year? You'd be more than welcome here with us, and there's a very nice International School in Vienna, I'm sure your dad would approve. Most of the teaching is in English, so you'd feel very much at home. Think it over. My own granddaughter Petra went there for a while,' Eva rattled on, 'and she got along quite well even though her mother tongue is Spanish – she's Mexican, you see.'

'I started with French in my school last year,' Sherrill volunteered unexpectedly. 'I could have taken German but I know someone who's working in Paris so I'm learning French instead. I hate it.'

'Is that so,' Eva said, little imagining that the someone might be a boyfriend. 'Well, I'm sure you'll catch up on your German in no time, once you're living here. You'll be quite comfortable; there's plenty of space as you can see for yourself, and I've a nice big old-fashioned desk you could use for your schoolwork. I'll see to it that you have a good lamp to study by, that goes without saying. Lighting is so important for the eyes and the concentration.'

Sherrill finished her egg cognac and licked up the last couple of drops with the tip of her tongue, gazing at Eva meditatively.

'And of course it would be your own room; you could have your music on whenever you pleased within reasonable hours, and after that with the headphones.' Enchanted with the scenario she had conjured up, Eva was giving her generous impulses free rein. 'And if you needed extra pocket money for the little things you might like to have, why, I could really use some help in the garden, and you could earn a bit by lending a hand there.' Never mind that the girl probably wouldn't know an orchid from a stinging nettle!

'That's very kind of you, I'm sure,' Sherrill said politely, and her eyes began flicking around Eva's bedroom, as if something just said had suddenly roused her interest in her surroundings as a possible future habitation. 'But I'd need to think it over a bit.'

'Oh, you must, my dear, of course you must.' Eva was coming down a bit from the clouds. 'Please don't feel you're under any pressure. I only thought it seemed like a promising solution … Your poor father is really upset, you know.'

'Upset, is he? My heart bleeds,' Sherrill retorted rudely. 'Listen, Dad'd have nothing to get upset about if he'd just stop trying to steam-roller me.' She got to her feet. 'Anyway, thanks for the drink. Mind if I have a look at these?'

She was already inspecting, with evident approval, the constellation of pictures (everything from Dürer's *Feldhase* to somebody's water-colour of an Indian temple scene) that adorns the wall by Eva's bed.

'Gosh, these are terrific.' Then she stepped across for a close look at the framed photographs displayed on Eva's Biedermeier dressing-table. There were pictures of S. in and out of uniform, a studio portrait of their parents in front of a Greek-temple backdrop, made a year after their wedding, pictures of Eva and S. as children, another formal por-trait of Dr Hebbar and his first wife in their younger days, and an enlarged snapshot, taken by Dr Hebbar, of Eva herself standing in front of the 'Beethoven House' on the Moelkerbastei, one of the great com-poser's seventeen Vienna residences.

This photo immediately caught Sherrill's notice. 'Oh, Mrs Berger, is that you?' she asked in a small sweet voice that contrasted grotesquely with the fishwife shouts from her bedroom a half-hour earlier.

'Well, if it looks like me it must be me,' Eva said shortly. 'But if family pictures interest you, I've got a lot more in here.' She was burrowing in her escritoire, her back to the girl, and presently produced a small tin chest brimful of family snapshots, for the most part neatly inscribed by Eva herself in years gone by.

Sherrill made a show of interest in these, but it soon became obvi-ous that her mind was elsewhere, so Eva found a pretext (the immi-nence of lunchtime) to put the box away and let the girl go back to her room while she herself went down to attend to the other guests.

A few minutes later she summoned S. to the kitchen and told him of the offer she had made to Sherrill. 'No, listen,' she said, thinking to calm him. 'I know I'm too impulsive, but nothing's settled. She only said she'd think about it, and for all her theatrics I don't think she's ready to do anything that drastic. But I think it took the pressure off. I think she and Brian should be able to talk, now that she's got another option.'

'Not if Brian won't agree to it, and he won't,' S. said.

'Well, in any case the two of them need to talk. And I don't think it's going to happen while they're cooped up here with us,' Eva said. 'Neither of them has seen anything of Vienna yet, and if we send them off for a bit of sight-seeing together … '

'If the girl will go.'

'Leave that to me. I'll have another little chat with her, and I'll slip her a hundred Schillings so that she can buy herself some sort of souvenir. And I want to give Brian one of those *Vienna for Visitor*s booklets they sell at the tobacconist's for forty schillings or so. Listen, would you be a dear and fetch my purse from my dressing-table upstairs? And run out to the tobacconist for the guidebook? I'd really like to spring it on them at lunch. Sherrill might have decided to break down and have some food today, I think.'

S. found his sister's shiny black patent-leather handbag in its usual resting-place atop the dressing-table, but the clasp was open and, to his surprise and shock, the morocco purse was not inside where she always kept it. He hurried back to the kitchen and informed Eva of this troubling circumstance.

Once a personal inspection had convinced her of the accuracy of her brother's report, Eva launched a general search, which ended only a few minutes later when Sherrill, acting as she said 'on a hunch', discovered the missing object on the floor by the hall coat-stand, just underneath Eva's cream-coloured Burberry spring coat.

'It must have fallen out of your pocket when you hung up your coat,' the girl suggested innocently.

Eva reluctantly agreed. 'But I really must be getting senile,' she said. 'Putting it back in my coat pocket, of all places! I think the last time I had it out was Easter Monday, when I gave Brother Sebastian ten schillings to light a candle for us at chapel. I was in a bit of a hurry, I remember. That must account for it. But how careless of me! And how clever of you to find it, Sherrill! I didn't even have to call on St Anthony!'

And with that the case was closed, so to speak, for Eva well knew that no one would be tactless enough to ask whether anything was missing from the purse. If so, there was only one person on whom suspicion could fall: the very person whose cause Eva had taken up and whom she seemed determined to protect!

* * *

Immediately after supper S. withdrew to his room with the intention of looking through the latest issue of *Modern Philatelist* which Eva had kindly bought for him some days earlier. Almost at his heels, Eva entered with his evening medication.

'I think I'll make an early night of it too,' she said. 'I feel I've had about all I can handle for one day.'

'You handled that lost-purse business pretty neatly, I thought,' S. said.

'Meaning?'

'Meaning that you probably fooled everybody but me. Tell me, how much was missing?'

'What on earth are you talking about?' she faltered. 'Oh, all right, you might as well know. Something over nine hundred schillings.'

'Well, that's no tragedy then, is it?' S. remarked coolly, though he hadn't realised that Eva carried such sums about with her. 'I just wonder whether you're doing her a favour in letting her get away with it. If I were Brian I wouldn't take it kindly, I can tell you that.'

'Of course you'd see it that way, wouldn't you? But there's something else you should see. The child's really alone, and she's desperate. If I play along with this pitiful little naughtiness of hers, she may just see that there's someone on her side. That the adult world isn't entirely against her. Whereas if I betray her to her father and the others, it'll prove that she's surrounded by enemies. And she'd escape, she'll run away for good. A child of fifteen, in a strange city, with nine hundred schillings in her pocket. A couple of meals, one night in a cheap hotel, and then what? It doesn't bear thinking about!'

Eva shut her eyes tightly, as if to shut out that vision.

'See, if we handle things right I think we can really save her. She could live here with us, be part of the family, you know. She'd enrol in the International School in Vienna and commute. Quite convenient, and you know they haven't got the sort of drug problems there that they do in England. Of course it wouldn't be easy, it's a big responsibility. Don't think I'm not aware of that,' she added, before S. could voice his own thoughts on the subject.

'Well, you'd better give it some more thought,' S. said drily. 'Sherrill's made it fairly obvious that she doesn't care for the idfea, hasn't she? But it's entirely up to you, I have no voice in the matter. So you can count on me not to interfere.' He got to his feet. 'Mind if I ask you to leave now? I've still got my yoga to do.'

For at least two decades S. had tried to adhere to a regular routine of yoga exercises, or rather a sequence of postures, called Surya Namaskara or 'greetings to the sun god'. Dr Hebbar, who had introduced him to this practice, had been at pains to impress on his pupil that they must be done daily without fail, otherwise their virtue is wasted.

Like writing, it's no good skipping your morning Surya Namaskara when you're not in the mood, then doubling up next day. As with so much else in life, it's the regularity that counts!

⊰ 30 ⊱

Aunt Mia was not greatly surprised by Sherrill's refusal to go back to her boarding school in England.

'That girl is pregnant if you ask me,' she remarked at brunch next morning. ('Brunch' is the American term for a late full-course breakfast, combined with an early light lunch.) It was practically the first time the family had been among themselves. Brian had shown up just long enough to wolf down several slices of salami on rye, followed by a jam tart and a cup of tea, before making a beeline for his daughter's room to renew his efforts to bring her to her senses.

Mia hadn't wanted to say anything earlier, she told the others, but on the day after the girl had arrived she had come knocking at her door in a dreadful state, saying she was in awful trouble and simply had to get away somehow. She had virtually begged Mia to take her with her back to New York.

'I could work for you to pay back the fare,' the girl had said. 'I'd be willing to do anything – scrub floors, clean windows, do laundry, anything – just so it gets me a long, long way from home, just as fast as possible.' And she had hinted that she had plans for 'later', once this mysterious emergency was past.

'Well, of course I knew better than to ask her what it was all about,' Aunt Mia said, 'but the first time I laid eyes on her I said to myself, "That girl's pregnant." Don't ask me how I knew, I just sensed it. Not that I blame her,' she went on, addressing herself exclusively now to her favourite nephew. (Force of habit, no doubt!) 'Look, I can sympathise with her up to a point. I was only sixteen myself when I started going out with my future husband. Some girls are just ready for it, others aren't. Of course I didn't say a word about that! What I told her was, "Sorry, darling, but I've got a marvellous cleaning woman in New York, she's been with me for a quarter of a century and she knows exactly how I want things to be done. And nobody but me dusts the piano," I told her.'

Aunt Mia extracted two sweetener pills from her little red-and-blue enamel saccharin box and dropped them into her cup. She normally limited herself to one, but Eva had made the coffee particularly strong that morning.

'Remember your grandpapa's piano, Beatrice?' she said suddenly. 'Remember how you used to sit on his knee, when he played *Hänschen klein*? About the little lad who left his mamma behind in tears, while he marched off to America?' She dabbed at her eyes with her nice old-fashioned monogrammed handkerchief. This was no pretence of sentiment: lately, such reminiscences often brought tears to the dear old lady's eyes.

'Oh, Granny, don't keep telling people how nobody's been allowed to touch the piano for thirty-odd years, they'll think you have a screw loose,' Beatrice said sensibly. She reached for a fresh piece of toast and started to butter it, absent-mindedly no doubt; S. had heard her proclaim her resolution to avoid fats.

A moment later she put down the knife and gazed at Aunt Mia fixedly. 'My God, Granny, I believe you could be right. That would account for the big rebellion, anyway. But what an appalling mess!' She stared at her plate. 'I can tell you one thing right now, though: anyone who expects me to jump in and sort it out is in for a shock. You all do as you please, or maybe Brian can pull the fat out of the fire. All I know is I'm not going to get involved, full stop! I've got my own life to live, haven't I?' (Looking up defiantly.)

* * *

No one had expected this unprovoked outburst from such a self-contained young woman, and it naturally had an upsetting effect on her brunch-mates. Eva, full of good will as usual, tried her best to ease the awkwardness and dispel the gloom. Many reassuring commonplaces fell from her lips: Every dark cloud has a silver lining; it's an ill wind that blows nobody good; man proposes, God disposes; it's always darkest just before the dawn; *et cetera*. And not content with that, she then proceeded to employ various terms from Brother Sebastian's vocabulary with regard to Sherrill and the drug incident: 'peer pressure', 'value shifts' and the like.

Yet behind this façade of calm rationality, Eva must have been deeply disturbed by Beatrice's outburst and Aunt Mia's revelation, for she presently asked S. to bring her a glass of water (a most unusual request from Eva) and used it to down three tablets from the strip of painkillers S. had procured for her the day before.

For that matter, S. himself wasn't feeling his best. He would have done better, no doubt, to have forgone the second cream puff from Berger's, and he should certainly not have touched a drop of Eva's home-made apricot liqueur. Self-indulgence had contributed not a little to the heaviness, lassitude and general drowsiness which finally compelled S. to excuse himself and retire to his room considerably earlier than usual for the afternoon nap which events had all week obliged him to forgo.

* * *

But as the old saying has it, nothing is eaten as hot as it's cooked. Having sworn she would never be drawn into the Sherrill problem, Beatrice was soon offering some extremely sensible suggestions which she was evidently not unwilling to help put into effect. So, by the time she and Eva and Aunt Mia had finished their repast, they had jointly devised what seemed to them a satisfactory solution.

Pregnant or not, they had decided, Sherrill could probably be bribed to stay on for a few weeks in Elisabethstrasse, doing light housework for Eva in exchange for her board and keep. Beatrice, meanwhile, would arrange a place for her at the St Magdalene Home for Young Ladies in New York, which she described as a 'better' (i.e. hard to get into!) hostel for young single women, offering, for an affordable fee or voluntary contribution, not only decent shelter and vocational counselling but also, for mothers-to-be, pre- and post-natal care and, where required, advice on adoption.

Cost did not appear to be a problem. Aunt Mia proposed to pay Sherrill's air fare when the time came. Meanwhile, she was ready to provide Sherrill with a reasonable allowance provided, she put it, Eva was 'masochistic enough to want to saddle yourself with another burden'.

Which, of course, was precisely what Eva had in mind, as if her own brother weren't already burden enough! It was as if, by taking on

Brian's erring daughter, a total stranger, she could somehow make amends for her treatment, years ago, of her own granddaughter Petra!

* * *

'Come now, my dear sir,' the sophisticated reader might very well challenge the author at this point. 'Surely it has been revealed long ago to modern audiences – even to the simplest-minded readers, to say nothing of theatre audiences or the vast multitude of television viewers – that human behaviour is rarely if ever ruled by moral impulses? Would you, an otherwise successful author, really have us believe that S.'s sister Eva, after all those years of what seems to have been, after all, a fairly self-centered existence, could be suddenly overwhelmed by a need to make amends in such an eccentric fashion for her denial of love to her own granddaughter? To atone for her cold heart by taking a stranger's disturbed offspring to her far from ample bosom? Absurd!'

Ah, gentle reader, who can fathom the human heart? Who can draw a line and say, here remorse ends, here pity enters. Not ALL love is sexual by any means. The author here begs to differ strongly with Dr Freud! In fact, given the choice of guru, as between Sigmund of Vienna and Carl Gustav of Zurich, S., though a loyal son of Austria, would unhesitatingly throw in his lot with Carl Jung!

* * *

'Another big plus for Sherrill in America is the job placement part,' Beatrice told her English friend as she laid before him the proposed strategy for dealing with his troublesome daughter. 'Look, Brian, chances are she isn't even pregnant; it could just as well be another of my grandmother's fantasies. You know, whenever Granny gets wind of my going out with someone on a casual date she's simply overjoyed. She probably thinks to herself, "Hurrah, he'll get her pregnant, he'll have to marry her!" I can't tell you how often she's said to me, "Beattie, my child, it's high time for you to settle down and start a family. You'd better hurry up and find yourself an eligible partner – " Oops, sorry, no offence intended,' she interrupted herself, blushing at the thoughtless *faux pas*. (The reader is reminded of Brian's confession that he had been left permanently sterile by the mumps.)

'Don't apologise, love,' Brian said, staring at the floor. 'I can't begin to tell you how sorry I am … how I wish … ' Sitting round-shouldered in the chair, hands hanging between his knees, he seemed to have shrunk together, and the pouches under his eyes were dark with fatigue.

Beatrice swiftly dropped the subject. 'But in any case, Brian, if it was me I certainly wouldn't try to force the child to come back to England. Chances are you wouldn't succeed, but if you did you might just lose her altogether.'

'Oh, you're perfectly right, Beatrice,' he agreed at once, no doubt relieved at the change of topic. 'It would be insane to get the police involved, and I certainly wouldn't dream of using force. But I don't know how I feel about having her stay on here alone, without her brother … '

'Only for another month or so, Brian. After that she'd be safe in St Magdalene and very well looked after indeed. You know it's really a first-class place. They don't take just anybody. The girls have to bring character references and everything, but I happen to know someone who knows a trustee, so there shouldn't be any hitches — '

'Look here, Beatrice, let me tell you right now, putting Sherrill in a hostel like that is totally out of the question,' Brian broke in with uncharacteristic firmness. He ran his fingers distractedly through his curly hair. 'Of course, Carrollton Hall isn't the ideal place for either Sherrill or Joel, but there simply wasn't any other choice, you see. At least they were together there, that counted for a lot.'

'It must count for something, certainly,' she readily conceded. 'I guess I hadn't realised that they were that close.'

'They weren't, really, but they do need each other now,' Brian said earnestly. His mood was changing; a sentimental note was creeping into his voice. 'You know, Beatrice, it was really tough on us when Jilly walked out on the family! Especially on Joel. He used to be a real loner – no interest in sports, no girlfriends, no great shakes at his lessons either. He cut classes a lot too. All he seemed to care about was amateur radio, and then his computer. Socialising with other loners at a safe distance, you see. You wouldn't understand, of course.'

Beatrice let this pass without comment.

'But after Jilly left us – ' he resumed ('us', not 'me', Beatrice registered) ' – Joel suddenly became very dependent, almost clinging. I mean, during the Christmas hols he'd hang about in the evenings with me, or Sherrill if she hadn't gone out, instead of heading straight for his room after dinner as usual. Not to talk, either; he hadn't much to say at all. He just seemed to need the company. And his next school term was pretty much of a disaster, his grades just plummeted, but he simply didn't seem to care. He'd got involved with a weird group of boys, three or four of them, that called themselves "punks" and more or less acted the part. Joel was thick as thieves with them. Real tough fellows, you know, football hooligans, that kind, you know,' Brian added hurriedly, no doubt fearing in the depths of his puritanical heart that if he were challenged on the point by Beatrice, he would find himself obliged to make a case for his son's heterosexuality! 'Even Sherrill was worried about him. I think he needs a total change of scene, maybe some American technical college where they concentrate on the kind of stuff that interests him. But the lad does need a place to come home to, a hearth. Everyone does at that stage of life.'

Beatrice listened with growing exasperation as Brian warmed to the theme of Home and its meaning for the growing 'child': the family hearth, a safe haven in turbulent times, always welcoming, always sheltering, always listening and sharing and supporting, 'a very present help in trouble'.

At last, unable to restrain herself longer, she broke in, 'Yes, I understand what you're saying, Brian. What I don't quite get is why you should uproot yourselves. You could accomplish everything you have in mind without ever leaving England. Why does it have to be America?' she added disingenuously.

'Because of you, of course,' Brian said with a boyish grin. 'I'm thinking about myself too, you know.'

'And about my apartment?' Beatrice suggested, dangerously calm.

'Yes, well, of course that was my first thought. But I've had another idea. It might sound crazy, but – what would you say to a complete change of scene? I've got a standing offer of a job with Reuters in L.A., and you'd be swamped with work, you know you would. The kids would love California too. It'd be great for all four of us.'

Beatrice stared at him, thunderstruck. 'Am I to take this as a proposal of marriage?' she said after a moment.

'Indeed you are,' Brian said gravely. 'I offer you my hand and heart, Beattie.' Embarrassingly, his eyes glistened with tears, and for a moment or two Beatrice was apprehensive lest he should take it into his head to fall on his knees before her. 'I want to spend my life with you. I need you so badly, my darling!'

'Oh, good grief!' In a panic, she covered her eyes with her hands.

Then she said in a small, stifled voice, 'All right, since you put it so nicely, I accept,' and burst into tears.

* * *

It may very well be the best feeling there is, being loved or needed or valued by someone, even though there may be nothing you really can do, or would even wish to do, to answer their need.

But Eva maintains it can be just as fulfilling simply to have someone with whom it's possible to share one's feelings and ideas.

One day during her visit to India she had travelled alone to Somnathpur, a place two hours by bus from Bangalore, because she wanted to see the great temple there. Dr Hebbar had been much distressed that arrangements for his niece's wedding made it impossible for him to take her there, but she laughed at his worry, telling him he had been reading too much E. M. Forster.

Somnathpur was not the Marabar Caves, and she was certainly no Miss Quested!

And in fact nothing untoward had occurred. She found the temple awesome, and the only thing that marred her pleasure in it was the persistence of a would-be guide, a thin, bony-faced little brown man who attached himself to her the moment she entered the temple compound and insisted on rattling off, in Indian English far too rapid for her to follow, elaborate explanations of the sculptures she had hoped to survey in solitude.

On and on he went, despite her efforts to shake him off. First she told him politely that she didn't require a guide, then she asked him loudly to go away, and finally she tried steadfastly ignoring her unwanted companion, but to no avail.

'I'd made it perfectly clear to him that he wasn't going to get any money from me,' she said, 'and after a bit I realized that he wasn't really after money at all, though I doubt if he'd have refused it. He loved that temple and he was just delighted to share it with this strange European lady who had come to see it all on her own. So by the time I was ready to go inside for a glimpse of the main deity, I'd given up trying to shake him off. So we went in more or less together.

'It was fairly eerie in there – very dark, you could barely make out the figure of the god in the inner chamber by the light of those little oil lamps. It was some sort of black stone, daubed with coloured chalk and hung with jasmine wreaths. Quite awesome, really. And suddenly I remembered my little man and looked around for him. He was just there at my elbow, and he gave me this ecstatic smile and whispered, "God Subramaniam, madam. So beautiful, so beautiful! You see also?" And suddenly I did see, and I felt terribly happy to be sharing this thing with another person. The glow lasted all through the bus ride back to Bangalore.'

'Nice story, but what does it prove?' S. said. 'How does it apply to Beatrice and Brian?'

'Well, he'll be company for her, won't he?' Eva replied gently. 'She may come to value that.' Which was no answer at all!

* * *

As soon as he could politely do so, S. had left the three ladies at the brunch table to carry on by themselves and retired to his room to nurse a slight headache and a faint feeling of discomfort from heartburn, no doubt the penalty for having taken not one but two extra cups of coffee!

He had carefully closed the door behind him, drawn the curtains, taken off his shoes and trousers to preserve the creases, stretched out on his bed and prepared to drift off into slumber when he was roused by a faint creaking of the floorboards. In an instant he was sitting bolt upright with every sense alert, a reflex from his soldiering days.

'Excuse me, sir.' It was Sherrill, standing in the middle of his room, barefooted and wearing, as far as he could tell, only a long, plain nightshirt.

Great-Aunt Mitzi used to wear the same style of garment. Today, half

a century later, it's once again in fashion, judging by the saucy man-
nequins in the windows of elegant ladies' wear shops like Palmers on
our town's principal square. On Sherrill the effect was waiflike and
pathetic, rather like Little Orphan Annie in the comics Hannah had
occasionally included in the stacks of reading matter she used to send
him from America, back in the days when she was eager for him to
learn as much as possible about her new homeland.

The dialogue that was to follow between S. and the girl Sherrill was
conducted *sotto voce* throughout, although in good old-fashioned
houses like ours the walls are so thick and the doors so substantial that to be heard in another room you really have to shout and
scream, like battling parents. Anyone wishing to know what might be
going on behind closed doors must literally press his earhole to the key-
hole!

'Sorry I scared you like that, sir.' As S. had already noticed, Sherrill's
speech was hurried and slurred compared with her father's. 'But I wondered if you might like to help me out with some money.'

'Money?' He was horrified. A scene from his first visit to a certain
establishment on the Guertel flashed before his mind. He shook his
head vigorously to banish it. 'My dear young lady, you are far too young!
You could be my granddaughter, do you realise that?'

'Oh, I didn't mean for sex, I know you wouldn't want to,' said the
girl blandly, gazing at him with her big brown eyes as if she half expected
to be contradicted.

S.'s mouth was very dry, but he maintained his composure. He
raised himself on his elbows. 'But, dear young lady, why on earth come
to me for money?'

'Oh, I just thought you might feel like helping me.' Sherrill stared
at the floor for a few seconds in silence. 'I've got to split, see? Leave. Get
away. Understand?' The explanation was superfluous, S. having picked
up this particular bit of slang from an American TV serial.

'I understand perfectly,' he told her.

The cold of early spring was in the room, and he was suddenly taken
by a fit of shivering. 'But I don't have any money to give you,' he told
her. 'I have nothing of my own, you see. I'm a patient at the asylum!
Didn't you know that, you wretched girl – ' here he broke down, shame-

fully, in violent but almost soundless sobs. There were tears as well, he could not stop them.

He buried his face in the pillow, hoping to find her gone when he looked again. But a moment later there was the weight of a body on the mattress beside him, the tentative weight of an arm around his shoulders, and her consoling whisper, 'There, there, Mr Burger, no need to get upset, it's all right. Sherrill didn't mean to upset you, honestly not! And you've got nothing to be ashamed of, Mr Burger, you're a really nice gentleman even if you are a bit mental.' (A ludicrous error, but how was she to know that the 'Berger' on the front-door nameplate was Eva's married name?)

The position in which he now found himself was causing S. intense discomfort. If the truth be told, he was becoming unsettled by the pressure of the girl's warm body, but she showed no sign of releasing him from her half-embrace and he feared offending her by too obvious a withdrawal.

And if, in this awkward situation, he briefly forgot himself and put his hand where it should not have been, the girl gave no sign of displeasure. Rather, it was S. himself who was startled into jerking not only his hand but his whole body away from hers. He got hastily to his feet, stammering something in the order of an apology.

The girl remained sitting on the bed, regarding him with a quizzical smile. 'No problem, Mr Burger. We all have our moments, don't we? But it's no big deal, no big deal at all.'

* * *

Shock, confusion and embarrassment naturally blurred S.'s memory of the next few minutes. It is also possible that he suffered one of the blackouts which still afflicted him from time to time.

What is certain, however, is that there was no further mention of money between them, and that Sherrill did not leave the room without a half-wave of the hand and a timid smile, tempting him to believe that even though she was obliged to leave empty-handed, each of them had gained a friend.

* * *

Was it the frustration of her hopes, or some impulse from a deeper level, triggered perhaps by her encounter with S., that moved Sherrill to tell her father about her Australian friend? Nineteen years old; an apprentice chef; Stavros by name (his dad was Greek). He and Sherrill had met the previous summer at a rock concert in Cardiff, and had secretly spent a bank-holiday weekend together at the seashore when Brian thought she was visiting her schoolmate Doris Updegraf in Devon. Stavros had been working since January in Biarritz, but now he was going back to Australia to take up a permanent job at a big Hilton hotel in Melbourne.

They had planned that Sherrill would go with him if she could get together half of her fare by the first of May; Stavros would put up the other half. Stavros had said she could get a waitress job for sure. They would work and save their money and get married and start a family. It was Sherrill's dream, and the only obstacle was money: she had saved a little and earned a little but was still three hundred and fifty pounds short of the needed four hundred and ten.

So that was it.

Oh yes: S., being a writer, understood the child. Long, long ago he forgave her for all the turmoil she had briefly caused in his life.

* * *

Brian, though shocked and distressed by her revelation, lacked the courage to oppose his fiercely determined daughter. After an emotional half-hour, he had not only consented to her plan but agreed to finance it, subject only to a sight of her fiancé before they both departed for Down Under, as the Australian continent is known in England.

Although Sherrill agreed to arrange this meeting once Brian had conceded that his approval was in no way at issue, it never actually came about.

* * *

Yet the saying 'Ends well, all's well' did in the end hold good for Brian's daughter. Writing from Los Angeles some eight months later, Brian was able to report to his Austrian friend the arrival on earth of 'a Christmas baby', Christofas Aristoteles Kalidopoulos, seven pounds two ounces (in metric terms, 2.85 kg), 'making me a grandfather *in absentia*', as Brian put it in the letter accompanying the printed birth announcement.

* * *

S. received this news with remarkable equanimity, considering the intimacy of his involvement with the persons concerned and the slender but appalling chance that the new baby might have been secretly marked (as Amy's child was openly marked) by destiny as another rotten branch of a diseased family tree!

That would surely be the case had Sherrill been impregnated by accident that Saturday afternoon. S. was indeed virtually one hundred per cent certain that no trace of his body fluid could have touched the girl. Yet the thing was possible, if only just; and had S. been in a more usual state of mind, he would have agonised endlessly over that possibility.

◀ 31 ▶

What lay behind S.'s state of mental disengagement during this very trying period of his life was mainly his deepening absorption in literary concerns. Thanks in no small measure to the influence of Prof. Dr Rosen, creative writing was exerting an ever-growing fascination on S. and providing him with ever-richer rewards.

Along with his daily Surya Namaskara exercises and regular morning and late-afternoon walks in the sanatorium's extensive meadows and woodlands, his literary endeavours so consumed his waking hours and his emotional energies that the world outside the walls had, happily, only the feeblest of claims on his attention.

* * *

Moreover, ever since the redemptive death of the infant, there dwelt somewhere in the depths of his consciousness a shadowy sense that the penance for ancestral sin had been accomplished in full measure, the slate wiped clean and the attention of the Almighty now focused elsewhere.

Cousin Hannah would no doubt scoff at that idea, having little tolerance for the very concept of an Almighty God!

'I no longer believe in a Lord of Heaven who deals out rewards and punishments in the next world in accordance with the way people have behaved in this,' she had written in an early letter.

Deeply disturbed at this apparent lapse into flagrant atheism, S. had challenged her to say what, if anything, she did believe.

Her reply, which arrived virtually by return of post, was a declaration of faith in a new religion which (she explained) holds that our souls must be repeatedly reborn through a long series of earthly lives, escaping from the wheel (the cycle of births and deaths) only when we succeed in living a life of perfect virtue in this world.

Bemused by this answer (as he would be by many other ideas Hannah was to embrace over the years to come), S. did not then pursue the subject, resisting the temptation to inform his cousin that her new doctrine smelt suspiciously of a religion which has been practised for millennia by hundreds of millions of people, very much including Eva's close friend Dr Hebbar.

Granted, there were certain basic differences between his belief and hers. Dr Hebbar's Hinduism, for instance, calls for detachment, indifference to the vicissitudes of life, whereas in Hannah's view the practice of any kind of virtue can be effective and meaningful only if it is motivated by love, which to her apparently meant a kind of disinterested, rather impersonal compassion, largely inspired by the influence of what she terms good spirits on the receptive soul.

It is all far too esoteric for S., and in truth a little tiresome as well, but Hannah, an ardent convert, has never given up hope of winning him over to her peculiar post-Christian theories!

* * *

With the advent and early demise of Amy's ill-starred baby, Eva's life, her outlook and her temper have taken a noticeable turn for the better. The improvement appears to have coincided with a greatly increased interest in music and a special enthusiasm for performances by a certain provincial symphony orchestra. Eva makes a point of attending as many of their concerts as possible, sometimes undertaking long train journeys for the purpose.

Her brother has grounds for suspecting that this sudden flowering of Eva's musical life is not unconnected with the orchestra's present conductor, an elderly but extremely dynamic person, formerly first-desk cellist of the Vienna Philharmonic, whose identity must for legal reasons remain unknown to the readers of these pages.

Eva first met this gentleman after a concert in Klosterneuburg which she had attended only because a friend had given her an extra ticket. Under the spell of Mahler's Ninth Symphony, she had gone up to the conductor's dressing-room after the performance to ask for his autograph and stammer her thanks for what she described as 'a transfiguring experience'. To her great surprise and delight the Herr Dirigent invited *die gnädige Frau* to join him and some friends for a glass of wine at the nearby Stiftskeller.

And so it was that Eva became a member of a congenial circle of a dozen or so of the orchestra's (that is, of Herr X's) devoted following, mostly women of indeterminate age like Eva herself, who not only pursue him, so to speak, from concert to concert but also meet socially at restaurants over good food and wine. A half-dozen of them, including Eva, have formed a Friday-afternoon discussion group at the Café Eiles (often joined by the conductor himself when he's in town) which takes up such weighty musical questions as 'What is an authentic performance?' and 'Are conductors really necessary?'

'I know it sounds like a waste of time, and sometimes the discussion does wander off into trivialities,' Eva said to S. (as if she needed to apologise!), 'but the group really does mean quite a lot to everyone. It's a big thing in my own life just now.'

S. shrugged. 'People are social animals,' he said, adding despite himself, 'Of course the true artist stands alone. Can you imagine Beethoven chattering away at the Café Eiles every Friday afternoon?'

'Not very likely, considering he was deaf as a post,' Eva retorted, with an inappropriate attempt at humour.

* * *

S., with his usual reticence, refrains from commenting in any way on Eva's new preoccupation; he simply listens in silence to her effusions about the orchestra and its conductor, with whom she is probably in love although he is married and, more to the point, 'pushing eighty'. His wife, a lady many years his junior, is said to be in delicate health. She resides year-round in their villa at St Gilgen, an area famous for its thermal springs.

After all, S. tells himself, if a harmless romantic attachment makes Eva happy, improves her temper and makes life easier for those around her, why not? Besides, a new situation of this kind provides fresh food for the creative writer's imagination!

* * *

Sadly, however, these positive changes in Eva's life have not altered her personality. She is still, for instance, barely able to conceal her envy of S.'s extensive stable of correspondents – Hannah first and foremost of course, but numerous others as well, such as Brian

Whiting and various editors of European and American publishing houses.

The only personal mail Eva herself regularly receives, apart from Aunt Mia's cheery short messages on picture-postcards from Florida, are lengthy, turgid, months-apart documents in Dr Hebbar's tiny, meticulous hand.

Typical of Eva is the behaviour pattern she exhibits when one of these missives arrives at the house in Elisabethstrasse. First she rips open the envelope with no care for the carefully chosen postage stamps, then she reads the letter herself, and only then does she bring it (in its torn envelope) to the sanatorium for S. to read aloud to her, as if she were not already familiar with its content. The reading-aloud, moreover, is punctuated by vigorous head-nodding on Eva's part, as if to say, 'I always sensed that, and now I know it.'

It must be admitted that these letters make interesting reading. They normally consist of three elements: a 'literary' section on the subject of Dr Hebbar's recent reading and the reflections it has inspired; a detailed account of the latest political intrigues in state political circles and their impact on 'his' education department reforms; and a report on the current welfare of each and every member, by blood or marriage, of the writer's extended family. They invariably end with 'warmest greetings' to Eva and her 'dear' brother, not only from Dr Hebbar himself but from the new Mrs Hebbar as well, regardless of the fact that S. has never in his life had the pleasure of meeting that lady!

* * *

Another unchanging feature of Eva's personality is her ambivalence on the subject of Hannah: one day spouting sentimental effusions about their dearest cousin, the next fairly spitting with hostility!

'You've really let Hannah take you in, haven't you?' she baited her brother one day, having just come off worst in an argument about the nature of God. 'It's easy enough to spout pieties about love and compassion and forgiveness when you're sitting in an easy chair with nobody to pity and nothing to forgive. All I can say is, actions speak louder than words. And don't you go about telling yourself,' she continued ruthlessly, 'that she really believes all that – well, ungodly stuff that she writes you, all that rubbish about good spirits, *et cetera*. She's playing with you. It's just a pose, it's a kind of coquetry, basically. It's pseudo-Hannah.'

'If that's pseudo-Hannah you must be pseudo-Eva,' S. suggested wittily. 'And I might be pseudo-Stefan, who knows?'

'Rubbish, you know quite well what I'm saying,' Eva went on doggedly. 'All that pretentious claptrap she fed you – you took it at face value. Whether she'd convinced herself or not is beside the point. It was claptrap and you swallowed it, dear brother. You might as well admit it to yourself!'

She leaned back in her chair, hugging her chest in the classic 'defensive' posture familiar to any student of elementary psychology. 'By the way, did you imagine I didn't know what went on between her and Herbert after the war? Well, I did. I heard all about it from Aunt Mia the summer I visited her in New York. Remember, when I had that Polish woman here look after Werner?'

'Frau Zabrovsky,' S. said, concealing the shock her words had dealt him. 'I got the impression she was afraid of me. That's why I never came home the whole two weeks you were away.'

'That was silly of you,' Eva said perfunctorily, then resumed her harping on the painful theme of Hannah. You needn't be in love with someone to be jealous of them!

'Of course Hannah knew all about the marriage and the baby,' she went on in an increasingly unsteady voice. 'It was all in the first letter I wrote to Aunt Mia after the war.'

'I remember,' S. said. 'It was a well-written letter. It had the desired effect.'

'I resent that,' Eva said angrily. 'It wasn't a begging letter in any sense and you know it. I just wanted us to be in touch, because she was the only one of the family left. Except for you, of course,' she corrected herself hastily.

S. waved his hand in a gesture of dismissal.

'Believe me, S.,' she went on, 'I'm the last person to be ungrateful for all she's done for us, and I'd love her just the same no matter what. But don't ask me to believe she wouldn't have passed on that bit of information to her daughter. Not that she'd have expected it to matter much to Hannah,' she added bitterly.

'Well, it's not as if you'd sworn Aunt Mia to secrecy, is it? And for that matter you didn't even know that Herbert was still alive.'

'It didn't matter to me whether he was alive or dead, or what he might have been getting up to with Hannah or anyone else,' she retorted with typical feminine illogic. 'I couldn't have cared less,' she went on, her voice rising. 'Werner was an accident, as you've probably guessed. What hurts is that Hannah should have found it in her heart to betray me like that, when we'd been so close. Close as sisters – ' She broke off, evidently on the verge of tears.

'Well, live and learn,' S. said philosophically, to mask his inner chagrin and distress at the discovery that Eva had known for so long about Hannah's perfidy. 'But do remember, my dear sister, that I knew nothing of this until that baby was born and I decided to look into the family background. In the interest of science, you might say. I thought the defect might be hereditary.'

His perfectly reasonable explanation only provoked her to turn on him abusively. 'Scientific curiosity, eh? Peeping-Tomism at your age! That's what it amounts to, this muckraking in the name of your so-called creative writing!' Her tone was bitterly sarcastic. 'Of course you're free to do as you please. Ask for scandal and filth and you'll get it, plenty of it too. But be warned, little brother! You can't play with other people's dirt and keep your own hands clean. It's a risky game, believe me, this poking into the murky corners of the past! If I were you I'd look for story material somewhere else, not besmirch my own family as you are evidently intending to do!' A pause for breath. 'And if you must know, that's precisely why I've never told you anything about this until today. Not that it's any of your business anyway!'

'If you could only hear yourself, dear sister,' S. remarked with cool objectivity. 'Jealousy, that's your problem. It speaks out loud and clear from every sentence you utter. You've seen Hannah as a rival ever since we were children, of course you have. That's why you're so concerned about my being "taken in", as you call it. You just can't stand the idea of me having a … a dialogue with somebody other than you. Somebody whose ideas I might find attractive.'

Eva was startled enough by this bit of plain speaking to hold her peace for a few moments.

She sat with closed eyes in S.'s one armchair, which he normally uses for television viewing but always gallantly relinquishes to Eva whenever she visits him in his 'new' room at the sanatorium. On these occasions he generally perches on the edge of his bed in preference to his Posturepedic office chair, a present ordered and paid for, like his desk and his computer, through the unstinting generosity of Aunt Mia. (The green-shaded desk lamp had been chosen by Eva, who believes green is beneficial to the eyes.)

'Well, true or false?' he challenged her. 'Can you deny that you're simply eaten up with jealousy?'

No answer.

'Because Hannah keeps on writing to me,' S. went on relentlessly. 'Because I'm her chosen confidant. Because I get a postcard from every blessed place her lecture tours take her. Do you think she does it to kill time? She has such a lot of time on her hands, hasn't she?' A bitter laugh escaped him. 'There couldn't be any other reason, could there? Such as a need for communion with a kindred spirit, maybe the one person she can trust to understand?'

Hearing his voice climb perilously, S. broke off at this point and struggled to regain control, clenching his fists inside his trouser pockets as he gazed fixedly out of the window, past Eva's head, at the tops of the acacias swaying in a light breeze.

'Me jealous of Hannah?' Eva finally burst out furiously. 'How dare you, S.? You know it's a wicked lie! We've loved each other like sisters always, and you know it! Nothing could ever come between us! Herbert? Don't make me laugh! He meant nothing much to either of us, really. But we were young and ready – ' She checked herself to regain control of her runaway emotions before going on, in somewhat calmer tones, 'Herbert, you see, just turned up at the right time, first on my doorstep and then Hannah's, in America. Made a short stay and then moved on again, without much grief on either part.'

Another pause, long enough for reflection on this situation before a renewed upsurge of her original grievance. 'So now you insult me with your talk of rivalry. Your own sister, who's stuck with you through thick and thin! Who's sitting here with you right now, when everyone else has deserted you!'

Unexpectedly, she pounded her chest with a clenched fist.

'Talk about love, what more proof can you ask for? God knows the last thing I'd want is to deprive you of anything your heart desires. Do you think it's so easy for me to sit hour after hour correcting a mountainous manuscript full of lies and innuendos churned out by an unstable mind? Oh, don't give me that silly look!' she fairly spat at him. 'And don't you dare pretend you don't understand what I mean.' She groped in her bag for a tissue. 'After all, I've asked nothing for myself all these years, have I, and all I'm asking now is understanding and a bit of loyalty. Loyalty from a person's own brother, is that too much to ask?'

S., startled at all these new twists and turns, shook his head mutely. His mind was blank. He stood up, took the two steps from the bed to the chair, knelt down beside his sister and rested his head gently on her forearm, making no effort to check his tears.

* * *

When he looked up she was still frowning with distress, but presently the frown dissolved into a wry little smile. 'Oh, what's the use?' she said. 'I say, let's just stop this nonsense. The last thing I want to do is get myself all excited. I'm invited to a concert tonight in Purkersdorf. There'll be a reception for the orchestra afterwards at the Palais Radetsky, and I certainly don't want to appear there looking like a ruffled old hen.'

'Well, you look fine to me,' S. said, getting to his feet. He noted with gratification that his voice had regained its usual deep sonority. Standing by the window, hands in pockets, he couldn't help adding a reminder. 'Actually it wasn't me who started us off on this silly discussion. It was madam herself, wasn't it!'

'I know, I'm sorry.' Eva reached into her bag for another tissue and patted her eyes with it very delicately, taking care not to smudge the carefully applied eye shadow or touch her eyebrows, which are a striking golden brown. Without cosmetic aid, they would probably, like her hair, have gone a little grey, but Eva insists that their colour is due not to dye but to the near-magical properties of some herbal root-oil she brought back from a visit to India some years ago.

Eva finally spoke again. 'One of these days you really could come with me to a concert in the city, there is no reason why you shouldn't,' she said, looking closely at her pocket mirror for a final check on her cosmetic artistry. 'You might enjoy it, you know. Anyway it would be better than spending another evening by yourself here, sitting all by yourself here in this room with the computer. Those letters of yours could always wait, I'm sure. And a little change of scene would do you so much good!'

But such efforts at persuasion fell on deaf ears. After the Friday of the abortive rendezvous, S. had no intention of wasting any more time on frivolous trips to the city. On his desk a veritable mountain of correspondence was clamouring for his attention!

* * *

Apropos of correspondence, this may be an opportune point for the author of these pages to record his heartfelt thanks to another faithful correspondent, his friend Brian Whiting, whose weekly letters from America have beguiled many a rainy afternoon, and whose generosity in regularly forwarding (by airmail!) to St Anselm the weekly book-review section of the prestigious Los Angeles Times has enabled the author to keep his finger on the pulse of intellectual life elsewhere in the world.

The continuing Brian connection has been particularly precious to the author in recent times, when the swish of the Grim Reaper's scythe and the removal of familiar figures to foreign parts have drastically reduced the circle of his English-speaking friends and others who share his interest in foreign cultures generally and the Anglo-American literary scene in particular.

The Brian & Beatrice partnership seems to be flourishing. While Beatrice flits from Caribbean islands to Rocky Mountain ski resorts in photographic pursuit of the rich and famous, Brian sits comfortably in their Los Angeles flat polishing their little stories and selling the joint product, via satellite, to newspapers and feature agencies as far afield as New Zealand and South Africa. It seems he cooks for them both when Beatrice is at home. He writes that food shopping and cooking have become quite a hobby with him. Beatrice, he says, loves good food almost as much as she loathes cooking, but she has recently complained that Brian is 'overdoing the L'Escoffier bit', and begun nagging him to take up some sport or other leisure activity that doesn't put the pounds on quite so fast.

'Altogether I'm a very lucky man,' Brian wrote in a recent letter to S., whom he rightly regards as an attentive reader with time to spare for the concerns of others. 'My main worries are over – Sherrill happily settled with husband and child in far Australia, Joel in London with his granny – my mother loves having him, of course! – while he works towards his degree in computer sciences. Joel's a computer freak, and we keep in close touch by e-mail. But his main interest seems to be biology. He wants to go into medical research. The lad has got brains and ambition, and I foresee that he will make a name for himself.'

And as for your daughter, my dear friend, S. thinks to himself with an inward chuckle, who knows what gift God may have put into the womb of that little baggage? Maybe tiny Christofas will turn out to be the long-awaited Second Coming! What adds piquancy to this reflection is the calculation that a child born on Christmas Day could well have been conceived in April, during what S. himself still thinks of as his time of turbulence.

* * *

Yet it must be admitted that with the passage of time, S.'s near-certainty that the almost-unthinkable was actually impossible has increasingly been clouded by doubts concerning his own mental competence and state of awareness at the time. What precisely happened in his room that afternoon, other than the clear fact of an involuntary seminal emission, he can no longer confidently say. Obviously he has never breathed a word about the matter to any living soul. Whether the veil should ever be drawn aside is now, perhaps regrettably, an empty question.

* * *

Brian and Beatrice have, of course, no children of their own. 'We have each other, and the business is our baby,' Brian wrote to S. in the only letter ever to touch on the subject. ('Our baby', an old-fashioned American slang expression, denotes a non-human entity on which as much love and devotion is expended as a parent might lavish on his or her very own infant.)

'You wouldn't believe it, but those two really dote on each other,' Aunt Mia once told Eva over the telephone during the time when she herself still lived in Queens, New York.

(Mysteriously, since she moved to Florida there have been no telephone calls from Aunt Mia. Eva guesses that because of the greater distance Aunt Mia may think it an extravagance to telephone, but S. suspects that she may very well be intimidated by modern telephone systems that require one to accurately press as many as twelve digits in swift succession or risk a stern computerised reprimand!)

Aunt Mia's remark had prompted S. to enquire of his sister, 'Do you think there's any real hope for those two? For the marriage, I mean? I don't think she even respects him very much.'

He immediately regretted this unkind question, for Eva was probably still smarting at Beatrice's past insinuations about Brother Sebastian and his supposed attentions to herself. Poor Eva, she cannot help her jealous nature! That old barb will doubtless go on festering in her brain until her dying day. At the same time, however, it must be said that Eva – much like her brother in this as in many other respects – is scrupulously fair, never allowing her own hurt to prejudice her judgement!

And so after giving the question some serious thought, Eva delivered a judicious reply to her brother's question.

'Hope? Yes, I'm sure of it,' she said. 'Beatrice isn't a fool. I think she needs him as much as he needs her. Isn't that why people marry?'

No doubt Eva has all the makings of a good writer, but she lacks confidence in herself and prefers to put her talents at the service of those she loves.

◦ 32 ◦

If the conviviality of the Easter Week, shadowed as it was by tensions and uncertainties, had brought S. a rare measure of happiness in the company of two splendid new friends (Brian and Charles), the Sunday that followed heralded a season of sadness and further loss: Brother Sebastian's transfer to a new posting in Africa.

* * *

The day had begun cheerfully enough, despite the imminent departure of all visitors from abroad. This meant, too, a parting from Aunt Mia – maybe for years, maybe forever! A painful prospect, somewhat lightened to be sure by having nearly had one's fill of canasta, not to mention the garrulity of one's *vis-à-vis* (however well loved) and a plethora of family gossip about persons long dead that has no relevance to present times.

But there would be compensations, once the door had closed behind the visitors and the siblings had the house to themselves again. S. welcomed the prospect of a quiet interlude alone with Eva, a leisurely perusal of the literary section of the Sunday *Presse* and, later in the day, afternoon tea with Brother Sebastian – afternoon coffee, rather, since Brother had long ago adopted that Austrian habit – and afterwards the homeward journey with Brother to the peace and tranquillity of the sanatorium, arriving (if Brother's old car played no tricks) in good time for the six o'clock Sunday service in the intimacy of the Brothers' chapel. (This is S.'s favourite service because of the concentrated brevity of the liturgy, and above all the joy of commending oneself to the protection and consolation of the Virgin, whom S. loves best among all the heavenly hierarchy for Her modesty and humility.)

All the guests were to leave at ten-thirty that morning. Aunt Mia and Beatrice, bound for New York, had to check in at Schwechat airport no later than noon. Brian and Sherrill's flight to London wasn't until three, but Sherrill was said to be keen to explore the airport shops, and Brian said he thought it would be a ridiculous extravagance to hire a separate taxi.

Eva and her brother, the first to rise, breakfasted alone together at seven, while the others busied themselves with last-minute packing or, in Sherrill's case, self-beautification. She spent more than an hour in the bathroom showering, washing her hair and engaging in other cosmetic activities involving lavish application of a pungent, musky perfume which haunted the entire upper floor for almost a week afterwards.

None of the travellers had left themselves enough time for a proper breakfast. Brian and Aunt Mia managed coffee and a roll, Beatrice drank coffee standing and Sherrill didn't appear at all until the last possible moment, when she tripped downstairs with an enormous bulky carry-all long after the man from Patzak's Limousines had, as he thought, finished stowing the party's baggage in the boot of his vehicle. He had to take everything out again and repack it to accommodate the carry-all, but did so with good grace.

At last, with goodbyes exchanged, kisses on either cheek bestowed by Aunt Mia and a few tears shed on both sides, the big Mercedes bearing their four house guests swung out of sight at ten-thirty on the dot, and with a 'So, then, that's over' from Eva, brother and sister turned and re-entered the house.

* * *

Much as he had looked forward to a solitude shared only with his sister, the house now seemed to S. disagreeably still and empty. He had settled himself in the sitting-room and started reading a critique of H. C. Atmann that had caught his eye by its provocative title, but soon found his mind straying from the text. Boredom and discontent made him wish for Eva's company, but she was upstairs checking the closets for articles that might have been forgotten by their departing guests. (In Beatrice's room she found a nice 'Thank you from both of us' note, which she failed to mention until questioned directly by her brother some time later.)

When at last she appeared, Eva let herself sink into the red velvet grandfather chair, Aunt Mia's gift years ago to Great-Aunt Mitzi. She reached down with a little groan to pull out the bulky footrest.

'Here, let me do it – ' S. said, but Eva, as is her wont, brushed him aside with a, 'No thanks, I can manage … Ah, it's good to be alone for a stretch, just the two of us, isn't it?'

'Why not let me do it? It's not beyond my capacities to shift a footstool, for God's sake!' S. said.

'Of course it's not, Stefan,' Eva said soothingly, 'but actually I'm not sure it helps to elevate the leg. My back still gives me a twinge now and then and I may be better off with my feet on the floor.' She lifted her feet from the stool and pushed it aside. 'But thank you.'

'Have it your way,' S. replied with a shrug. Slipping his hands into his trouser pockets, he wandered over to the window and stared out into the garden. The flowerbeds had a sadly neglected look, and the grass wanted mowing. 'But you know if you need me, I could easily stay with you here,' he said without turning around. 'Help you in the garden, and so on. I'm not their prisoner, you know.'

'Of course you're not, whatever gave you that idea?'

S. clenched his fists in his trouser pockets. 'Legally, you know, I can leave the sanatorium any time, In fact, Dr Rosen has already raised that possibility.'

'Oh, Stefan, do I have to tell you you're welcome to stay here whenever you please, or simply to move in if you like,' Eva said with a show of warmth. 'After all, it's your home as much as it is mine.'

S. ignored this. 'I've got my disability pension. It would be cash in hand, if I weren't up there on the Hill. That would help with the groceries, wouldn't it? Because I wouldn't really need anything for myself.'

'Oh, do stop talking nonsense, Stefan! – '

'I could do the shopping and the housekeeping and all the other work that's hard on your back,' he told her.

Silence from Eva, in which the clock ticked loudly.

'Gardening, too,' S. persisted. 'As I said, the flowerbeds need turning over.'

'I know,' Eva said fretfully. 'But Stefan, you've got to realise all that would take time. It can't be done overnight.' She shifted laboriously in her chair. 'Besides,' she said after a moment or two, 'I'm planning to fly to India in the autumn. I've had such an nice invitation from the Hebbars. He says they won't take no for an answer and I'm sure they mean it. For at least six weeks, he said in his last letter. I was going to tell you a week ago, but then with all the upset – '

'To India,' S. repeated numbly, and closed his eyes. 'I see. Of course. In that case I'd only be a problem for you here.'

'No, no, not a bit of it, Stefan! What are you thinking of?' his sister said hastily. 'I wouldn't stay as long as six weeks anyway, if I do go this year, and who knows if I'll be able to, with this stupid back of mine?' She grimaced. 'You know, according to Hebbar there's a swami only a couple of hours from their place who does some amazing healing work, "Verging on the miraculous", Hebbar says, and you know what a sceptic he is,' she chatters on. 'On the other hand, it might make more sense for me to go to a spa for a few weeks, somewhere like Bad Tatzmannsdorf. I really don't know. But in any case it would hardly suit you, would it, to stay on here all by yourself when you've been so accustomed to company up on the Hill?'

Blah blah blah, S. said to himself bitterly. 'Yes, yes, do whatever you think is best for you,' he said aloud, and took a step to the window to adjust the white net curtains. When he was a child they had been starched and always hung stiff and straight. These days they were invariably a bit crooked. 'People will miss you, you know. Brother Sebastian –'

'Brother Sebastian?' Eva said. 'Yes, perhaps.'

'No "perhaps" about it. He's very fond of you.'

'People like him always get along well with women,' Eva said. 'Old, young, it makes no difference.'

'Are you suggesting he's a skirt-chaser?' S. demanded, pretending indignation.

Eva smiled a tired smile. 'Men like Sebastian don't chase after women, little brother.'

'What does that mean? Do you think he's "queer"?' S. said, feeling a wave of heat mount to his face and scalp.

'I never said such a thing, and don't you either, it's plain wicked,' Eva said sharply. 'Now let's stop this silly talk. It serves no purpose. No purpose at all,' she added. 'He might be a saint, for all I know.'

'A saint,' S. repeated. 'What an idea.'

The word hung in the silence.

Then Eva said, 'Brother has applied for mission work in Africa, to the same place where those five priests were killed last year. The Central African Republic. But please, Stefan, keep it to yourself. He told me last Sunday, but don't let him know you know. He'll want to tell you himself, I'm sure.'

'Africa,' S. repeated dully. The name summoned up vast expanses of sandy desert, herds of wild elephants, man-eating tigers and hyenas. Starvation, desolation, madness. Scenes from Conrad's *Heart of Darkness*, on the English Literature first-term reading list for extramural studies at the University. Images of bleak mission stations, corrugated-iron barracks, brightly painted gypsum saints, artificial altar flowers.

Drooping, faded vegetation.

Natives' flesh corrupted by unspeakable diseases.

Gaunt white priests, preparing their sacrifices for the Second Coming.

Outwardly he remained calm and collected, saying with a sigh, 'Poor Brother … What exactly did he tell you?' he queried after some moments.

'No, there was no misunderstanding, if that's what you're thinking,' Eva in a tremulous voice. 'What could he say? I'd always known he wanted to work in a mission. He must have applied for a transfer long ago. But I find it hard to believe that it's actually happening.'

She turned her face away, pulled out another tissue and dabbed at her eyes. It occurred to S. that he had never before seen her actually shed tears. Not as a child, when she fell and bloodied her knees. Not when her son left her without a word of farewell. Not when her brother was committed and she saw that people were beginning to shun her.

Indeed, she had reported to S. with great amusement how Frau Hayd across the street had begged her tearfully not to encourage the attentions of her son Karli. Fat, self-conscious Karli, who wore thick glasses and whose thighs chafed together at every step!

'Oh well, I suppose we must try to see it from Brother's side too,' Eva said finally. 'It's something he needs to do. And in a way I'd rather see him risk his life to help the poor Africans than stay on here and get ensnared by worldly things.' She blew her nose loudly. 'It's only a physical parting, anyway. Brother won't forget us; we'll always be included in his thoughts and prayers, I'm sure of it!'

'I'm sure Brother will always think of you, in Europe or Africa or Timbuktu!' S. said, and his clumsy bit of doggerel – made up on the spur of the moment – at last attracted the trace of a smile to Eva's drawn face!

In his heart S. knew that Brother Sebastian would soon forget both of them, along with the sanatorium on the Hill that had been his home as well as S.'s. Other people, other rooms and other landscapes would displace their memory. Time hardens the heart.

Only Art can preserve life, remould it, transcend it.

Thanks to his formal academic studies as well as his experience as disciple to Professor Rosen, S. has learned to deal with life's sad but inescapable realities in a way inaccessible to others like his sister, who because they lack this armour are vulnerable to all manner of psychic dangers!

* * *

Poor Eva must really have felt Brother Sebastian's impending departure as a deliberate desertion, a blow that might almost have been aimed at her personally. Wounded on the one hand, crushed with guilt on the other by her not wholly unconscious impulse to tempt a man of God, would she not at this moment have welcomed even death with open arms?

But that was wrong thinking on S.'s part! He should have recalled how, from the very beginning of their professional relationship, Dr Rosen had sought to dissuade him from further attempts to end his life by arguing that from the philosophical point of view alone, death should be welcomed only when one knows that one's life has reached its apogee – not before that, and most emphatically not after!

◀ *33* ▶

As usual, Brother Sebastian arrived at four-thirty on the dot: late enough for him to have overseen the portioning-out of evening medicines for the patients on his station, early enough for a leisurely afternoon tea (i.e. coffee!) with Eva and her brother before driving S. back 'home' to the sanatorium.

'Your apfelstrudel is excellent as ever, Frau Eva,' he complimented her as usual, lifting a last forkful to his lips.

'How nice of you to say so, Sebastian,' Eva replied calmly. She was very pale this afternoon, and the rings under her eyes told of sleepless nights. 'I was afraid the apples might be too sweet. Believe it or not, I couldn't find a single native apple at the co-operative, they're all imported from somewhere. They look pretty enough, but they're too bland for a strudel. For a really good apfelstrudel you need tart apples, the tarter the better.'

'For cider, too,' S. put in.

'A glass of wine, Sebastian?'

'Just half. Thanks, that's plenty.'

'Oh, but it's a Moselle, very light. Remember, you once brought us a bottle. On my birthday – ' she broke off, blushing.

'And when my story was published in *Die Presse*,' S. recalled for her. 'We celebrated here then too, just like today. With a bottle of wine.'

'*Ja, natürlich ich erinnere mich sehr gut,*' Brother Sebastian said. His German was still stilted enough to bring a smile to the lips of most patients who had any idea of what was going on around them.

Whilst Eva filled up his glass – no toasts this time – Brother enquired of S. how he was getting on with his writing. Eva reported that she was thinking of taking serious piano lessons, and Brother Sebastian recalled that when he lived in California he had taken up the guitar and learned just enough to be able to accompany himself a bit. Oh yes, everyone tried to sing in those days. They were all into Phil Collins … Chatter, chatter, all through the meal!

Listening to them, S. thought how strange it is that old friends can pass time together like this and never say a word about the things that lie most heavily on their hearts and need most urgently to be shared!

* * *

At the front door, when Brother was finally ready to take his leave, he took Eva's hand in both of his and bowed so deeply that his forehead must have touched their joined hands.

Murmurs: Thank you, Eva, for everything. Always a pleasure, Brother. (A sniff.) Goodbye, dear lady. Goodbye. Farewell, Brother. Farewell. Goodbye, then.

* * *

Not a word had been said the whole time about his imminent farewell to the green pastures of Austria. He was to leave on the Tuesday for a month's retreat at the order's mother house in Carinthia, in preparation for his posting to the mission deep in the Central African bush.

Strange, too, that with years of service to the sick behind him, Brother Sebastian should seemingly have taken no notice of Eva's extreme pallor, the trembling of her hand as she unlocked the outside door, or the strangled voice in which she bade him goodbye. Could Brother have been too preoccupied to mark these signs that all was not well with Eva? Yet no word of concern escaped his lips.

Perhaps, though, silence was really best. Even if he had noticed, what could Brother have done to help? Even if he now regretted his decision and wanted to stay? His long-planned-for new posting was imminent, his visas issued, his bags already packed.

Already that Sunday, on their way back to the sanatorium, Brother was becoming for S. a shadowy figure, ever more remote, as it were, in time and space. Neither of them spoke much during the short journey. A glance at his companion's profile suggested to S. that Brother might at that moment be sending up a silent prayer – for Eva and her brother, perhaps, as well as for himself.

* * *

Following their departure, Eva confessed to S. later, she had lacked even the energy to clear away the remains of their repast. In fact, she had felt ill enough to take to her bed, and later that evening the thermometer showed two degrees of fever. By Monday afternoon her temperature was down, but her back was hurting badly again. Dr Müller prescribed an analgesic and bedrest, but the backache continued for most of the week. Even on Friday, when S. rang to see about her driving him home for the weekend in place of the departed Brother Sebastian, her back would not allow it.

* * *

'Have you ever considered the possibility that your backache might be of neurotic origin?' S. suggested. 'Perhaps it's your body's expression of the grief you feel over the departure of people dear to us.'

'What a clever suggestion,' Eva snapped. 'Quite the psychotherapist, aren't you? You'll be telling me next that the accident never happened, I suppose!'

'Not at all,' S. replied seriously. 'It started with the accident, of course. But this latest relapse seems puzzling on a purely physical basis. And if it is neurotic, maybe you need to open up to someone, talk it through.'

Eva, of course, would have none of this. Twenty-four hours later, in fact, she had sufficiently recovered to take the train to Vienna for a concert rehearsal of *Don Quixote* at the Konzerthaus, an event which was to give the wheel of fortune a decisive turn in her favour!

* * *

S.'s words had been uttered without much premeditation, but as soon as they were spoken he saw that they were heavy with implications for his own situation.

In fact, his late mentor and friend Dr Rosen would no doubt have detected, in that moment, the birth in S.'s mind of the idea of a public confession with all its possible consequences, not least among them the mobilisation of a rescue mission that might well bring absent friends thronging to his aid!

* * *

In the last two days before his departure Brother Sebastian was busy with his own affairs and no longer made the rounds of the wards. On

Monday morning Sister Monika, a red-headed agency nurse, young and reasonably pretty but distinctly short-tempered, had temporarily, with no explanation to the patients, taken over his nursing duties. Since patients are not allowed in the Brothers' quarters, S. did not see Brother Sebastian again until Tuesday, at two thirty-five in the afternoon.

S. was seated at his table soaking the stamps off a stack of old post-cards and envelopes that Eva had picked up for him at last month's St Anselm flea market when Brother knocked and entered.

'I've come to say goodbye to you, S.,' he announced needlessly.

S. acknowledged the information with a nod. 'Please be seated, I'll be finished with this shortly,' he said.

Brother drew up the second chair and watched for a while as S., using a pair of delicate pincers that had seen years of use in his father's veterinary surgery, lifted the wet stamps one by once from the paper squares soaking in a small steel bowl borrowed from the canteen.

'I'm sorry to intrude on you without prior warning,' Brother Sebastian began in a casual tone, 'but tomorrow will be hectic with winding things up and packing, so I thought I'd come to see you today.' He leaned back in the chair, his bony ankles crossed. 'I'm off to our Mother House here for a month's retreat before I take up my new posting.'

'So I understand,' S. said, briefly raising his eyes from his task. 'Deep in the bush of Central Africa, isn't it?'

'That's right,' Brother said briskly. 'Graz to London and London to Lagos and Lagos to Bangui by air, then by jeep into the bush. It will be a real challenge.' He uncrossed his legs and leaned forward towards his host. 'I'll keep you posted in any case. And let me know how things are going with you too, will you?'

This was confirmed by S. with a brief nod.

'Look, S., be sure too to keep me posted on your writing,' Brother said quickly, passing his hand through his hair. 'Tell your sister to send me a copy of any new draft. I'm really keen to see what you've done.'

'Why ask Eva? I can still manage a trip to the post office, I suppose,' S. said, retaining control of himself despite the innuendo.

'Very well, you do it then.' There was an unexpected touch of impa-tience in Brother's voice.

'How do you know you'll even find time to read it?' S. retorted.

'Enough of that, now! I've already told you I want to read it,' Brother Sebastian said with unaccustomed sharpness. 'And do remember to ask for commemorative stamps. And stick them on carefully, with a good margin all around, otherwise they're no good for anything.' He suddenly broke off and brushed the back of his hand across his eyes. 'But of course you know that anyway. You must forgive me ... it's difficult ... I shall miss you, you know, and Frau Berger – '

Nothing else could, at that moment, have more adversely affected S.'s composure than such words of kindness and affection!

'Brother, please don't go – don't leave, Brother, we need you, Brother. Stay with us, Brother – ' and so on and so forth, in an uncontrolled, shamefully high-pitched voice.

It wouldn't have been surprising at all if Brother Sebastian himself had been affected by this sudden unabashed upsurge of long-suppressed feelings – feelings which could hardly have been quite unreciprocated on his own part but which, at that particular moment, must have seemed to him threateningly powerful!

But Brother Sebastian never lost control over himself. His response to S.'s outburst was calm and sympathetic. No matter how far separated in space, he said, they would always remain united in thought and prayer. Again he urged S. to keep him posted on his creative efforts. Then, composedly and collectedly, he rose and took his leave, repeatedly assuring S., by way of consolation, that he would be included daily in his prayers.

* * *

One must of course bear in mind that Brother Sebastian is a monk who has solemnly vowed to devote his life exclusively to God in the service of his religious order!

* * *

The more, therefore, it should be reckoned to his credit that after less than a week's prayerful contemplation in his order's mission house in Graz, two hundred kilometres away, Brother Sebastian broke off his stay and returned, at the request of Dr Rosen, on a rescue mission to the Hill.

◄ 34 ►

Much as it might have helped to advance his case, after the first few sessions S. gave up trying to provide Professor Rosen with credible answers to his incessant volley of questions. He was relentlessly grilled about the how and when and where and why of the genesis of (a) the idea that the baby would be better off dead, (b) the conception of the plan and (c) the circumstances of its (supposedly imaginary) execution. Of special importance to the great man, it seemed, was the question why S., as the author of the story, should have elected himself as the chosen instrument to carry out the deed.

'I've been thinking over your ideas on the subject again, and I must say it all makes pretty good sense,' Dr Rosen would remark at some point, as casually as his acquired Britishness would allow. 'But there are still some points that keep on troubling me … '

And then the inquisition resumes.

'How can you portray your protagonist as someone driven by what you call "an overpowering urge" to kill, that is, someone not in control of his actions, and at the same time defend his act by dragging in these supposed moral justifications – that he was ending a "fundamentally hopeless" existence in the interest of the victim and those close to him, and so on? Not very consistent, is it? Or very credible. Of course, as a device for achieving and maintaining personal dominance it might have served very well indeed!'

Etc., etc. For a time S. had put himself to a great deal of trouble formulating detailed and precise answers to Dr Rosen's questions, but soon he realised that his responses merely provoked a multitude of further questions – questions that often, under the pretext of scientific research, trespassed shamelessly into the most private recesses of his patient's mind!

Yet at the end it was the instigator of this process on whom his self-imposed task finally took its toll.

From one month's meeting to the next, Dr Rosen's voice betrayed increasing bodily frailness and fatigue. In spite of having given up smoking in late summer, he had noticeably lost weight since the spring, and his gait was no longer so brisk and self-assured. Only the pale blue eyes behind the gold-rimmed spectacles had retained their arrogant sharpness, betraying the inquisitor's confidence in his victory.

Until finally, late in October, Dr Rosen paid an unscheduled visit to the Hill. He had flown to Vienna the day before to receive the keys to the city from the mayor in a special ceremony honouring 'great sons of Austria' who had fled with the coming of Hitler. So it was that S., who had spent the weekend at the house in Elisabethstrasse, found a message in his room that Sunday evening, unexpectedly inviting him to a therapy session the next morning at ten.

Dr Rosen's demeanour was more subdued, it seemed to S., and his questions and observations, if not actually rambling, less incisive than usual. S., who had been almost looking forward to a resumption of hostilities with his old friend and intellectual sparring partner, found himself wondering whether Dr Rosen had any real purpose in mind, or had simply found himself with an empty hour in his schedule. In any case, S. himself was in a communicative mood and used the opportunity to air some fresh concerns about certain changes in Eva's attitudes and behaviour that seemed to bode ill for her future emotional stability.

As the hour was drawing to its close, a brief pause in S.'s account – a new-paragraph pause, as it were – gave Dr Rosen the opportunity to drop the bombshell that he had evidently prepared well in advance of their meeting.

'Excuse me for interrupting, S.,' he said drily, 'but there is something I have to tell you. This will be our last meeting, at least for the foreseeable future. My health is not what it should be. I have been told that if I wish to live to the biblical threescore years and ten I must drastically curtail my foreign travel. That means, among other things, relinquishing my consultancy here. – I am going while the going is good,' he added with a little deprecatory smile, as if a cliché could soften the blow.

'I understand perfectly, Herr Professor,' S. replied swiftly. 'While the going is good, and it has been very good indeed for you, as nobody can deny. What a success your life has been! Your work has won recognition all over the globe, academic honours have been heaped on you, your citizenship has been restored, you hold – if the rumour is true – the

keys to the city of Vienna. Doubtless your biographers are already waiting in the wings. If ever a man deserved to be congratulated it is yourself, and I do congratulate you with all my heart. You stand at the apex
of your career. You must be a very happy man, Herr Professor.' He
allowed himself a little smile. 'Time to take our leave, then, as we might
have said in olden times. Or don't you agree?'

* * *

Reflecting on the painful nature of that meeting, S. wonders how he
could have been so blind as to expect any further profit from philosophical discourse with anyone so inextricably embedded in a narrow
clinical cocoon that neither hatred for his former enemies nor love for
a friend had any longer the power to move him. How sad it was that this
famous man should so wantonly have rejected the ideals and convic-
tions of his youth, disowning his former admiration for the great
philosophers of classical times who exalted Happiness as the crown of
human existence, and embraced Death at the moment of fulfilment!

   Or had that great man's whole life too been built, like everyone
else's, on nothing but lies, deception and betrayal?

* * *

No reply from Dr Rosen, who was now busying himself leafing through
the last entries in his patient's dossier. S., studying his friend's face with
compassion, noticed for the first time a tiny vein pulsing in the papery
skin of his temple. Clearly not a well man, was S.'s judgement. Perhaps
his bout with Asian influenza months earlier had drained some part of
his vital energies that the body had been unable to regain. Yet he had
not let illness stop him from coming all the way from Cambridge to help
his old friend and debating partner out of – as he had put it – 'a difficult spot'.

   S. decided to press the issue. 'Do you really think it was wise of you,
Herr Professor, to make such a journey for purely ceremonial purposes,
against medical advice? Surely honours conferred in absentia are
equally valid. I can hardly believe that you would risk your health on
such a tiring flight merely to shake the mayor's beefy hand!'

   Having closed S.'s dossier, Dr Rosen felt his jacket pockets, pulled out a packet of Gauloises and immediately put it back unopened, as was lately his wont.

'Whatever did prompt you to come to come here?' S. persisted. 'It was nothing to do with me, I hope! I would hate to feel that I had any involvement in any self-destructive behaviour on your part.'

He shook his head reflectively.

'Had I been in your place, Dr Rosen, I'd have handled matters quite differently from the outset, I can tell you that! I'd never have let myself be taken in so outrageously by a patient of certified "diminished responsibility",' S. continued steadily, defying the adverse effect of agitation on his vocal register. 'And in your position I would most certainly never have preened myself on my professionalism to the point of tolerating insults to my person from such a patient! And people of your faith are supposed to be so clever!' S. concluded, just as emotion threatened to quench his voice entirely.

Dr Rosen, as usual, heard S. out without interruption. At some point he had got up and gone to the window, where he stood for some time in silence, gazing at the familiar vista: the gravel walk, rainswept today, that leads straight upwards in the direction of the famous Walterskirche, a modern architectural marvel that countless foreigners come to gape at. The bare acacia trees lining the *Allee* were whipped by sheets of rain. It was a wintry scene, although many trees still had most of their foliage.

'My friend, you have won the argument. You have won on every score. I happily concede you the victory.' Professor Rosen said. He turned from the window to face S., took off his spectacles and passed his hands over his eyes. Without the glasses his face was naked and vulnerable, the cheeks drawn and nose bonily prominent. He looked strangely reduced, as if he had shrunk inside his clothes. He stared at S. for a moment blankly, then recovered himself and managed a weak smile.

'You are right, my friend,' he resumed in an unexpectedly firm voice. 'This is the point where we must make an ending. A happy ending indeed, *ein glückliches Ende*,' he repeated in German, slowly and softly as if luxuriating in the sound of the words. He smiled again at S., but the smile swiftly gave way to a frown of puzzlement, then to a mask of acute distress. Without a word or a sound he tottered two steps to his chair, fell into it and started frantically searching his pockets for something. Cigarettes and a pocket comb fell to the floor. Moments later the man grunted and collapsed, striking his face and shattering his glasses against the edge of the desk.

S., not quite in time to catch him as he fell, cradled the beloved head in his lap as his noble friend expired on a series of long, rasping breaths which S. recognised as a textbook example of Cheyne-Stokes breathing.

* * *

While mindful of the risk of over-sentimentalising or even offending against good taste, it deserves mention that after some moments of stunned immobility, it was S.'s first instinct to kneel beside his fallen hero, whispering, in lieu of panegyric, a few words of a song that had become the traditional German soldier's farewell to a fallen comrade:

> *Ich hatt' einen Kameraden,*
> *Einen bessern findst du nit …*

The full text, in English translation:

> *I had a comrade,*
> *a better you'll not find;*
> *the drum summoned to battle,*
> *he marched at my side,*
> *keeping step.*
> *A bullet came whizzing –*
> *Will it strike you or me?*
> *Him it tore away;*
> *he lay at my feet*
> *like a piece of my very self.*
> *He tried to reach me his hand*
> *just as I was loading:*
> *'Can't reach you my hand –*
> *may you live on forever,*
> *my good comrade!'*

* * *

The obituaries and memorial tributes for Dr Rosen mentioned in Chapter 13 have been assembled from various sources by Frau Dr Eva Berger and are available in photocopy form from the author, on written request, for a postage and handling fee of AS 70. Return of cancelled stamps will be appreciated by collectors.

35

That Professor Rosen's sudden demise in the very presence of his star patient should have left an indelible imprint on the latter's psyche is not, of course, open to question.

But it should not be assumed that the relationship between doctor and patient had been a one-way affair, with the former playing the role of benefactor and the latter that of grateful recipient. Helmut Rosen himself would have been the first to insist that fruitful relations between two persons must be based on mutual affinity and trust. He would surely have encouraged future biographers to search out the underlying cause that had first moved a young doctor to take more than a purely professional interest in a certain patient, his exact contemporary, who until very recently had been, technically speaking, his enemy. Was the answer anything as simple as unacknowledged sexual attraction? Elective affinities in the broader sense? Thirst for revenge on the son of Nazi parents? A morbid itch for self-abasement, an unconscious need to be once more the loser? Vanity, curiosity, compassion? Love? Coincidence?

As usual, Eva thinks she has all the answers.

'You impressed him with your creative talent. You were a great find for him, the ideal creative schizophrenic,' she tells her brother.

'How so, creative?' S. may object. 'The one thing I've done was the *Presse* story, and when we first met it hadn't been written. In fact it was Dr Rosen who gave me the idea of the story, don't you remember? And encouraged me to try my hand at it. And supplied me with the historical detail. No, my dear sister, in this case the chicken definitely came before the egg.'

But instead of conceding her error, Eva will adroitly shift her ground. 'Well, in the end he succeeded in acting out his ideas, didn't he?' she will say, as if clinching a point.

'But it wasn't a suicide, was it? And if it had been, it still wouldn't fit the story,' S. will patiently point out. 'The idea there is of suicide as a solemn ritual, suicide without squalor.'

From the look on Eva's face, she is tempted to tell the story's author that he doesn't really understand his own work, but she merely says 'Hm,' and changes the subject, as if convinced of the pointlessness of further discussion with anyone so unreasonable!

* * *

Gradually at first, S.'s life forces, grievously depleted as they had been by the loss of two dearly beloved friends, began to reassert themselves. Thanks to the marvels of modern pharmacology and the devotion of his sister and other well-wishers both here and abroad, it now seems within the realm of the possible that S.'s name may yet one day find a place on the roster of St Anselm's most renowned artists, in the company of the great – such as Franz Kafka (3 July 1883–3 June 1924) and Rainer Robert Gütersloh (1 April 1913–29 December 1966)!

* * *

His sister, too, has shown much courage in bearing the double wound inflicted by fate. Brother Sebastian's final departure for Africa had been followed by a sudden worsening of her back condition which seems to have set at naught all her plans and contrivances for a return visit to India and a possible renewal of the attachment between herself and Dr Hebbar. (Though she must of course have realised, long before the event, that her hopes in that direction would in any case come to nothing in the end!) It was yet another of the many disappointments that life had dealt her.

All their lives long, in fact, neither Eva nor her brother had ever known the favour of Fortune, hard as she tries to deny it.

'There you are wrong, my darling brother, quite wrong. I'm perfectly happy, thank you very much,' Eva might retort to this assertion in the chirpy manner she sometimes playfully adopts with him. 'Look at me: reasonably healthy if you don't count the stupid back, financially independent, intelligent enough to be interested in music and books and ideas. And able to be useful to someone I love. Last but not least,' she would add with a wry little smile.

S.'s only comment is a dry laugh and a laconic, 'Well, I'm glad to hear you say that!' while thinking to himself: Well, if that's all it takes to make you happy … There is her friend the renowned conductor, tottering (actuarially speaking) on the edge of the grave. There are the two young gallants Hans and Lothar, her escorts these days to many a concert, 'art film' and *vernissage*, who plainly find Eva an agreeable accessory but are sadly unresponsive, except on the most superficial level, to feminine airs and graces!

But credit where credit is due: despite Eva's defeats on various fronts, despite her lack of vision and purpose – what a gallant lady she is, soldiering on cheerfully and bravely in the face of life's adversities!

* * *

The most recent example of Eva's enterprising spirit are the fortnightly musicales she has begun to hold at Elisabethstrasse on Sunday afternoons for a circle of a dozen or so friends and fellow admirers of X, their distinguished conductor.

The idea is that at each of these affairs a member of the orchestra appears as 'guest soloist', giving an hour-long recital of a not too demanding nature, usually accompanied by the aforementioned Lothar on Eva's ancient but adequate Bechstein upright piano.

In addition to the music, and probably more attractive to some, are coffee, wine, strudel and home-made poppyseed cake. Eva deals them out with a liberal hand, buzzing happily about among the guests and contributing her full share to their chatter about 'sacred art', the creative process and other matters of which they know absolutely nothing!

Attendance varies according to the season and the weather, although the house could hardly be more accessible to visitors from Vienna. It is barely five minutes by foot from the train which terminates at a railway station in the centre of the city which is named for the last royal and imperial ruler over the Dual Monarchy Austria-Hungary. As an Austrian poet has written:

> *Much that we held precious has gone under,*
> *And the fairest things are Time's first plunder.*

S. had attended a few of these musicales. One that stands out in his memory, because it marked the first time than any music had brought real tears to his eyes, was a recital of songs by Schubert in which a young miller-lad (in the inappropriate person of a large middle-aged soprano) sings of love, betrayal and self-chosen death by water.

He could, of course, have attended any of these affairs he chose, having already been allowed up to twelve consecutive hours leave from the sanatorium, provided only that the same companion signs him both out and in.

But the fact is that outings of any kind hold little attraction for S., since they consume much time that could be far better spent at his desk, not only in creative writing but in correspondence with friends as far away as Mexico (Eva's Werner and family), Africa (Brother Sebastian), Florida (Aunt Mia), California (Brian & Beatrice, though mostly it's Brian who writes) and Bangalore, India (who else but Dr Hebbar?).

Also the annual Christmas greetings to be sent to the 'family' in Australia. (Sherrill, after all, is Brian's daughter, and Brian is Beatrice's husband, and Beatrice is Hannah's child.) There is an occasional letter of thanks to Charles Hawkins in Maple Harbor, acknowledging another consignment of New World postage stamps. No word, however, from Amy, who after all has only once laid eyes on S., and then only for a few moments in her hospital room. Charles has custody of the girls.

Hannah continues to be S.'s most faithful and diligent correspondent. Undaunted as ever by S.'s laconic responses to her lengthy effusions, she continues to bombard him with enthusiastic reports on the latest esoteric 'alternative' craze she has chosen to embrace and burns to share with her deeply sceptical cousin.

Since Amy's baby is buried in Maine, no one has any reason to return to Vienna for All Souls' Day.

* * *

More than ever, these days, writing serves as his only lifeline to the outside world. This is the result of radical changes in his personal circumstances in the course of recent months. Undoubtedly (though this is strenuously denied by the Deputy Director) as punishment for his stubborn insistence on the truth with regard to the demise of little Stefan, S. has been transferred from the creative pavilion, with all its amenities and privileges, to the west wing of the main building.

He still, however, has a private room, with telephone and TV. He still has his trusty computer and his big German-English Langenscheidt, an invaluable aid with his voluminous correspondence. Best of all, he has the unshakeable assurance, thanks to dear Aunt Mia's will, that all this is secure for whatever future remains to him, safe behind the familiar, sheltering walls.

* * *

The broad, well-kept grounds stretch down, on the eastern side, almost to the Danube. At about the halfway point, under an oak tree, there stands a bench (donated by one Ludwig Birnbaum in memory of his mother) from which you can see a stretch of the river with its constantly changing traffic of barges, freighters flying the flags of many countries and pleasure ships from Vienna and Budapest and points east, whose passengers will sometimes return your wave.

And then there are the creatures. A troop of grey squirrels, bold and shamelessly greedy. Sparrows and finches, some so tame they can almost be tempted to snatch a bit of biscuit from one's hand. And, strangely, a little wild cat, lame in the left hind leg, that sometimes emerges from the shrubbery but will never venture to approach the bench, even when tempted with a scrap of meat saved over from last night's dinner.

Other amusements too are on offer: reading, writing long letters, wandering along the walks on windy autumn days. Now and again a good film on television. Not too frequently, a chat with the crippled stamp-collector across the hall who is so pathetically eager for any human contact that everyone gives him a wide berth.

S.'s physical health gives little cause for concern. His days are active, and – largely, he supposes, as a result of a recent change in his medicines – he has become a heavy sleeper. His dreams, if he dreams at all, entirely elude the waking memory.

What will follow when, sadly, the last page of the last manuscript is written; or, sadder yet, when nothing more remains to be written; or, saddest of all, he wearies entirely of the whole business of writing – that is a question best left unasked.

Epilogue

Little remains to be added before the present manuscript is formally offered to several carefully selected English-speaking publishers through the good offices of Mr Brian Whiting. Provisionally entitled (subject to publisher's approval)

THE DANUBE TESTAMENT

it is the last and perhaps most mature work of the Austrian writer Hans Stefan Zimmermann, who wrote and published under the pseudonym of Stefan Rosenfeld.

* * *

The author is, alas, no longer of this world, having perished in the recent spring floods of the Danube.

Seeking peace in nature – 'the peace that the world cannot give' – he had taken his usual walk that March morning towards a favourite rustic seat on the dam, easily accessible through a broken-down gate at the easternmost corner of the grounds. Less than a kilometre away, as it happens, is the picnic spot where he and his cousin Hannah had rested during their first and only bicycle ride together.

The 'Birnbaum' bench affords an extensive view of the river, from the gentle undulation of the Bisamberg to the lowlands of the Czech border country, with gaily beflagged barges and freighters silently passing on the ancient river: a healing view indeed, evocative of that long-ago April afternoon.

Sometimes his thoughts would roam back towards his childhood, and his mind's eye would conjure up the images of Papa and Mamma sitting shoulder to shoulder on a sandy bank somewhere up-river where they had taken him on an outing, Krems perhaps, or Stein an der Donau. They were watching the ships pass while Stefan and some older children played at the water's edge, where it was shallow and safe.

Then Papa was saying, 'I'm going for a swim, are you coming,

Bärbel?' and reaching his hand to help her up. She gets to her feet and follows him, reluctantly at first, but soon they are both running hand in hand, laughing as they make a dash for the shining water. Remembering this, S. addresses them in his mind: Mamma, Papa, before you died together did you think that you might meet your child there in the beyond, and were you disappointed? Papa, Mamma, will you be there waiting, will you ever sit watching us children again? Thoughts such as these were increasingly in his mind of late, but they were too private ever to be shared with his sister.

On this last day in the life of our Austrian storyteller, the ancient river was in an angry mood. A heavy late snowfall the week before had swollen the waters to a raging torrent. Banks had crumbled, bushes had been swept away, trees uprooted, boats torn from their moorings. Except for the solitary figure of the writer, no living thing was in sight, and nothing could be heard above the dull, mindless roaring of the river ceaselessly assaulting the ear.

Until suddenly, amid that elemental fury, there appeared a living creature, a kitten clinging to the slender trunk of an uprooted alder momentarily swept into a backwater by the powerful current, miaowing pitifully no doubt and too frozen with fear to scramble for the nearby bank.

Almost certainly S. acted on instinct, dashing down the embankment to the tiny creature's rescue. Flinging himself into the flood – he was still a strong swimmer – he succeeded in catching hold of the alder and dragging its tiny passenger to safety. But it must be presumed that the icy floodwaters had delivered a fatal shock to his system. Wading to the bank he staggered, clutched his breast and fell face down into the flood, which carried the now lifeless body a long way down river.

Washed ashore within sight of the Hungarian border, it was recovered, identified by his weeping sister, and, in due course, solemnly laid to rest in sanctified ground, mourned by relatives, friends and a few devoted sanatorium staff.

The grave is little visited today. Hardly anyone who was not present at the funeral rites is even aware of its location. But there will surely be a few among the lovers of the storyteller's art who will grieve the loss sustained by world literature when the floods of spring silenced the modest voice of Stefan Rosenfeld.

Appendix

THE SUICIDE SOCIETY

BY STEFAN ROSENFELD

Robert Ell had reason to regard his situation as hopeless, and he decided to end his life. He was financially ruined, he was ethically and morally bankrupt, he was philosophically at a dead end. He was without hope. Hoping, to him, meant harbouring false expectations of life. Vulnerant omnis, ultima necit *(Each hour wounds, the last one kills) reads the inscription on a medieval sundial.*

Ell put in order the few affairs of possible concern to others after his death, reviewed his life's history of missed opportunities, put a record on the gramophone, emptied at a draught the waiting glass and abandoned himself to the music. As the choir intoned, 'For all flesh is as grass,' Ell lost consciousness.

But Ell, a failure at living, proved a failure at dying as well. He woke in hospital with a pumped-out stomach, and his first emotion was contempt for a society which, having deprived him of any reason to live, was now bending its efforts to prevent him from expiring.

These efforts were successful. Ell survived and was committed to a psychiatric clinic, since his wish to die was regarded as a mental aberration. Every day he was brought before the chief physician, a thin little professor with restless eyes, who asked him a great many sensible and many apparently senseless questions. Had he ever dreamt he could fly like a bird? Did he know how to play chess? Were chess players intelligent? Had he ever stolen anything? In the course of these interviews Ell gave a multitude of answers about his childhood, his outlook on life and his personal situation.

Ten days later, having completed his exploration of Ell's personality, the professor said to him, 'You are one of those extremely rare cases whom nothing, absolutely nothing, impels to the maintenance of physical existence. The unique feature of your split personality is that mentally and spiritually you have already arrived at that point on the circle where Being and Not-Being merge into one, whereas your physical existence appears to be programmed according to the normal human clock, with a substantial amount of time still due to run.' He smiled and leaned back in his chair. 'In ancient Marseilles, poison for the purpose of suicide was provided at the cost of the municipality, provided the city fathers were satisfied that one had good reason for wishing to die. You and I live in a different culture, where suicide is regarded as a form of murder. And you, Ell, are fortunate that society is not consistent enough to apply the same sanctions to a suicide attempt as to an attempted murder.' Again he paused, took out a card from the desk drawer, rose and said in an expressionless voice, 'You will be discharged from the clinic today. Take this card and go to the indicated address. You will find help there. Good-day.'

Only on returning to his sickroom did Ell examine the card. He read:

Society of Suicides, 8 Holy Cross Court. From 6 p.m.

After leaving the clinic he asked himself whether he should follow the professor's invitation. In the days when he was still governed by principle, he had shunned all human gatherings as something unclean. But he had long since said goodbye to principles: having learned that any harbour will serve for living or for dying, he no longer strove to sail against the wind. The professor had given him the address; so he went.

The door was opened by an orderly. Ell gave his name, mentioned the professor as a reference, and showed the card he had been given. The orderly invited Ell to enter, offered him a chair and vanished. After several minutes a friendly young man appeared, saying, 'Herr Ell?' and introduced him-

self as the secretary of the society. He led Ell to his office, offered him coffee and chatted about the weather. Then he said, 'But let me tell you about the society. We were founded during the reign of the Emperor Joseph the Second. Our mission is to transform the act of suicide, for a chosen élite, into a celebration; a celebration performed with solemn joy and power, as in ancient days. For more than two hundred years the members of our society have trod the path of voluntary self-extinction unhampered by squalid circumstance, unconstrained by crippling anxiety, in full, free, joyous awareness of their act.'

He lowered his voice and added, kindly, 'Your own suicide attempt did not, of course, fulfil our criteria, but as an individual you had no possibility of attaining to that. Only later will you learn the full significance of being invited to apply for membership in our society.'

The secretary paused to give Ell an opportunity to respond. As Ell was silent, he continued, 'The initiative must come from you, however. Henceforth you will have access to our library. Make use of it. Read the Annals of the Society, read in the Golden Book. When the fruit is ripe enough to drop from the tree, you will know, and so shall we.'

Day after day Ell haunted the library. It was rich in philosophical works which contained little new to him, as well as in biographies and historical treatises, some of these by authors previously unknown to him. At length he came upon the twelve-volume Annals of the Society of Suicides, in which he now regularly immersed himself. He was amazed to find that among the signatories of the society's original constitution, whose text was printed there, had been Wolfgang Amadeus Mozart! A biography of the great composer informed him that Mozart had composed his Requiem for the society, acting in complicity with that Count Walsegg who is commonly supposed to have commissioned it anonymously in order to pass it off as his own. Walsegg had in fact been *master of ceremonies of the society at that time. It could only be ascribed to a malign fate that a fatal illness had prevented Mozart from consecrating his work by a solemn act of self-destruction within the circle of his friends.*

The lives and deaths of several hundred members were described in the Annals. *Besides the names of famous known suicides, such as Kleist, van Gogh and Weininger, Ell discovered names of others, like Herkheim and Eliozi, whom the world supposed had died from natural causes.*

In the centre of the library, on a lectern draped in black velvet, lay the Golden Book. *It contained handwritten dedicatory messages to the society from those on the threshold of death. These consisted mainly of citations from philosophical and literary works already known to Ell, mostly from Stoic sources. But a few were new to him, such as this from Pascal:*

Man is equally unable to grasp the Nothingness from which he sprang and the Infinite that lies before him.

or Lichtenberg's aphorism:

Being born is a business of such beastlike passivity that it ought to occur to someone to take the full intellectual measure of dying.

Weeks passed, and Ell increasingly gave himself over to the longing for death. One evening he went to the secretary of the society and told him, 'I am ready.'

'We have been waiting for you,' the secretary answered. He led Ell through narrow corridors, down staircases and through darkened rooms into a brightly candlelit vaulted chamber, where twelve persons sat at a festively laid table. The secretary addressed them: 'Revered Master, and friends! I hereby introduce Robert Ell, who desires to become a member of our society.'

Those seated at the table clapped their hands in token of their goodwill. The man who had been addressed as 'Master' approached Ell and solemnly extended his hand, whereupon Ell recognised him as the professor from the psychiatric clinic. He bade Ell take the seat to his left; the secretary seated himself next to Ell. Food and drink were brought, and the talk around the table, hesitant at first, presently became livelier and louder. The man seated at the Master's right hand was addressed with special cordiality and respect by the others. Ell asked the secretary what the occasion for this might be. 'That is the poet Augarten,' came the reply. 'In a few hours he will be dead.'

Before the dessert course the Master proposed a toast to the guest of honour, Augarten, praising his works, which in his last period had centred on one great theme: death, the central question of existence. He pointed out that the unique artistic value of his work could be perfected only in death. This Augarten had recognised; it was the source of his ardent wish to take this final step to consummation.

The rules of the society prescribed, he went on, that a new member should be elected to fill the place soon to be vacant, and the society's choice had fallen on Robert Ell. He was now about to impart to their friend Augarten something which the poet might rightly regard as the crown of his life's work: the most distinguished publisher of the German-speaking world had decided to bring out a special commemorative edition of Augarten's collected works!

The Master raised his glass; the members of the society rose to their feet, emptied their glasses to Augarten and applauded. Augarten was too deeply moved to express his thanks, but the Master embraced him. When the last course was finished, the Golden Book *was brought and laid before Augarten, who wrote in it a verse from Horace:* Mors ultima rerum est (Death is the goal of all things).

Night was nearing its end, and the friends took solemn leave of Augarten. Last of all, the poet offered Ell his hand and said with a smile, 'I am happy to have made your acquaintance on this of all days.' Then he nodded to the

Master and, without a further glance at the others, left the chamber in his company.

The secretary went to a wall cabinet, took out a dozen pairs of binoculars and handed them out to each of the others, with the single exception of Augarten. Thus equipped, the members of the society passed into a courtyard just outside, where three cars stood in readiness. The car driven by the secretary, in which Ell was riding, led the way. Through the brightly lit nocturnal streets, seemingly frozen in immobility, they drove towards the distant mountains. Up the steep, sinuous roads the cars climbed, their headlamps piercing the forest darkness. As a greying of the eastern horizon heralded the morning, the twelve members of the society reached their goal: a high mountain ridge which plunged at their feet into an abyss. A vertical wall of rock formed the opposite side of the chasm.

The members of the society silently focused their binoculars on the top of the rock wall, where a little patch of meadow marked the end of a path that led up from the other side to the very edge of the abyss. In the perfect stillness of early dawn, some minutes passed.

Suddenly Augarten entered their field of vision. Behind him Ell recognised the Master. They stopped, conversed briefly and shook hands. The Master handed Augarten something wrapped in a cloth. Augarten unwrapped it; it was a pistol. Now the Master gestured towards the ridge opposite, where the members of the society were gathered. Augarten raised his arm in greeting; the members of the society doffed their hats. Augarten stepped to the edge of the abyss, put the pistol to his temple, fired and pitched head first into the chasm. From far below they heard the sound of the impact and the clatter of the avalanche of loose rock set off by the shattered body. The members of the society replaced their hats and drove in silence back to the city.

Robert Ell had now taken Augarten's place as a member of the society. He took part in the friends' festivities, each of which began with the initiation of a new member (in voting, *a single black ball sufficed to disqualify the applicant) and ended with a solemn leavetaking from one of the friends. Eleven times more Ell was permitted to witness the death of one of his fellow-members; then it was his turn.*

As his last dawn approached, Ell, in the half-sleep that precedes full consciousness, pondered the words that he in his turn would inscribe in the Golden Book. Then he opened his eyes. The objects in the room appeared to be swimming in a mist. He had a burning pain in his mouth, his heart was racing, a frightful nausea gripped him. Near his bed a light was burning, beside it an empty glass. Something in the room was ticking slowly. It was the gramophone needle, tracing and retracing the last groove of the record. Ell found he was powerless to move. His muscles were cramping in intolerable pain. He felt himself losing the power to draw breath. His ribcage was paralysed, he fought for breath, he was at the point of suffocation.

The Master and his disciples had been nothing but a fevered dream. Robert Ell's last thought was that he would now die as he had wished to do from the beginning: without a friend, without a God.

This edition published
in Great Britain in 2004 by

ELLIOTT & THOMPSON
27 John Street
London WC1N 2BX

First published
by Bellew Publishing 1998

ISBN 1 904027 12 1

First Edition

Book design by Brad Thompson
Printed and bound in Malta by Interprint